PE JORDAN
COLLECTION

Christmas nights

Published in Great Britain 2012
Mills & Boon, an imprint of Harlequin (UK) Limited,
Eton House, 18-24 Paradise Road, Richmond, Surrey TW9 1SR

ISBN: 978 0 263 90228 0

028-1112

Harlequin (UK) policy is to use papers that are natural, renewable and recyclable products and made from wood grown in sustainable forests. The logging and manufacturing processes conform to the legal environmental regulations of the country of origin.

Printed and bound
by CPI Group (UK) Ltd, Croydon, CR0 4YY

Dear Reader,

Christmas is a particularly poignant time of year for me as I was privileged to be able to spend part of Christmas day with Penny, one of my dearest friends, before for this courageous, witty, dignified lady passed away just a few days later.

I will never forget Penny, or how we met.

I have a very special envelope on my desk. On the front it says: Lot 4. Be An Author For A Day. Your chance to work with local author Penny Jordan.

Author for a day? A friend for life, as it turned out.

My husband bought this lot for me at a 'Pride and Prejudice' charity auction, which we attended in full costume—ate the food and danced the dances of those long-ago times.

After the ball I was in awe at the thought of meeting one of my favourite authors, though less so when Penny opened the door and her four dogs bounded out to greet me, as I had three dogs of my own. Our friendship was cemented the moment we noticed matching dog slobber on our identical trousers.

Grace, elegance, kindness, thoughtfulness—none of these could do sufficient credit to a woman who brought reading pleasure into so many people's lives. I was with Penny shortly before she died and her most urgent request was that I tell you, her readers, how much you meant to her. You were Penny's inspiration, and her only regret was that she couldn't finish all the books she wanted to write for you. But as, I told Penny, however many books she wrote we, her loyal readers, would always want more.

I know you will enjoy this collection of wonderful stories as much as I have.

With my warmest wishes to you all,

Susan Stephens

Penny Jordan is one of Mills & Boon's most popular authors. Sadly Penny died from cancer on 31st December 2011, aged sixty-five. She leaves an outstanding legacy, having sold over a hundred million books around the world. She wrote a total of a hundred and eighty-seven novels for Mills & Boon, including the phenomenally successful *A Perfect Family, To Love, Honour & Betray, The Perfect Sinner* and *Power Play*, which hit the *Sunday Times* and *New York Times* bestseller lists. Loved for her distinctive voice, her success was in part because she continually broke boundaries and evolved her writing to keep up with readers' changing tastes. *Publishers Weekly* said about Jordan: 'Women everywhere will find pieces of themselves in Jordan's characters' and this perhaps explains her enduring appeal.

Although Penny was born in Preston, Lancashire, and spent her childhood there, she moved to Cheshire as a teenager and continued to live there for the rest of her life. Following the death of her husband she moved to the small traditional Cheshire market town on which she based her much-loved Crighton books.

Penny was a member and supporter of the Romantic Novelists' Association and the Romance Writers of America—two organisations dedicated to providing support for both published and yet-to-be published authors. Her significant contribution to women's fiction was recognised in 2011, when the Romantic Novelists' Association presented Penny with a Lifetime Achievement Award.

A Bride for His Majesty's Pleasure

PENNY JORDAN

PROLOGUE

'AND if I refuse to marry you?' Although she did her best not to allow her feelings to show, she was conscious of the fact that her voice trembled slightly.

Max looked at her.

'I think you already know the answer to your own question.'

The dying sun streaming in through the tower window warmed the darkness of her hair and revealed the classical beauty of her facial bone structure, before stroking golden fingers along the exposed column of her throat.

A twenty-first-century woman, caught in an ancient and powerful trap of savagery and custom, Max acknowledged wryly, if only to himself.

The intensity of the powerful and unwanted emotional and physical reaction that punched through him caught him off guard. It was a dangerous mix of sympathy and desire, neither of which he should be feeling. But most especially not the desire. Immediately Max turned away from her—like a schoolboy desperate to conceal the over-enthusiastic and inappropriate reaction of his developing maleness, he derided himself.

But he was not a schoolboy, and furthermore he was perfectly capable of controlling both his emotions and his physical desire. So his own body had momentarily caught him off guard? It would not happen again.

What he was doing wasn't something he wanted to do, nor was it in any way for his own benefit. It was a duty, and she was the doorway via which he could access what he needed to help those who needed it so desperately. It was a loathsome situation; either he sacrificed her, and in a sense himself, or he risked sacrificing his people. He did not have the luxury of indulging in personal and private emotional needs. His duty now obliged him to channel his thoughts and feelings towards those to whom he had given his commitment when he had accepted the crown and become the ruling Prince of Fortenegro. His people. This woman's people.

He turned back towards her. So much was at stake; the future of a whole country lay in this woman's hands. He would have preferred to be honest with her—but how could he, given her family background? She was a rich man's grandchild. Her grandfather a man, he knew now, who had alternated between both over-indulging his grandchildren and over-controlling them—to the extent that they had become adept at deceit and were motivated only by self interest.

Ionanthe looked at the man facing her—a man who represented so much that she hated.

'You mean that I'll be thrown to the wolves, so to speak? In the form of the people? Forced to pay my family's debt of honour to you?'

When he gave no reply she laughed bitterly.

'And you dare to call yourself civilized?'

'I own neither the crime nor its punishment. I am as impotent in this situation as you are yourself,' Max defended himself caustically.

Impotent. It was a deliberately telling choice of word, surely, given that he had just told her that she must marry him and give him a son as recompense for her sister's crimes against him. Or be handed over to the people to be tried by a feudal form of justice that was no justice at all.

As he waited for her response Max thought back over the events that had led them both to this unwanted impasse.

CHAPTER ONE

'THERE must be vengeance, Highness.' The courtier was emphatic and determined as he addressed Max.

The Count no doubt considered him ill fitted for his role of ruler of the island of Fortenegro—the black fort, so named originally because of the sheer dark cliffs that protected the mainland facing side of the island.

'Justice must be seen to be done,' Count Petronius continued forcefully.

The Count, like most of the courtiers, was in his late sixties. Fortenegro's society was fiercely patriarchal, and its laws harsh and even cruel, reflecting its refusal to move with the times. A refusal which Max fully intended to change. The only reason he had not flatly refused to step into his late cousin's shoes and become the new ruler of the principality was because of his determination to do what he knew his late father had longed to do—and that was to bring Fortenegro, and more importantly its people, out of the Dark Ages and into the light of the twenty-first century. That, though, was going to take time and patience, and first he must win the respect of his people and, just as importantly, their trust.

Fortenegrans were constitutionally opposed to change—especially, according to his courtiers, any kind of change that threatened their way of life and the beliefs that went with that way of life: beliefs such as the need to take revenge for insults and slights both real and imagined.

'An eye for an eye; a tooth for a tooth—that is the law of our people,' the Count continued enthusiastically. 'And they will expect you to uphold it. In their eyes a prince and a ruler who cannot protect his own honour cannot be trusted to protect theirs. That is their way and the way they live.'

And not just them, Max reflected grimly as he looked one by one at the group of elderly courtiers who had been his late cousin's advisers and who, in many ways, despite the fact that he was now ruler of the island, were still reluctant to cede to him the power they had taken for themselves during his late cousin's reign. But then Cosmo had been a playboy, unashamedly hedonistic and not in the least bit interested in the island he ruled or its people—only the wealth with which it had provided him.

Cosmo, though, was dead—dying at thirty-two of the damage inflicted by the so-called 'recreational' drugs to which he had become addicted. He'd been without a son to succeed him, leaving the title to pass to Max.

Justice must indeed be seen to be done, Max knew, but it would be *his* justice, not theirs, done in his way and according to his judgement and his beliefs.

The most senior of his late cousin's advisers was speaking again.

'The people will expect you to revenge yourself on the family of your late wife because of her betrayal of you.'

Max knew that the Count and Eloise's grandfather had been sworn enemies, united only by their shared adherence to a moral code that was primitive and arcane. Now, with Eloise and her grandfather dead, he was being urged to take revenge on the sole remaining member of the family—his late wife's sister—for Eloise's betrayal of their marriage and her failure to provide him with the promised heir.

In the eyes of his people it was not merely his right but his duty to them as their ruler to carry out full vengeance according to the ancient laws relating to any damage done to a man's honour. His late wife's family must make full restitution for the shame she had brought on them and on him. Traditionally, that meant that the dishonoured husband could set aside the wife who had betrayed him and take in her place one of her sisters or cousins, who must then provide him with the son his wife's betrayal had denied him.

These were ancient laws, passed down by word of mouth, and Max was appalled at the thought of giving in to them and to those who clung so fiercely to them. But he had no choice. Not if he wanted to win the trust of his people. Without that trust he knew that he could not hope to change things, to bring the island and those who lived there into the modern world. He had already sacrificed his personal beliefs once by marrying Eloise in the first place. Did he really want to do so a second time? Especially when it meant involving someone else? And if so, why?

The status and wealth of being the island's ruler meant little to him. He was already wealthy, and the very idea of one person 'ruling' others went against his strongest beliefs.

But he *was* the island's ruler, whether he wanted to be or not, and as such he owed its people—his people—a duty of care. He might never succeed in bringing change to the older generation, but for the sake of their children and their children's children he had to win the trust of the leaders and the elders so that those changes could be slowly put in place.

Refusing to accept their way of life and ignoring the laws that meant so much to them would only create hostility. Max knew all these things, but still the whole idea of honour and vengeance was repugnant to him.

A year ago he would have laughed in disbelief at the very idea that he might find himself the ruler of an island in the Aegean off the coast of Croatia.

He had known about the island and its history, of course. His father had spoken often of it, and the older brother with whom he had quarrelled as a young man—because his brother had refused to acknowledge that for the sake of the island's people it was necessary to spend some of his vast fortune on improving the quality of their lives and their education.

Max's father had explained to him that the island was locked in its own past, and that the men who had advised his grandfather and then his own father were hostile to modernisation, fearing for their wealth and status.

His father, with his astute brain and compassion for the human race, had proved that being wealthy and being a philanthropist were far from mutually exclusive, and after the death of his parents Max had continued with their charitable work as head of the foundation his father had started. Under Max's financial guidance both his own personal wealth and that of the foundation had grown, and Max had joined the exclusive ranks of that small and discreet group of billionaires who used their wealth for the benefit of others. Anonymity was a prized virtue of this group of generous benefactors. Max was as different from his late cousin as it was possible to be.

Physically, Max had inherited through his father's genes the tall, broad-shouldered physique of the warrior princes who had coveted and conquered the island many generations ago, along with thick dark hair and a profile that could sometimes look as though it had been hewn from the rock that protected the island from its enemies, so little did his expression give away.

Only his slate-blue eyes came from his English mother; the rest of him was, as his father had often said, 'pure Fortenegro and its royal house.' The evidence of the truth of that statement could be seen in the profile stamped into the island's ancient coinage, but whilst outwardly he might resemble his ancestors, inwardly Max was his own man—a man who fully intended to remove from the people of the island the heavy yoke of custom and oppression under which they lived.

When he had first come to the island to take up the reins of ruling he had promised himself that he would bring the people out of the darkness of poverty and lack of opportunity into the light. But it was proving a far harder task than he had anticipated.

The men who formed his 'court', instead of supporting him, were completely antagonistic towards any kind of modernisation, and continually warned him of the risk of riots and worse from the people if their way of life were to be challenged.

In an attempt to do the right thing Max had married the granddaughter of one of his nobles—a marriage of mutual convenience, which Eloise had assured him she wanted, saying that she would be proud to provide the island with its next ruler. What she had not told him was that whilst she was happy to become his Princess, she had no intention of giving up her regular pasttime of taking a lover whenever she felt like it—foreigners, normally, who had come to the island for one reason or another.

Within hours of the deaths of Eloise and her current lover, when their car had plunged over one of Fortenegro's steep cliffs, gossip about her relationship with the man she had been with had begun. A maid at the castle had seen Eloise in bed in her grandfather's apartment with her lover, and before too long the whole island had known.

Now, six months after her death and following the death of her grandfather, his barons were pressing him to exact revenge on her family for her betrayal.

'It is your duty,' his courtiers had insisted. 'Your late wife's sister must make restitution. She must provide you with the son your wife denied you. That is the way of our people. Your wife shamed you. Only by taking her sister can that shame be expunged and both your honour and the honour of her family be restored.'

'I doubt that Eloise's sister would agree with you.'

Neither his wife nor her grandfather had ever spoken much about Eloise's sister. All Max knew about her, other than the fact that she existed, was that, having trained as an economist, she now lived and worked in Europe.

'She no longer lives here,' Max had pointed out. 'And if she is as intelligent as she seems she will not return, knowing what awaits her.'

'She is already on her way back,' Max had been told by Count Petronius, who had continued smoothly, 'I have taken it upon myself to summon her on your behalf.'

Max had been furious.

'So that she can be threatened into paying her family's supposed debt of honour?' he had demanded angrily.

The Count had shrugged his shoulders. 'I have told her that the apartment in the palace occupied by her late grandfather must be cleared of his possessions. Since he occupied the apartment for many years she will naturally wish to remove from it those things that may be of value.'

Max hadn't been able to conceal his loathing for the Count's underhanded behaviour.

'You have tricked and trapped her.'

'It is your own fate you should be considering, not hers,' the Count had pointed out. 'The people will not tolerate being shamed by a ruler who allows his wife to cuckold him. They will expect you to demand a blood payment.'

And if I do not? Max had wanted to demand. But he had known the answer.

'We live in troubled times,' the Count had told him. 'There are those on the mainland who look at this island and covet it for their own reasons. If the islanders were to rise up against you because they felt you had let them down then such people would be pleased. They would be quick to seize the advantage you will have given them.'

Max had frowned. The Count might have spoken theatrically, but Max knew that there was indeed a cadre of very very rich and unscrupulous businessmen who would like very much indeed to take over the island and use it for their own purposes. The island was rich in minerals, and it would be a perfect tax haven. And so much more than that. With its natural scenic beauty—its snow in winter on the high ridge of its mountains, and its sea facing beaches that basked in summer sunshine—it would make a perfect tourist destination, providing year-round enjoyment.

Max was already aware of the benefits that tourism could bring to the people of the island—handled properly—but he was equally aware of the billions it could make for the unscrupulous, and the destruction and damage they would cause if they were allowed to gain control of the island. He had a duty to ensure that did not happen.

'Your late wife's sister is on her way here, and once she is here you must show the people the power of your vengeance. Only then will you have their respect and their trust,' the Count had continued.

And now he must wait for the woman standing opposite him to give him her answer—and he must hope, for her sake and the sake of his people, that she gave him the right one, even whilst he abhorred the way she had been tricked into coming to the island, and the nature of the threats against her personal safety.

If nothing else, he told himself grimly, when she married him he would at least be able to protect her from the appalling situation the Count had outlined to him—even if that protection did come at the cost of her personal freedom.

Certain aspects of his current position were never going to sit comfortably with his personal moral code, Max acknowledged grimly. It was all very well for him. He was making the decision to sacrifice his freedom of choice for the sake of his people. Ionanthe did not have that choice. She was being *forced* to sacrifice hers.

CHAPTER TWO

THE sun was sinking swiftly into the Aegean sea whilst the man who had been her sister's husband—who now wanted her to take Eloise's place—stood in silence by the window. The evening breeze ruffled the thick darkness of his hair. With that carved, hawkish over-proud profile he could easily have belonged to another age. He *did* belong to another age—one that should no longer be allowed to exist. An age in which some men were born to grind others beneath their heels and impose their will on them without mercy or restraint.

Well, she wasn't going to give in—no matter how much he threatened her. She had been a fool to let herself be tricked into coming here, especially when she knew what the old guard of the island were like. That was why she had left in the first place. Was it really only a handful of hours ago that she had been promising herself that finally, with her grandfather's death and the money she would inherit, she would be free to do what she had wanted to do for so long. Offer her services as an economist to what she considered to be the most forward-thinking and socially responsible charitable organisation in the world—The Veritas Foundation.

Ionanthe had first heard about Veritas when she had been working in Brussels. A male colleague to whom she had taken a dislike had complained about the charity, saying that its aims of alleviating poverty and oppression by offering education and the hope of democracy to the oppressed was just a crazy idealist fantasy. Ionanthe had been curious enough about the organisation to want to find out more, and what she had learned had filled her with an ambition to one day be part of the dedicated team of professionals who worked for the charity. The Foundation was about doing things for others, not self-aggrandisement, and she approved of that as much as she did *not* approve of her homeland's new ruler.

As far as she was concerned, the island's new Prince was every bit as bad as those who had gone before him. He expected her to take Eloise's place and wipe out the shame staining both his reputation and that of her family—to give him the son Eloise had not. A son who would one day rule in his place.

A son, an heir. A future ruler.

All of a sudden a sense of prescient awareness so powerful that it reached deep down into the most secret places of her heart shuddered through her, warning her that she stood at a crossroads that would affect not just her own life but more importantly the lives of others—not for one generation, but for the whole future of her people.

She might originally have studied law and gone to Brussels hoping to make changes that would benefit the lives of others, but she had gradually become disillusioned and the bright hopes of her dreams had become tarnished. Now she could do something for others—something just as important in its way as the work she might have been able to do via the Veritas Foundation.

The man confronting her needed an heir. A son. *Her* son. A son born of her who, with her love and guidance, would surely become a ruler who would be everything a good ruler should be—a ruler who would honour and love his people, who would guide them to a better future, who would understand the importance of providing them with proper education. A ruler who would build hospitals and schools, who would give his people pride in themselves and their future instead of tethering them to the past.

Hope and determination gathered force inside her like a tidal wave, surging up from the depths of her being, refusing to allow anything to stand in its way. Her breath caught in her throat, lifting her breasts. The movement caught Max's attention. His late wife had considered herself to be a beauty, a *femme fatale* whom no man could resist, but her sister had a darker, deeper female magic that owed nothing to the expensive beauty treatments and designer clothes Eloise had loved. The promise of true sensuality surrounded her like an invisible aura. Max frowned. The last thing he wanted was another wife whose sex drive might take her into the arms and the beds of other men. But against his will, against logic and wisdom, he could feel the magnetic pull of her sensuality on his own senses.

He dismissed the warning note being struck within him—he had been too long without a woman. But, since he was thirty-four years old, and not twenty-four, he was perfectly capable of subsuming his sexual desire and channelling his energies into other less dangerous responses.

Unexpectedly, irrationally and surely foolishly a small thrill of excitement surged through Ionanthe. She had the power to give Fortenegro a prince—a leader who would truly lead its people to freedom.

She looked at Max. He exuded power and confidence. His features were strongly drawn into lines of raw masculinity, his cheekbones and jaw carved and sculpted and then clothed in flesh in a way that drew the female eye. Yes, he was very good-looking—if one liked that particular brand of hard-edged arrogant male sexuality and darkly brooding looks. He carried within his genes the history of all those who had ruled Fortenegro: Moorish warriors, Crusaders, Norman knights, and long before them Egyptians, Phoenicians, Greeks and Romans. He wore his pride like an invisible cloak that swung from his shoulders as surely as a real one had swung from the shoulders of those who had come here and stamped their will on the island—just as he was now trying to stamp his will on her.

But she had her own power—the power of giving the island a ruler who would truly be an honourable man and a wise and just prince—her son by this man who had brought her here to be a flesh-and-blood sacrifice—a destiny that belonged in reality to another age. But she was a woman of this modern age, a twenty-first-century woman with strong beliefs and values. She was no helpless victim but a woman with the strength of mind and of purpose to shape events to match her own goals.

She was no young, foolish girl with a head and a heart filled with silly dreams. Yes, once she had yearned to find love, a man who would share her crusading need to right the wrongs of the past and to work for the good of her people. She had known that she would never find him on the island, governed by men like her grandfather, who adhered to the old ways, but she had not found him in Brussels either, where she had quickly learned that a sincere smile could easily mask a liar and a cheat. Powerful men had desired her—powerful married men. She had refused them, whilst the men she *had* accepted had ultimately turned out to be weak and incapable of matching her hunger for equality and justice for those denied those things. She was twenty-seven now, and she couldn't remember whether it was five or six years since she had last slept with a man—either way, it didn't matter. She was not her sister, greedy and amoral, craving the shallow satisfaction of the excitement of sex with strangers.

Her sister—to whom the man now waiting for her response had been married. She was surprised that Eloise had cheated on him. She would have thought that he was just Eloise's type: good-looking, sexy, rich, and in a position to give her the status she and their grandfather had always craved.

Ionanthe might have acknowledged that she would never fulfil her dream of meeting a man who could be her true partner in life and in love, but she still had that same teenage longing to change the world—and for the better. That goal could now be within her reach. Through her son—the son this man would demand from her in payment of her family's debt to him—she could change the lives of her people for the better. Was that perhaps not just her fate but more importantly her destiny? That she should provide the people with a ruler who would be worthy of them?

The sun was dying into the sea, burnishing it dark gold. Ionanthe shook back her hair, the action tightening her throat, the last of the light carving her profile into a perfect cameo.

There was a pride about her, a wildness, an energy, a challenge about her, that unleashed within him an unfamiliar need to respond. Max frowned, not liking his own reaction and not really understanding it. Eloise had been sexually provocative and had left him cold. But Ionanthe challenged him with her pride, not her body or her sexuality, and for some reason his body had reacted to that. He shrugged, mentally dismissing what he did not want to dwell on. Ionanthe was a beautiful woman, and he was a man who had been without sex for almost a year.

Ionanthe turned away from the window and looked at Max.

'And if I refuse?' she demanded, her head held high, pride in every line of her body.

'You already know the answer to that. I cannot force you to marry me, but, according to my ministers and courtiers, if I do not show myself to the people as a worthy ruler by taking you, and if you do not submit to me in blood payment for the dishonour and shame your sister has brought on both our houses, then the people may very well take it upon themselves to exact payment from *you*.'

The starkness of his warning hung between them in the stern watching silence of the tower—a place that had held and held again against the enemies of the rulers of Fortenegro, protecting their lives and their honour.

The blood left Ionanthe's face, but she didn't weaken. Just the merest whisper of an exhaled breath and the movement of her throat as she swallowed betrayed what she felt.

She was as spoiled and arrogant as her sister, of course. They shared the same blood and the same upbringing, after all, and like her sister and her grandfather she would despise his plans for her country. But she had courage, Max admitted.

'I expect that it was Count Petronius who suggested that you bully me into agreeing by threatening to hand me over to the people,' she said scornfully. 'He and my grandfather were bitter enemies, who vied to have the most control over whoever sat on the throne.'

'It *was* Count Petronius who told me that in some of the more remote parts of the island the people have been known to stone adulterous wives,' Max agreed.

They looked at one another.

She was *not* going to weaken or show him any fear, Ionanthe told herself.

'I am not an adulterous wife. And I am not a possession to be used to pay off my family's supposed debt to you to save your pride and your honour.' Her voice dripped acid contempt.

'This isn't about my pride or my honour,' Max corrected her coldly.

Ionanthe gave a small shrug, the action revealing the

smooth golden flesh of one bare shoulder as the wide boat neckline of her top slipped to one side. She felt its movement but disdained to adjust the neckline. She wasn't going to have him thinking that the thought of him looking at her bare flesh made her feel uncomfortable.

She was an outstandingly alluring woman, Max acknowledged, and yet for all her obvious sensuality she seemed unaware of its power, wearing what to other women would be the equivalent of a priceless *haute couture* garment as carelessly as though it were no more than a pair of chainstore jeans.

If she was oblivious to her effect on his sex, he was not, Max admitted. There had been women who had shared his life and his bed—beautiful, enticing women from whom he had always parted without any regret, having enjoyed a mutual satisfying sexual relationship. But none of them had ever aroused him by the sight of a bared shoulder. Merely feasting his gaze on her naked shoulder felt as erotic as though he had actually touched her skin, stroked his hand over it, absorbing its texture and its warmth.

Angered by his own momentary weakness, Max looked away from her. His life was complicated enough already, without him adding any further complications to it. Certainly it would be easier and would make more sense to let her think that he expected her to provide him with a son than to try to tell her the truth, Max acknowledged.

'The people are anxious for me to secure the succession,' he told her, his voice clipped.

The succession. Her son. The key that would unlock the medieval prison in which the people were trapped.

'My grandfather would say that it is my duty to do as you ask and take my sister's place.'

'And what do *you* say?' Max prompted.

'I say that a man who tricks and traps a woman into marriage and threatens her with death by stoning if she refuses is not a man I could either respect or honour. But you are not merely a man, are you? You are Fortenegro's ruler—its Prince.'

Even as she spoke a powerful sense of destiny was filling her. A demand. And her own answer to it rose up inside her and would not be denied. A sacrifice was being demanded of her, but the thought of the potential benefit for her people was so filled with hope and joy that her own heart filled with them as well.

She took a deep breath, and told Max calmly, 'I will marry you. But I will live my own life within that marriage. No, before you make any accusation, I do not wish to copy my sister and crawl into the beds of an endless succession of men. But there is a life I wish to live of my own, and I *shall* live it.'

'What kind of life?' Max demanded. But she refused to answer him, simply shaking her head instead.

As Max's wife, as Crown Princess, she could surely begin to do some of those things she had argued so passionately for her grandfather to do, which he had told her so angrily he would *never* do nor allow her to do either. She could start on their own estates; she would have the money. Her grandfather had been a wealthy man, and had had power. Education for the children, better working conditions for their parents—there was so much she wanted to do. But she must move carefully; she could, after all, do nothing until they were married.

Why was he standing here feeling such a sense of loss, such a sense of a darkness within himself? Ionanthe had given him the answer he needed.

Yes, she had given him that—but he sensed that there was something she was concealing from him, some sense of purpose, something that might affect his own plans to their detriment.

Max shrugged aside his doubts. Their marriage was as necessary to him for his purpose as it was to her for her safety. They would both gain something from it—just as they would both lose something.

'So we are agreed, then?' he asked her. 'You understand that you are to take your late sister's place in my life and in my bed, as my wife and the mother of my heir?'

They were stark and dispassionate words, cold words that described an equally cold marriage, Max acknowledged. But they were words that had to be said. There must be no misunderstanding on her part as to what would be expected of her.

Ionanthe lifted her chin, and told him firmly, 'Yes. I do.'

'Very well, then,' he acknowledged.

They looked at one another: two people who neither trusted nor liked one another but who understood that their future lay together and that they were trapped in it together.

CHAPTER THREE

'*ASIIEEE*—how cruel it is that your poor mother did not live to see this day. Her daughter marrying our Prince and being crowned Princess.'

'I too wish that my mother was still alive, Maria,' Ionanthe told the old lady who had been part of her grandfather's household for as long as Ionanthe could remember.

She had the happiest of memories of her parents, who had died in a skiing accident in Italy when she had been thirteen. She had missed them desperately then and she still missed them now. Especially at times like this. She felt very alone, standing here in what had once been her grandfather's state apartment. The weight of the fabric of the cloth-of-gold overdress—a priceless royal heirloom in which all Fortenegro brides were supposed to be married but which apparently her sister had refused point-blank to wear—was heavy, and felt all the more so because of the old scents of rose and lavender that clung to it, reminding her of previous brides who had worn it. But its weight was easier to bear right now than the weight of the responsibility she was about to take on—for her country and its people, she told herself fiercely, for them and for the son she would give them, who would transform their lives with the light of true democracy.

There was a heavy knock on the closed double doors, which were flung open to reveal the Lord Chamberlain in his formal regalia, flanked by heralds wearing the Prince's livery and supported by the island's highest ranking dignitaries, also wearing their ancient formal regalia.

The gold dress, worn over a rich cream lace gown that matched her veil, no longer seemed so garishly rich now that she was surrounded by her bridal escort in their scarlet, and gold.

Since she had no male relative it was the Lord Chamberlain who escorted her. The heavy weight of her skirt and his cloak combined to make a surging sound as they walked ceremoniously through the open doors of the staterooms.

Max looked down at the bent head of his bride as she kneeled before him in the traditional symbolic gesture that was part of the royal marriage service whilst the Archbishop married them.

It made her blood boil to have to kneel to her new husband like this, but she must think of the greater good and not her own humiliation, Ionanthe told herself as one of the other two officiating bishops wafted the sacred scented incense over her and the other dropped gold-painted rose petals on her.

'Let the doors be thrown open and the news be carried to the furtherest part of his kingdom that the

Prince is married,' the Archbishop intoned. 'Let the trumpets sound and great joy be amongst the people.'

From her kneeling position Ionanthe couldn't see the doors being opened, but she could see the light that poured into the cathedral.

Max reached down and took hold of Ionanthe's hands, which were still folded in front of her.

Ionanthe looked up at him, ignoring the warning she had been given that it was forbidden by tradition for her to look at her new husband until he gave her permission to do so.

Also according to tradition she was now supposed to kiss his foot in gratitude for being married to him. Ionanthe's lips compressed as she deliberately stood up so that they were standing facing one another. The triumph she had been feeling at breaking with tradition and showing her own strength of character and will was lost in the Archbishop's hissed gasp of shocked breath when Max stepped forward, clasping her shoulders and holding her imprisoned as he bent his head towards her.

When she realised what he intended to do Ionanthe stiffened in rejection and hissed, 'No—you must not kiss me. It is not the tradition.'

'Then we will make our own new tradition,' Max told her equably.

His lips felt warm against her own, warm and firm and knowingly confident in a way that her own were not. They were alternately trembling and then parting, in helpless disarray. He had undermined her attempt to establish her independence far too effectively for her to be able to rally and fight back. His lips left hers and then returned, brushing them softly.

If she hadn't known better she might even have thought that his touch was meant to be reassuring—but that couldn't possibly be so, since he was the one who had mocked her with his kiss in the first place. Had he perhaps confused her with Eloise, assuming that she was like her sister and would welcome this promise of future intimacy between them? If so he was going to be in for a shock when he discovered that she did not have her sister's breadth of sexual experience. It was too late now to regret not taking advantage of the ample opportunities over the years when she had preferred her studies and her dreams to the intimacies she had been offered.

'It is not the custom for the Crown Prince's bride to stand at his side as his equal until she has asked for permission to do so,' the Archbishop was saying, with disapproval.

'Sometimes custom has to give way to a more modern way of doing things,' Ionanthe heard Max saying, before she could react herself and refuse to kneel. 'And this is one of those occasions.'

'It is our custom,' the Archbishop was insisting stubbornly.

'Then it must be changed for a new custom—one that is based on equality.'

Ionanthe knew that she was probably looking as shocked as the Archbishop, although for a different reason. The last thing she had expected was to hear her new husband talking about equality.

The Archbishop looked crestfallen and upset. 'But, sire....'

Max frowned as he listened to the quaver in the older man's voice. He had told himself that he would take things slowly and not risk offending his people, but the sight of Ionanthe kneeling at his feet had filled him with so much revulsion that he hadn't been able to stop himself from saying something.

The Archbishop's pride had been hurt, though, and he must salve that wound, Max recognised. In a more gentle voice he told him, 'I do not believe that it is fitting for the mother of my heir to kneel at any man's feet.'

The Archbishop nodded his head and looked appeased.

The new Prince was a dangerously clever man, Ionanthe decided as Max took her arm, so that together they walked down the aisle towards the open doors of the cathedral and the state carriage waiting to take them back to the palace.

An hour later they stood on the main balcony of the palace, looking down into the square where people had gathered to see them.

'At least the people are pleased to see us married. Listen to them cheering,' said Max.

'Are they cheering as loudly as they did when you married Eloise?' Ionanthe couldn't resist asking cynically. She regretted the words as soon as they had been uttered. They reminded her too sharply of the way she had felt as a child, knowing that their grandfather favoured her sister and always trying and failing to claim some of his attention and approval—some of his love—for herself. Her words had been a foolish mistake. After all, she didn't want anything from this man who had been her sister's husband.

'That was different,' he answered her quietly.

Different? Different in what way? Different because he had actually *loved* her wayward sister?

The feeling exploding inside her couldn't possibly be pain, Ionanthe denied to herself. Why should it be?

The scene down below them was one of pageantry and excitement. The square was busy with dancers in national dress, the Royal Guard in their uniforms—sentries in dark blue, gunners in dark green coats with gold braid standing by their cannons, whilst the cavalry were wearing scarlet. The rich colours stood out against the icing-white glare of the eighteenth-century baroque frontage that had been put on the old castle.

The church clock on the opposite side of the square, which had fascinated her as a child, was still drawing crowds of children to stand at the bottom, waiting for midday to strike and set off the mechanical scenes that took place one after the other. Eloise had always been far more interested in watching the changing of the guard than looking at the clock.

Ionanthe closed her eyes. She and her sister had never been close, but that did not mean she did not feel any discomfort at all at the thought of taking what had been her place. Tonight, when she lay in Max's arms fulfilling her sacrificial role, would he be thinking of Eloise? Would he be comparing her to her sister and finding her wanting? They would have been well matched in bed, her sister and this man who somehow remained very sensual and male despite the formality of the dress uniform he was wearing. It caused her a sharp spike of disquiet to know that it was his sensuality, his sexuality, that was somehow foremost in her mind, and not far more relevant aspects of his personality.

Max watched the crowd down below them, laughing happily and enjoying themselves as they celebrated their marriage—the same crowd that, according to the Count, would have threatened to depose him if he had not followed the island's tradition and accepted its cruel ancient laws. Once again he had a wife—this time one who had been blackmailed and forced into marrying him. Max wished he knew Ionanthe better. Eloise had never talked about her sister or to her, as far as Max knew, other than to say that Ionanthe had always been jealous of her because their grandfather had loved her more than he did Ionanthe.

Had he known her better, had he been able to trust her, then he might have talked openly and honestly to her. He might have told her that he loathed the way she had been forced into marriage with him as much as she did herself. Told her that as soon as it was within his power to do so he would set her free. And, had he thought there was the remotest chance that she would understand them, he might have revealed his dreams and hopes for their people to her. But he did not know her, and he could not trust her, so he could say nothing. It was too much of a risk. After all, he had already made one mistake in thinking he could trust her sister.

In the early days of their marriage, when he had still been foolish enough to think that they could work together to create a marriage based on mutual respect and a shared goal, he had talked to Eloise about his plans. She had sulked and complained that he was being boring, telling him that she thought he should let her grandfather and the other barons deal with the people, because all she wanted to do was have fun. Eloise had quickly grown bored with their marriage once she'd realised that he was not prepared to accede to her demands that they become part of the spoiled wealthy and well-born European social circle she loved.

Max had soon come to understand that there was no point in blaming Eloise for his own disillusionment at her shallowness and her adultery. The blame lay with their very different assumptions and beliefs, and the fact that they had each assumed that the other felt as they did about key issues.

Eloise and Ionanthe had been brought up in the same household, and whilst Ionanthe might *seem* to have very different values from those of her sister, that did not mean that he could trust her. As he had already discovered, the elite of the island—of which Ionanthe was a member—were fiercely opposed to the changes Max wanted to make. Given that, it made sense for him not to say anything to her.

Count Petronius appeared at Max's elbow. 'The people are waiting for you to walk amongst them to present your bride to them and receive their congratulations,' he informed them both.

Max frowned, and told him curtly, 'I don't think that would be a good idea.'

Ionanthe drew in a sharp breath on another fierce stab

of angry pride. Before she could stop herself she was demanding, 'I presume that you followed the custom when you married Eloise? That you were happy to present *her* to the people?'

How many times as a child had she been forced into the shadows whilst her grandfather proudly showed off Eloise? How many times had she been hurt by his preference for her sister? Those he had appointed to care for them had pursed their lips and shaken their heads, telling her that she was 'difficult' and that it was no wonder her grandfather preferred her prettier and 'nicer' sister. The feelings she had experienced then surged through her now, overwhelming adult logic and understanding. For a handful of seconds her new husband's unwillingness to present her to the people with pride in their relationship became her grandfather's cruel rejection of her, and she was filled with the same hurting pain as she had been then.

But analysing logically just why she should feel this angry rush of painful emotion would have to wait until she was calmer. Right now what she wanted more than anything else was recognition of her right to be respected as her sister had been.

Max's clipped 'That was different' only inflamed rather than soothed her anger.

Gritting her teeth, Ionanthe told him fiercely, 'I will not be humiliated and shamed before the people by being bundled out of sight. I may not be the bride—the wife—of your free choice, but you are the one who has forced this marriage on both of us. In marrying you I have paid my family's debt to you and to the people. I am now their Princess. They have a right to welcome me as such, and I have a right to that welcome.'

She spoke well and with pride, Max recognised, and maybe the fears he had for her safety amongst a crowd who not so very long ago might have turned on her in fury and revenge were unnecessary. She, after all, would know the people, the way they thought and felt, far better than he.

'The Princess is right, Highness. The people will expect you both to walk amongst them.'

'Very well, then,' Max agreed.

The square was crowded, the air warm from the many food stalls offering hot food. The heavy weight of the gold overdress added to Ionanthe's growing discomfort as they made their slow and stately progress through the crowd.

Initially, when they had set out from the palace steps, they had been surrounded by uniformed palace guards, but the square was packed with people and gradually they had broken through the ranks of the guards. The people might be enjoying themselves, but Ionanthe couldn't help contrasting their general air of shabbiness and poverty with the extreme richness of the appearance of those connected with the court—including, of course, herself. Here and there amongst the sea of faces, Ionanthe recognised people from her grandfather's estate, and a wave of self-revulsion washed over her as she acknowledged that *her* family was responsible for their poverty. That must change. She was determined on that.

A courtier was throwing coins into the crowd for the children, and it filled Ionanthe with anger to see them scrabbling for the money. Right in front of them one small child burst into tears as an older child wrenched open his chubby hand to remove the coins inside it. The small scene wrenched at Ionanthe's heart. Automatically she stepped forward, wanting to comfort the smaller child, but to her astonishment Max beat her to it, going down on one knee in the dust of the square to take the hands of both children. To the side of him the families looked on, their faces tight with real fear. Cosmo had treated the poorest amongst the people particularly badly, Ionanthe knew, raising taxes and punishing them for all manner of small things, laughing and saying that they were free to leave the island and live elsewhere if they did not like the way he ran his own country.

Obedient to Max's grip on their wrists, both children opened their hands. Max felt his heart contract with angry pity as he looked down at the small coins that had caused the fracas. A few pennies, that was all, and yet—as he already knew from studying the island's financial affairs—for some of the poorest families a few pennies would be vitally important. One day, if he was successful, no child on Fortenegro would need to fight for pennies or risk going hungry.

Sharing the coins between the two children equally, he closed their palms over them and then stood up, announcing firmly, 'My people—in honour of this day, every family in Fortenegro will receive the sum of one hundred *fortens*.'

Immediately a loud buzz of excitement broke out as the news was passed from person to person. The Count looked aghast and complained, 'Such a gesture will cost the treasury dear, Highness.'

'Then let it. The Treasury can certainly afford it; it is less, I suspect, than my late cousin would have spent on the new yacht he was planning to commission.'

There were tears of real gratitude in the eyes of the people listening to him, and Ionanthe could feel her own eyes starting to smart with emotion as she reacted to his unexpected generosity. But he was still Cosmo's cousin, she reminded herself fiercely. Still the same man who had threatened and forced her into this marriage with him rather than risk losing his royal status and everything that went with it. One act of casual kindness could not alter that.

It appalled and shocked her to realise how easily swayed her emotions were; in some way she seemed to want to believe the best of him, as though she was already emotionally vulnerable to him. That was ridiculous—more than ridiculous. It was impossible. The emotion she felt stemmed from her concern for the people, that was all, and she must make sure he knew it.

When the Count had turned away, she lifted her chin and told Max fiercely, 'It is all very well giving them money, but what they really need is the freedom to earn a decent wage instead of working for a pittance as they do now for the island's rich landowners.'

'One of which was your grandfather,' Max pointed out coolly. Her words stung.

What had he expected? He derided himself. That she

would turn to him and praise him for his actions? That she would look at him with warmth in her eyes instead of contempt? That she would fling herself into his arms? Of course not. Why should it matter *what* she thought of him? She was simply a means to an end, that was all. A means to an end and yet a human being whose freedom of choice was being sacrificed to appease an age-old custom. For the greater good, Max insisted to himself—against his conscience.

'It is time, I think, for us to head back to the palace.'

Delicate, but oh-so-erotic shivers of pleasure slid wantonly over Ionanthe's skin in the place where Max's warm breath had touched it. Her reaction took her completely off guard. Shock followed pleasure—shock that her body was capable of having such an immediate and intense reaction to any man, but most of all to this one. It was totally out of character for her—totally unfamiliar, totally unwanted and unacceptable—and yet still her flesh was clinging to the memory of the sensation it had soaked up so greedily. She had gone years without missing or wanting a man's sensual touch—so why now, as though some magical button had been pressed, was she becoming so acutely aware of this man's sensuality?

Infuriated with herself for her weakness, Ionanthe moved out of reach of a second assault on her defences, firmly reminding herself of the reality of the situation. This was a man who was already dictating to her and telling her what to do. To him she was merely a possession—payment of a debt he was owed. And tonight in his arms she would have to make the first payment.

A shudder tore through her. She should not have allowed herself to think of that, of tonight.

As she moved away from him he reached out to stop her, placing his hand on her arm. Even though he wasn't using any force, and even though her arms were covered, thanks to her unwanted heightened state of awareness she could feel each one of his fingers pressing on her as though there was no barrier between them. His touch was that of flesh on flesh. Disturbing and unwanted images slid serpent-like into her mind—images of him with her sister, touching her, caressing her, admiring and praising her. Once again emotion spiked sharply through her, reminding her of the jealousy she had felt as a child. This was so wrong, so foolish, and so dangerous. She was *not* competing with her dead sister for this man's approval. There was only one thing she wanted from him and it was not his sexual desire for her. The only reason she had married him was the people of Fortenegro, for the son who would one day rule benignly over them. For that she was prepared to undergo and endure whatever was necessary. She pulled away from him, plunging into the crowd, determined to show him her independence.

'Ionanthe! No!' Max protested, cursing under his breath as she was swallowed up by the crowd, and forcing his way through it after her.

People were pressing in on her, the crowd was carrying her along with it, almost causing her to lose her balance. Fear stabbed through Ionanthe as she realised how vulnerable she was in her heavy clothes.

An elderly man grabbed hold of her arm, warning

her, 'You had better do better by our Prince than that whore of a sister of yours. She shamed us all when she shamed him.'

Spittle flecked his lips, and his eyes were wild with anger as he shook her arm painfully. The people surrounding her who had been smiling before were now starting to frown, their mood changing. She looked round for the guards but couldn't see any of them. She was alone in a crowd which was quickly becoming hostile to her.

She hadn't thought it was in her nature to panic, but she was beginning to do so now.

Then Ionanthe felt another hand on her arm, in a touch that extraordinarily her body somehow recognised. And a familiar voice was saying firmly, 'Princess Ionanthe has already paid the debt owed by her family to the people of Fortenegro. Her presence here today as my bride and your Princess is proof of that.'

He was at her side now, his presence calming the crowd and forcing the old man to release her, as the crowd began to murmur their agreement to his words.

Calmly but determinedly Max was guiding her back through the crowd. A male voice called out to him from the crowd.

'Make sure you get us a fine future prince on her as soon as maybe, Your Highness.' The sentiment was quickly taken up by others, who threw in their own words of bawdy advice to the new bridegroom. Ionanthe fought to stop her face from burning with angry humiliated colour. Torn between unwanted relief that she had been rescued and discomfort about what was being said,

Ionanthe took refuge in silence as they made their way back towards the palace.

They had almost reached the main entrance when once again Max told hold of her arm. This time she fought against her body's treacherous reaction, clamping down on the sensation that shot through her veins and stiffening herself against it. The comments she had been subjected to had brought home to her the reality of what she had done; they clung inside her head, rubbing as abrasively against her mind as burrs would have rubbed against her skin.

'Isn't it enough for you to have forced me into marrying you? Must you force me to obey your will physically as well?' she challenged him bitterly.

Max felt the forceful surge of his own anger swelling through him to meet her biting contempt, shocking him with its intensity as he fought to subdue it.

Not once during the months he had been married to Eloise had she ever come anywhere near arousing him emotionally in the way that Ionanthe could, despite the fact that he had known her only a matter of days. She seemed to delight in pushing him—punishing him for their current situation, no doubt, he reminded himself as his anger subsided. It was completely out of character for him to let anyone get under his skin enough to make him react emotionally to them when his response should be purely cerebral.

'Far from wishing to force you to do anything, I merely wanted to suggest that we use the side entrance to the palace. That way we will attract less attention.'

He had a point, Ionanthe admitted grudgingly, but

she wasn't going to say so. Instead she started to walk towards the door set in one of the original castle turrets, both of them slipping through the shadows the building now threw across the square, hidden from the view of the people crowding the palace steps. She welcomed the peace of its stone interior after the busyness of the square. Her dress had become uncomfortably heavy and her head had started to ache. The reality of what she had done had begun to set in, filling her with a mixture of despair and panic. But she mustn't think of herself and her immediate future, she told herself as she started to climb the stone steps that she knew from memory led to a corridor that connected the old castle to the more modern palace.

She had almost reached the last step when somehow or other she stepped onto the hem of her gown, the accidental movement unbalancing her and causing her to stumble. Max, who was several steps below her, heard the small startled sound she made and raced up the stairs, catching her as she fell.

If she was trembling with the fragility of new spring buds in the wind then it was because of her shock. If she felt weak and her heart was pounding with dangerous speed then it was because of the weight of her gown. If she couldn't move then it was because of the arms that imprisoned her.

She had to make him release her. It was dangerous to be in his arms. She looked up at him, her gaze travelling the distance from his chin to his mouth and then refusing to move any further. What had been a mere tremor of shock had now become a fiercely violent shudder that came from deep within her and ached through her. She felt dizzy, light-headed, removed from everything about herself she considered 'normal'. She had become, instead, a woman who hungered for something unknown and forbidden.

Was this how her sister had felt with those men, those strangers, she had delighted in taking to her bed? Hungering for something she knew she should not want? It was a disturbing thought. She had always prided herself on being different from Eloise, on having different values from the sister, whose behaviour she had never been able to relate to and had privately abhorred.

It was because her heart was racing so fast that his own had started to pound heavily, Max told himself. It was because the walls either side of the steps enclosed them that he was so conscious of the scent of her hair and her skin. It was because he was a man and she was a woman that his body was flooded with an unwanted surge of physical arousal that had him tightening his hold on her.

He wanted her, Max knew. The knowledge rushed over him and through him, possessing him as he ached to possess her, threatening to carry with it every moral barrier and code that should have held it back. Why? It was illogical, unfathomable, the opposite of so much about himself he had believed unchangeable. He felt as though he had stepped outside his own skin and become a hostage to his own need in a way that filled him with mental distaste and rejection. Yet at the same time his body renewed its assault on those feelings as though it was determined to have its way.

To travel so far and in such an unfamiliar direction so unexpectedly and in so short a space of time had robbed him of the ability to think logically, Max decided.

An aeon could have passed, or merely a few seconds. She was quite unable to judge the difference, Ionanthe admitted, because she was too caught up in the maelstrom of sensations and emotions that had somehow been created out of nothing and which were still controlling her. And would probably continue to control her for as long as Max was holding her. She was quite literally spellbound, and he was the one who had cast that spell, binding her senses to his will, forcing from them a response she would never willingly have given him, stirring up within her a dark mystery of maddening longing that had seized and held captive her ability to think or reason.

All she knew was that his lips were only a sigh away from her own. All she wanted to know was the possession of them on her own. There was nothing else in this moment but him.

The normal Ionanthe—the Ionanthe she knew—would never have closed her eyes and swayed closer to Max, exhaling on a breath that was a siren's call. But this Ionanthe was not her normal self. This Ionanthe was not prepared to listen to any objections from its alter ego.

He should resist. Max knew that. This trick of pretended longing and faked intimacy had been one of Eloise's favourites, and it had been a ploy he had found easy enough to withstand when she'd used it against him. Somehow, though, with Ionanthe things were different. Her lips, soft and warm with natural colour, were surely shaped for kisses and sensuality. They pillowed the touch of his own, igniting within him a need that roared through him like a forest fire.

Extreme danger. How often had she heard those words and dismissed them and those who lived to experience it, those who holidayed in places that offered it? Now she could only marvel that they should go to such lengths when all the time it was here, so close at hand, in a man's arms and beneath the hard pressure of his lips.

Extreme danger and extreme desire went hand in hand, producing between them an extreme pleasure that was an almost unbearable delight. A delight that was merely a foretaste of what the night that lay before them would hold for her. How could Eloise have wanted someone else when she'd had a husband who could give her this kind of pleasure?

Eloise! Abruptly Ionanthe pulled back from Max before he could stop her, telling him in a voice designed to conceal the shaky vulnerability she was really feeling, 'My sister may have welcomed being treated like a sex object, but I don't.'

Her angry contempt coming hard on the heels of her earlier eagerness rasped against Max's already dangerously charged emotions. How the hell had he managed to lose control of himself so easily and so quickly?

'You could have fooled me,' he responded grimly. 'In fact I'd have gone as far as to say you were positively…'

'What? Asking for it? Is that what you were going to say?' Ionanthe rounded on him angrily. 'How typical of a man like you—but then I suppose I shouldn't have expected anything else. Cosmo was a sexist bully, and you are obviously cut from the same cloth.'

Her accusation cooled Max's own anger to sharp-edged ice.

'What I was going to say was that you seemed to be positively enjoying it. But if we're talking about shared family flaws, then perhaps *I* should have remembered that your sister also had a taste for playing the tease, blowing hot when she wanted something and then blowing cold when it suited her.'

I am not Eloise, Ionanthe wanted to say. But she remembered how often her grandfather had distanced himself from her and withheld his love from her with the words, 'You are not Eloise.' Instead she picked up her heavy skirts and turned her back on Max as she headed down the empty corridor.

CHAPTER FOUR

SHE was free now of the presence of the stiffly correct lady's maid she had needed to help her out of the heavy formality of her wedding gown, alone in the bedroom she would be sharing with her new husband.

Over the handful of days that had elapsed between Max presenting her with his ultimatum and their marriage Ionanthe had told both Max and the Count that she did not want to be surrounded by ladies-in-waiting or a large staff, and it had eventually been agreed that two ladies-in-waiting would attend her on only the most formal occasions, and that she would have only one personal maid who would attend her only when she needed her.

It was a relief to be wearing her own clothes again—even if the maid had eyed them with disdain.

The suite of rooms she was to share with Max had surprised her. She had assumed that he would be occupying the Royal State Apartments, which she remembered from her childhood, but Max had created his own far more modern living quarters in the older part of the building—the castle itself—rather than opting to live in the seventeenth-century addition of the palace. The 'new' royal apartments comprised a drawing room, a dining room with a small kitchen off it, the bedroom she was now in, two bathrooms and two dressing rooms, which were entered via doors on either side of the large bed that she was trying desperately hard to ignore.

The drawing room had large glass doors that opened out onto a private terrace, complete with an infinity swimming pool, and the view from the apartments' windows was one of wild rugged splendour over the cliffs and out to sea.

Unlike the rest of the palace, with its grand and formal decor and furniture, these rooms had a much more modern and relaxed air to them. In fact they were rooms in which she would have felt very much at home in other circumstances.

She had deliberately chosen to change into a pair of jeans and a simple tee shirt, as though wearing them was somehow like wearing a badge of independence, making a statement about what she was and what she was not. And because she wanted to distance herself in every way from what had happened earlier, so that he knew it had been a momentary aberration—her response to him alien to everything she believed she stood for and something never to be repeated.

She did not desire him. She simply desired the son he would give her. When she lay beneath him, enduring the possession of his body, it would be because of her belief that the people on this island deserved to be freed from their servitude. Not because she wanted to be there, and certainly not because she gloried in being there. There would be no repetition of that earlier kiss. She would show him no weakness or vulnerability.

Abruptly she realised that she was pacing the floor. Why? She already knew that he would claim payment of her family's debt to him. If he thought to draw out her torment by making her wait, because he thought she would be anxious until it was over and done with, then she would show him that he was wrong.

She opened the glass doors and stepped out onto the terrace. The air on this side of the island smelled and felt different, somehow—sharper, stronger, more exhilarating. The sea both protected the castle and reminded those who had built it that it was a dangerous restless living force that could never be ignored. Like love itself.

Love? What had *that* to do with anything?

Everything, she told herself sombrely. Because she would love the son this marriage would bring her, and in turn would ensure that he loved his people.

Late autumn had long ago faded into winter and now the tops of the mountains that lay inland were capped with snow as icy and remote as the heart of this marriage she had made.

Where was he? When was he going to come to her and demand his pound of flesh? Ionanthe paced the terrace as she looked towards the bedroom she would have to share with Max.

At least it was not the same bedchamber he had shared with her sister. Yania, the young woman who had been appointed to attend her, had told her that when she had mentioned that Max had moved out of the Royal State Apartments immediately after Eloise's death.

Because he couldn't bear to sleep there alone without her?

What did it matter to her *what* he felt?

She turned round to stare out to sea.

'I'm sorry. I got involved in some necessary paperwork which took longer than I had anticipated.'

Was it the fact that she hadn't heard him come towards her or the fact that she hadn't expected his apology that was causing her heart to thump so unsteadily against her chest wall?

'Have you eaten? Are you hungry?'

'No, and no,' Ionanthe answered him shortly, adding, 'Look, we both know what we're here for, so why don't we just get it over with?'

Max frowned. Her dismissive, almost critical manner was so different from the come-on she had given him earlier that it struck him that it must be just another ploy—and that irritated him. He'd expected anger, resentment, bitternes—those were the things he had been prepared for her to display, the things he'd promised himself he'd try to find a way to soothe for both their sakes. Fiery, ardent passion followed by icy disdain were not. She was challenging his pride, needling him into a retaliation he couldn't subdue.

'"Get it over with"?' he repeated grimly. 'Are you sure that's what you really want?'

He was referring to that…that incident on the stairs, Ionanthe knew, trying to humiliate and mock her because of her response to him then. The memory of that response was a taste as sour as the bitter aloes her nursemaid had painted on her nails as a child to stop her from biting them. Ionanthe looked down at those nails now, immaculately neat, with well-shaped cuticles, buffed to a soft natural sheen.

Max saw Ionanthe look down at her own hand. Her nails were free of the polish with which Eloise had always painted hers, and he had a sudden urge to reach for her hand, with its slim wrist and elegant fingers, and hold it within his own in an age-old gesture of comfort. Comfort? For her or for himself? Why not for both of them? After all, they were entering the unknown and uncertain world their marriage would be together, weren't they?

What was wrong with him? He already knew that there could be no real intimacy between them. Far better that they kept their emotional distance from one another. After all, she had made it plain enough to him that she didn't look for anything from their physical union other than getting it 'over with.'

He had moved closer to her, Ionanthe recognised. She hadn't seen him move, but her body knew that he had. Her senses had registered it and were still registering it; her nerve-endings were going into overload as they relayed back the effect his closeness was having on them.

'Yes. That is what I want,' Ionanthe confirmed, her pride pushing her to add recklessly, 'What else is there for me to want?'

'Pleasure, perhaps?' Max suggested.

Pleasure. Her muscles locked against the images his mocking words had evoked, but it was too late. Those same feelings she had experienced on the steps were running riot inside her like a gang of skilled pickpockets, overturning the barriers put up to deter them and plundering the vulnerable cache they had discovered.

'I don't look for pleasure in a relationship such as ours.' Her words were as much a denial of what she could feel within her own body as they were of what she was sure was his taunting mockery of her.

'But if you were to find it there…' Max persisted.

'That's impossible. There could never be any pleasure for me in having sex with a man I can't respect. I wouldn't want there to be. It would shame me to want such a man,' she declared furiously, desperate to stop him from thinking she had actually wanted him when they had shared that kiss.

Max felt the swift running tide of his own pride, its power and speed sucking away reason and impartiality. She was challenging him as a man—challenging his ability to arouse her and pleasure her. Telling him that she would rather lie ice-cold in his arms than permit her body to be warmed by any shared need or desire.

Ionanthe saw the glint of anger in Max's eyes. A quiver of something that was more than mere apprehension feathered across her nerves. Perhaps she had gone too far? she admitted. Said more than was wise? Now, in the chill of her growing anxiety, it was easy to admit what she had not been prepared to see in the heat of her prideful anger. Her husband was a powerful, sexual man—a man who knew how to touch a woman's body to draw the most sensual response from it. In her determination to stop him from thinking that she wanted him, and so spare her pride, had she unwittingly triggered his own pride?

'I am sure we are both agreed that we have in our different ways made a commitment that it is our duty to honour,' Ionanthe told Max hastily, trying to repair the damage she feared she might have caused. 'That being the case, I am sure we are also agreed that there is no need for either of us to look for anything more than the…the satisfaction that comes from doing that duty.'

'Your views on sex are obviously very different from those of your late sister,' Max responded wryly.

'My views on many things differ from those of Eloise,' Ionanthe hit back. 'I did not want to marry you,' she added when he made no response. 'You were the one who forced me into this marriage.'

'You are right,' Max announced. 'We might as well "get it over with".'

Was it because he was thinking about Eloise, comparing her sexuality to her late sister's and finding her wanting that he had made that abrupt statement? Ionanthe wondered.

The light had faded whilst they had been arguing, the sun sinking down into the sea and turning it a dull molten gold.

In their absence an ice bucket containing a bottle of champagne and two crystal champagne flutes had been placed on one of the modern black-marble-topped tables just inside the glass doors.

Ionanthe watched as Max opened the bottle with a single economically fluid movement, expertly filling the two glasses and then holding one out to her.

She rarely drank, but she suspected that to refuse

now would open her up to another unfavourable comparison with her late sister.

'What shall we toast?' Max asked as she took the glass from him.

What did you toast on your wedding night with Eloise? Ionanthe was tempted to ask, but of course she didn't. Instead she looked at him and said quietly, 'I would toast freedom. But of course it is not a toast we can share.'

Max could feel the anger burning up under his skin.

'You toast freedom, then, and I shall toast pleasure,' he told her mockingly, slanting a glance at her that made her whole body burn.

She was trembling so much she could barely hold the glass, never mind drink from it.

When she replaced it on the table, Max said coolly, 'You're right—we're wasting time when we should be performing our duty.' He shot back his cuff and looked at his watch—a plain, serviceable watch, not at all the kind of ostentatious rich man's toy she would have expected him to be wearing.

'Shall we agree to meet in the bedroom in, say, fifteen minutes' time? Dressed, or rather undressed for action?'

Ionanthe could feel her heart bumping along the bottom of her ribcage. She wasn't going to let him see the despair she was beginning to feel, though. Instead she lifted her chin and agreed, 'Very well.'

Max drained his glass, and was just turning away from her when after a brief knock the drawing room door was hurriedly opened. The Chancellor came in, looking very concerned, Count Petronius hard on his heels,

'I told you there was no need for us to disturb His

Highness, Ethan. I can deal with this matter,' said the Count.

'What matter?' Max demanded.

The Chancellor needed no further invitation. Ignoring the Count's obvious irritation he addressed Max. 'Highness, there has been a disturbance in the city—fighting in the streets among some of the men of your new bride's people, claiming that it is wrong that she has been forced to make a blood payment on behalf of her sister—'

'They have been arrested and are now, as we speak, being held in the square by the Royal Guard,' the Count broke in. 'There is no need for you to concern yourself on the matter, Highness. They will be treated with appropriate severity.'

'No!' Ionanthe defended her people automatically. These were men who had been loyal to her late parents and to their land. Now they stood firm to support Ionanthe. 'They will have meant no real harm.'

'They threatened the person of their ruler,' the Count insisted. 'And they must be punished accordingly.'

Max looked from the Count's implacable expression to Ionanthe's flushed face. So, *something* could apparently arouse his bride to passion, even if it wasn't him.

'I shall speak to these men myself,' he told the Count.

'And I shall come with you,' Ionanthe told them both firmly.

Max looked at her. Her announcement and her determination were very different from the reaction he had expected, knowing from experience what the reaction of both her sister and her grandfather would have been. He would have pursued the subject, to satisfy what he admitted was his growing curiosity about the differences he was observing between his late wife and the sister who had taken her place, but this was not the time for that.

'Sire, I would urge you not to risk either your own safety or that of Her Highness,' the Count was warning. 'Far better to allow the authorities to deal with the situation.'

Max listened to him, and then pointed out coolly, 'I disagree with you, Count. In fact I believe that it is time that all the people of Fortenegro recognised that *I* am this island's final authority, and that *my* word is law.'

With a brisk nod of his head, and without waiting to see what the Count's reaction was to his none-too-subtle challenge to the older man's determination to hold on to the power he had made on his own, Max strode towards the main doors to the castle.

'Open the doors,' he told the waiting guards firmly.

Was he going to order that those who were loyal to her family be punished? Ionanthe worried as she half ran to catch up with him.

'The Count is right when he says that you should not be exposed to danger,' Max told her.

'I am coming with you,' Ionanthe repeated, raising her voice so that he could hear it above the noise pouring in through the now open doors from the square below.

Somehow or other, without the need of heralds or trumpets, the crowd seemed to sense their presence, even though Max had descended the steps in silence. The words 'the Prince' seemed to pass from one person to another, to become a hush that gathered in force and intensity until the whole square was silently expectant. A shiver ran through Ionanthe as she felt the ancient power of the people's belief in and dependence on their ruler.

On the other side of the square the lights on the walls clearly illuminated the ceremonial uniforms of the Royal Guard, highlighting the disparity between their richness and the poverty of the small group of men they had herded into a corner and were keeping captive. *Her people.* A huge lump formed in Ionanthe's throat and her eyes stung with tears of mingled pity and pride for the men who had been brave enough and foolish enough to want to protect her.

Without thinking, she turned to Max and hissed fiercely, 'You must not hurt them.'

From deep within her memory she heard an echo of Cosmo as a young boy, saying savagely to her in the middle of a childhood quarrel, '*You* cannot tell me to do anything. I am Fortenegro's ruler. No one can tell me what to do, and those who try have to be punished.'

Max was ignoring her, and instead was striding towards the captives and their captors. The mass of people in the square parted before him.

When he reached the guards, Max demanded, 'What is going on here?'

'We have arrested these troublemakers, sire,' the most senior of the guards told him.

'You have forced our Duchess to marry you under duress. It is our duty to protect her and her honour,' one of the men under guard shouted.

Immediately someone in the crowd who had heard him yelled out, 'Listen to how the traitor speaks of our

Prince and the honour of a family that has no right to any honour. His words are an insult to His Highness.'

Despite herself, Ionanthe shivered as she saw the speed with which anger burned its way through the crowd.

Max saw the colour leave Ionanthe's face, and without being able to reason why he should want to do so he reached for her hand, holding it within his own and giving it a comforting squeeze.

Any prideful attempt she might have wanted to make to pull away was demolished as the crowd started to surge around them, almost knocking Ionanthe off her feet. Small stones were being thrown at the captive men.

Quickly Max pulled her close to him, holding her protectively and then commanding, 'My people, listen to me. Today has signified a very special moment in our shared history. For your sake, and out of her love for you, the Duchess Ionanthe consented to become my wife. Those who have served her family have every right to feel great pride in the sacrifice she has made for the sake of our principality. Together we will work for the good of this island and its people—all its people. It is my will and my decree that our wedding day should not be marred by violence and punishment.'

Although initially shocked to hear Max speak in such a powerful and flattering way about her, Ionanthe recovered quickly, seizing the moment to join her own voice to that of her new husband and address the now silent and watchful crowd.

'Your Prince speaks the truth.' She turned to where the captive men were standing stiffly and resentfully and told them, 'You do me great honour, but it is no exaggeration to say that your Prince has done me an even greater honour in taking me as his wife.'

A low rumble of dissent from her people and an even stronger rumble of contempt from the rest of the crowd swelled ominously into the silence, but Ionanthe refused to be deterred. She could feel the warmth of Max's arm against her back and she could feel too the protective clasp of his hand on her shoulder.

'Out of our shared love for you, if God wills it, the Prince and I will create the son who will one day rule you all. It is for him that I have submitted to my duty in the eyes of our ancient law, for him that your Prince has accepted my sacrifice. My people—our people—we do this for you.'

The whole square had fallen silent once more, but it was a tense, watchful and judging silence, Ionanthe knew. A silence that brooded and threatened. And then, unbelievably, Max caught hold of her hand and lifted it to his lips. Placing his kiss not on her knuckles but rather opening her palm and placing a kiss into it. Those close enough to witness the emotional intimacy and intensity of the small gesture gasped.

'My wife is right,' Max told the crowd. And, raising his voice, he commanded them, 'My people, this is not a time to dwell on past quarrels or injustices. It is a time to celebrate. Those who would have fought for the honour of my wife are to be praised, not punished, because in serving her best interests they also serve mine. I commend their loyalty, just as I promise my loyalty to all of you. Captain—' he turned to the captain of the Guard '—these men are to be allowed to go free.'

There was a great cheer from the crowd, and then another, and then suddenly the people were surging all around them, laughing and cheering, the earlier mood of hostility wiped clean away.

'Thank you for…for freeing them,' she managed to say to Max, even though she knew her voice was stilted.

The movement of the crowd suddenly threw Ionanthe against Max's chest. His arms came round her to hold her steady. Her hands were on his shoulders as she too sought to steady herself. She looked up at him, and then couldn't look away. The noise of the crowd seemed to fade, and all her senses registered was contained within the encirclement of Max's arms. He bent his head towards her own. Her heart was beating far too fast—and for no sensible reason. Her people were safe now, there was no need for her heart to thud or her pulse to race.

Max's lips touched her own, their possession hard and purposeful. She should pull away, she *wanted* to pull away, but the dominating power of his mouth on hers wouldn't let her. Instead she felt as though she was being carried by a swift and dangerous current that was taking her deeper with every breath she took. Until she was giving in to it and sinking down into its hot velvet darkness, allowing it to take her and possess her. Reality and everything that went with it was forgotten, sent into oblivion by what she was feeling, as though those feelings and her own senses had united against her, treacherously allowing an enemy force to overwhelm her defences.

Her whole body had turned soft and heavy, as though she had drunk some potion brewed by the witches who centuries ago were supposed to have inhabited the high mountains of Fortenegro. Desires, longings, needs that less than half an hour ago she would have fiercely claimed it was impossible for her to feel for any man, much less this one, were now burning through her, invading her belly, making her breasts ache, making her long with increasing sexual urgency for the most intense and intimate possession of her flesh by the man who was holding her.

And then the darkness beyond the town square was broken as a firework display began, the sound bringing her back to reality. Above them in the night sky showers of multi-coloured stars exploded and then fell back to earth, their effect a mere shadow of the explosion of desire inside her. Shocked, Ionanthe pulled herself out of Max's arms.

His arms felt cold and empty, and his body was racked with a physical ache that gnawed at him; all he wanted right now, Max acknowledged, was to take Ionanthe back to the castle and his bed. Her response to his kiss had ignited a need inside him that had taken him completely by surprise. And, more than that, during those intense moments a hope had come to life inside him that went against everything he had told himself he believed with regard to any marriage he might make. It should have been a salutary experience, or at the very least one which left him feeling wary and concerned about his own misjudgement, but instead what he actually felt was a feeling that was far sweeter.

Could it be that against all the odds—miraculously, almost—they shared a mutual desire for one another which could prove to be an unexpected foundation stone on which they could build a strong marriage? Max asked himself ruefully. If so… He looked at Ionanthe.

Sensing Max's gaze focusing on her, and dreading what she suspected she would see in it if she were foolish enough to meet it, Ionanthe fought to keep her burning face, with its scarlet banners advertising her folly, to herself.

She knew perfectly well what Max would be thinking. She had experienced male sexual arrogance—if mainly second hand—often enough during the course of her work in Brussels to know full well that the average man's reaction to a woman who responded as passionately as she had just done to Max was to assume that she must find him irresistible, must be desperate for even more sexual intimacy with him. There was no way Ionanthe wanted Max to think that about her. It offended her pride more than enough that she had to acknowledge to herself that she had responded to him, without having to endure *him* smirking over her vulnerability as well. She had to say something that would convince him that she had not really been affected by his kiss at all.

Ionanthe took a deep breath and said, as coolly as she could, 'Well, now that I've played my part and done everything I can to convince everyone that I've married you willingly, including that faked display of wifely adoration, perhaps we could return to the palace?'

Ionanthe took care to wait for the silence that followed with a small frosty smile that was more a baring of her pretty white teeth than a real smile, before actually risking a look at Max.

The stony expression carved on his face should have been reassuring—as should the icy-cold tones in which he informed her, in a very distancing manner, 'Very well. I'll get the Captain of the Guard to escort you back.'

Instead, for some silly reason, they actually made her feel abandoned and forlorn.

So much for his stupid hopes, Max reflected grimly as he watched the Captain of the Guard escorting Ionanthe back to the hotel. At least the Captain was a middle-aged, heavily set man, and not the kind of Adonis-like youth his first wife had seemed to find so irresistible—just in case her sister should have the same proclivities. What a fool he'd been to think for even a moment that there could be something personal between them. Hell, he'd already told himself that that was the last thing he wanted. Didn't he already have more than enough on his plate, with all the problems involved in bringing a new era to subjects without wanting to burden himself with some more? He simply could not take the risk of allowing himself to become sexually or emotionally vulnerable to Ionanthe. He knew that.

Cerebrally he might know it, but what about his body?

His body would have to learn, Max told himself grimly.

It was late in the evening—far later than he had initially envisaged having this conversation, thanks to the incident in the square—and the formal surroundings of the Grand Ministerial Chamber were hardly suited to its subject matter. But he had been determined to sign the necessary declaration that would ensure the freedom of the protestors without any delay.

Not that their earlier surroundings had been any more intimate—their first shared evening meal as a newly married couple having taken place in the equally formal and grand State Dining Room, where they had been seated at either end of a table designed to accommodate formal state dinners. With the length of a polished mahogany table that could easily seat fifty people separating them, and a silver-gilt centrepiece from the Royal Treasury between them, even if they had wanted to talk to one another it would have been impossible.

However, despite the cold hauteur with which Ionanthe had made plain exactly what her expectations of their marriage were, Max felt duty bound to have this conversation.

'As there hasn't been time to arrange a formal honeymoon—' he began.

'I don't want one.' Ionanthe stopped him quickly.

He had taken her sister to Italy—surely one of the most romantic honeymoon venues there could be?—but that wasn't the reason for her immediate interruption. That owed its existence to what had happened to her out in the square, when Max had kissed her. How easily she had risked humiliating herself. She could just imagine how much it would please her new husband's male ego if he thought that he could arouse her so easily. Men had no conscience when it came to women's emotions and desires. She had seen that so often in Brussels. She had seen how men exploited the vulnerability of women, persuading them to give up their own moral beliefs for their own advantage. She certainly wasn't going to put herself in that position—not when there was so much at stake for the country, for the son she hoped to have who would one day rule it.

There must be no further impulsive and unnecessary intimacies between Max and herself. It was her duty to consummate their marriage—how else could she conceive the son she was so determined to have for the people?—but she was determined not to put herself in a position where she might be sucked back into that dangerous state she had experienced earlier. A cool, calm and controlled execution of her marital and royal duty was her goal.

'Maybe not,' Max agreed calmly, 'but it is expected. Therefore I plan to arrange for us to spend several days at the hunting lodge.'

Ionanthe looked at him in dismay.

The Royal Hunting Lodge was up in the mountains, and in winter doubled as a ski lodge as it was above the snow line.

'Surely it will be inconvenient for you to be away from the centre of government?' she protested. Not for anything was she going to admit to him that the hunting lodge's remoteness and the fact that they would be alone there were filling her with panic.

When Max made no response she shrugged and affected a cool logic she was far from feeling, telling him, 'I can't see any purpose in us isolating ourselves in the mountains. It is our duty, I know, to produce an heir to succeed you, but we can do that just as well here.'

Such a pragmatic and logical, unemotional approach to their union was surely something he should applaud, Max told himself. After all, it reflected everything he had already told himself their marriage must be. Why, then, was he finding that he felt not just repelled but also in some dangerous way actively challenged as a man by Ionanthe's attitude to the intimacy they must share?

'You showed great passion this evening in your defence of your people.'

Ionanthe stiffened. What was he hinting? Was he going to ask her to deny that she had also shown great passion for him? Her pride writhed in agony at the thought.

'Their safety is my responsibility,' she answered coldly. 'Your sexual pleasure is not. I refuse to fake passion for the sake of a man's ego. You may have been able to force me to marry you, but you cannot force me to desire you and nor will I do so. Having said that, however, as I have already confirmed, I am fully prepared to fulfil my duty to the crown and to the people.'

The red mist of savage male sexual anger that rose up inside him shocked Max. He had to bring this conversation to a close before he was tempted to do something he considered beneath him, something he knew ultimately he would regret. He had never before wanted to overwhelm a woman's resistance and arouse her to the point where she succumbed and gave herself completely and mindlessly to him out of the white-hot desire he had brought her to. But right now the images imposing themselves on his thoughts were of Ionanthe on a bed—a very large bed—on which their naked bodies were passionately entwined. Even without closing his eyes and focusing his senses he could imagine the silky softness of her hair against his own skin, its scent—her scent—heated by desire to release its erotic fragrance into the air, filling his nostrils. Her head would be thrown back against his arm, her eyes a passion-glazed glitter between thick dark lashes, her lips swollen from their shared kisses and eagerly parted, proclaiming her pleasure and her desire for more as she smiled invitingly up at him.

Angrily Max dragged his thoughts back to reality. He had no business allowing his mind to create such images. They were an offence, a mental assault that he could not allow to continue and that he would not tolerate in himself.

Even so, he could not stop himself from saying curtly, 'You have a very clinical and detached attitude to the creation of a new life. A child deserves to be loved by those who give it life.'

'The fact that I can remain clinical and detached about the process that will create the next ruler of Fortenegro does not mean that I will not love my son any more than a woman who seeks medical intervention in order to conceive does not love *her* child,' Ionanthe retaliated sharply.

How much longer was she going to have to wait? Lying alone in the darkness of the large bed, waiting for Max to come to her, Ionanthe tried not to feel anxious. She had promised herself that she would remain calm, that she would not repeat her foolishness of earlier in the evening, but now, with the chimes of the cathedral clock striking midnight dying into silence, it was growing harder for her to quell her over-active imagination.

What would she do if he refused to adopt the same clinical manner she had sworn to show him and instead kissed her as he had done in the square? Why was she asking herself such a silly question? If he did that, then of course she would not respond to him. But if he were to persist? If he were to persist then she must just continue to remain unaffected.

How much longer would it be before he came to her? Was he delaying deliberately, in order to torment her and to break down her resistance? Did he think by leaving her here alone in their marriage bed that when he did choose to join her she would be so grateful that she would fling herself into his arms? If so, then he was going to learn just how wrong he was.

She looked at her watch. It was half past twelve. Had her sister found him such a reluctant bridegroom? Somehow Ionanthe doubted it.

Where *was* he?

It had been a long day, but despite her physical tiredness she knew that it would be impossible for her to sleep until the final act cementing their union had been completed. Beyond the huge windows which she had deliberately asked to be left uncurtained she could see the bright sharpness of the late autumn moon. Not many weeks ago it would have had the heavy fullness of the ripe harvest moon, signalling the culmination of nature's seasons of productivity, emblazoning her fertility across the night sky. Ionanthe touched her flat stomach. There was a season for all things, for all life, a time of planting and growing. An ache sprang to life inside her, urgent and demanding: the desire for a seed that would create the most precious gift Mother Nature could give.

Tears came out of nowhere to burn the backs of her eyes, accompanied by a helpless yearning and longing. Her body was waiting to conceive this son she wanted so very much. She was ready to give herself over to the sacrifice she must make for the future of the people. More than anything else right now she wanted to feel that necessary male movement within her, giving her the spark of life she ached so physically for. It must be her longing for the conception of their child that was driving into her, possessing her, filling her with restless longing. It couldn't possibly be anything else.

Where *was* he?

CHAPTER FIVE

'I UNDERSTAND that you wanted to speak to me?'

It would have been wiser for him to accede to Ionanthe's formal request to his aide by seeing her somewhere other than in this bedroom. All the more so when he had spent the last eight nights avoiding coming anywhere near it—because he couldn't trust his own self-control to prevent him from reacting to the dangerous mix of fierce anger and equally fierce sexual desire she aroused in him, Max recognized. But it was too late for him to regret that error now. He could hardly have ignored it, after all—not when she had delivered it so very publically, via his *aide de camp.*

What did she want? he wondered. Money? Jewellery? Her sister had asked for both those things and more. He thought angrily of the obvious and pitiful poverty of that group of men who had been prepared to risk their lives, if necessary, for the sake of Ionanthe's honour.

'Yes,' Ionanthe confirmed. She couldn't bring herself to look at Max. She didn't trust herself to do so. They had been married for just over a week—eight days, in fact, and eight long, humiliating nights. All of which she had spent alone in a bed that was obviously designed to accommodate two people—the bed that she was determined not to look at now, even though its presence in the room dominated her thoughts almost as much as Max's absence from it had dominated them during these last eight days of a marriage that was in effect no marriage at all.

Because she was not her sister? The pain of her childhood, with its lack of love and her grandfather's rejection, must not be allowed to affect her now. She must not allow herself to appear vulnerable or needy. She must demand what was her right—not for her own sake, of course. She had no desire to share the intimacy of sex with a man who, having forced her into marriage, now chose to ignore her. After all, she had never been the kind of woman who was driven by her own sexual need—far from it. In fact, going without sex had, if anything, become her preferred way of life, and one she had been happy with. No. It was for the sake of the people that she was forcing herself to put aside her own personal feelings. Alone, she could not change things for them. She knew that. The island's society was one rooted in the past, in which the male head of the family held absolute control. It would take a man to change that—a very strong, very aware, very courageous man. A son. *Her* son. A man who would be enlightened enough to change things for his people.

Despite her own lack of any need to be a sexually desired woman, there was still the undeniable fact that Max's very public rejection of her had left her feeling humiliated. Theirs was not, after all, a 'normal' marriage. As the island's ruler Max had to live very much in the public eye, and as his wife so did she. It would have been easy enough to bear if only *she* had known about her husband's sexual rejection of her, but of course the rest of the court was bound to know. Ionanthe hadn't missed the sympathetic looks her maid had been giving her every morning for the last eight mornings. The fact that everyone knew that Max had married her because he needed a son, and yet had not consummated their marriage shamed and insulted her, turning her into a laughing stock. She was not prepared to tolerate the situation any longer.

Max could feel his muscles, in fact his whole body, tensing against Ionanthe's presence, whilst at the same time his senses strained to absorb as much of it and her as they could. The room smelled of her, of the scent she always wore, which somehow he had learned to search for in the rooms from which she herself was absent. In the long, aching reaches of the empty nights it had tormented him, conjuring up for him images of it cloaking her skin and scenting the darkness until he'd felt he was being driven close to madness by the folly of his own savage hunger for her. How had it come to this? How was it possible for him to want her so deeply and so compulsively?

Max didn't have the answer to that question. The manner in which his physical hunger for her suspended all that was rational and normal for him was something he couldn't analyse to any satisfactory conclusion. Not that he hadn't tried; he had. And in the end all he'd been able to tell himself was that the desire that burned inside him was simply the result of some primitive male instinct within himself that had been unleashed by her behaviour towards him.

He had been with his personal aide, the son of one of the island's barons when Ionanthe's lady-in-waiting had brought the message that Ionanthe wished to speak with him, so it had been impossible for him to ignore it.

Ionanthe took a deep breath and, still keeping her back to the bed, began. 'Your absence from our marital bed has humiliated me and made me the subject of court gossip.'

Max fought to control his body's reaction to her words. Only he knew how hard it had been for him to keep to his decision not to give in to his growing desire for her. He would not partner her in the kind of cold and clinical intercourse she had described to him as the manner in which she wished to consummate their marriage. He would not, or did he fear that he *could* not? Max was forced to ask himself. Wasn't it true that he was staying away from the bed they should have shared because he was afraid that if he did share it with her he would not be able to control the desire she aroused in him? The fact that she should arouse that desire was difficult enough for him to come to terms with, without having to add his concern that he would not be able to control it. It had, after all, come out of nowhere, with such speed and power that it had left him punch-drunk, reeling and, worst of all, feeling that he could no longer trust his own carefully set inner controls. No woman had ever affected him as Ionanthe did. No woman had ever aroused him to such a pitch of aching need combined with furious anger—

severing him from the man he had always thought himself to be when it came to sexual needs. That man had been willing to follow his partner's wishes, been very careful to keep the emotional temperature on merely warm. That man had certainly never had to deal with the kind of raw, demanding need he was experiencing now.

Why? He had barely registered the fact that Ionanthe even existed before he had met her, and yet now here he was…

Here he was *what*? Here he was wanting her so desperately and so passionately that he barely recognised himself any more?

Max's mouth hardened—the only outwardly visible sign of his inner demons and one that Ionanthe registered as antagonism towards her.

Max was trying to force her to back down. Well, she wasn't going to.

The proud arching of her neck as she lifted her chin to confront him brought a sharp shock of physical reaction to Max's senses. He wanted to cover the distance between them—to cover *her* in the most basic and intimate way. He wanted to slide his hand and then his mouth down the tormenting oh-so-proud and yet vulnerable arch of her creamy-fleshed neck. He wanted to pushed aside the neat fawn cashmere sweater she was wearing and explore the curve of her shoulder, tasting her, knowing her, feeling her breast swell into his hand and her nipple harden and tighten in his palm.

Oblivious to Max's reaction to her, Ionanthe pressed on.

'Either you bring that humiliation to an end by consummating our marriage,' she told him determinedly, ' or…'

Her words were like the worst kind of sharp blows against already dangerously raw and open wounds, overloading his self-control, inflaming him, driving him into an unfamiliar place where the red mist that came down over him obliterated everything else, Max acknowledged. All he could think, all he knew, was that she was tormenting him to the point where he had to put some distance between them or risk them both facing the consequences.

'This isn't a discussion I want to pursue,' he told her flatly, turning his back on her and heading for the door.

For a second Ionanthe was too frozen with anger and disbelief to say or do anything. But then desperation drove her, and she ran for the door, reaching it ahead of Max and flattening her back against it, her arms outspread as she told him fiercely, 'That's not good enough. I won't be treated like that. I want an answer from you, and I am not going to let you leave this room until I get one.'

Max was so close to her that he could feel the sweet warmth of her breath against his skin. He wanted to close his eyes to blot out her image, but he couldn't. How ironic it was that, whilst all Ionanthe wanted from him was a clinical and detached act of consummation, her sister had actively wanted to reduce him to wanting her, with all her wiles and coquettish well-used tricks. But she had never once come anywhere near arousing him to one tenth of the desire rampaging through him right now—for Ionanthe. A desire he had to control.

'Stand aside,' he commanded Ionanthe, stepping up to her and reaching out to grasp the handle of the door.

'No,' Ionanthe refused.

Her denial was all the spark the dry tinderbox of tensions within him needed. Max's self-control snapped. With one swift movement he imprisoned her against the door, the hand he had previously curled round the door handle now gripping her hip, whilst his other hand pinioned her shoulder.

'You want an answer? Very well then—let *this* be your answer,' Max told her, crushing his mouth down on hers, imprinting the shape and taste of it on her lips just as the weight of his body was imprinting itself against her flesh, forcing her to accept his domination.

This wasn't what she had wanted—so why was she allowing him to impose the bruising pressure of his kiss on her? How had she moved so quickly from holding the high ground with justifiable anger to this place where she was now, where her whole body was awash with a flood of sensations she didn't want and *he* was the one in control?

Somehow she managed to break the kiss, straining back from him, her heart racing from the exertion—the exertion or the excitement? The exertion, of course. He didn't excite her. How could he? She tried to pull away from him, and for a second, as his hands lifted from her body, she thought she had succeeded. But he didn't let her get very far.

His hands closed on her shoulders as he swung her round, so that he was the one leaning on the door and somehow or other she was leaning on him—on him and into him—her whole body pressed into his, making her aware of her own flesh and its sexuality in a way that shocked through her like lightning. Why had she never known before that the pressure of a man's hard muscular chest against her breasts could turn their rounded softness into a mass of sensually receptive nerve-endings? Or that the pump of a male heartbeat lifting its owner's chest against her could translate into something that her breasts interpreted as a caress, and to which they responded with a fierce ache that tore at her flesh?

That ache sent images into her head that were visually and sensually erotic—images of Max's dark head bent over her naked body, his lips capturing the flaunting demand of her puckered nipples and drawing on them until her pleasure reached a crescendo that made her want to moan out loud—she could hardly believe that she was experiencing them.

But she was. And she was experiencing too the heavy low drag of need that was filling her lower body as it rested against his, making her want to press closer to him, making her want to grind her hips eagerly against him, making her *want*. A shudder of wild delight gripped her when Max's hands slid down to her hips, pulling her even more intimately against him whilst his lips pillaged the vulnerable flesh of her throat.

Something unfamiliar and dangerous slid through her veins, like a heady, intoxicating potion that stripped her of her will to deal in the factual and logical. It carried her with it on a tide that reacted to Max's maleness with the same kind of magnetic pull that the moon had on the oceans of the world.

He should have stopped before this, Max knew,

whilst he had still been able to stop. Now it was too late. He swept Ionanthe up into his arms and carried her towards the bed.

As he placed her on it Ionanthe tried to listen to the inner voice warning her that she was in danger—tried to draw back from him as he started to undress her.

'You were the one who wanted this,' Max reminded her as he leaned over her, removed her skirt and then her sweater.

'Not like this,' Ionanthe protested.

Not like *what*?

He was kissing her again, nuzzling her throat, stringing kisses against it so delicate and yet so sensual that they dizzied her senses and robbed her of any ability to verbalise her true feelings. Instead she was arching her throat, offering it up to him and then shuddering in mute pleasure when the heat of his mouth became more possessive.

His hands on her bra had somehow become an aid, an ally, understanding her need to be clothed only by his touch. But Max seemed more disposed to linger over the silky underwear that was her one concession to the demands of her femininity rather than remove it speedily. Her frustration grew.

Through the fine silk of her underwear Max could see the dark thrust of Ionanthe's nipples, and the even darker softness of the hair covering her sex. She dressed so primly on the outside that to see her clothed in such a way underneath was somehow unbearably erotic. Was it possible that her outwardly cold manner could conceal a passionate heat? Desire kicked fiercely through him at the thought of her meeting and matching him in the white-hot conflagration of shared need. He kissed the exposed upper slope of her breast, savouring the sweetness of her flesh, slowly easing away the silk until he could stroke his tongue-tip against her nipple.

Ionanthe cried out sharply, the sound torn from her in response to the shockingly intense stab of pleasure that pierced her, lifting her from the bed to arch against Max's mouth. Her hand rose to cup the back of his head, her fingers curling into the thickness of his hair as she gave herself up to the hot pleasure his mouth was spilling through her. In response his hand covered her sex, probing the barrier of fragile silk and lace that was no barrier at all, slipping beyond it to find the warm wetness that waited for him.

The late afternoon light slipped away into darkness without Ionanthe being aware of the passage of time. She was capable only of measuring time by the acceleration of the growing ache of need that had possessed her. The whole purpose of her life, what she had been born for, had become distilled into this concentration of her entire being, so that it could be given up to the moment that would create life even while everything she had thought she was fell away and burned, dying in the conflagration of creating that spark of new life.

These thoughts and many others whirled inside her head kaleidoscope-like, meaning nothing. Her thoughts were incapable of doing anything to bring to a halt what she herself had set in motion, and nor did she want them to.

But this was not a time for thinking. It was a time for feeling, for knowing, for believing, for giving herself up to the sensation of Max's hands and lips on her body. Every part of her pulsated with the urge for completion that was driving her. Every nerve-ending within her was so sensitised to and by his caresses that she felt that he could take her no higher, that the moment of culmination was there, a mere tantalising half a breath out of reach.

But Max would not allow her that culmination. By some alchemic force and power surely only he alone possessed he drew the fine skein of thread linking her to her desire higher and tighter, to her gasped litany of pleas and protests. Ignoring her plea to him not to torment her any further, he continued to prove to her that she was wrong and that he could. With the deliberate and lingering stroke of his tongue-tip against the pulsing thrust of flesh that was her sex and the intimate caress of his fingers within her he brought her time and time again to the point where the release she wanted was within reach—only to change his caresses to a gentler pace, brushing butterfly wing kisses against her inner thighs whilst he stroked the soft flesh there, keeping her at an unbearable pitch of need whilst refusing to satisfy it.

He couldn't hold out much longer, Max acknowledged as he tried to separate his body from his mind and ignore the furious clamour and the almost physical pain of his self-denial. He ached with every cell he possessed to slide himself fully and deeply into the warm eager wetness Ionanthe was so eagerly offering him and take them both to orgasm. But he couldn't; not yet. Not until he was sure she was ready to give him what he had to have.

The winter sunlight had long ago given way to the silvery light of the rising moon, painting Ionanthe's body in silver and charcoal. She would make a magnificent subject for an artist's eye, he thought. Her hair a dark tumbling mass around her shoulders, the bone structure beneath her skin delineated by the stardust silver brush on her shoulder, her hip, her thigh, whilst her flesh itself was moonlight-pale, her nipples charcoal-rose and the secret places of her body an inviting velvety night-sky-dark.

He wanted to lose himself completely with her and within her. No woman had ever made him feel like this, want like this, need like this—but no other woman had made him question her purpose and her beliefs either. Because no other woman had been important enough for him to *have* such feelings.

The sensual intimacy he was using against Ionanthe was a two-edged sword, Max recognised. He might be breaking down her contemptuous claim that for her sex between them could only be a cold, clinical matter, but in doing so he was creating within himself an emotional awareness of her, a closeness to her that could run totally counter to his determination to put his people and their needs before anything else.

He was creating problems where none needed to exist, Max told himself. This was a one-off—a response to the challenge Ionanthe had thrown at him.

He bent his head and painted slow, sensual circles of erotic delight on Ionanthe's inner thigh, drawing the thread of her desire even tighter. Helpless to stop herself, Ionanthe reached down between her parted thighs to cup the back of Max's head, unable to tell whether she wanted to keep him where he was or urge him to return and repeat the earlier, previously unknown intimacy he had shown her. She knew only that she could not bear it if he withdrew from her.

But he did, lifting his head to look at her through the moonlit darkness to demand softly, 'So tell me now, Ionanthe, whilst you are still capable of saying the words and I am rational enough to hear them, how do you *really* prefer your sex? Cold and clinical? Or like this? Which is best?'

His touch stroked slowly, warmly, wetly the length of her, and then rested firmly against her clitoris before once more he lifted his head for her answer.

He hadn't said that this would be the end—an end that would be no end at all since it would leave her gripped by agonising need—but the fear that that was what he had in mind was enough for her body to command her brain.

'*This* is best,' she admitted, closing her eyes as her body forced aside her pride, making her lips form words she had never thought she would utter. '*You* are the best,' she added helplessly. "I have nev—' She gasped and cried out—a low, guttural sound of aching pleasure as Max responded to her initial admission with the slow, powerful, deep thrust of his body within her own.

How could something so primitive, so basic, designed by nature and not the human mind, meet so perfectly the needs of flesh and the senses? Ionanthe wondered dizzily, instinctively tightening her muscles around the slick, hot male flesh that was not just filling her but stroking into her, receiving back from her a growing urgency. But then whilst nature might have provided the ingredients for her pleasure, it was Max who had taken them and honed them.

The climb grew steeper, making demands on her she had never known existed. Ionanthe fought for breath, for the strength to endure—and for purchase, so as not to lose her place on the sharp incline.

The summit was there, within reach—so dazzlingly beautiful, so immortal, so achingly needed that its promise brought the sting of tears to her eyes. And somehow he knew, even through his own journey. Just for a beat of time she wavered, half afraid of reaching the pinnacle, knowing that once she did she must fling herself headlong into its glory and give up all her sense of self. And then Max was there, whispering to her. 'Now…' His hand reached for hers, his fingers entwining with hers, holding her safe as the moment came and together they defied time and mortality. Together…

As the force of the moment shook her body, the knowledge burned into Ionanthe's spirit that in those final seconds, with the peak so close and yet not reached, all she had wanted—all she had ached and yearned for—was to reach it with Max. Not one thought had she had for the son for whom she had married Max and begun the journey they had just completed. Not one thought had she given to the people. Her sacrifice of self had not been for them but instead for the need that had burned in her for the man who was now holding her.

'Max?'

The sound of his name, spoken in a voice drenched with a heart-aching mix of emotions, had Max drawing Ionanthe closer to him, covering her body with the protective warmth and strength of his own in the same way that he suddenly longed to cloak her emotions and keep her from pain. He had driven her hard, fuelled by anger to punish her for the damage she had done to his pride, but now, rather than flaunt his triumph to her, he wanted instead to protect her.

As he held her Max felt Ionanthe slip into sleep, her breathing becoming even and soft against his skin. Very carefully and gently he detached himself from her, stilling when in her sleep she frowned, as though reluctant to let him go. He continued when she didn't wake. There were things he had to do, duties he had to perform, responsibilities he could not and should not evade.

CHAPTER SIX

SOMETHING sweetly juicy was moistening her dry lips, causing her to part them the better to taste it. The pleasurable sensation woke Ionanthe from her sleep.

Fresh peach! A luxury in December, and grown, she remembered, in the hothouses of the summer palace, built in the eighteenth century on the site where centuries before the Moorish rulers of the island had also taken advantage of the most southerly facing coastline of Fortenegro to cultivate dates and grow peaches.

A more concerned and less selfish ruler would have used that fertile and protected land for the good of his people, rather than himself, ordering that the land be turned over to the production of fruit and vegetables for the export markets of Northern Europe. It was equally selfish of her to enjoy the taste of something grown only for the pleasure of one selfish man. But her mouth was dry, and the scent of the fruit as well as its taste was tormenting her senses. Slowly, Ionanthe opened her eyes.

Beyond the windows the sky was still night-dark, but now in the room beyond the bedroom a fire burned in the modern central fireplace, throwing out from its flames soft colour and warmth.

It was Max who was tempting her, his skin tanned against the whiteness of the towelling robe he was wearing, his feet bare—as he would be beneath his robe. A huge lump formed in her throat. She reached up to push away his hand, chagrin charging her emotions. But Max was ready for her rejection, his free hand firmly cupping the side of her face.

'You should eat.'

The words were calm enough, but something her body heard in them that her ears could not sent a stab of something primitive and shamefully sweet kicking through her, and this time when he offered her the fruit her fingers rested on his wrist, as though she feared he might withdraw before she could bite into the slice of juicy peach.

Its taste was heavenly, sharply sweet, quenching her thirst.

'More?' Max asked softly.

Again her body responded ahead of her mind—her breath quickening, her gaze sleepily possessive as it fastened on his lips, watching him speak to her. Her assent might only have been a brief nod of her head, but it was enough. More than enough, she recognized, when Max held out to her the cream silk peignoir she had bought on impulse in Paris whilst waiting for her connecting flight to the island. Little had she known then just where and how she would be wearing it.

Ionanthe trembled a little as she turned her back on him to slip her arms into its sleeves. She had had to step from the bed naked, and she had been aware when she did so of the unashamed and intent way in which he had openly absorbed her nakedness. Now, with the warmth of that watchful caress still upon her, she trembled slightly. Because of the way he had looked at her, or because of her own secret but equally unashamed deep-rooted enjoyment of that visual caress from a sexually triumphant man in possession?

Out of nowhere a new road had been carved through the once impenetrable barriers of her mind, allowing her access to places within herself she didn't really want to go. It was easier to focus on other things—such as the fact that Max had obviously been busy whilst she had slept, as evidenced by the lit fire and the small banquet she could now see laid out on low tables within reach of the sitting room's luxuriously comfortable and deeply upholstered sofas. She could see fruit from the royal succession houses—peach, fig, nectarines—and almond sweets dusted with sugar—an Island speciality like the delicately flavoured local goats cheese, roasted and mixed with salad, served with seeded flat unleavened local bread and island-grown olives. There was even a bottle of the island's wine, although it was a glass of champagne that Max now poured for her.

Her sister's favourite drink. Her hand trembled, her heart chilling.

Max watched Ionanthe, trying to hold on to his resolution. He had chosen their food deliberately, focusing on what the island produced in an attempt to remind himself of his duty instead of giving way to his personal need.

Only now, in the aftermath of their shared passion,

was the true legacy of what he had done hitting him. He had allowed his pride and his anger to push him into ignoring the warnings he had already registered, which he *should* have listened to. Warnings such as the unexpectedly powerful effect Ionanthe had had on his senses at their first meeting. Warnings regarding his increasing awareness of his desire for her. Warnings which had urged him to recognise that it would be fatally easy to step off the path he had chosen for himself. Because—most dangerous of all—it wasn't merely physically that she affected him.

Was she aware that the small banquet in front of her comprised food and drink that came from the island but which was available only to the very wealthy? This kind of food and drink could and should provide not only a better diet for the people of the island but could also be exported, to provide them with a better income and bring in money which could be invested to the benefit of everyone—helping to pay for an improved infrastructure, for schools and hospitals and ultimately, through them, bringing better jobs for people and brighter futures. Or was she oblivious to all of that? Unknowing and uncaring?

Even worse, was she, as her sister had been, not just oblivious to but actively *against* the plans he had to persuade those who held most of the island's fertile land by virtue of nothing more than inherited titles to allow it to be let out at a peppercorn rent for the benefit of the people? He planned to do so with much of the land he himself as Prince now owned. But her grandfather, after all, had been the most antagonistic of all his courtiers, and Max had swiftly come to recognise that the Baron's plan to marry his granddaughter to him had not just been to secure for her the highest status in the island but, more ambitiously, because he had hoped to influence and if possible rule the island from behind the throne.

Max could still remember the quarrel between them after he had told Eloise that he would not take her to South of France to attend a celebrity party because he had set up a meeting with some Spanish growers whose advice he wanted to seek. She had announced with semi-drunken spite that he was a fool, and that her grandfather would never allow him to put his plans into practice.

He had known then that their marriage was dead. The revulsion with which Eloise had filled him had ensured that.

And Ionanthe was her sister. Brought up by the same man and in the same manner. He must not forget that.

He waited for her to take the glass of champagne he had poured for her, but Ionanthe shook her head.

'Some, wine, then?' he offered. 'Although I should warn you that it is strong and…'

'You should warn me?' Ionanthe stopped him. 'You seem to be forgetting that I grew up here—that I am perfectly well aware of the strength of our home-grown wine.' As she spoke Ionanthe reached for the bottle and poured herself a glass. She would rather have drunk poison, she told herself bitterly, than to drink her sister's beloved bubbly.

The truth was that she rarely drank alcohol at all, but she wasn't going to tell him that. Lifting her glass to her lips, she took a deep swallow. The firelight on the glass warmed the potent darkness of its contents, just as the wine itself was now warming her, spreading a heat that relaxed the angry tension that had been clutching tight fingers round her heart.

She drank some more, grateful for the wine's immediate and empowering effect on her senses. And then she made the mistake of looking directly at Max, and immediately that empowerment transformed itself into a dizzying and weakening surge of female awareness of his maleness, heightened by her body's memory of the pleasure he had already shown it.

Could two gulps of wine be enough to make her feel like this? Far more likely her blood sugar level had plunged and she needed something to eat, Ionanthe reassured herself, turning abruptly towards the table. Embarrassingly, she almost stumbled, so that Max had to step forward and take hold of her.

Wide-eyed, she looked up at him. Why was it that the expensive fabric of her peignoir suddenly felt oppressive? Its touch was making her nipples feel so acutely sensitive that she wanted to pull it off. Why was it, too, that her heart was thudding so heavily and so unsteadily?

Steadying her with one hand, Max removed the wine glass from her hold with the other, putting it down and then telling her, 'I think you should sit down, don't you?' He guided her towards the sofa.

No, Ionanthe thought rebelliously as he calmly but firmly urged her onto the sofa. What I should do is go back to bed, so that you can do everything you did before all over again.

Shock spiralled through her. Was she really having such alien thoughts? Where had they come from?

Max watched her with a small frown. She'd hardly touched the wine and yet her cheeks were flushed, her eyes brilliant, her lips swollen with promise.

His groin began to ache. His frown deepened. More sex wasn't what he had had in mind when he had ordered this intimate supper and instructed the staff to leave them alone. What he had wanted to do was find out what basis they might have for beginning a relationship that might work.

He reached for the plate of figs that was close to his hand, intending only to ensure that Ionanthe had something to eat. But when he offered the plate to her she used her free hand to hold his wrist as she took one, so that he could not put the plate down or step back from her without pushing her away.

Her gaze on his, she bit into the fruit, causing its dusting of powdered sugar to cling to her lips and fall to her body, speckling the flesh exposed by the opening of her robe.

The fig was sweet and sticky. When she had finished eating it Ionanthe looked round for a napkin, and then put one of her fingers in her mouth and licked it.

Max felt reaction implode inside him, wiring his whole body to immediate fierce desire. He put down the plate and reached for Ionanthe's arm, taking the sticky fingers one by one into his own mouth and sucking slowly on them.

Ionanthe drew in her breath and then exhaled it on a small sob of physical delight, silenced when Max released her hand to kiss the sweetness from her mouth. When she wanted to demand something more intimate he used his tongue to lick the sugar from her skin at the V her robe exposed—the tantalisingly small area of flesh where her breasts started to rise from the valley between them. Her nipples pressed eagerly against her peignoir, the agitation of her breathing increasing the silk's movement against them so that the delicate friction became a torment of aroused sensitivity. Wild thoughts flashed though her head, filling her with reckless excitement.

She pushed Max away, giving him a small secret smile when he obeyed, but looked as though he had done so with reluctance. She reached for the plate Max had put down and then, balancing it on her lap, unfastened her wrap and shrugged her arms free of it. It slipped down to pool round her waist, leaving the top half of her body to be clothed only by firelight. Then, watching Max as she did so, she picked up one of the figs and began to eat it, very slowly, whilst its sugar coating drifted down onto her naked breasts.

Liquid fire ran through Max's veins. Ionanthe's playful sensuality intoxicated him far more than any amount of alcohol might have done. Had she somehow *known* what was going on inside his head earlier, when he had licked the sugar from her skin? Had she read his mind and guessed then that mentally he was visualising her exactly as she was now? No, not *exactly* as she was now, he admitted. His imagination had not had the power to do her full justice. It had not, for instance, painted her nipples with such dark swollen crowns that the sugar speckling them made him want not merely to lick it from them but to taste them and suck them.

Ionanthe watched Max with the liquid-dark secret knowledge of a woman. The kind of knowledge that came not just from knowing a man in the most intimate physical way there was, but also from seeing the pure essence of him laid bare through the power of mutual desire and need. Without having to question or doubt Ionanthe knew beyond mere ordinary knowing that the desire running through her, the images inside her head, the need driving her, were all things that were in their different ways reflections of what Max himself was experiencing.

When he came to her without haste, his desire so charged that she could feel its heat burning her own skin, she was ready for him. There was no need for any words between them. She bit deeply into the small fruit he was holding out to her, and then offered him the unbitten half, keeping his gaze even when his fingers gripped her wrist and his lips brushed her fingertips as he took the fruit from her hold.

Without words to accompany them, somehow the symbolic gestures they were sharing took on an almost sacred intimacy—as though in some way they were enacting a ritual that went all the way back into the mists of human time, as though the blood of the ancestry they shared mingled with their own to move powerfully and quicken within them, taking them to heights that for Ionanthe would have been unimaginable twenty-four hours beforehand.

As the firelight played and glistened on their desire-drenched bodies they came together, to ascend the peak and then to freefall from it into infinity—not just once, but throughout all the night hours as the desire within them rose higher to new heights by way of new pleasures.

And not once, as her body strained for pleasure and release, did Ionanthe think of the son she had sworn to herself was the only purpose for her being here.

The morning came slowly and kindly, waking Max first, so that he had the pleasure of watching Ionanthe whilst she slept, her body resting against his, her skin smelling of the musky intimacy of the night and of *her*, the heady combination sending a slow wave of freshly burgeoning desire uncurling within him.

Whilst he watched her Ionanthe's eyes opened. Perhaps mystically she had sensed his need, as though it had called out to her, bringing her from the depths of sleep. Max derided himself inwardly for the danger of such thoughts. It was simply because he had moved that he had woken her. Nothing more. And yet without a word Ionanthe leaned over him, seeking his lips with her own, her hand sliding down his naked body until she reached the rigid swell of his penis.

Her kiss deepened, and her swift movement to straddle him surprised and delighted him. His hands immediately went to her hips to assist her as he lifted her onto his erection.

Max's eyes closed in mute pleasure as she took him slowly into her body, tormenting him a little with the soft caress of her muscles. And then, just when he thought the torment would be too much for him, Ionanthe began to rise and fall on him, slowly at first, taking him deeper and deeper within herself, holding him there, and then faster—until he was the one holding her down onto him, and she was the one crying out the ache of her need and the glory of its fulfilment.

Afterwards they showered together—Max quickly, leaving Ionanthe alone to enjoy the warmth of the water.

When she returned to the bedroom she saw that he had made a small breakfast for them of tea and toast.

'Of course if you'd also like some fruit…' Max teased her, but Ionanthe shook her head even whilst the colour bloomed in her face.

She felt too languid to quarrel with him. Too… Too satisfied? Her face burned hotter.

CHAPTER SEVEN

IT WAS six hours and ten minutes since she had woken up alone in bed to the realisation of what she had done. And it was over eight hours since she had last seen Max—longer since they had last…

Ionanthe made an agitated turn of the floor of their private sitting room. What she had done, the way she had behaved, was unforgivable, unacceptable, unbearable. The more she relived the events of the night the more she hated and despised herself. It was impossible now for her to cling to the excuse that her behaviour had been caused by her desire to conceive a son—a future ruler for the people. The truth was that there had been no thought of him in her head or driving her body when she had hungered over and over again for Max's possession.

What was the cause of her behaviour, then? Too many years of celibacy? Too many years of low sexual self-esteem after living in the shadow of her sister? If she was going to go down that track then why not shift the blame from herself altogether? Ionanthe derided herself. Why not blame the wine, or the figs, or—? She stood completely still, not even drawing breath. Or why not blame the one who had conjured desire from her flesh—the man who had put her under his spell and who had brought from her the need that had overwhelmed her? It was easier, surely, to blame Max—who, after all, had been the one to start the conflagration that had destroyed everything she had previously thought about her own sexuality—than to accept the sharply painful suggestion that she might have been the authoress of her own downfall.

As she struggled to battle with her responsibility for protecting herself and her responsibility to acknowledge the truth, unconnected, barely formed, but still very distracting thoughts weaved themselves though her pain. Thoughts such as how she would never, ever forget the scent of Max's flesh, pre-arousal, during it, and in its final culmination. Such as how there had been a certain look in his eyes, a certain tension in his body that her senses would forever recognize. Thoughts such as how could her sister have wanted to have sex with other men when she'd had Max—a man, a husband, so able to satisfy her every sexual need?

Had he held Eloise as he had held her? Had he touched her? Aroused her? Satisfied her?

Pain ripped through her, savaging her, stripping back the protective layer of her emotional skin to leave its nerve-endings exposed and raw.

Dear God, what was she doing to herself? Hadn't she caused herself enough harm already without adding more? Right now, in order to protect herself, she must not think about what had happened. Instead she must summon all her mental powers and somehow ignore it.

Why not demand that her brain go one step further and attempt to convince herself that it had never happened at all? Ionanthe derided herself. Why not simply pretend that last night had never been?

By rights she ought to have the courage to face up to what had happened. Was she a woman capable of producing and guiding the boy who would become the man who would stand tall and strong for the causes of right and justice for the weak and poor? Or was she simply a coward?

This wasn't a contest between bravery and cowardice, Ionanthe told herself. It was instead a matter of survival—of living with the weakness and the vulnerability she had found within herself whilst continuing to pursue her objectives. And that could start right now, with her making sure that Max understood that what had happened last night had been a one-off. After all, even though shamefully she had not thought of it last night, she might already have conceived her son. It would take time for her to know, of course, but until she did there was no reason for her to continue to have sex with Max, was there? She had been weak, but here was her chance to regain the self-respect she had lost. All she had to do was convey her decision to Max.

And when and where would she do that? In his arms? In bed? In the silvery moonlight with his hands on her body? While he knew her and possessed her so intimately and completely that they were almost as one?

A deep shudder wrenched at her body.

'And then there is the matter of the consortium wishing to apply for permission to excavate a coal mine on Your

Highness's land. You will remember that I informed you that your late cousin was on the point of granting them a licence just before his death?'

Max frowned as he listened to the Count. 'As I remember, that land is usually let out to—'

'Sheep farmers. Yes. But there is no formal agreement. You have the right to move their stock off the land if you wish to do so.'

Max's frown deepened. He was keen to invest in renewable energy sources for the island, but these plans were still in their infancy and he was not yet ready to go public with them or discuss them with the Count.

'I am due to fly to Spain tomorrow,' he pointed out instead.

'Indeed? Shall the Princess be accompanying you?'

The Count's question was, on the face of it, justified. But Max still gave him a sharp look. He was rewarded when the other man continued smoothly, 'If I may be permitted to say so, Your Highness, I am delighted to see that things are working out so well between you. Had I been consulted in the first place, I would have suggested then that if you were determined to marry one of the late Baron's granddaughters then his younger granddaughter would be by far the better choice. Whilst Ionanthe may never have found favour in her late grandfather's eyes, it was always obvious to those with the wit to see it that she far outshone her sister. As a child Ionanthe was always the one who felt more passionately about the island and its people. It was a source of great sorrow to her parents, I know, that she was not born a son. For then the traditions of their family—a family that has always upheld the way of life of our island—would have been assured. But Ionanthe will make you an excellent consort. She is well versed in our ways.'

The Count sounded as pleased with himself—as though he himself had created Ionanthe.

Max gave him a sharp look. It was, of course, impossible to keep anything hidden from the members of a court who virtually lived together. Everyone would know by now that he and Ionanthe had spent the night together, and would have drawn their own conclusions from that. Was the Count hoping that through Ionanthe pressure could be brought to bear on him to accept their way of life rather than insist on changing it? It had, after all, been the Count who had been so instrumental in forcing this marriage on them. On them, or on *him*?

Half an hour later, alone in the Chamber of State, Max reminded himself that he had warned himself all along of the dangers inherent in becoming intimately and emotionally involved with Ionanthe. Now was the time to take a step back, to remember the reason why he was here, playing a feudal role in an equally feudal country that was surely more akin to a Gilbert and Sullivan creation than part of the modern world.

And what of Ionanthe's own beliefs? Max had no need of anyone to tell him that Ionanthe's sexual and moral code was a world away from that of her sister, or that she was one of life's givers rather than one of its takers. But, as he had already discovered, those who by their own decree had long held the right to high office on the island felt passionately about the traditions they upheld, and were passionate in their refusal to allow any change. And Ionanthe was a very passionate woman.

He might not need her support to put in place the changes he planned to make, but neither did he intend to put himself in a position where he was afraid that confidences he let slip to Ionanthe in the intimacy of their bed might be passed on to those who opposed his plans.

It was perhaps as well that he was flying to Barcelona tomorrow.

Tonight would be different; tonight she would not give way or weaken. Tonight she would be the woman, the Ionanthe, she had to be from now on, she had assured herself as she had dressed for the formal dinner that was being held tonight for Philippe de la Croix, a French diplomat who was visiting from Paris.

But that had been before she had seen Max—before he had thrust open the door to their private quarters and come striding towards her, causing her heart to slam into her ribs and her whole body to go weak.

The pleasure he had shown her was not hers alone, she tried to remind herself. He had been married to her sister, after all—a woman who had been far more sexually experienced and desirable than she was herself. The savagery of the pain coiling through her shocked her. So this was jealousy, red-hot and raw, filling her with a fierce, possessive need to obliterate the memory of her sister from his mind and his senses, shaming her with its primitive message. She tried to block the destructive thoughts from her mind, but still they went on forcing themselves onto her, burning her where they touched her vulnerable places.

Today, studying the cooling ashes of last night's passion, had he compared her to Eloise and found her wanting? *Aaahhh,* but that hurt so very much, reducing the pain of the rejection she had known as a child to nothing—a shadow of this so much greater agony. Was it because she had known all along that she would feel like this that she had fought so hard against loving a man?

Loving a man? But she did not *love* Max. She could not. It was impossible. She barely knew him.

She knew enough of him to know his touch and its effect on her senses. He had marked her indelibly as his, and nothing could change that. If that was not a form of loving then— No. She would not allow it to be. It must not be. She must escape from what was happening to her, from him.

She took a deep breath and announced shakily, 'I should like your permission to withdraw to my family's estate. There are matters there that need my attention following my grandfather's death, and if I delay going there much longer the castle will be cut off by the winter snows.'

In truth Ionanthe knew that there was not likely to be any real need for her to visit the castle. Her grandfather had disliked it because of its isolation, and had rarely gone there after the death of her parents, preferring to base himself here, in his State apartment. Eloise had loathed the castle, and had always treated the simple country people who lived close to it, working manually on the estate as their families had done for many generations, with acid contempt.

Their parents, though, *had* spent time there—her mother encouraging Ionanthe when she had tried to teach the young children of the estate workers to read. Those had been happy days—until her grandfather had found out about her impromptu classes and roared at her in anger, telling her mother that she was not to encourage the 'labourers' brats' to waste their time on learning skills they did not need.

That had been when Ionanthe had recognised that even her parents were not strong enough to stand up to her grandfather.

Max listened to her in silence. He did not for one minute believe that she really felt any urgent desire to visit the remote castle she had inherited from her grandfather. He suspected, in fact, that the real reason for her request was a desire on her part to distance herself from last night. But he was not going to challenge her on that point. Why should he, when it suited him so well? And yet there was a feeling within him of antagonism towards her announcement—a latent need to assert the right that his body felt last night had given it to keep her close, a surge of male hostility at her desire to separate herself from him.

All merely primitive male ego drives that must be ignored, Max told himself firmly. And to prove that he intended to do exactly that, he nodded his head and told Ionanthe calmly, 'Of course you may have my permission.'

Her relief was immediate, and visible in the exhalation of her breath. Was it her relief that speared him, conjuring up his swift response?

'There is, after all, no reason for me to withhold it. I trust that you are thoroughly satisfied now that we have consummated our marriage?' He gave emphasis to the word 'satisfied' rather than the far less dangerous and emotive 'now' that followed.

Was this man now deliberately tormenting her the same man who only last night had fed her—fed on the desire he had created within her? She ought to despise him, not be in danger of loving him, Ionanthe told herself angrily.

'I am satisfied that I have performed my duty.' It was all she could think of to say in response.

'Duty—such a cold word, and so wholly inappropriate for—'

To Ionanthe's relief, before Max could finish delivering his intended taunt someone had knocked on the door, bringing their conversation to a halt and allowing her to escape to prepare herself for the evening's formal dinner.

If growing up observing her grandfather's Machiavellian attitude to court politics had taught Ionanthe a great deal about how the world of wealth and power operated, and in addition given her a private antipathy towards it, then her working life in Brussels had given her an inner resilience, equipped her to deal with it whilst keeping her own private counsel. She knew the rules of engagement that governed the subtle wars of status and power that underwrote policy and the way it was managed: via a tightly woven mesh of lobbyists, business interests, law-makers and law-breakers. As a child, witnessing the court of Fortenegro's crushing need for power as evidenced by her grandfather had hurt her. But now, returning to the island as a woman, and with the experience of Brussels behind her, Ionanthe intended to equip herself with all the information she would need to enable her to work behind the scenes and improve the lot of the people.

Tonight's dinner, in honour of Philippe de la Croix, would be a good place for her to start honing the skills she would need.

The dinner was to be a formal event, and Ionanthe had dressed accordingly in one of the two designer evening gowns she had purchased for similar events in Brussels. The one she was wearing this evening was a deceptively simple column of dull cream heavy silk jersey that skimmed rather than hugged her body, with long sleeves and a high neckline slashed across her collarbone.

Luckily the ladies' maid the Count had found for her was a skilful hairdresser, and she had drawn Ionanthe's dark hair back off her face and styled it in a way that reminded Ionanthe of the Shakespearean heroine in a film she had once seen.

Her maid had insisted that the dinner necessitated the wearing of what she had described 'proper jewellery, from the Crown Jewels'.

Ionanthe had flatly refused to wear the heavy and ornate crown, opting instead for a far simpler tiara set, along with a diamond necklace and a pair of matching wide diamond cuff bracelets worn over the sleeves of her gown.

Since the castle could be cold, and it was a long walk

from the Princess's robing room, where the Crown Jewels were stored, to the reception and dining rooms in the newer part of the building, Ionanthe had agreed that she would need some kind of warm covering. She had, though, refused the ermine-lined cloak the maid had wanted her to wear, and was instead wearing a far simpler cloak in rich dark ruby velvet.

Max, who had gone through much the same arguments with his valet as Ionanthe had with her maid, felt his heart unexpectedly contract when he saw Ionanthe coming towards him down the long gallery. That she would look every inch a princess he had expected—but that she would do so with such elegance, stamping what was obviously her own style on the position she now held, caught at his emotions before he could check his reaction to her. Her sister's interpretation of regal splendour had been a wardrobe full of tight-fitting rhinestone-covered designer clothes—more suitable, in Max's opinion, for a media-attention-hungry C-list celebrity.

After Eloise's death he had instructed that the clothes be packed up and sent to an appropriate charity shop.

Max suspected that the dress Ionanthe was wearing had been chosen because she believed that its flowing style did not draw attention to her body. But as a man Max knew that the cream fabric's gentle skimming of her body drew the gaze far more intently than her sister's tight, cleavage-revealing clothes had ever done.

Had things been different—had they met in different circumstances, had they chosen freely to be together, had he been able to trust her in a way that would have made them true partners, working together for a shared cause—Max knew that this moment would have been very special indeed. In the privacy of their marital bed they would, for instance, already have discussed the French diplomat's visit, and would have agreed a shared plan for maximising its potential for the benefit of the people. Max was keen to explore the possibility of making more of the island's small wine-producing area, and Monsieur de la Croix belonged to a renowned dynasty of French wine-producers.

Ionanthe had almost reached him. Automatically Max went towards her, formally offering her his crooked arm.

Unable to stop herself, Ionanthe hesitated, and then mentally rebuked herself. What was there to fear, after all? She would not be touching his bare flesh, would she? She was wearing clothes, and Max, as hereditary holder of the office of Commander of the Royal Guard, was wearing its winter dress uniform—dark green jacket ornamented with gold frogged fastenings and gold epaulettes—whilst his second in command stood to one side of him holding the large plumed helmet that denoted Max's status.

The colour of dark green for the uniform had originally been chosen so that the men who wore it would merge with the pine trees of the island's mountains, where fighting had frequently taken place when rebels had had to be subdued.

Privately Ionanthe had always disliked the wearing of what was, after all, a symbol of what had been the oppression of the poorest people of the island by its richest. However, she was forced to admit that Max carried the uniform off unexpectedly well. He gave off an air free from the louche arrogance of his late cousin. Max was a man who did not need a fancy uniform to garner respect from others.

Her mouth felt uncomfortably dry with tension as she rested her fingertips as lightly as she could on his sleeve.

Together they traversed the long gallery—together, and yet so very far apart, Ionanthe acknowledged painfully as they made their journey in silence.

Only when they had reached the double doors that led to the Audience Chamber where the reception was to take place did Max give any indication that he was aware of her. He turned his head to look at her for a second as the liveried flunkeys pulled open the doors and the heralds in their gaudy medieval tabards blew a shrill clarion call to attention for the waiting audience. His free hand covered her gloved fingers. She had been wrong to think that the formal barriers of gloves and sleeves would protect her from being affected by his touch. If anything those barriers made things worse, because they caused her to compare the satisfaction of the sensation of naked flesh on naked flesh with the ache of frustration that came now with the layers of cloth between them.

The dinner was almost over. The gold plate and the Sèvres china commissioned by the same Prince who had been responsible for the baroque decor of the rooms in this eighteenth-century addition to the original castle still gleamed in the light from the three ornate chandeliers illuminating the room. That same light also struck brilliant reflections from the facets of the diamonds worn by the female guests.

The main course had been served accompanied by wine from the diplomat's family vineyards, which Max had chosen especially, and the mood around the table had grown as mellow as it was possible to be under such circumstances.

Ionanthe was listening dutifully to their guest. She had seen him once before in Brussels—very briefly—at a large corporate event, and was well aware of his reputation as a womaniser. As she listened intently to him her heart contracted on a sharp stab of emotion—but not because of the attention he was paying her. On the contrary, she found his compliments as unappealing as the deliberately sexual looks he was giving her. No, it was the subject of his current self-satisfied monologue that was causing her muscles to tighten with angry anxiety.

'So is it true, then?' he pressed her, obviously seeking confirmation of what he had heard. 'This talk that your husband plans to allow other countries to bid for a licence to mine your coal reserves?'

Ionanthe couldn't answer him. She was too busy trying to conceal her angry dismay. Fortenegro's coal reserves lay beneath land owned by the Crown but grazed by the sheep of some of the poorest people on the island. They would be made even poorer—destitute, in fact—if, as the diplomat seemed to think, Max had agreed to allow foreign corporations to mine the coal.

It was impossible for her either to ignore or deny the intensity of the anger and the sense of betrayal she felt. Not because she herself was personally in any way disappointed by Max's callous disregard of his people's needs—of course not—her feelings were on behalf of those people, against Max's betrayal of them.

Cosmo might have been a selfish, self-satisfied egotist, who had thought only of his own pleasure, but at least *he* had had the virtue of being too lazy to think of adding to his own personal wealth by further pauperising his people. Max, who was shrewder and more business aware, could do far more damage to the island than Cosmo had if he literally mined its assets for his own personal benefit.

The diplomat was still awaiting her response. 'I'm afraid I'm not the person you should be asking,' she responded with ease. 'It is my husband who rules Fortenegro.'

'Ah, but even a man who is a ruler can be putty in the hands of a beautiful and intelligent woman who herself knows how the business world works. Should there be future opportunities here of international interest I am sure any astutely managed conglomerate would want to court your personal support.'

Was the Frenchman sounding her out as a possible aide in the future asset-stripping of the island? Ionanthe concealed her outraged revulsion, and her desire to inform Monsieur de la Croix that she wanted to protect her country from exploitation, not assist in it. After all, it was far better to allow him to think they might be future allies. That way she would have more chance of learning what deals were being discussed—although she had no idea how she might prevent them. It sickened her to remember how she had felt in Max's arms now that she knew what he was planning to do.

It had been the Count's idea that Monsieur de la

Croix should be seated next to Ionanthe rather than the Prince himself, even though he was the guest of honour, and now, watching the other man focusing so intently on Ionanthe and quite obviously flirting with her, totally ignoring the elderly dowager on his left-hand side, Max was finding it more and more difficult not to watch them—like some passionately in love fool who was being ridiculously and unnecessarily jealous.

It was a relief to Ionanthe when the evening finally came to an end and the French diplomat was escorted to a car waiting to take him to the airport for his homeward flight. Tomorrow morning Max would be leaving for Barcelona from that same airport, and then in the afternoon she herself would be leaving for her ancestral home—the Castle in the Clouds as it was known locally, because of the height of the mountain range on which it was built.

Of course it wasn't really loneliness and disappointment she felt, she reassured herself later, as she lay alone in the bed she had so briefly shared with Max. How could she live with herself, after all, if she were to admit to those feelings for a man who stood for and championed so much that she hated and despised?

If she had any longings, then they were simply longings to conceive the son who now more than ever she knew she must have to protect the people. It was not the thought of Max himself that made her body quicken and her pulse race, whilst her flesh was seized with a thrill of aching need. It was her growing sense of urgency with regard to conceiving a son. The ache now flaring hotly inside her came from her impatience to conceive—

from the knowledge that she had to have the most intimate sexual contact there was with Max to achieve her ambition. Not from any desire for Max himself…

CHAPTER EIGHT

THEY had almost reached the airport. Max put down the geological survey reports which had only arrived that morning and leaned back in the seat of the large Mercedes. He had commissioned the reports some months earlier, when he had first come to the throne, having heard rumours that certain factions within his court had been making enquiries about the possibility of Fortenegro's mountainous region possessing reserves not just of coal but of other valuable minerals and ores as well. One of the most likely areas to yield the more valuable commodities, according to the reports, was the mountain land owned by the late Baron—now owned by his granddaughter, Ionanthe.

Max exhaled. He did not welcome having to be so suspicious. He placed a very high value on mutual trust, and it was an important principle of his foundation. However, he also valued instinct, and his instinct was telling him—as it had done right from the start—that Ionanthe had had an undeclared purpose in agreeing to marry him.

That undeclared reason could, of course, be something personal that would not impact on anyone other than herself. It might well be that he was being overly cautious. It might be that he'd simply have to put his thoughts to her for her to supply him with an answer to his question. Ionanthe might not even be aware of the value of what lay beneath the surface of her family's land.

On the other hand, it might also be that Ionanthe *did* know—she had worked in Brussels, after all, and would be well aware of the importance and the value of certain raw materials. It was possible that she was now playing for very high stakes with the island's natural resources, in a 'winner takes all' throw of the dice. Was she contemplating selling out those who depended on her? Or was he allowing the grit of an instinct that had jarred on him to grow into something that owed more to his imagination than true fact?

Legally, of course, she had every right to dispose of any riches on or in the land which she owned—although Max deplored the immorality of anyone depriving such a very poor people of their living to add to their own already extensive wealth. It was impossible for her to know of his very private wish to bring an end to such feudal ownership of huge tracts of the island by a handful of powerful families—and that included much of the land owned by the Crown—in order to give it instead to the people. He had already known and accepted that he would have to move very carefully and tactfully, unfortunately perhaps even in secret in the early stages of this endeavour. It was essential for its success that none of the resources were sold on to someone outside the island before he could complete the process.

Now the situation with regard to Ionanthe further

complicated the issue—and all the more so because Max knew that what had happened between them meant that he could not really trust his own judgement. It would forever be clouded by the desire he felt for her. Had that desire damaged his ability to judge her correctly? Already he had told himself that she was a giver, not a taker; already he was not just prepared but actively wanting to believe the best of her. But Max knew that he could not afford to let his emotions control his judgement. There was far too much at risk for that. Little though he liked doing so, he owed it to his people to look suspiciously upon Ionanthe's possible motives.

Was it possible that Ionanthe had married him to provide herself with a smokescreen behind which she could sell off the mineral rights she now owned? Was that why she wished to visit her family home? Had she deceived him all along with her apparent inability to control her sensuality, using it as a means to lull him into a false state of security?

No wonder history recorded so many long-dead monarchs as suspicious paranoids, Max thought wryly.

Ionanthe had been asleep when he had gone into the bedroom this morning, tempted by an emotion that should have had no place in his thinking to reveal his concern to her. Thinking about her now, it was that image that filled his head: her hair a dark silky cloud on the white pillow, her face free of make-up. She'd slept on, oblivious to his presence, whilst his body had been all too acutely aware of hers.

The need he was fighting was far more skilled at getting past his barriers than he was at maintaining them, Max recognized, as his body began its familiar assault on his mind. And it wasn't just his body that was susceptible, over-printed with its memories of her. His emotions were now at war within themselves as well. But when you stripped back everything else, it was trust, or rather the lack of it, that lay at the core of his dilemma. And not just his personal trust in her as a woman he was perilously close to loving. He was by virtue of his position the designated protector of his people's trust. Trust in himself and in those with whom he chose to share his most intimate confidences and beliefs. He might judge that his need for Ionanthe outweighed his wish that he could trust her, but he could not make that choice with his people's trust. That was a risk he must not and would not take.

In another couple of hours Ionanthe would be leaving for the mountains. Was it, as he had initially assumed, because she wanted to put some distance between them? Or did she have another, far more devious purpose?

He wasn't going to find the answer to his question in Barcelona.

He reached for his mobile phone, and then leaned forward to attract the attention of his driver.

CHAPTER NINE

SHE could have driven herself to the castle—she had wanted to. But the Count had protested that it was unseemly for her to do so in her new role, so Ionanthe had given in, even whilst reminding the Count that the road to the castle was badly maintained, and because of that it would be necessary for her to travel there in a sturdy four-wheel drive rather than the kind of car more suited for pomp and State occasions.

Initially she might have made the impetuous decision to visit her childhood home to escape from Max and her vulnerability to him, but Ionanthe hadn't forgotten the vow she'd made to herself to use the wealth she had inherited from her grandfather to improve the lives of their tenants and those who worked for the family. As an ambition it came nowhere near matching the truly awesome achievements of the Veritas Foundation she so admired, but it was a small step in the right direction. Ionanthe smiled ruefully to herself at the thought of the reaction of the chairman of Veritas in the unlikely event of him ever getting to know how much the foundation's achievements had inspired her.

It was a cornerstone of the foundation's ethos that inherited wealth should be used for the greater good of those people who were most in need—mainly through health incentives followed by education. The island had a desperately poor record on both issues. There was one exclusive private hospital for the rich, and a handful of shamefully ill-equipped and badly run clinics for the poor. The wealthy sent their sons abroad for private schooling and groomed their daughters for the right kind of marriage, whilst the poor—if they were lucky—made do with state education which ended when a child reached fourteen. Fortenegro did not have proper senior schools for its brighter children, never mind colleges or a university. There was no middle class. Any islander who did well enough to make any money tended to leave the island, seeking better opportunities for themselves and their families.

It could all have been so very different. Fortenegro was rich in natural assets, which included its mineral deposits, its climate, and its scenery.

Max would probably be in Barcelona by now. Ionanthe looked at the telephone on the desk. In a normal relationship a man separated from his partner would surely telephone her, ostensibly to assure her of his safe arrival, but in reality because of their shared need to hear one another's voice. But of course hers was not a normal relationship, and even less a normal marriage. Her own thoughts pressed on her heart like hard fingers on a painful bruise, making her want to withdraw from the hurt they were causing.

'Highness, the car is waiting.'

Ionanthe nodded her head in response to the Count's information.

The air was colder today—a warning that winter was almost here, Ionanthe recognised, as she looked up towards the hills already cloaked in snow.

In only a few days it would be Christmas. *Christmas.* She could feel the familiar sadness settling on her like the drift of winter snow. Christmas had once been her favourite time of year. But Christmas was a time for sharing, for loving, and she had no one with whom to share her love or the deepest secrets of her heart. She had no loving, caring family with whom to spend this special time of year.

In Brussels she had dreaded the build-up to the season, forced to listen and watch as her co-workers prepared excitedly for their Christmas break, talking of their happiness at the thought of 'going home' or being with someone special. Christmas could be the cruellest time of year for those without love, as she well knew.

According to the Count, the court made no special plans for Christmas; when Cosmo had been alive he had always spent from late December until the end of January away from Fortenegro, 'enjoying himself'.

Ionanthe burrowed deeper into the camel-coloured cashmere coat she was wearing—another item she had worked and saved hard for. Ionanthe was a believer in 'investment' items of clothing. Throw-away clothes, like throw-away relationships, held no appeal for her. Perhaps because of her childhood, she yearned for those things that would endure and on which she knew she could depend.

A little to her surprise, the waiting equerry was holding open the front passenger door of the sturdy four-wheel drive vehicle waiting in the courtyard. Its darkened windows were an affectation that made Ionanthe suspect that the vehicle must have been one of the many carelessly purchased by Cosmo.

Even more unexpected was the fact that the car was without its driver. But Ionanthe didn't realise that until she was in her seat and the equerry was closing the door and moving round to the driver's side of the vehicle, holding it open for the man now coming down the steps towards them.

Ionanthe's heart whooshed to the bottom of her ribcage as though caught up in an avalanche. Max! It surely couldn't be him? But it was! Just for a moment the sweetest and most intoxicating surge of joy filled her—but then reality cut in. He couldn't possibly have changed his mind because he wanted to be with her. And she shouldn't want that to be the case.

She watched guardedly as he got into the car, unable to stop herself from saying, almost accusingly, 'You're supposed to be in Barcelona.'

'I am supposed to be,' Max agreed. 'But my meeting was cancelled.' It was the truth, after all—even if he himself had been the one to do the cancelling. 'And I decided it would be a good idea if we were to visit your castle together. It will help to reassure people of our unity, and of course of our commitment to one another and to them.'

Ionanthe gave a small shiver, despite the delicious warmth of the car's interior. 'I really don't think that would be a good idea,' she protested.

'You don't? Why not?'

Why not? Because her escape had been about preventing any intimacy between them, not promoting it. But of course she could hardly tell him that.

'My grandfather didn't use the castle very much. It's old-fashioned, and not very well equipped with mod cons.'

'Really? I understood from your sister that your parents had spent what she described as "a fortune" on installing modern plumbing and central heating.'

Ionanthe's heart sank. Her parents *had* modernised the castle—much to the anger of her grandfather, who had never ceased complaining about what he considered to be a waste of money. Eloise had taken the same attitude as their grandfather, begrudging the money spent and claiming that such luxuries as bathrooms and central heating were wasted on the staff who looked after the castle.

'That was nearly twenty years ago. I'm not even sure the central heating system will still be working.'

'If it isn't then we shall just have to find some other way to keep warm, then, shan't we?'

The swift hiss of Ionanthe's betraying breath should have pleased him, but instead it made him feel like stopping the car and taking her in his arms.

To punish himself, Max continued briskly, 'After all, I'm sure your staff must have found one. It would be uncomfortable if not impossible for them to endure the cold of the mountain winters if they had not.'

Was Max genuinely expressing concern for others? Or was he simply using them as a means of mocking her?

'The boiler and the fires are fed by logs cut from trees that fall or have to be felled,' she explained. 'It is hard work, and the logs have to be eked out carefully when there are bad winters.'

'You make it sound very unpleasant, but I dare say those who live there are accustomed to it. Or do they wish for an easier life in a less harsh environment?'

Max's question made Ionanthe tense. What was the true purpose of his questions and his obvious determination to visit the mountains? Was he merely making conversation, or did he have a darker purpose in suggesting that her people might wish to abandon the mountains and live somewhere else? It was, after all, beneath the mountains that the coal lay—on land he owned, which bordered what was now hers.

What was he trying to prove in giving Ionanthe the opportunity to confide in him? Max wondered grimly.

She wasn't going to play Max's game, Ionanthe decided. She had already learned the painful cost of doing so, hadn't she?

'It is their choice to live where and how they do,' she answered, giving a small shrug as she did so in an attempt to express a lack of interest in the subject that would bring his questions to an end.

But Max gave her a hard look and suggested, in an even harder voice, 'And since *you* do not have to endure their hardship it is of no concern to you? Your sister expressed much the same view. I should perhaps have expected that you would share it.'

Was he trying to suggest that she didn't care about the lives of those who depended on her? Now Ionanthe was really angry.

'For your information, I do *not* slavishly adopt the views of others. I formulate my own. And if you knew anything about history then you would know that in many instances—from the Scottish Highland clearances to the wholesale movement of people from their terraced houses to the planners' rabbit hutch post-war flats—when people have been taken from their environment and resettled against their will it has led to the destruction of their sense of community, adding to their ills rather than lessening them. If my people wish to move and change their way of life then of course I shall do my best to aid them in that endeavour. But I will never force it upon them.'

There was real passion in her voice, Max acknowledged. Passion and conviction. But was there also honesty?

They were approaching the turn-off they needed to take from the coast road, but before Ionanthe could let Max know it was coming up he was signalling to make the turning.

As though he knew what she was thinking, he told her curtly, 'I visited the castle with Eloise, shortly before our marriage.'

'She wouldn't have liked that.'

The words were out before Ionanthe could stop them. Now he would think she was jealous and mean as well as everything else, Ionanthe thought miserably, unable to look at Max for fear of what she might see in his eyes.

'Eloise was always a city and bright lights person,' she explained lamely. 'Neither she nor our grandfather liked the castle.'

'But you did?' Max guessed.

'It was my family home when our parents were alive. My mother loved it, and because my father loved her he was happy for them to make their home there.'

Ionanthe's voice softened and warmed as she spoke of her parents. Eloise had barely spoken of them or her sister at all, Max remembered.

'My parents had so many plans—especially my mother. She wanted—' Abruptly Ionanthe stopped. That was what you got from allowing your emotions to take over. You were in danger of saying things it was best not to say. Her mother had been a reformist, a pioneer in her way, who had felt passionately about the importance of education and who had proved her commitment to her beliefs by setting up her own small school for the children of those who worked in the castle and on its lands. It had been Ionanthe's own special and much loved task to help the very little ones with their letters.

Watching the way her expression softened, Max thought she had never looked lovelier. Her emotions had brought a luminosity to her skin and her eyes, a sweet approachability that was not vulnerability but something stronger and deeper—as though a path had opened up between them. As though…

Lost in her memories, Ionanthe continued softly, 'At this time of year my mother would send my father out into the forest to bring back a Christmas tree. It had to be tall enough for the star to touch the ceiling in the grand hall, and its lower branches wide enough for there to be space beneath them for all the presents my mother would wrap for the children. She always seemed to know exactly what each child most longed for. Many of the toys were made in secret in the estate's carpentry shop—dolls' houses and cribs for the girls, forts and trains for the boys, puppets and so much more… We made our own decorations too—my mother was very artistic. The time around Christmas always seemed to be filled with our parents' laughter.

'At New Year my parents held a large party, with lots of guests coming to stay, but Christmas itself was always for the children. We'd have snow, of course, being in the mountains, and there'd be snowball fights and ski races. To me as a child Christmas was the best time—magical and filled with love and happiness. When my parents died it was as though they had taken Christmas with them, because it was never the same afterwards. That was when my grandfather moved permanently to his apartment in the royal castle.'

Her words had brought an ache to Max's throat, a need to open his arms to her and hold her safe within them, a longing to tell her that somehow he would find a way to make Christmases magical again. How on earth was he going to be able to stick to his principles if just listening to her talk about her childhood was going to put his judgement in the balance and weight the scales heavily in her favour?

Max told himself that he was glad that he was driving, because that at least stopped him from touching her. 'And you and Eloise? Where did you live after your parents' death?' he asked, trying to sound detached.

His question caused Ionanthe to look at him. Hadn't Eloise told him *anything* about their childhood?

'Grandfather took Eloise with him. They were always close.' She wasn't going to say that Eloise had been their grandfather's favourite and make herself sound even more pathetic and jealous. The plain, unwanted grandchild who had been pushed into the background to mourn the loss of the parents who had loved her as her grandfather had not.

'And you?' Max persisted. He was frowning now, as though angered by something.

'I went away to school. It was what I wanted and what my parents had always planned.'

No need to say that their parents had planned to send them both, not separate them and favour one above the other.

'What about you and your childhood?' Ionanthe asked him, wanting to divert their conversation away from herself.

'Me? I was an only child.'

'And your parents?'

'Dead. An accident.'

The curt voice in which the information was delivered warned Ionanthe not to pursue the subject—and yet she wanted to. Because she wanted to know all there was to know about him.

And so what if she did? Wasn't there an old adage about knowing one's enemy?

Enemies? Was *that* what they must be?

Whilst they had been talking the road had started to climb steeply. Small patches of snow lying in the hollows gradually became more widespread, until up ahead of them the whole landscape was white—apart from where the trunks of the trees were etched dark and the sheer face of the rocks showed grey with age.

A flight of geese cut their perfect V formation across the sky—heading, Ionanthe guessed, for the large natural lake that lay just below the snow line.

'Some of the older estate workers swear that there were once bears in the mountains,' she told Max with a small smile. 'But my father always used to say it was simply a story to scare us children.'

It had started to snow. Thick fat flakes drifting down from a grey sky. How she had once loved the first snows of winter, hoping they would fall thick and deep enough to keep her parents in the castle with them. She hadn't recognised then how hard the harsh weather made the lives of those who worked on the land—tenant farmers, in the main, with flocks of goats and sheep. If there was mineral wealth beneath these sometimes cruel mountains then surely it belonged to those farmers?

Christmas. He hadn't realised how close it was, Max admitted. The foundation had a special fund that provided money for various charities to help those in need at this special time of year.

Max remembered the year his parents had given him the best present he had ever received. He had been sixteen, and he could still remember the thrill of pride he had felt when they had told him that they were giving him his own small area of responsibility within the foundation. He had been given a fund-raising target to meet. He had delivered newspapers, cleaned cars and run errands in order to earn the money to make that target, and no target he had met since had been as sweet.

Because his parents had been killed shortly after his eighteenth birthday, and from then on there had been no one to praise him for his endeavours.

The four-wheel drive was equipped with snow tyres, and they were needed now that they were above the snow line.

They were nearly there. Once they had gone round the corner they would be able to see the castle. Ionanthe folded her hands in her lap. It was foolish to feel so excited. She wasn't a child any more, after all. Even so she caught and held her breath as they rounded the next bend, expelling it on a long sigh at the sight high above them, on its small plateau on the mountainside, of the castle, its topmost turrets disappearing into the heavy snow clouds.

It was truly a fairytale castle—all turrets and crenulated battlements, its exterior faced with a white limestone that made it look more as though it was made from icing sugar than the granite the facing concealed.

The small ornamental lake in the grounds where she had learned to skate would be frozen. Her parents had held skating parties there with coloured lanterns suspended from the branches of the trees that overhung the lake to illuminate the darkness. Ionanthe remembered lying in bed with her window wide open, despite the cold, so that she could listen to the adult laughter.

They had reached the long drive to the castle now, and the trees that bordered it were so heavy with snow that their branches swept right down to the ground.

The light had started to fade, and one by one the lights were coming on in the castle, to cast a warming welcoming glow from the windows. In the courtyard people were waiting for them, eager hands opening the car doors, familiar voices exclaiming proudly, 'Your Highness.'

Retainers she remembered as formidable adults not afraid to chide an over-active child were now bowing and curtsying low to her.

Impulsively Ionanthe reached out to take hold of the arms of the cook, remonstrating with her. 'No, Ariadne, please. There is no need.'

'Hah, I see you still hold the same republican views as your mother,' the elderly woman snapped sharply. 'Well, there are those of us who still respect our Sovereign, and if we want to show that respect then we shall.'

Max was hard put to it not to laugh. The small red-cheeked woman reminded him very much of a Greek cook his parents had once employed. She had run the whole household, and Max suspected that this woman did the same.

'So you're a republican at heart, are you?' He couldn't resist teasing Ionanthe as they were ushered inside.

'Ariadne likes to think so,' was all Ionanthe would allow herself to say.

The great hall was ablaze with lights, a fire roaring in the large fireplace, although Max suspected that it was the radiators that in reality kept the double-height room so warm.

The room's heat made Ionanthe frown and say accusingly to Ariadne, 'You've got the heating on.'

'Of course. You don't think we'd allow our Prince to freeze to death, do you?'

Ionanthe's lips compressed. She knew how much

wood it took to warm the great hall, and what back-breaking labour it was to provide that wood.

'I don't want you using a whole winter's supply of logs to keep the castle warm just because we're here,' she told Ariadne.

When they got back to the royal palace she must make arrangements, somehow, for extra supplies of wood to be delivered to the castle, to replace that which would be burned keeping the place warm for them, she decided.

'You needn't worry about that,' Ariadne assured her. 'Pieter has turned off all the radiators except those down here and in the drawing room—and in the state bedroom, of course. Made up the bed with that special linen your mother liked so much, Magda has.'

As the full meaning of Ariadne's words sank into Ionanthe's head, a trill of horror shot through her. 'You've put us both in the state bedroom?' she demanded.

'Well, of course I have. Where else would you sleep?' Ariadne demanded. 'Decorated especially for His Highness's great-grandfather, that room was.'

Ionanthe didn't dare look at Max.

'I suppose you'll be wanting Pieter and the men to go out and bring you a Christmas tree in? Wouldn't be a proper Christmas without one, after all. It's time we had you here for Christmas. A place isn't a proper home without family in it.'

Ionanthe listened to the older woman with growing dismay as she realised that Ariadne thought they were here for Christmas. Ariadne was attempting to sound disapproving, but Ionanthe could see how pleased she was. She hated having to disappoint her, but she would have to put her right and correct her misapprehension.

'Ariadne, this is only a brief visit—' she began. But to her astonishment Max put his hand on her arm and shook his head.

'What the Princess means, Ariadne, is that we are unable to stay as long as we'd like.'

'Well, as to that, it's the mountains that says how long a person stays. *You* should know that,' she reminded Ionanthe. 'You've been snowed in here often enough, after all. I remember the year that sister of yours kicked up such a fuss because she couldn't go to some party or other. Chasing after some boy, I expect, and in no mind to be stopped. Always spoiled, she was. The old Baron could never see her for what she really was. Always did favour shine over substance, he did. More fool him.'

Ionanthe shot a quick look at Max, wondering how he was reacting to Ariadne's criticism of Eloise, but it was impossible to guess his thoughts from his expression.

Ariadne hadn't finished. 'You'll find this one a different kettle of fish from the other,' she informed Max bluntly. 'You've got the better bargain with her.'

'I'm sure you're right,' Max agreed, keeping his face straight.

'I am right. Watched them both growing up, I did. That Eloise always did think too well of herself and not well enough of others. Of course this one's just the opposite—always putting others first. What you want, my girl, is a nursery full of little ones to keep you busy.'

Ariadne might be speaking to her, but she was looking

at Max, Ionanthe recognised, with a roguish glint in her small currant-dark eyes. She'd even put her head on one side, as though inviting Max to agree with her.

CHAPTER TEN

'BEFORE you complain, let me remind you that none of this is my fault. I didn't ask you to come here with me,' Ionanthe told Max sharply.

They were in the state bedroom, and the flush on Ionanthe's cheeks was caused more by her emotions than by the heat or the fire—even if she *was* desperately trying not to look as though she cared about the fact that the room possessed only one double bed, and not a particularly wide double bed at that.

'What exactly is it that you expect me to complain about?' Max asked quizzically.

Ionanthe gave him a suspicious look. 'You know perfectly well what I mean. We're going to have to share this…this room, or risk Ariadne making a dreadful fuss.'

Max grinned at her. 'Well, we certainly don't want that, do we? She might send us to bed supperless.'

To her own disbelief Ionanthe discovered that she desperately wanted to giggle.

'She can't help it,' she defended the elderly woman. 'She's always been the same. Grandfather used to get infuriated with her and threaten to sack her, but she'd just ignore him.'

'Sensible woman.' Max flicked back the heavy silk linen window hanging and informed her, 'It's still snowing.'

'Then you'd better work some royal magic to make it stop,' Ionanthe told him shortly, adding, 'I don't know why Ariadne assumed we'd be here for Christmas. I certainly never said that. When I telephoned I simply said that I'd be staying for a couple of nights.'

'It won't be the end of the world if we do have to stay, will it? Or do you have some special reason for wanting to leave?'

Ionanthe frowned. 'No, of course not. I was thinking of you. It will be expected that you spend Christmas at the palace.'

Max crooked one eyebrow and asked wryly, 'Why?'

For a reason Ionanthe didn't want to dwell on, something about the way Max was looking at her made her feel stupidly flustered—hot and flustered, she acknowledged. Treacherously, the image of a fig, luscious and ripe and dusted in sugar, slipped tauntingly into view inside her head. Now she didn't only feel flustered, she felt flushed as well—hot and flustered and— She licked uncomfortably dry lips. Surely this wasn't what was going to happen to her every time she was alone in a bedroom with Max?

Ionanthe struggled to replace the teasing image inside her head with a blank screen, knowing that she still hadn't answered Max's question and that he was quite obviously expecting her to do so.

'I wouldn't have thought that state business comes to a halt just because it's Christmas,' she eventually replied, in a stuffy, righteous voice she hardly recognised as her own.

Max looked less than impressed by her argument, one dark eyebrow inclining even more steeply. 'I can conduct what state business I have to attend to just as easily here as there. One of the benefits of modern technology,' he informed her dryly, indicating the Blackberry he had just removed from his jacket pocket.

Ionanthe took a deep breath in an attempt to steady herself, and was then forced to exhale it faster than she'd wanted when she saw that Max had turned away from her to remove the jacket of his business suit. The fabric of his shirt stretched across the breadth of his shoulders as he did so. Beneath that shirt lay flesh so smooth and honed that just looking at it was an intensely sensual experience, never mind what happened when she actually touched it—and him.

What was the matter with her? Hadn't she sat through innumerable business meetings during which men had removed their suit jackets without reacting like this?

But they hadn't been Max.

Like the muffled sound of a warning bell rung so hard and deep that its echo shook the depths, Ionanthe felt a tremor of warning deep within her body.

No! It was inconceivable that this man should be the one to affect her like this. The adage that it was too late to lock the stable door after the horse had bolted had surely never been more appropriate.

Ionanthe knew that if Max were to turn to her now and take her in his arms she would not be able to resist him—or herself. But when he did turn back to her he merely said casually, 'Didn't Ariadne say something about having made you some of your favourite soup?'

'You're hungry?' Ionanthe guessed.

She couldn't look at him. She was too afraid that he might see her disappointment and guess its cause. It was so unfair that, having taken flight here to protect herself from him, all she had done was leave herself more vulnerable. They would be thrown far more into one another's company here than they would ever have been at court.

Max studied Ionanthe's downbent head. The fall of her hair revealed a glimpse of the elegant length of her neck, her skin as luminous as a pearl. Desire flamed through him, hot and urgent. He wanted to go to her and draw her back against him, tasting the soft warmth of her skin as he did so, waiting for her to turn in his arms and press herself into him, silently saying that she shared his need, offering him her lips, herself, her love…

Her *love*? Was that really what the hunger gnawing at him was? A need not just for the sexual pleasure he had already shared with her, but for something richer and deeper, something stronger, more primitive and eternal?

Was he hungry? Ionanthe had asked, and the true answer was *yes*, he was. Hungry for Ionanthe. Hungry for exactly what he had told himself he must not want because of the danger attached to it.

How had it happened? Max had no idea.

'Yes, I'm hungry,' he agreed.

His voice was flat and hard, and for some reason it left Ionanthe with an ache in her throat and smarting eyes.

* * *

The large, comfortable kitchen was busy. A young woman whom Ionanthe vaguely recognised was whisking about, whilst two young children were seated at the table crayoning.

'You'll remember Marta, Gorge's youngest,' Ariadne informed Ionanthe, and the pretty young woman gave Ionanthe a shy smile. 'Married to our Tomas, she is now, with two young ones of her own.'

Ionanthe returned the young woman's smile.

'I'm teaching my two their letters, Highness, just like you taught me mine. Ever so grateful to you and your mother we were, for telling our parents that we should have our schooling. I've told my Tomas that our girls are going to get their schooling no matter what.'

Ariadne, who was stirring a large pot on the stove, gave a derisory snort. 'Soft as butter, Tomas is—not like fathers were in my day. Them parents of yours have a lot to answer for, filling folks' heads with ideas above their station with all that talk of schooling and the like.'

'Take no notice of Mam,' Marta told Ionanthe cheerfully. 'Proud as punch of our two girls, she is, and always telling them that they've got to pay attention to their lessons. Teachers is what I'd like them to be. But they'd have to go to the mainland for that, and that costs money.'

Watching Marta's bright smile give way to uncertainty and anxiety, Ionanthe reached out towards her, telling her without thinking, 'Don't worry, Marta. The money will be there for them. I'm planning to set up a fund in my parents' name, out of the money my grandfather left. It will provide scholarships for children like yours to get all the education they need.'

It was Ariadne who spoke first in the silence that followed Ionanthe's impulsive declaration, saying triumphantly to her daughter-in-law, in whose eyes emotional tears were beginning to glisten, 'There—you see. I told you our Princess would see to it that something was done. Not that you'll have an easy time persuading *some* folk to send their children to school,' Ariadne added darkly.

'All the children of Fortenegro should have the right to a good education. It is my duty as Fortenegro's ruler to ensure that they do.'

Max's voice was firm and uncompromising, causing them all to look at him.

'My wife is to be applauded for what she plans to do, but there must come a day when the children on this island receive their education as a right, not as a gift.'

Ionanthe couldn't take her gaze from Max's face. They might almost have been alone as her expression showed him how much his declaration meant to her.

'Do you really mean that?'

'Yes,' he confirmed.

CHAPTER ELEVEN

'CONVINCING the barons and some of the community elders that no child should leave school before sixteen won't be easy, never mind winning them round to the idea of Fortenegro having its own colleges and university,' Ionanthe warned Max.

They were alone in the great hall, having just finished their dinner, and Ionanthe's face was flushed with delight and the hope that Max really shared her belief that changes needed to be made, allowing the children of the island to receive the educational opportunities they were currently denied.

'There will be opposition, I know,' Max allowed.

'A great deal of opposition,' Ionanthe agreed.

She paused. The French diplomat's comment about the licensing of coal mining was a spectre she desperately wanted to banish.

'What you're planning will be very expensive,' she began hesitantly. 'You will need to increase the island's revenue to the Crown.'

'I have several plans in mind for that,' Max told her. Should he bring up the subject of the mineral reserves on her land? He wanted to do so. The realisation that she shared at least one of his plans, and the sense of being at one with her that had created over dinner, made him want to be open and honest with her. But now was perhaps not the time for a further potentially lengthy discussion.

The fire was burning low; Ionanthe was smothering a small yawn. There were more intimate ways in which he wanted to communicate with her right now; more personal bonds he wanted to forge with her.

'You're tired?'

Max's words were a statement, not a question, and the smile which accompanied them made Ionanthe's heart leap and flounder inside her chest.

'Yes,' she admitted.

'We've travelled a long way today, sometimes over difficult and unfamiliar territory, but for my own part I have to say that the journey has been very worthwhile,' Max told her, before emphasising softly, '*Very* worthwhile.'

Ionanthe looked at him and saw that she had been right to sense that he was not referring to their journey to the castle.

'I agree,' she responded, picking her words as carefully as she could.

From the smile Max was giving her, it had obviously been the response he wanted.

'Time for bed?' he suggested.

Ionanthe struggled to control the leap of delight in her body.

'I'm sorry that Ariadne has put us both in the same room.'

Max stood up and came towards her, reaching down to take her hand and pull her gently out of her chair.

'Are you? That's disappointing. Perhaps I can persuade you to change your mind?'

Ionanthe's breath caught in her throat, her thoughts a giddy whirl of mingled disbelief and excitement. Did Max really mean what he seemed to be saying? The evening and their shared conversation had brought them so close that for her there was only one way she wanted it to end.

It was because it was so cold on the stone stairs and walking down the long passage that led to their room in the tallest turret tower of the castle that they had to walk so close together, with Max's arm around her, holding her close to his side. That was what Ionanthe told herself, but it was not a valid excuse for what happened outside their bedroom door, when Max pulled her into his arms and kissed her.

'You taste of cold mountain air and magic,' Max told her, tracing the shape of her lips with the pad of his thumb.

'Magic hasn't got a taste,' Ionanthe objected huskily.

'Yes, it has,' Max corrected her. 'It tastes of wonder and witchery and woman—the woman I want more than any other woman I have ever wanted before.'

Ionanthe couldn't believe what she was hearing. She hardly dared breathe in case she broke what she knew must be some kind of spell.

Her eyes dark with emotion, she asked, 'Do you want me more than you wanted Eloise?'

There was a small pause, during which she trembled

and Max's arms tightened around her, and then he answered her truthfully.

'There is no comparison.'

He kissed her again, his mouth hot and hard on hers, before he withdrew from her to say gruffly, 'I can't kiss you as I want to out here, and if I don't stop now I won't be able to.'

They were inside the room and Max was locking the door. The room's warmth welcomed them, the soft glow of the fire casting softly caressing shadows.

Ionanthe went to the window and drew back the heavy curtain to perch on the small window seat and look out. Almost immediately Max joined her, coming to stand behind her, his body close to hers and his hand on her shoulder.

'It's still snowing,' Ionanthe announced.

'Yes,' Max agreed, turning her to him.

There were no figs this time, but Max said softly that he didn't care, that Ionanthe herself was all he needed and wanted.

Ionanthe couldn't bring herself to voice her own feelings. She was half afraid that doing so might break the spell that was binding them together. It was enough that he was there and they were together.

The dying embers of the fire in the grate threw out enough light for her to see as well as feel the muscles and the strength of Max's body as she caressed him with secretly avid hunger and delight. Now she could marvel at the ease with which he could arouse her to those heights she had never imagined existed, instead of fearing it as she had done that first time.

They touched and caressed and kissed in a sensual warmth of absorbed pleasure, accompanied by the music of their soft sounds of mutual arousal which grew less soft and more urgent as their passion took fire.

The touch of Max's hand cupping the underside of her breast whilst his thumb-tip rubbed slowly against her nipple had Ionanthe crying out to him in sweet pleasure. When his lips took possession of her eager flesh in response to that cry Ionanthe held his head to her breast, arching her back in delight. Their bodies threw erotic shadows on the wall.

This time Ionanthe was bolder, determined to take her own pleasure from caressing and tasting Max as ardently as he had done her. Experimentally she drew her fingertips along the inside of his thigh—just the merest brushing of her nails in slow circles that at first held him rigid and then, when she persisted, drove him to groan and offer himself up to her with an intimate longing she couldn't resist.

Her lips followed her fingertips, until Max groaned out loud and pulled her to him.

She was eager and ready for him, welcoming the feel of him sinking deep into her, holding him there so that she could savour the sensation.

In silence they held one another, neither of them moving.

This was where he was meant to be—here, with this woman who made him feel that holding her like this was worth more than a thousand kingdoms, Max admitted to himself. It was too late now for him to tell himself that he mustn't love her. He *did* love her. He loved everything about her.

Now. Now she was whole and complete—holding Max to her and within her, Ionanthe acknowledged. She loved him more than she had thought it possible to love anyone.

They breathed together and their flesh quickened. Max began to move, driven by an age-old need, and Ionanthe opened herself to him, obeying a primitive instinct of her own.

Their pleasure rose and then plateaued, allowing them to rest their sweat-soaked bodies and ease their laboured breathing. The climb had been steep and urgent, claiming from them everything they had to give. And then, as though nature herself had grown impatient with the delay, the very act of their breathing set off within Ionanthe a small but cataclysmic tightening of eager muscles accompanied by a ripple of pleasure. Her hands tightened on Max's shoulders and immediately he responded, driving hard, feeling her taking him deep within her. Their rhythm changed, tightening, hurrying, rushing frantically as they laboured to meet the demands being made on them.

The end came fiercely, with a final paroxysm of shared pleasure leaving them clinging together at the pinnacle, their hearts thudding in unison.

Ionanthe woke to a morning of snow-bright light and the gentle caress of Max's hands on her body.

How delicious it was to wake to such sensual pleasure. She turned to Max and smiled sleepily at him, her smile turning to a soft gasp when his touch grew more intimate.

'We'll be late for breakfast,' she warned him.

'Mmm…breakfast, or this and you?' Max murmured, as though pretending to consider his choice.

His lips feathered kisses against her skin and his fingers teased nipples that were already showing how eager they were for him to make *them* his choice.

CHAPTER TWELVE

'I THOUGHT that since we shall have to spend Christmas here now, after last night's snowfall, we could perhaps have a party for everyone here at the castle on Christmas Eve. My parents used to do it.'

'It sounds a good idea to me,' Max agreed.

'We'll need a Christmas tree, of course.'

'I'll take some of the men and see what we can find.'

They exchanged smiles.

They'd breakfasted on homemade bread and honey from the estate's bees, whilst Ionanthe explained to Max that the estate was almost self-sufficient.

'The people live simply, but well, in the same way they have lived for many, many generations. That is why the elders of the communities are so opposed to change. They cannot see what benefits it could bring. They believe they have everything they need. They cannot see that we live in different times, and that they are denying the younger generation the right to make their own choices. They think that life can continue as it has always done without any change for ever, but it can't. The world is growing smaller; the island itself will have to change. That is inevitable.'

Max put down his coffee cup. Was one of the changes Ionanthe was envisaging the mining of the island's minerals? Last night, hearing her speak so passionately about the need for education for the island's children, he had admired and applauded her, allowing his heart to rule his head, but now once again the responsibilities of his role were reminding him that there were questions that had to be answered.

'When you say that the island will have to change, what kind of changes do you have in mind?' he asked.

Ionanthe shook her head.

'There are so many. Fortenegro has many natural resources—'

'And you favour utilising them?'

'I think that we have to. But in a controlled way, of course.'

'Of course.' Max's heart had grown colder with every word Ionanthe uttered. 'Have you thought of the disruption this will cause to people's lives? The antagonism there will be?'

'Yes, but it is still my belief that it must be done.'

Something was wrong. Ionanthe could sense it. The warmth had gone from Max's voice, and although he hadn't actually said anything critical Ionanthe felt that inwardly he was hostile.

Why, when last night they had seemed so much in accord? Was it that despite his apparent enthusiasm yesterday he was now having cold feet?

It hurt to think that the closeness she had believed they shared could vanish so easily.

She wasn't going to change her mind or backtrack, though. She couldn't—no matter how much she loved him. She owed it to the children of Fortenegro to stick to her plan. Marta's comments last night had shown her that.

She lifted her chin and told Max firmly, 'And here on this estate—my estate and my land—I intend that it *shall* be done.'

'No one can dispute that you have that right.' Max's voice was clipped and sharp. He wanted to get her to reconsider, to tell her that he would give her all the money she could want if only— If only what? If only she would be the woman he wanted her to be?

Max had enough experience of the world to know that there were far more people who would do exactly as Ionanthe planned to do, were they in her shoes, than those who would not. He couldn't blame her. Not really. If he wanted to blame someone then he should blame himself, for wanting her to be different, for wanting her to be the woman he had created out of his own need for her to be that way. And he didn't want to admit that it was possible for him to love a woman who did not share his outlook on life or his fierce attachment to working for the benefit of others.

Ionanthe hadn't deceived him. He had deceived himself.

Sitting alone in the castle library, Ionanthe closed her eyes to control the sting of unwanted tears. She hadn't wanted to come back to Fortenegro, after all, or to fall in love with Max. But now that she was here she had a duty to her people. They were the ones who really deserved the fortune her grandfather had left to her. Blood money, in her view, tainted with the blood, sweat and tears of those who had worked all their lives to earn it for her family without getting anything in return.

Last night, discussing her plans with Max, she had felt buoyed up with hope and the joy of sharing her dreams with him. She had felt as though everything she longed to do was possible and achievable, because she had thought he felt the same. But now, this morning, with that joy stripped from her, she felt as though she had a mammoth task in front of her and she wondered if she would ever achieve it.

If the reality was that Max was opposed to reform, then what chance had she of seeing it happen even here on her own land? The old guard—the barons and the community elders—would oppose her every step of the way.

Had she forgotten that it was because of that that she had agreed to marry Max? She had known then that an island like Fortenegro, locked fast in ancient tradition and a paternalistic society, could only be reformed by a very strong man. Her son. The son who would have to be what his father was not.

Then she had not cared about what Max was not, but neither had she known that she would love him, and that it would hurt her more than anything else ever had or ever would to know that there was this divide between them.

Max had gone out with the men to seek out a suitable Christmas tree. Ionanthe had watched him in the courtyard from the shelter of the kitchen, as he trod through the snow wearing an old pair of her father's ski boots.

Some of the men who worked on the estate, summoned by Tomas, Marta's son, had quickly gathered around him, making awkward semi-bows and tugging on dark tufts of hair exposed to the sharp wind as they removed their caps. They had responded to him, respecting him, respecting his natural air of authority, willing to let him take charge in a way they would never have done with her.

Wasn't there a saying that the hand that rocked the cradle ruled the world? Women like Marta were the future; they and their children had to be.

How much did it cost to build a school? To provide it with teachers and equipment? To provide its pupils with further education, with university education? The Veritas Foundation was helping to build and finance educational projects every day of the week. Ionanthe longed for just a fraction of their expertise, and for the dedication and the wisdom of the mystery man who was responsible for it.

She could understand why he clung to his anonymity, but nevertheless she wished that she might meet him. To speak with such a man must be a little like sitting at the feet of a very wise guru.

Ionanthe got up from her seat and looked out of the window. It had started to snow again. The library overlooked the castle gardens, and the snow there was pristine and untouched.

Already she was missing Max. She left the library and, although she could have sworn it wasn't what she had intended, for some reason she headed for the bedroom, frowning when she saw that the window was open. Snow had blown in and was covering the laptop case Max had left on the window seat.

Automatically Ionanthe picked it up, brushing the snow off with her hand as she did so. At the same time she accidentally dislodged some papers which must have been in the case's outer pocket. As she made to push them back, Ionanthe glanced at them and then stiffened.

Very carefully she sat down and pulled the papers free of the case, her hands trembling as she read the report she was holding—a report on the mineral assets of Fortenegro.

The sick feeling within her intensified, making her shake with a mixture of mouth-drying nausea and a longing to run away like a child and hide from what she did not want to see.

But she was not a child. And no matter how hard her heart might pound, or how much despair she might feel, she had to read on.

Frantically Ionanthe flicked through it, searching for what she hoped she would not find even whilst somehow knowing that she would. After all, hadn't this been what she had dreaded ever since Philippe de la Croix had told her about the coal mining consortium's approach?

And finally there it was—a full-page map of the mountains, *her* mountains, showing quite clearly where the rich veins of mineral deposits lay beneath them. The salient facts were there in print, heavily underlined as though to remind the reader of their importance.

Was this why Max had married them both? First her

sister and then her? Because he had *known* the value of what lay beneath the harsh granite? Did he, like so many others, value that more than he valued the rights of the people who lived on that land? More than he valued her and what they might have had together?

She couldn't cry. She had gone beyond that. But inwardly she was weeping hot tears that blistered her heart and would leave it forever scarred.

She had been a fool, of course; she had known from the start—from that first sharply dangerous and sweetly alluring spark of reaction to him which she had felt at their first meeting and then denied—that her feelings would lead to this pain. Hadn't she tried to guard against her own vulnerability by giving herself a higher purpose in agreeing to marry Max than merely her own safety and that treacherous spark? Shouldn't she have stuck to the path she had chosen then, and ignored the fatal temptation to stray from it? If she had, then what she had just read would only have strengthened her resolve to help her son to be a very different man from his father. If she had, then right now she would be feeling justified and vindicated in her choice of action, not guilt-ridden and heartbroken. She had no one but herself to blame.

Oh, but she hurt so badly—quite literally sickened by the incontrovertible evidence that Max was not worthy of the love and trust of either her or, more importantly by far, his people.

Given free choice she would have fled then, as fast and as far as she could, seeking somewhere to hide herself away from her pain. But she could not do that.

She must stay and face what had to be faced for the sake of those who could not protect themselves. She must stay and stand between Max and his plans. She was the only person who could, since the land belonged to her. She must not allow him to seduce her into giving away her people's rights in the same way that he had seduced her into giving him her love.

The door opened and Max came in.

'I think we've found you your tree, but you'd better come and inspect it before we bring it in,' he began, only to stop when he saw the report Ionanthe was holding.

'You've been through my papers?' he accused her.

'No.' Ionanthe denied his accusation fiercely, shaking her head. 'Someone left the window open and there was snow on your laptop case. I merely intended to move it out of harm's way. The papers fell out.' When she saw the cynical look he was giving her she cried out, 'It's the truth. Not that I have any need to justify myself to you now that I've seen what you plan to do.'

'What *I* plan to do?'

'You can't deny it. I've seen the evidence with my own eyes. When Philippe de la Croix told me he'd heard rumours that you were going to foreign conglomerates about a coal mining contract I wanted to believe that he was wrong, that unlike Cosmo you *don't* see the island simply as a means of filling your own bank account. No wonder you were so keen to marry both of us. You *knew* about the mineral ore and you wanted to make sure that you had a legal right to it. That's why you took me to bed and seduced me, making me believe that there could be something more between us than merely a cold dynastic marriage. And I dare say that's why you went out with the men this morning as well. What were you really doing? Trying to take rock samples? Well, you were wasting your time. I would only ever allow this land to be mined if it was the wish of those who live on it, for *their* benefit, to provide them and their children with all those things that the rule of your family has denied them. No, don't come near me,' she told him when Max closed the door and started to walk towards her. 'I don't want you anywhere near me.'

'Have you finished?' Max's voice was even, but there was a white line of anger round his mouth.

'Finished? I've finished thinking that I can trust you to do the best for the people of Fortenegro, and I've certainly finished feeling that I can respect you, if that's what you mean.'

'For your information I did not commission that report, as you have accused me, because I want to benefit personally from the island's resources. Far from it.'

'I don't believe you,' Ionanthe told him flatly.

'That is your choice. But think about this. I too heard about plans to sell off the island's mineral assets to benefit the few who owned them.'

'So you thought you'd get in on the act?' Ionanthe interrupted him contemptuously.

'No such thing. In fact the very accusations you are laying against me are exactly those that I should lay against you. *You* are the one who will stand to benefit if the minerals lying beneath your land are to be mined.'

Ionanthe was too shocked to conceal what she felt,

and her response betrayed her emotions. 'You thought that of me?'

'Why not? Both your grandfather and your sister proved themselves to be duplicitous, intent on putting their own interests first. Why should you be any different?'

Max knew that he was goading her, but he had to be sure she was saying what he thought she was saying.

'But I am not like them. You said yourself that you knew that I was different.'

Ionanthe's reaction was everything he'd hoped for. Even if she had originally thought about selling her mineral rights she would change her mind, see things differently, come to understand and share his views, share all those things he wanted to do for the island and those who lived there. She *must* care about them. She had already shown that in the way she had spoken about the need for more schools. But he must be sure. He must hear her say categorically that she had no ulterior motive for marrying him.

'You could have been deliberately deceiving me—deliberately creating a fake persona for yourself to conceal your real intentions. When there are millions at stake, then people…'

'You really think I would take that money for myself when the people need it so much, to pay for education and health care and a better infrastructure?' Tears burned her eyes.

'You had no real reason to come back to Fortenegro,' Max pointed out. 'You must have known that by doing so the feudal law of atonement would be invoked against you.'

'I knew it existed, yes, but it never occurred to me that a modern man of the twenty-first century would be governed by it. Were you the ruler you should be, you would have such antiquated laws repealed.'

Her unexpected attack on him hit a raw nerve. He would already have repealed those laws had he felt that the people would accept such changes. He still intended to repeal them—once he had won their trust.

'Such an act would merely have been empty words,' he felt obliged to tell her. 'It takes the will of the people to make a law work, and as you must know there any many people here on Fortenegro who, either through fear or ignorance or pride, or a mixture of all those things, are not willing to relinquish the control and power they believe such demanding laws give them. Do not deny it. That mindset is operating here within this castle and its lands every time a father refuses to allow his child an education. You have as good as said so yourself.'

'They do that because they have no choice.' Ionanthe immediately defended her people. 'Because they cannot afford to take their children off the land. Because the law allows landowners to demand a set number of days of work per year from their tenants.'

When Max didn't respond she shook her head in angry despair.

'Oh, it is hopeless trying to make you understand.' Tears of frustration gathered in her eyes. 'The other night when we were discussing education you let me think that you shared my views and my hopes for the people,' she accused him. 'But you were just deceiving me. Why would you do that if not to lull me into a false sense of security? To make me think that we shared a similar purpose?'

'I could just as easily use that argument against *you*,' Max told her curtly.

He shouldn't be doing this, Max knew. As Fortenegro's ruler, he knew he had a duty of care to his people which involved questioning her motives and acting on his suspicions. But he wasn't just Fortenegro's ruler. He was also a man. And as that man who had held her in his arms, who had known whilst holding her there that he never wanted to let her go, surely he had a duty to that feeling?

There was only one thing he could do now—one question he had to ask. The whole of his future personal happiness was balanced on the answer.

Ionanthe possessed strength of will, she possessed courage, and she was passionate about what she believed in. He could think of no one better to share both his personal and his public life. But he also had to know that he could trust her with Fortenegro's future; he had to know that she would put what was best for the island above her own personal gain. He could not and would not blame her for wanting to realise the wealth beneath the surface of her land for herself. From what he had learned, it was her grandfather who was to blame. He had taught his granddaughters to value wealth and pride, and to follow his example of always putting himself first.

'If you are not lying about the mineral deposits, then tell me that you had no ulterior motive whatsoever in agreeing to marry me other than the need to protect your own safety.'

Ionanthe looked at him, her expression anguished. She desperately wanted to win his trust, but lying was an anathema to her. She hesitated, and then admitted, 'I did have an ulterior motive, yes. But—'

Max didn't want to hear any more. He had been a fool to hope that he might be wrong. He turned back towards the door, but Ionanthe moved faster.

'You will listen to me,' she told him. 'Because for the sake of my people I cannot allow you to think what you are thinking. I did have an ulterior motive, yes, but it was *not* the one of which you are trying to accuse me. This island has a long history of rulers who have abused their position, and its people have suffered as a result. As you have said yourself, they are set in their ways and bound by ancient customs and laws which imprison them in a feudal system that denies their children so very much. I grew up witnessing that. I saw my parents' attempts to change things, and I saw the power of those who opposed those changes—including my own grandfather. I saw greed and pride and a lack of compassion. And I saw too that what this island needed more than anything else was a ruler strong enough and courageous enough to lead his people to freedom.

'When I heard that Fortenegro had a new ruler in you, I hoped so much that you would be that man—but then you married my sister, a woman I knew to be rapacious and selfish. Had you married her because you shared her belief that the island existed merely to fund her expensive lifestyle? I wondered. Or did you love her without sharing her views? I knew she did not love you. She wrote to me and said so. But then Eloise loved only herself, and the blame for that lay with our grandfather. I watched to see what changes you might make to benefit the people of Fortenegro, but I could find none. So I compared you with the man I admire more than any other man who walks this earth and I found you wanting.'

Max was shocked by the violent surge of savage male jealousy that gripped him to hear Ionanthe speaking of admiring another man.

In a manner that was completely out of character for him, he demanded contemptuously, 'And who *is* this paragon you so admire? Some Brussels eurocrat who makes laws he himself will never have to obey and plays God with other people's lives?'

Ionanthe's breath hissed out in furious denial.

'No. He is not. He is a man who works selflessly for the benefit of others. Through the auspices of the foundation which he heads he has heard and answered the cries of the poor and the sick. He has viewed them with compassion and understood their need. He has provided money for wells for clean water, for schools to educate, for hospitals to heal, for crops to grow and for peace, so that all those who use what he has given them can flourish.'

The passion in her voice showed how she felt, and Max had to look away from her. What she had just told him changed everything—but he could not tell her that.

Ionanthe's throat hurt, and her eyes ached with the tears she was not going to let Max see.

'Once it was my dream and my hope that I might work for the Veritas Foundation and learn from such a master. That was not to be, but there is *something* I can do for the people of Fortenegro, even if it is merely a small shadow of what he has done. Just as he educates the children of today so that they can grow to be to the leaders of tomorrow, I thought that as your wife *I* could provide Fortenegro with the ruler it so desperately needs.'

'You planned to convert me to follow the teaching of this…this man you admire so much?' he suggested.

Ionanthe shook her head.

'No. I hoped to conceive and raise a son who would be all the things that he will need to be to help this island. *That* was my hidden agenda in marrying you. No scheming to sell off the minerals that lie beneath the mountains,' Ionanthe told him on a slightly shaky breath.

She had wanted those last words to sound proud and scornful, but she was miserably aware that in reality they sounded closer to tearful and upset.

Battling through the complex mass of emotions Ionanthe's speech had aroused in him, for the first time in his life Max simply did not know what to say or do to make things right. He knew what he wanted to say; he knew what he wanted to do. But he also knew that the very last thing Ionanthe would want to hear from him right now was that her hero—the man she admired more than any other, the man she had placed on a pedestal and at whose feet she had openly and proudly confessed she yearned to sit and learn—was no other than himself.

Giving her that news now would hurt her dreadfully. Fiercely Max blinked away the telltale moisture that would have betrayed how much the thought of her pain hurt him.

It wasn't that he had deliberately set out to deceive her. No, it was simply that it had never occurred to him that it might be necessary for him to tell her about the foundation and his role in it.

He breathed in, and then exhaled.

'So you agreed to marry me hoping that I would give you a child—a son who, with your guidance, would in time become the ruler you believe the island needs?'

He sounded remarkably accepting of her plan, Ionanthe acknowledged, but instead of reassuring her that only served to increase her hostility and pain.

'Yes,' she confirmed.

'And those times when you lay in my arms, when my body possessed yours, for you it was only because you wanted me to give you my child?'

Ionanthe's heart bumped treacherously into her ribs. She looked at Max, and then wished she hadn't.

'Yes…of course.' Something about the way in which Max was looking back at her drove her into adding recklessly, 'What other reason could there be?'

Max's silence made her nerve-endings prickle with tension.

Please God, don't let him tell her mercilessly and truthfully that he *knew* from the minute he had touched her she had had no thoughts in her head for anyone or anything but him and the need he aroused in her.

'And now—if I have? If you *are* carrying my child?'

The question slipped under her guard and made her eyes widen and her heart thud.

'It's…it's too soon to know,' she protested.

'That was not what I asked you,' Max pointed out. 'You have told me of your plans for my son's adult future, but what of his childhood? You have said nothing of that.'

Ionanthe frowned.

'What I want to know is how will he grow up?'

'What do you mean?'

'You and I both lost our parents before we were fully adult. You were pushed into the shadows by a grandfather who lavished all his attention on your sister. You must know as I do how much every child yearns for the security of being loved?'

'Yes, of course I do. I shall love my son.'

'But you do not love me, and he will sense that and be confused and hurt by it. Children always are when their loyalties are claimed by two parents who are opposed to one another.'

Both Max's voice and his expression were grave and heavy.

He genuinely cared about the emotional welfare of a child who might never exist, Ionanthe realised, with a small ache of surprise and sadness.

'You've been so long I've had to come and find you, and it's a long walk from my kitchen.'

Ariadne's arrival as she puffed towards them brought an immediate end to their conversation.

'The men are still waiting for you to come and look at the tree,' she told Ionanthe in a chivvying voice.

'I'll come and look now,' Ionanthe said.

'Christmas trees! A whole lot of fuss and bother, if you ask me,' Ariadne complained.

CHAPTER THIRTEEN

THE Christmas tree was a perfect fit, with the star which Max had placed on its topmost branch just touching the ceiling of the great hall. Its branches were now decorated with the homemade garlands and painted cones that she and the children had been busy making for the last two days, along with the familiar decorations Ionanthe remembered from her own childhood.

She touched one of the fragile glass baubles with a tender finger. It was from the set that her parents had bought one year when they had taken them to a German Christmas market. The bauble might be slightly tarnished, but Ionanthe saw it with the eyes of love and it was still beautiful. Just looking at it reminded her of the smell of warm gingerbread and the wonderful warmth of her father's large hand holding her own.

So many happy memories of a childhood in which she had felt loved and safe until her parents' deaths. Her mother and father had adored one another. Even as a young child she had somehow sensed that and been warmed by it. Ionanthe frowned. She was *not* going to allow Max's comments underlining the fact that he did not love her and that any child they had would suffer because of it to affect her.

They were still sharing the same bedroom and the same bed, but for the last two nights, since the confrontation between them in the library, they had slept in it as though they were miles apart. Max hadn't made one single move to approach her, or to apologise for what he had said. She certainly wasn't going to be the one to approach *him*. After all, she had done nothing wrong.

Except plan to bring up his son and heir to ultimately act against him and everything she thought he stood for.

It wasn't easy trying to pretend that nothing was wrong, but for the sake of the children so excitedly waiting for Christmas, and for the sake of their parents and grandparents who had made it plain how thrilled and honoured they felt to have them both here, Ionanthe felt that she had to make an effort. It was hard when she was having to strive desperately to pretend that she felt nothing for Max other than anger and contempt when the truth was—

Blindly she stepped backwards, gasping in shock as she bumped into the heavy wooden step ladders she had forgotten were there, striking her funny bone against one of the steps. A wave of nauseating dizziness from the sharply acute pain surged over her, causing her to sway slightly.

Max, who had been talking to Tomas, saw Ionanthe bump into the ladders and then clutch at her elbow, her face losing its colour as she swayed giddily. Immediately he hurried to her side, taking hold of her hand and demanding, 'Are you all right?'

'Of course I'm all right,' Ionanthe lied, trying to pull free.

The truth was that she felt terribly weak and sick, and would have given anything to rest her head on Max's shoulder and feel his arms close round her.

'All I did was catch my elbow,' she continued, when he refused to let her go.

A surge of love for her so strong that it felt as though it was drawn from the deepest core of him rolled over Max. Initially, in the aftermath of their quarrel, he had handled things badly, Max admitted to himself. He had spent most of the previous night lying awake, longing to turn back the clock. And not just because of the suspicions they'd had, the misjudgements they had both made about one another which had led to their quarrel.

Ionanthe's impassioned outburst about the Veritas Foundation and the man who controlled it, her obvious partisanship and admiration for both the organisation and the man behind it had, even if she herself could not know it, put him in a completely untenable position. He could not in all good conscience continue to withhold the truth from her—but how was he to tell her?

She was very angry with him, and her pride was hurt by his misjudgement of her. He knew that and he understood why. But that meant that this was not a good time to tell her that the man she so admired and had put on a pedestal, scornfully telling her husband of her hero's moral and charitable achievements, and how far short of him he fell, was actually the same man—him. She would be justifiably angry and—far more important to him—she would also be hurt.

On the other hand, if he didn't tell her, now that he knew how she felt, wasn't he going to be guilty of an even less excusable offence? One which in the long term would cause even more damage to their relationship because it would inflict a wound that would fester? They needed to be able to *trust* one another if the love Max was sure they felt for one another was going to be able to grow and flourish.

His only excuse for his omissions and failures was that he had never loved before, and that therefore everything he was learning was new. No matter how careful he was, no matter how much he wanted her happiness before anything else, he was fallible and liable to make mistakes.

Right now what they needed more than anything else was the two things they did not have: privacy and time. He looked round the hall; the ebb and flow of everyday life was going on around them but at that moment they were in some sense isolated from it in this shadowy corner of the great hall. The time was far from perfect, but Max admitted to himself that he couldn't trust himself to endure another night of the torture of sharing a bed with her—knowing that she was so close and yet at the same time so very far away from him, without reaching for her. He might not know much about love, but he did know that breaking down Ionanthe's barriers so that they could share the intimacy of sex without telling her that *he* was Veritas would be unforgivable.

He had to tell her now. He couldn't endure another day of cool silence, during which he was deprived of those small, sometimes silent exchanges of mutual awareness to which he had become accustomed without knowing it until the intimacy was denied him. He had misjudged her, and without meaning to he had also misled her.

When she made to pull away from him a second time, Max bent his head and begged in a low voice, 'Wait. There's something I have to say to you.'

Ionanthe's heart lifted. Hope swelled and rose inside her. He was going to tell her that he loved and needed her more than life itself. He was going to apologise and beg her forgiveness.

She looked over his shoulder. Although the great hall was busy with people, none of them were paying them any particular attention. The hope that he was going to say the words she most longed to hear grew inside her and took wing—only to crash to earth to die painfully when he said, 'You won't like it, I know, but it has to be said.'

The words were enough to send an icy trickle of despair down her spine. She couldn't, she *mustn't* let him see how she really felt.

'If you're going to make more accusations,' she threw back at him, rallying her pride to her defence, 'then I dare say I shan't.'

Max shook his head.

'No, I'm not going to accuse you of anything. The truth is…'

His voice died away as he struggled to find the right words. He was still holding her hand, and now he played with her fingers, stroking them and holding them, his actions such that, had he been a different kind of man, Ionanthe might have thought they betrayed uncertainty. But Max was never uncertain—about anything, she decided bitterly.

'The truth is what?' she pressed him.

'You may remember that you mentioned the Veritas Foundation to me?'

Ionanthe nodded her head, although she couldn't imagine what her praise of Veritas had to do with Max telling her something she wasn't going to like hearing.

'You said how much you admired the…the man who runs it?'

'Yes, I did,' Ionanthe agreed, her eyes darkening with anger. 'You want me to retract what I said because if offends your pride? Is that it?' she guessed.

'No.' Max's voice was terse. His fingers interlaced with her own. 'The truth is—'

'Yes?'

'I should have told you this before, but at the time I didn't think there was any need. It never occurred to me that you'd even *heard* of Veritas, never mind…' He said the words. 'The Veritas Foundation was originally set up by my father. I inherited it from him.'

'No…' Ionanthe protested, but somehow she knew that Max was telling her the truth.

'I'm sorry. I never imagined… If I'd known…'

This was so humiliating, so shaming. Hot blood forced its way up under her skin, but she couldn't afford to give way to the chagrin she was feeling. She had made a fool of herself, but Max surely had made even more of a fool of her. Her pride stung, as though it had received a thousand savage cuts.

'You never imagined *what*?' she demanded angrily. 'You never imagined that I might be someone who admired everything I believed Veritas and the man in charge of it stood for?'

Red flags of angry pride might be burning in Ionanthe's face, but because he loved her Max knew that what she was really feeling was pain—the same pain he himself would have felt had their situation been reversed. More than anything he longed to hold her and to take that pain from her.

'I'm sorry.'

'For what? Misjudging me? Destroying my illusions? Believing that I wasn't good enough to know the truth? That I wasn't worthy of sharing your ideals?'

'Ionanthe, don't—please…'

He'd hurt her, and she was justifiably angry. Max understood that, but there was something he still had to tell her. 'I was a fool for not realising that you—'

'No, *I* am the one who was the fool. But not any more, Max,' Ionanthe cut across him bitterly.

Before she could continue Tomas was approaching them, looking self-conscious and uncertain as he addressed himself to Max.

'Highness, the people are asking if you will lead them in the sled race tomorrow, Christmas Eve morning.'

'What sled race is this?' Max asked, looking at Ionanthe. But she shook her head, leaving Tomas to explain whilst her heart sank like a lead weight inside her chest. Her father had led the traditional sled race, and now she wanted to protest in bitter anger that Max should be asked to stand in her father's place.

'It is a tradition of the estate that on the day before Christmas there is a sled race from the top of the ridge behind the castle, and that the race is begun by our lord,' Tomas was explaining eagerly to Max. 'For many years we have not had anyone here to do it, and the old ones are saying that it will bring us luck to have our Prince commence the race for us.'

The people—her people—were showing their approval of Max and their willingness to accept him. Ionanthe felt very alone. Alone and unloved, deceived and misjudged.

Max *had* misjudged her and hurt her, but she had also misjudged him, honesty compelled her to admit. Yes, that was true—but at least he had always known who she was. She hadn't hidden her true self away from him. She hadn't let him talk about his dreams knowing that in comparison to her achievements they were as a child's drawing compared to the work of a master. That was what hurt so badly: knowing that he had excluded her from such an important part of his life; knowing that he had already done all those things she longed so much to do.

Now she could admit to herself what she hadn't really known before. That it was important to her that they met and recognised one another as equals. In her grandfather's eyes she had always been a poor substitute for Eloise. Knowing that, growing up with it, had diminished her. She couldn't allow herself to love a man whose very existence and achievements could not help but do the same.

Their marriage would have to be brought to an end. There was no purpose to it now, after all. Max was the perfect man to rule Fortenegro and to give its people all that they needed. He was also the best role model there could be for his son. Max—the Max she now knew him to be—could achieve far more than she had ever envisaged being able to achieve. There was no purpose in her staying—no need, no role for her, nothing. Ionanthe prayed that fate had been wiser than she had herself, and that she had not yet conceived Max's child.

Max looked towards Ionanthe for guidance as to how he should answer Tomas's request, but her expression was remote and cold. Tomas's interruption had come at the wrong time.

'I shall be pleased to begin the race,' he told Tomas, when Ionanthe continued to ignore his silent request for advice.

The beaming smile with which Tomas received his reply told Max that at least one person was pleased with his response.

She would have to wait until they returned to the palace—until she was sure that she was not carrying Max's child—to inform Max that she wanted their marriage brought to an end, Ionanthe decided. Or maybe she should just leave the island and then tell him. Although of course that would be cowardly. And what if she had conceived? The frantic despairing leap of her heart told her how easy it would be for her to clutch at the excuse to remain married to him.

How Max must have inwardly laughed at her when she had confided to him her admiration for the head of Veritas, unknowingly extolling his virtues, for all the world like some naive teenager filled with hero-worship. All she had to hold on to now was her pride. But she had survived before without love, without anyone to turn to.

That had been different, though. Then she had had hope. Now there was nothing left for her to hope for other than that she did not make even more of a fool of herself than she already had.

Max had married her because his very nature impelled him to want to improve the lot of the islanders. Every move he had made *had* to have been part of a carefully orchestrated plan designed to eliminate what stood in the way of his progress and to move forward with his plans. She couldn't argue with or object to his underlying motivation—after all, she had married him with her own agenda. She couldn't either logically or clinically refuse to understand why he'd had to be so suspicious of her. But pretending to want her—and he *had* done that, even if he had not said the words—allowing her to believe that they shared a mutual desire for one another, that was unforgivable.

And she never would forgive herself for believing even momentarily that he *did* want her. Hadn't she known all along that he had been married to Eloise? Hadn't she known that there were questions she should ask, doubts she should have? But she had wilfully ignored the inner voice that had been trying to protect her.

Whenever she had asked Max about Eloise he had answered that his marriage to her sister had been 'different.'

But it hadn't. He had married them both for exactly the same reason. He had married them because he believed that marriage within their family would help him to gain the acceptance of the islanders and protect their mineral rights. As a person she meant nothing to him. She was simply a means to an end.

CHAPTER FOURTEEN

'SO YOU are not going to watch the sled race, then?' Ariadne kneaded the dough on which she was working with a fierce pummelling motion that matched the ferocity of her expression.

'No,' Ionanthe confirmed.

'Hah—I always said that you had your grandfather's stubborn pride, and look what that got him! So you and the Prince have had a few sharp words? That's no reason for you to be sitting here in my kitchen sulking.'

'I know you mean well, Ariadne, but you don't understand.'

Ariadne gave a cross snort.

'I understand well enough that our good Prince deserves better than a sulking wife—especially when anyone can see how much he thinks of you.'

Ionanthe shook her head grimly. 'He married me because of who I am, Ariadne…'

'Well, I dare say he did. A man would be a fool not to look about him for a wife who can bring some benefit to a marriage. But you can't tell me that those soft looks he keeps giving you when he doesn't think anyone else is looking don't mean anything, because they do. Look at the way he went out and got you that Christmas tree. It's as plain as plain can be how much he wants to please you, and a man doesn't do that for no reason. I'll tell you now that your father would have had something to say if your mother had behaved like you're doing—showing him up in front of everyone instead of supporting him. I thought our Prince had chosen himself a good wife in you, but now I'm beginning to think I was wrong. You aren't just his wife, and he isn't just your husband. He's our Prince and you are our Princess. That means a lot to folk like us—even if it doesn't to you.'

Ionanthe flinched under the lash of Ariadne's outspoken criticism. The old lady saw things in black and white, but that didn't mean there wasn't an element of truth in what she was saying.

'Quarrel all you want with him in the privacy of your bedroom,' Ariadne continued bluntly. 'There you and him can be just like everyone else. But don't you go forgetting that he's our Prince and you're his wife. The people have expectations of you.'

Ionanthe gave in. 'What is it you're trying to say, Ariadne?'

'I'm saying that your place isn't here in this kitchen, sulking like a child—those days are gone. You should be up on that mountainside, showing yourself as our Princess. It's what the people expect, even if His Highness himself doesn't.'

Ariadne had a point. Her people wouldn't understand why she wasn't there. Her absence would hurt them, and she had neither the wish nor the right to do that.

She looked at her watch, and as though Ariadne had read her mind the cook told her, 'You've still got time. Tomas won't start the race without you being there.'

Ionanthe gave her a grim look, recognising that she had been manipulated and outmanoeuvred.

It was crisp and fresh on the snowy ridge above the steep slope down which the home-made sleds would race. In his teens Max had been a keen winter sportsman, so he was no stranger to the cold and the snow. No stranger to that, but a stranger here nonetheless. An outsider, a man obliged to stand alone, without the woman he loved. Instinctively he looked towards the castle. Only he knew how alone he felt, and how painful that feeling was. How much he wished things were different and he could be free to give all his time and energy to showing Ionanthe how much he loved her.

Ionanthe spotted Max immediately, in a group of men clustered together at the starting point.

'It was lucky I had your father's ski suit stored away,' Ariadne had told Ionanthe earlier. 'The Prince is taller than your father, though.'

Her father's old black racing suit now outlined the breadth of Max's shoulders. Ionanthe knew that there hadn't been a single heart's breath of a second when she had looked at the men from a distance and not known exactly which one he was long before she'd recognised the suit.

She started to walk faster as she climbed the last few yards of the incline.

Those planning to take part in the race had already claimed their sleds from the waiting pile, and the children were watching excitedly as their fathers and elder brothers prepared themselves. The race should have started already, and the children were getting impatient.

One father was smiling at the baby held tight in its mother's arms. An unfamiliar feeling tugged at Ionanthe's heart. The father looked so proud, the mother so lovingly indulgent. It was a matter of great pride and respect to these people that the head of the family showed his bravery and skill on an occasion like this one.

Something made her lift her head and look again to where Max was standing. When she saw he was looking back at her, that he must have been watching her, her heart rolled over inside her chest as fiercely as though it was about to start an avalanche.

She loved him so much.

Her breath made small puffs of white vapour on the cold air as she climbed.

She had almost reached him when a sudden anxious cry went up, and a small boy—no more than five or six years old, Ionanthe guessed, who must have been sitting on his father's sled—suddenly somehow dislodged the sled, which began to rush down the mountainside with him clinging to it.

The course was fast and dangerous, and for that reason the race was forbidden to children. A wave of horror gripped them all for a split second, and then, before anyone else could react, Max dropped down onto his sled and kicked off in pursuit of the little boy.

Ionanthe had watched the race many times, and always admired the skill of the contestants, but never with her heart in her mouth like this, or her partisanship for one man's skill so strong.

Max steered the sled more skilfully than she had ever seen anyone do, Ionanthe acknowledged as she joined in the concerted gasp the onlookers gave as he raced downhill in pursuit of the child. The boy was clinging precariously to his own sled, heading right for the darkly dangerous outcrop of rocks that lay outside the formal lines of the run.

Max would never catch the boy in time, and he too would end up crashing into the rocks. Ionanthe felt sick with dread for them both. What woman watching the man she loved risk his life in such a fashion would not feel as she did now? Her heart leapt into her throat as somehow Max expertly spun his sled sideways across the snow.

He was going to try to cut off the other sled—put himself between it and the rocks. He would never be able to do it—and if he did then the extra weight of the little boy would take Max crashing right into them, the child's life spared at the cost of his own.

'No!' Her denial was torn from her lungs on an agonised cry, and then, just when she feared the worst, somehow Max managed to intercept the other sled and turn it so that it was running alongside his own.

The rocks were so dreadfully close, and getting closer. Max was reaching for the little boy, pulling him off his sled and into his arms, then rolling off his own sled so that he became a human snowball.

Other men were racing down the hill towards them. Ionanthe wanted not to have to watch, not to have to see Max's beautiful body lying still and unmoving in the snow. But she couldn't *not* look—just as she couldn't stop herself from following the men's headlong flight down the steep slope, falling herself a couple of times, only to pick herself up and then wade knee-deep through the snow in her desperation to get to Max.

Incredibly, when she did get there, when she flung herself down in the snow next to his inert body, Ionanthe realised that she was in fact the first to reach him.

Whilst her tears fell unheeded on his snow-frosted face and eyelashes, the small boy he was still holding wriggled out of his grip, wide-eyed and unbelievably unharmed, to be snatched up in the arms of his father who had reached them within seconds of Ionanthe.

A firm strong hand—Max's hand—grasped Ionanthe's and held it. Max's eyes opened and he smiled at her. The voices of the men gathering round them faded as Ioanthe clung to Max's hand, Max's gaze. She was only able to say tremulously, 'You're alive. I thought…' The weight of what she had thought brought fresh tears.

Max lifted his free hand, the one that wasn't holding hers, and brushed them away, telling her tenderly, 'You mustn't cry. Your teardrops will freeze.'

'I thought you were going to be killed.'

'I couldn't let that happen,' Max told her. 'Not when I hadn't told you or shown you how important you are to me—how much I love you and value you. How much I respect you, and how much I can't bear the thought of my life without you. How much hearing you praise the work of Veritas—work which is so important to me and whose importance I haven't been able to share with anyone since my parents died—blew me away with pride and delight. We haven't known each other very long, Ionanthe, but I can tell you honestly that being with you has been like finding the true heart of my life, its true purpose and its true meaning.'

'Oh, Max…'

As she leaned towards him Max cupped her face and lifted himself up so that he could kiss her.

'No—you mustn't,' Ionanthe protested. 'You could be injured. You mustn't move.'

'I won't move—if you stay with me.' His voice grew strong as he added, 'Stay with me, Ionanthe. Stay with me for the rest of our lives and help me to become worthy of the values and hopes we share.'

There was no time for her to do more than nod her head, because the village doctor had arrived, quickly pronouncing that Max had had a remarkable escape and hadn't broken anything, but that he was likely to be badly bruised.

The father and the grandfather of the child whose life Max had saved had, of course, to shake his hand and thank him, and then all the men were hoisting him up on their shoulders for a triumphant journey back to the castle. Ionanthe joined the women and children following in their footsteps.

Surely there could be no frustration as tormenting as that which kept the one you loved at your side but out of the intimate reach you both craved? Ionanthe thought ruefully, as she and Max played their roles in the great hall at the party around the Christmas tree.

They hadn't even been able to snatch a few precious minutes alone together after their return from the accident, such had been the eager demand of her people to thank Max for his bravery.

Now the youngest children were snuggling sleepily in the arms of mothers and fathers as the final carol came to an end and the last cup of spiced wine was drunk.

A sweet, sharp thrill of excitement mingled with apprehension zinged through Ionanthe when at last they were free to leave—circumspectly saying their goodnights, and even more circumspectly walking down the long stone corridor together in silence. But what if she had misunderstood Max earlier? What if he had not meant those oh-so-sweet words he had said, which had completely taken away the sting of her earlier pain?

Ionanthe's heart started to beat faster. They had reached their room. Max put his hand on the door handle and looked down at her.

'It's gone midnight. That means that I can give you my gift.'

He'd got her a Christmas present? Ionanthe felt guilty. 'I haven't got anything for you—' she began.

Max shook his head and told her softly, 'Oh, yes, you have.'

They were inside the room, private and shadowed, warmed by the fire in the hearth and even more by their love.

As Max took her in his arms, Ionanthe protested, 'You're going to be so dreadfully bruised and sore.'

'Tomorrow,' Max agreed. 'But not tonight.'

And then he was kissing her, fiercely and hungrily and demandingly, and she was kissing him back with all the sweetness of her love and all the heat of her desire. And nothing, but *nothing* mattered other than that they were together.

Still holding her, Max reached into the inside pocket of his jacket and removed an envelope, which he handed to her.

'What is it?' Ionanthe asked uncertainly. It looked bulky and formal, and for some reason the sight of it had made her heart plummet.

'It's your Christmas present,' Max told her. 'Open it and see.'

Reluctantly Ionanthe detached herself from him and opened the envelope, hesitating a little before she removed the folded sheets of papers inside it.

That it was some kind of legal document she could see immediately, but it took her several minutes and three attempts to read the first page before what exactly it contained could sink in.

> I appoint my wife, Ionanthe, to the board of the Veritas Foundation as co-CEO, with powers equal to my own within that role…

There was more—a great deal more legal jargon—but the meaning was plain enough: Max was entrusting to *her* a half share in the operation of his foundation.

'You really trust me that much?' was all Ionanthe could manage to say.

'More,' Max told her truthfully.

He had wanted to show her beyond any doubt how he felt about her in so many different ways, and he could see from her expression that she knew and understood that.

'Oh, Max. I was so hurt that you hadn't told me about Veritas. I felt… I thought I'd have to leave… I love you too much to have been able to go on as things were. But in reality I misjudged you just as much as you did me.'

'We are equally at fault,' Max comforted her, and he drew her back into his arms. 'We both judged one another because of what our experience with others has taught us.'

'You were right to listen to your instinct and to question my reasons,' Ionanthe admitted. 'I did after all have an ulterior motive for marrying you. I can't deny that.'

'An altruistic motive,' Max corrected her tenderly.

'That *is* something we share—our desire to help the people of Fortenegro,' Ionanthe murmured.

'And is it the only desire we share?' Max teased, asking softly, 'You hesitate—but haven't we come far enough to be as honest with one another in words as our hearts and our bodies have already been? Would it help if I were to go first and proclaim my love and my desire for you?'

He was caressing her body as he spoke, stroking his hands over her back, making her want to melt into him.

'I am not a desirable woman—not like Eloise.' That

pain still remained, and with it some insecurity. 'You were married to her and—'

'In name, but never in deed,' Max told her truthfully.

Ionanthe pushed back to look up at him. 'You mean you never—?'

'Never. I couldn't,' Max told her simply. 'A fact about which she taunted me on more than one occasion—although oddly her taunts never had the same effect on me that yours did.'

Ionanthe went slightly pink. 'That was because I wanted to conceive your son.'

'Yes, I know.' Max's voice was mock-stern. 'You wanted to raise a ruler who would be all the things you believed his father was not—whilst *I* very much want to raise daughters who are everything their mother already *is*. Which of us will be first to get their wish, do you suppose?'

When had they moved towards the bed Ionanthe didn't know. She was just glad that they were there, and that Max was reaching out to her with familiar much loved hands to slowly remove her clothes whilst she did the same to him, accompanied by slow, sweet kisses.

'I can think of nothing I want more than for any son I might bear to grow up to match the goodness of his father,' Ionanthe breathed against Max's skin.

'Nothing?' he teased. 'Can't I tempt you to want anything a little more immediate and personal?'

Ionanthe's smile was warm.

'Mmm…' She joined in the game. 'Do you know, I have the *strangest* longing for a fig?' Her breath caught in her throat when she saw the look Max was giving her.

'But,' she told him, holding his gaze, 'what I long for far more is *you*, my dearest love.'

There was no need for any further words. They were locked in one another's arms and the kiss they were exchanging said everything they needed to know.

Her Christmas Fantasy

PENNY JORDAN

CHAPTER ONE

LISA PAUSED HESITANTLY outside the shop, studying the very obviously designer-label and expensive outfits in the window doubtfully.

She had been given the address by a friend who had told her that the shop was one of the most exclusive 'nearly new' designer-clothes outlets in the city, where outfits could be picked up for less than a third of their original price.

Lisa was no fashion victim—normally she was quite happy with her small wardrobe of good-quality chain-store clothes—but Henry had seemed so anxious that she create a good impression on his family and their friends, and most particularly his mother, during their Christmas visit to his parents' home in the north that Lisa had felt obliged to take the hints he had been dropping and add something rather more up-market to her wardrobe. Especially since Henry had already indicated that he wanted to put their relationship on a more formal basis, with an official announcement to his family of their plans to marry.

Lisa knew that many of her friends found Henry slightly stuffy and old-fashioned, but she liked those aspects of his personality. They indicated a reliability, a dependability in him which, so far as she was concerned, outweighed his admitted tendency to fuss and find fault over minor details.

When the more outspoken of her closest friends had asked her what she saw in him she'd told them quietly that she saw a dependable husband and a good father.

'But what about romance?' they had asked her. 'What about falling desperately and passionately in love?'

Lisa had laughed, genuinely amused.

'I'm not the type of woman who falls desperately or passionately in love,' she had responded, 'and nor do I want to be!'

'But doesn't it annoy you that Henry's so chauvinistically old-fashioned?' Her friends had persisted. 'Look at the way he's fussing over you meeting his parents and family—telling you how he wants you to dress.'

'He's just anxious for me to make a good impression,' Lisa had argued back on Henry's behalf. 'He obviously values his parents' opinion and—'

'And he's still tied to his mother's apron strings,' one of her friends had scoffed. 'I know the type.' She had paused a little before adding more seriously, 'You know, don't you, that he was on the point of becoming engaged to someone else shortly before he met you and that he broke off the relationship because he wasn't sure that his family would approve of her? Apparently they're very old-fashioned and strait-laced, and Janey had been living with someone else when she'd first met Henry—'

'Yes, I do know,' Lisa had retorted firmly. 'But the reason that they broke up was not Janey's past history but that Henry realised that they didn't, simply *didn't* have enough in common.'

'And you and he do?' her friend had asked drily.

'We both want the same things out of life, yes,' Lisa had asserted defensively.

And it was, after all, true. She might not have fallen deeply in love with Henry the night they were introduced by a mutual friend, but she had certainly liked him enough to accept his invitation to dinner, and their relationship had grown steadily from that date to the point where they both felt that their future lay together.

She might not be entirely comfortable with Henry's insistence that she buy herself a new wardrobe in order to impress his wealthy parents and their circle of friends, but she could sympathise with the emotion which had led to him making such a suggestion.

Her own parents would, she knew, be slightly bemused by her choice of a husband; her mother was a gifted and acclaimed potter whose work was internationally praised, whilst her father's stylish, modern furniture designs meant that he was constantly in demand, not just as a designer but as a lecturer as well.

Both her parents were currently in Japan, and were not due to return for another two months.

It would have been a lonely Christmas for her this year if Henry had not invited her to go north with him to the Yorkshire Dales to visit his parents, Lisa acknowledged.

He had already warned her that his parents might consider her work as a PA to the owner of a small, London-based antique business rather too bohemian and arty. Had she worked in industry, been a teacher or a nurse, they would have found it more acceptable.

'In fact they'd probably prefer it if you didn't work at all,' he had told Lisa carefully when they had been discussing the subject.

'Not work? But that's—' Hastily she had bitten back the words she had been about to say, responding mildly instead, 'Most women these days expect to have a career.'

'My mother doesn't approve of married women working, especially when they have children,' Henry had told her stiffly.

Firmly suppressing her instinctive response that his mother was very obviously rather out of touch with modern life, Lisa had said placatingly instead, 'A lot of women tend to put their career on hold or work part-time when their children are young.'

She had hesitated outside the shop for long enough, she decided now, pushing open the door and walking in.

The young girl who came forward to help her explained that she was actually standing in for the owner of the shop, who had been called away unexpectedly.

The clothes on offer were unexpectedly wearable, Lisa acknowledged, and not too over-the-top as she had half dreaded. One outfit in particular caught her eye—a trouser suit in fine cream wool crêpe which comprised trousers, waistcoat and jacket.

'It's an Armani,' the salesgirl enthused as Lisa picked it off the rail. 'A real bargain… I was tempted to buy it myself,' she admitted, 'but it's only a size ten and I take a twelve. It's this season's stock—a real bargain.'

'This season's.' A small frown puckered Lisa's forehead. Who on earth these days could afford to buy a designer outfit and then get rid of it within a few months of buying it—especially something like this in such a classical design that it wasn't going to date?

'If you like it, we've got several other things in from the same per…the same source,' the girl was telling her. 'Would you like to see them?'

Lisa paused and then smiled her agreement. She was beginning to enjoy this rather more than she had expected. The feel of the cream crêpe beneath her fingertips was sensuously luxurious. She had always loved fabrics, their textures, differing weights.

An hour later, her normally immaculate long bob of silky blonde hair slightly tousled from all her trying on, she grimaced ruefully at the pile of clothes that she had put to one side as impossible to resist.

What woman, having bought such a luxuriously expensive and elegantly wearable wardrobe, could bear to part with it after so short a period of time?

If she had been given free rein to choose from new herself, she could not have chosen better, Lisa recognised as she sighingly acknowledged that the buttermilk-coloured silk, wool and cashmere coat she had just tried on was an absolute must.

She was, she admitted ten minutes later as she took a deep breath and signed her credit-card bill, buying these clothes not so much for Henry and his family as for herself.

'You've got an absolute bargain,' the salesgirl told her unnecessarily as she carefully wrapped Lisa's purchases in tissue-paper and put them into several large, glossy carrier bags.

'I think these are the nicest things we've had in in a long time. Personally I don't think I could have brought myself to part with them… That coat…' She gave a small sigh and then told Lisa half enviously, 'They fitted you perfectly as well. I envy you being so tall and slim.'

'So tall.' Lisa winced slightly. She wasn't excessively tall, being five feet nine, but she was aware that with Henry being a rather stocky five feet ten or so he preferred her not to wear high-heeled shoes, and he had on occasion made rather irritated comments to her about her height.

She was just on her way out of the shop when a car drew up outside, its owner double parking in flagrant disregard for the law.

He looked extremely irritable and ill-tempered, Lisa decided as she watched him stride towards the shop, and wondered idly who he was.

Not a prospective customer, even on behalf of a woman friend. No, he was quite definitely the type who, if he did buy clothes for a woman, would not need to exercise financial restraint by buying them second-hand.

Lisa was aware of his frown deepening as he glanced almost dismissively at her.

Well, she was equally unimpressed by him, she decided critically. Stunningly, almost overpoweringly male he might look, with that tall, broad-shouldered body and that hawkish, arrogant profile, but he was simply not her type.

She had no doubt that the more romantic of her friends would consider him ideal 'swoon over' material, with those frowning, overtly sexual, strongly drawn male features and his dominant masterful manner. But she merely thought him arrogantly over-confident. Look at the way he had dismissed her with the briefest of irritable glances, stalking past her. Even the silky gleam of his thick dark hair possessed a strong air of male sexuality.

He would be the kind of man who looked almost too hirsute with his clothes off, she decided unkindly, sternly suppressing the impish little demon of rebellion within her that immediately produced a very clear and highly erotic mental image of him thus unclad and, to her exasperation, not overly hirsute at all… In fact…

Stop it, she warned herself as she flagged down a cruising taxi and gave the driver the address of the friend who had recommended the shop to her.

She had promised her that she would call round and let her know how she had fared, but for some reason, once her purchases had been duly displayed and enviously approved, she discovered that Alison was more interested in hearing about the man she had passed in the street than discussing the likelihood of her forthcoming introduction to Henry's parents going well.

'He wasn't my type at all,' she declared firmly to Alison.

'He was far too arrogant. I don't imagine he would have the first idea of how to treat a modern woman—'

'You mean that Henry does…?' Alison asked drily, stopping Lisa in her tracks for a moment before she valiantly responded.

'Of course he does.'

'You just wait,' Alison warned her. 'The moment he gets that ring on your finger, he's going to start nagging you to conform. He'll want you to stop working, for a start. Look at the way he goes on about what a perfect mother his own mother was…how she devoted her life to his father and himself…'

'I think it's rather touching that he's so devoted to her, so loyal and loving…' Lisa defended.

'Mmm… What's he like in bed?' Alison asked her curiously.

Even though Lisa was used to her friend's forthrightness, she was a little taken aback by her question, caught too off guard to do anything other than answer honestly.

'I…I don't know… We…we haven't… We don't…'

'You don't *know*. Are you crazy? You're planning to *marry* the man and you don't know yet what he's like in bed. How long have you two known one another?'

'Almost eight months,' Lisa replied slightly stiffly.

'Mmm… Hardly the type to be overwhelmed by passion, then, is he, our Henry?'

'Henry believes in old-fashioned courtship, that couples should get to know one another as…as people. He doesn't… he doesn't care for the modern approach to casual sex…'

'Very laudable,' Alison told her sardonically.

'Look, the fact that we haven't…that we don't…that we haven't been to bed together yet isn't a problem for *me*,' Lisa told her vehemently.

'No? Then it should be,' Alison returned forthrightly. 'How

on earth can you think of marrying a man when you don't even know if the two of you are sexually compatible yet?'

'Easily,' Lisa replied promptly. 'After all, our grandparents did.'

Alison rolled her eyes and mocked, 'And you claim that you aren't romantic.'

'It takes more to build a good marriage than just sex,' Lisa told her quietly. 'I'm tired of men who take you out for dinner and then expect you to take them to bed as a thank-you… I want stability in a relationship, Alison. Someone I can rely on, depend on. Someone who respects and values me as a *person*… Yes, all right, Henry might be slightly old-fashioned and…and…'

'Sexless?' her friend came back, but Lisa shook her head and continued determinedly.

'But he's very loyal…very faithful…very trustworthy… and…'

'If that's what you're looking for you'd be better off with a dog,' Alison suggested critically, but Lisa wasn't prepared to argue the matter any further.

'I'm just not the type for excitement and passion,' she told her friend. 'I like stability. Marriage isn't just for now, Alison; it's for the future too. Look, I'd better go,' she announced, glancing at her watch. 'Henry's taking me out for dinner this evening.' As she got up and headed for the door, she added gratefully, 'Thanks for recommending that shop to me.'

'Yes, I'm really envious. You've got some lovely things and at a knock-down price. All current season's stuff too… Lucky you.'

As she made her way home to her own flat Lisa was ruefully aware of how difficult her friends found it to understand her relationship with Henry, but then they had not had her upbringing and did not possess her desire—her craving in a sense—for emotional tranquillity, for roots and permanence.

Her parents were both by nature not just extremely artistic—and because of that at times wholly absorbed by their work—they were also gypsies, nomads, who enjoyed travelling and moving on. The thought of basing themselves somewhere permanently was anathema to them.

During her childhood Lisa couldn't remember having spent a whole year at any one school; she knew her parents loved her, and she certainly loved them dearly, but she had a different nature from theirs.

All right, so she knew that it would be difficult persuading Henry to accept that there was no reason why she should not still pursue her career as well as being a mother, but she was sure that she would be able to make him understand that her work was important to her. At the moment Henry worked for a prestigious firm of insurance brokers, but they had both agreed that once they were married they would move out of London and into the country.

She let herself into her small flat and carefully carried her new purchases into her bedroom.

After she had had a shower she intended to try them all on again, if she had time before Henry arrived. However, when she replayed her answering-machine tape there was a message on it from Henry, cancelling their date because he had an important business dinner that he had to attend and reminding her that they still had to shop for suitable Christmas presents to take for his family.

She had already made several suggestions based on what Henry had told her about his family, and specifically his parents—a very pretty petit point antique footstool for his grandmother, some elegant tulip vases for his mother, who, he had told her, was a keen gardener. But Henry had pursed his lips and dismissed her ideas.

She had been tempted to suggest that it might be better if he chose their Christmas presents on his own, but she had warned herself that she was being unfair and even slightly petty. He, after all, knew their tastes far better than she did.

She had just put on her favourite of all the outfits she had bought—the cream wool crêpe trouser suit—when her doorbell rang.

Assuming that it must be Henry after all, she went automatically to open the door, and then stood staring in total shock as she realised that her visitor wasn't Henry but the man she had last seen striding past her and storming into the dress agency as she'd left it.

'Lisa Phillips?' he demanded curtly as he stepped past her and into her hall.

Dumbly Lisa nodded her head, too taken aback by the unexpectedness of his arrival to think to question his right to walk uninvited into her home.

'My name's Oliver Davenport,' he told her curtly, handing her a card, barely giving her time to glance at it before he continued, 'I believe you purchased several items of clothing from Second Time Around earlier today.'

'Er…yes,' Lisa agreed. 'But—'

'Good. This shouldn't take long then. Unfortunately the clothes that you bought should not have been put on sale. Technically, in fact, the shop sold them without the permission of their true owner, and in such circumstances, as with the innocent purchase of a stolen car or indeed any stolen goods, you have no legal right to—'

'Just a minute,' she interrupted him in disbelief. Completely taken aback by his unexpected arrival and his infuriatingly arrogant manner, Lisa could feel herself becoming thoroughly angry. 'Are you accusing the shop of selling stolen clothes? Because if so it should be the police you are informing and not me.'

'Not exactly. Look, I'm prepared to refund you the full amount of what you spent plus an extra hundred pounds for any inconvenience. So if you'll just—'

'That's very generous of you,' Lisa told him sarcastically. 'But I bought these clothes for a specific purpose and I have no intention of selling them back to you. I bought them in good faith and—'

'Look, I've just explained to you, those clothes should never have been sold in the first place,' he cut across her harshly, giving her an impatiently angry look.

Lisa didn't like the way he was filling her small hall, looming almost menacingly over her, but there was no way she was going to give in to him. Why should she?

'If that's true, then why hasn't the shop been in touch with me?' Lisa challenged him.

She could see that he didn't like her question from the way his mouth tightened and hardened before he replied bitingly, 'Probably because the idiotic woman who runs the place refuses to listen to reason.'

'Really?' Lisa asked him scathingly. 'You seem to have a way with women. Has it ever occurred to you that a little less aggression and a good deal more persuasion might produce better results? Not that any amount of persuasion will change my mind,' she added firmly. 'I bought those clothes in good faith, and since the shop hasn't seen fit to get in touch with me concerning their supposedly wrongful sale I don't see why—'

'Oh, for God's sake.' She was interrupted furiously. 'Look, if you must know, the clothes belong to my cousin's girlfriend. They had a quarrel—it's a very volatile relationship. She walked out on him, vowing never to come back—they'd had an argument about her decision to go on holiday with a girlfriend, without him apparently—and in a fit of retaliatory anger he gave her clothes to the dress agency. It was an impulse…something he regretted virtually as soon as he'd done it, and when Emma rang him from Italy to make things up he asked me to help him get her things back before she comes home and discovers what he's done.'

'He asked *you* for help?'

There was very little doubt in Lisa's mind about whose girlfriend the absent Emma actually was, and it wasn't Oliver Davenport's fictitious cousin.

The look he gave her in response to her question wasn't very friendly, Lisa recognised; in fact it wasn't very friendly at all, but even though, concealed beneath the sensual elegance of her newly acquired trousers, her knees were knocking slightly, she refused to give in to her natural apprehension.

It wasn't like her to be so stubborn or so unsympathetic, but something about him just seemed to rub her up the wrong way and make her uncharacteristically antagonistic towards him.

It wasn't just the fact that he was demanding that she part with her newly acquired wardrobe that was making her combative, she admitted; it was something about the man himself, something about his arrogance, his…his maleness that was setting her nerves slightly on edge, challenging her into a mode of behaviour that was really quite foreign to her.

She knew that Henry would have been shocked to see her displaying so much stubbornness and anger—she was a little bit shocked herself.

'He was about to go away on business. Emma's due back at the end of the week. He didn't want her walking into the flat and discovering that half her clothes are missing…'

'No, I'm sure you…he…' Lisa corrected herself tauntingly '…doesn't…'

She saw from the dark burn of angry colour etching his cheekbones that he wasn't pleased by her deliberate 'mistake', nor the tone of voice she had delivered it in.

'You have no legal claim over those clothes,' he told her grimly. 'The shop sold them without the owner's permission.'

'If that's true, then it's up to the shop to get in touch with me,' Lisa pointed out. 'After all, for all I know, you could want them for yourself…' She paused. His temper was set on a hair-trigger already and although she doubted that he would actually physically harm her…

'Don't be ridiculous,' she heard him breathe softly, as though he had read her mind.

Inexplicably she realised that she was blushing slightly as, for no logical reason at all, she remembered exactly what she had been thinking about him—and his body—earlier in the day. Just as well he hadn't second guessed her private thoughts *then*!

'So you're not prepared to be reasonable about this?'

She be reasonable? Lisa could feel her own temper starting to rise.

'Doesn't it mean anything to you that you could be putting someone's whole relationship at risk by your refusal?'

'*Me* putting a relationship at risk?' Lisa gasped at the unfairness of it. 'If you ask me, I'm not the one who's doing that. If your relationship is so important to you, you should have thought of that before you lost your temper and decided to punish your girlfriend by selling her clothes—'

'Emma is not *my* girlfriend,' he told her with ominous calm. 'As I've already explained to you, I am simply acting as an intermediary in all of this for my cousin. But then I suppose it's par for the course that you should think otherwise. It goes with all the rest of your illogical behaviour,' he told her scathingly.

'If you ask me,' she told him, thoroughly incensed now, 'I think that Emma…whoever's girlfriend she is—yours or your cousin's…is better off without you. What kind of man does something like that…? Those clothes were virtually new and—'

'Exactly. New and expensive and paid for by my cousin, who is a rather jealous young man who objects to his girlfriend wearing the clothes he bought her to attract the attentions of other men…'

'And because of that he stole them from her wardrobe and sold them? It sounds to me as though she's better off without you…without him,' Lisa corrected herself fiercely, her eyes showing her contempt of a man—any man—jealous or otherwise, who could behave in such a petty and revengeful way.

'Well, I'm sorry,' she continued, patently anything but. 'But explaining to Emma just exactly what's happened to her clothes is your problem and not mine. I bought them in good faith—'

'And you'll be able to buy some more with the money I'm willing to refund you for them, especially since… Oh, I get it,' he said softly, his eyes suddenly narrowing.

'You get what?' Lisa demanded suspiciously, not liking the cynicism she could see in his eyes. 'Those clothes were virtually brand-new, this season's stock, and I'd be very lucky indeed to pick up anything else like them at such a bargain price, especially at this time of year, and—'

'Oh, yes, I can see what you're after. All right then, I don't like blackmailers and I wouldn't normally give in to someone who plainly thinks she's onto a good thing, but I haven't got time to waste negotiating with you. What would you guess was the full, brand-new value of the clothes you bought today?'

'The full value?' A small frown puckered Lisa's forehead. She had no idea at all of what he was getting at. 'I have no idea. I don't normally buy exclusive designer-label clothes, especially not Armani…but I imagine it would have to be several thousand pounds…'

'Several thousand pounds.' A thin, dangerous smile curled

his mouth, his eyes so coldly contemptuous that Lisa actually felt a small, icy shiver race down her spine.

'Why don't we settle for a round figure and make it five thousand pounds? I'll write you a cheque for five thousand here and now and you'll give me back Emma's clothes.'

Lisa stared at him in disbelief.

'But that's crazy,' she protested. 'Why on earth should you pay me five thousand pounds when you could go out and buy a whole new wardrobe for her for that amount…?' She shook her head in disbelief. 'I don't—'

'Oh, come on,' he interrupted her cuttingly. 'Don't give me that. You understand perfectly well. Even *I* understand how impossible and time-wasting an exercise it would be for me to go out and replace every single item with its exact replica… even if I knew what it was I was supposed to be buying. Don't overplay your hand,' he warned her. 'All that mock innocence doesn't suit you.'

Mock innocence!

As she suddenly recognised just what he was accusing her of, Lisa's face flushed a brilliant, furious scarlet.

'Get out… Get out of my flat right now,' she demanded shakily. 'Otherwise I'm going to call the police. How dare you accuse me of…of…?' She couldn't even say the word, she felt such a sense of outrage and disgust.

'I wouldn't give you those clothes now if you offered to pay me ten thousand…twenty thousand,' she told him passionately. 'You deserve to lose Emma… In fact, I think I'm probably doing her a favour by letting her see just what kind of a man you are. I suppose you thought that just because you bought her clothes for her you had a right to…to take them back… If I were her… If I were her…'

'Yes? If you were her, what?' he goaded her, just as furious as she was herself, Lisa recognised as she saw the small pulse beating fiercely in his jaw and the banked-down fury in his eyes.

'I wouldn't have let you buy them for me in the first place,' she threw emotionally at him, adding, 'I'd rather—'

'Rather what?' he challenged her, his voice dropping suddenly and becoming dangerously, sensually soft as he raked her from head to foot in such a sexually predatory and searching way that it left her virtually shaking, trembling, her body overreacting wildly to the male sexuality in the way he was looking at her, the sensual challenge in the way his eyes deliberately stripped her of her clothes, leaving her body vulnerable…exposed…naked.

'You'd rather what?' he repeated triumphantly. 'Go naked?'

Lisa couldn't speak; she was too shocked, too outraged, too aware of her feminine vulnerability to the blazing heat of his sexuality to risk saying anything.

'But then in actual fact, according to you—since you refuse to believe the truth and accept that I am acting for my cousin and not for myself—you are wearing clothes that I have chosen…bought…' he added softly, his glance slipping suggestively over her body for a second time, but this time more slowly, more lingeringly…more…more seductively, Lisa recognised as she felt herself responding helplessly to the sheer force of the magnetic spell he seemed to have cast over her.

From somewhere she managed to find the strength to break free. Stepping back from him, putting a safer distance between them, averting her eyes and her over-flushed face from his powerful gaze, she demanded huskily, 'I want you to leave. Now. Otherwise…'

'You'll call the police. I know,' he agreed drily. 'Very well, since it's obvious I can't make you see reason… I won't forget how co-operative you've been,' he added, sending a small shiver down her spine as she saw the look in his eyes. 'Although I can understand why you're so loath to part with your borrowed finery.

'The suit looks good on you,' he added unexpectedly as he turned towards the door, pausing to look at her before lifting his hand and outrageously tracing a line with the tip of his index finger all the way along the deep V of the neckline of the waistcoat just where the upper curves of her breasts, naked underneath it, pressed against the creamy fabric.

'It's a bit tighter here on you than it was on Emma, though,' he told her. 'She's probably only a 34B whereas you must be a 34C. Nice—especially worn the way you're wearing it now, without anything underneath it…'

Lisa swallowed back all of the agitated, defensive remarks that sprang to her lips, knowing that none of them could do anything to wipe out what he had just said to her, or the effect his words had had on her.

Why, she wondered wretchedly as he opened her front door and left her flat far more calmly than he had entered it, did her body have to react so…so…idiotically and erotically to his touch? Even without looking down she knew how betrayingly her nipples were still pressing against the fine fabric of her waistcoat—as they certainly hadn't been doing when he'd first arrived. As they had, in fact, only humiliatingly done when he had reached out and touched her with that lazily mocking fingertip which had had such a devastating effect on her senses.

It was because she was so overwrought, that was all, she tried to comfort herself half an hour later, the front door securely bolted as she hugged a comforting mug of freshly made coffee.

She would have to ring the shop, of course, and find out exactly what was going on, and if they asked her to return the clothes then morally she would have no option other than to do so.

How dared he accuse her of trying to blackmail him…? *Her.* The coffee slopped out of the mug as her hands started to shake. As if she would ever…ever do any such thing. She felt desperately sorry for the unknown Emma. It was bad enough that he should have sold her clothes, but how would she feel, knowing that he had touched her, another woman, so…so…? No, in her view Emma was better off without him. Much better off.

How dared he touch her like that…as though…as though…? And he had known exactly what he was doing as well. She had seen it in those shockingly knowing steel-grey eyes as she'd read the message of male triumph and awareness that they'd been giving her. He had known that he was arousing her—had known it and had enjoyed knowing it.

Unlike her. She had hated it and she hated him. Emma was quite definitely better off without him and she certainly wasn't going to be the one to help him make up their quarrel by returning her clothes.

At least he was not likely to be able to carry out that subtle threat of future retribution against her—thank goodness.

CHAPTER TWO

LISA STOOD IN FRONT of the guest-bedroom window of Henry's parents' large Victorian house looking out across the wintry countryside.

They had arrived considerably later than expected the previous evening, due, in the main, to the fact that Henry's car had been so badly damaged whilst parked in a client's car park that their departure had been delayed and they had had to use her small—much smaller—model, much to Henry's disgust.

They had arrived shortly after eleven o'clock, and whilst Henry had been greeted with a good deal of maternal anxiety and concern Lisa had received a considerably more frosty reception, Henry's mother giving her a chilly smile and presenting a cool cheek for her to kiss before commenting, 'I'm afraid we couldn't put back supper any longer. You know what your father's like about meal times, Henry.'

'It was Lisa's fault,' Henry had grumbled untruthfully, adding to Lisa, 'You really should get a decent car, you know. Oh, and by the way, you need petrol.'

Lisa had gritted her teeth and smiled, reminding herself that she had already guessed from Henry's comments about his family that, as an only child and a son, he was the apple of his mother's eye.

Whilst Henry had been despatched to his father's study, Lisa had been quizzed by Henry's mother about her family and background. It had subtly been made plain to Lisa that so far as Henry's mother was concerned the jury was still out on the subject of her suitability as Henry's intended wife.

Normally she would have enjoyed the chance to visit the Yorkshire Dales, Lisa acknowledged—especially at this time of the year. Last night she had been enchanted to discover that snow was expected on the high ground.

Henry had been less impressed. In fact, he had been in an edgy, difficult mood throughout the entire journey—and not just, Lisa suspected, because of the damage to his precious car.

It had struck her, over the previous weekend, when they'd been doing the last of their Christmas shopping together, that he was obviously having doubts about her ability to make the right impression on his parents. There had been several small lectures and clumsy hints on what his family would expect, and one particularly embarrassing moment when Alison had called round to the flat just as Henry had been explaining that he wasn't sure that the Armani trouser suit was going to be quite the thing for his parents' annual pre-Christmas supper party.

'What century are Henry's parents living in?' Alison had exploded after Henry had left the room. 'Honestly, Lisa, I can't—'

She had stopped when Lisa had shaken her head, changing the subject to ask instead, 'Any more repercussions about the clothes you bought from Second Time Around, by the way?'

Lisa had told Alison all about her run-in with Oliver Davenport, asking her friend's advice as to what she ought to do.

'Ring the shop and find out what they've got to say,' had been Alison's prompt response.

'I've already done that,' Lisa had told her. 'And there was just a message on the answering machine saying that the owner has had to close the shop down indefinitely because her father has been taken seriously ill.'

'Well, if you want my opinion, you bought those clothes in all good faith, and I feel that their original owner deserves to know exactly what kind of miserable rat her boyfriend is... I mean...selling her clothes... It's...it's... Well, I'd certainly never forgive any man who tried to pull that one on me. I think you did exactly the right thing in refusing to give them back,' Alison had said comfortingly.

'No. No further repercussions,' Lisa had told her in response to her latest question. 'Which I find surprising. I suppose I did overreact a little bit, but when he virtually accused me of trying to blackmail him into paying almost more for them than they had originally cost...'

Her voice had quivered with remembered indignation as she recalled how shocked and insulted she had felt to be confronted with such a contemptuous assessment of her character.

'You overreacting—and to a man... Now that's something I *would* like to see,' Alison had told her.

'Who are you discussing?' Henry had asked, coming back into the room.

'Oh, no one special,' Lisa had told him, hastily and untruthfully, hoping that he wouldn't question the sudden surge of hot, guilty colour flooding her face as she remembered the shocking unexpectedness and intimacy of the way Oliver Davenport had reached out and touched her, and her even more shocking and intimate reaction to his touch.

The whole incident was something that was best forgotten she told herself firmly now as she craned her neck to watch a shepherd manoeuvring his flock on the distant hillside. She felt very sorry for Emma, of course, in the loss of her clothes, but hopefully it would teach Oliver Davenport not to behave so arrogantly in future. It was certainly a lesson he needed to learn.

Lisa glanced at her watch.

Henry's mother had announced last night that they sat down for breakfast at eight o'clock sharp, the implication being that she suspected that Lisa lived too decadent and lazy a lifestyle to manage to get up early enough to join them.

She couldn't have been more wrong, Lisa acknowledged. She was normally a very early riser.

The build-up to Christmas, and most especially the week before it, was normally one of her favourite times of the year. Her parents might live a rather unconventional lifestyle by Henry's parents' standards, but wherever they had lived when she'd been a child they had always made a point of following as many Christmas traditions as they could—buying and dressing a specially chosen Christmas tree, cooking certain favourite Christmas treats, shopping for presents and wrapping them. But Lisa had always yearned for the trappings of a real British Christmas. She had been looking forward to seeing such a traditional scenario of events taking place in Henry's childhood home, but it had become apparent to her the previous evening that Henry's parents, and more specifically Henry's mother, did not view Christmas in the same way she did herself.

'The whole thing has become so dreadfully commercialised that I simply don't see the point nowadays,' she had commented when Lisa had been describing the fun she had had shopping for gifts for the several small and *not* so small children who featured on her Christmas present list.

Her father in particular delighted in receiving anything toy-like, and had a special weakness for magic tricks. Lisa had posted her gifts to her parents to Japan weeks ago, and had, in turn, received hers from them. She had brought the presents north with her, intending to add them to the pile she had assumed would accumulate beneath the Christmas tree, which in her imagination she had visualised as tall and wonderfully bushy, dominating the large hallway that Henry had described to her, warmed by the firelight of its open hearth and scenting the whole room with the delicious aroma of fresh pine needles.

Alas for her imaginings. Henry's mother did not, apparently, like real Christmas trees. They caused too much mess with their needles. And as for an open fire! They had had that boarded up years ago, she had informed Lisa, adding that it had caused far too much mess and nuisance.

So much for her hazy thoughts of establishing the beginnings of their own family traditions, her plans of one day telling her own children how she and their father had spent their first Christmas together, going out to choose the family Christmas tree.

'You're far too romantic and impractical,' Henry had criticised her. 'I agree with Mother. Real Christmas trees are nothing but a nuisance.'

As she turned away from the window Lisa was uncomfortably aware not only of Henry's mother's reluctance to accept her, but also of her own unexpectedly rebellious feeling that Henry was letting her down in not being more supportive of her.

She hadn't spent one full day with Henry's family yet, and already she was beginning to regret the extended length of their Christmas stay with them.

Reluctantly she walked towards the bedroom door. It was ten to eight, and the last thing she wanted to do now was arrive late for breakfast.

'Off-white wool... Don't you think that's rather impractical?' Henry's mother asked Lisa critically.

Taking a deep breath and counting to ten, Lisa forced herself to smile as she responded politely to Mary Hanford's criticism.

'Perhaps a little, but then—'

'I never wear cream or white. I think they can be so draining to the pale English complexion,' her prospective mother-in-law continued. 'Navy is always so much more serviceable, I think.'

Lisa had arrived downstairs half an hour ago, all her offers to help with the preparation of the pre-Christmas buffet supper having been firmly refused.

So much for creating the right impression on Henry's parents with her new clothes, Lisa reflected wryly, wishing that Alison was with her to appreciate the ironic humour of the situation.

She could, of course, have shared the joke with Henry, but somehow she doubted that he would have found it funny… He had, no doubt, inherited his sense of humour, or rather his lack of it, from his mother, she decided sourly, and was immediately ashamed of her own mean-spiritedness.

Of course, it was only natural that Henry's mother should be slightly distant with her. Naturally she was protective of Henry—he was her only son, her only child…

He was also a man of thirty-one, a sharp inner voice reminded Lisa, and surely capable of making his own mind up about who he wanted to marry? Or was he?

It hadn't escaped Lisa's notice during the day how Henry consistently and illuminatingly agreed with whatever opinion his mother chose to voice, but she dismissed the tiny niggling doubts that were beginning to undermine her confidence in her belief that she and Henry had a future together as natural uncertainties raised by seeing him in an unfamiliar setting and with people, moreover, who knew him far better than she did.

In the hallway the grandfather clock chimed the hour. In a few minutes the Hanfords' supper guests would be arriving.

Henry had already explained to her that his family had

lived in the area for several generations and that they had a large extended family, most of whom would be at the supper party, along with a handful of his parents' friends.

Lisa was slightly apprehensive, aware that she would be very much on show, which was one of the reasons why she had chosen to wear the cream trouser suit.

Henry, however, hadn't been any more approving of her outfit than his mother, telling her severely that he thought that a skirt would have been more appropriate than trousers.

Lisa had no doubt that Oliver Davenport would have been both highly amused and contemptuous of her failure to achieve the desired effect with her acquired plumage.

Oliver Davenport. Now what on earth was she doing thinking about such a disagreeable subject, such a contentious person, when by rights she ought to be concentrating on the evening ahead of her?

'Ah, Lisa, there you are!' she heard Henry exclaiming. 'Everyone will be arriving soon, and Mother likes us all to be in the hall to welcome them when they do.

'I see you didn't change after all,' he added, frowning at her.

'An Armani suit is a perfectly acceptable outfit to wear for a supper party, Henry,' Lisa pointed out mildly, and couldn't help adding a touch more robustly, 'And, to be honest, I think I would have felt rather cold in a skirt. Your parents—'

'Mother doesn't think an overheated house is healthy,' Henry interrupted her quickly—so quickly that Lisa suspected that she wasn't the first person to comment on the chilliness of his parents' house.

'I expect I'm feeling the cold because we're so much further north here,' she offered diplomatically as she followed him into the hallway.

Cars could be heard pulling up outside, their doors opening and closing.

'That's good!' Henry exclaimed. 'Mother likes everyone to be on time.'

Mother would, Lisa thought rebelliously, but wisely she kept the words to herself.

Henry's aunt and her family were the first to arrive. A smaller, quieter edition of her elder sister, she was, nevertheless, far warmer in her manner towards Lisa than Henry's mother had been, and Lisa didn't miss the looks exchanged by her three teenage children as they were subjected to Mary Hanford's critical inspection.

Fifteen minutes later the hallway was virtually full, and Lisa was beginning to lose track of just who everyone was. The doorbell rang again and Henry went to answer it. As Lisa turned to look at the newcomers her heart suddenly stood still and then gave a single shocked bound followed by a flurry of too fast, disbelieving, nervous beats.

Oliver Davenport! What on earth was he doing here? He couldn't have followed her here to pursue his demand for her to return Emma's clothes, could he?

At the thought of what Henry's mother was likely to say if Oliver Davenport caused the same kind of scene here in public as he had staged in the privacy of her own flat, Lisa closed her eyes in helpless dismay, and then heard Henry saying tensely to her, 'Lisa, I'd like to introduce you to one of my parents' neighbours. Oliver—'

'Lisa and I already know one another.'

Lisa's eyes widened in bemused incomprehension.

Oliver Davenport was a neighbour of Henry's parents! And what did he mean by implying that they knew one another… by saying her name in that grossly deceptive, softly sensual way, which seemed to imply that he…that she…?

'You do? You never said anything about knowing Oliver to me, Lisa,' Henry said almost hectoringly.

But before Lisa could make any attempt to defend herself

or explain, Oliver Davenport was doing it for her, addressing Henry in a tone that left Lisa in no doubt as to just what kind of opinion the other man had of her husband-to-be, as he announced cuttingly, 'No doubt she had more important things on her mind. Or perhaps she simply didn't think it was important…'

'I…I…I didn't realise you two knew one another,' was the only response Lisa could come up with, and she saw from Henry's face that it was not really one that satisfied him.

She nibbled worriedly at her bottom lip, cast Oliver Davenport a bitter look and then was forced to listen helplessly whilst Oliver, who still quite obviously bore her a grudge over the clothes, commented judiciously, 'I like the outfit… It suits you… But then I thought so the first time I saw you wearing it, didn't I?'

Lisa knew that she was blushing. Blushing…? She was turning a vivid and unconcealable shade of deep scarlet, she acknowledged miserably as she saw the suspicious look that Henry was giving her and recognised from the narrow, pursed-lip glare that Henry's mother must have also overheard Oliver's comment.

'Oliver, let me get you a drink,' Henry's father offered, thankfully coming up to usher him away, but not before Oliver managed to murmur softly to Lisa,

'Saved by the cavalry…'

'How on earth do you come to know Oliver Davenport?' Henry demanded angrily as soon as Oliver was out of earshot.

'I don't *know* him,' Lisa admitted wearily. 'At least not—'

'What do you mean? Of course you *know* him…and well enough for him to be able to comment on your clothes…'

'He's… Henry…this isn't the time for me to explain…' Lisa told him quietly.

'So there *is* something to explain, then.' Henry was refusing to be appeased. 'Where did you meet him? In London, I suppose. His business might be based up here at the Hall, but he still spends quite a considerable amount of time in London… His cousin works for him down there—'

'His cousin…?' Lisa couldn't quite keep the note of nervous apprehension out of her voice.

'Yes, Piers Davenport, Oliver's cousin. He's several years younger than Oliver and he lives in London with his girlfriend—some model or other…Emily…or Emma…I can't remember which…'

'Emma,' Lisa supplied hollowly.

So Oliver hadn't been lying, after all, when he had told her that he was acting on behalf of his cousin. She glanced uneasily over her shoulder, remembering just exactly how scathingly she had denounced him, practically accusing him of being a liar and worse.

No wonder he had given her that look this evening which had said that he hadn't finished with her and that he fully intended to make her pay for her angry insults, to exact retribution on her.

Apprehensively she wondered exactly what form that silently promised retribution was going to take. What was he going to do? Reveal to Henry and his parents that she had bought her clothes second-hand? She could just imagine how Mary Hanford would react to that information. At the thought of her impending humiliation, Lisa felt her stomach muscles tighten defensively.

It wasn't all her fault. Hers had been a natural enough mistake to make, she reminded herself. Alison had agreed with her. And Oliver had to share some of the blame for her error himself. If he had only been a little more conciliatory in his manner towards her, a little less arrogant in demanding that she return the clothes back to him…

'I do wish you had told me that you knew Oliver,' Henry was continuing fussily. 'Especially in view of his position locally.'

'What position locally?' Lisa asked him warily, but she suspected she could guess the answer. To judge from Mary Hanford's deferential manner towards him, Oliver Davenport was quite obviously someone of importance in the area. Her heart started to sink even further as Henry explained in a hushed, almost awed voice.

'Oliver is an extremely wealthy man. He owns and runs one of the north of England's largest financial consultancy businesses and he recently took over another firm based in London, giving him a countrywide network. But why are you asking me? Surely if you know him you must—?'

'I don't know him,' Lisa protested tiredly. 'Henry, there's something I have to tell you.' She took a deep breath. There was nothing else for it; she was going to have to tell Henry the truth.

'But you evidently do know him,' Henry protested, ignoring her and cutting across what she was trying to say. 'And rather well by the sound of it… Lisa, what exactly's going on?'

Henry could look remarkably like his mother when he pursed his lips and narrowed his eyes like that, Lisa decided. She suddenly had a mental image of the children they might have together—little replicas of their grandmother. Quickly she banished the unwelcome vision.

'Henry, nothing is going on. If you would just let me explain—' Lisa began.

But once again she was interrupted, this time by Henry's mother, who bore down on them, placing a proprietorial hand on Henry's arm as she told him, 'Henry, dear, Aunt Elspeth wants to talk to you. She's over there by the French windows. She's brought her god-daughter with her. You remember Louise. You used to play together when you were children—such a sweet girl…'

To Lisa's chagrin, Henry was borne off by his mother, leaving her standing alone, nursing an unwanted glass of too sweet sherry.

What should have been the happiest Christmas Eve of her adult life was turning out to be anything but, she admitted gloomily as she watched a petite, doe-eyed brunette, presumably Aunt Elspeth's god-daughter, simpering up at a Henry who was quite plainly wallowing in her dewy-eyed, fascinated attention.

It was a good thirty minutes before Henry returned to her side, during which time she had had ample opportunity to watch Oliver's progress amongst the guests and to wonder why on earth he had accepted the Hanfords' invitation, since he was quite obviously both bored and irritated by the almost fawning attention of Henry's mother.

He really was the most arrogantly supercilious man she had ever had the misfortune to meet, Lisa decided critically as he caught her watching him and lifted one derogatory, darkly interrogative eyebrow in her direction.

Flushing, she turned away, but not, she noticed, before Henry's mother had seen the brief, silent exchange between them.

'You still haven't explained to us just how you come to know… You really should have told us that you know Oliver,' she told Lisa, arriving at her side virtually at the same time as Henry, so that Lisa was once again prevented from explaining to him what had happened.

What was it about some people that made everything they said sound like either a reproach or a criticism? Lisa wondered grimly, but before she could answer she heard Mary Hanford adding, in an unfamiliar, almost arch and flattering voice, 'Ah, Oliver, we were just talking about you.'

'Really.'

He was looking at them contemptuously, as though they were creatures from another planet—some kind of subspecies provided for his entertainment, Lisa decided resentfully as he looked from Mary to Henry and then to her.

'Yes,' Mary continued, undeterred. 'I was just asking Lisa how she comes to know you…'

'Well, I think that's probably best left for Lisa herself to explain to you,' he responded smoothly. 'I should hate to embarrass her by making any unwelcome revelations…'

Lisa glared angrily at him.

'That suit looks good on you,' he added softly.

'So you've already said,' she reminded him through gritted teeth, all too aware of Henry's and his mother's silently suspicious watchfulness at her side.

'Yes,' Oliver continued, as though she hadn't spoken. 'You can always tell when a woman's wearing an outfit bought by a man for his lover.' As he spoke he reached out and touched her jacket-clad arm—a brief touch, nothing more, but it made the hot colour burn in Lisa's face, and she was not at all surprised to hear Henry's mother's outraged indrawn breath or to see the fury in Henry's eyes.

This was retribution with a vengeance. This wasn't just victory, she acknowledged helplessly; it was total annihilation.

'Have you worn any of the other things yet?' he added casually.

'Lisa…' she heard Henry demanding ominously at her side, but she couldn't answer him. She was too mortified, too furiously angry to dare to risk saying anything whilst Oliver Davenport was still standing there listening.

To her relief, he didn't linger long. Aunt Elspeth's goddaughter, the same one who had so determinedly flirted with Henry half an hour earlier, came up and very professionally broke up their quartet, insisting that Oliver had promised to get her a fresh drink.

He was barely out of earshot before Henry was insisting, 'I want to know what's going on, Lisa… What was all that about your clothes…?'

'I think we know exactly what's going on, Henry,' Lisa heard his mother answering coolly for him as she gave Lisa a look of virulent hostility edged with triumph. So much for pretending to welcome her into the family, Lisa thought tiredly.

'I can see what you're *both* thinking,' she announced. 'But you are wrong.'

'Wrong? How can we be wrong when Oliver more or less announced openly that the pair of you have been lovers?' Mary intoned.

'He did not announce that we had been lovers,' Lisa defended herself. 'And if you would just let me explain—'

'Henry, it's almost time for supper. You know how hopeless your father is at getting people organised. I'm going to need you to help me…'

'Henry, we need to talk.' Lisa tried to override his mother, but Henry was already turning away from her and going obediently to his mother's side.

If they married it would always be like this, Lisa suddenly recognised on a wave of helpless anger. He would always place his mother's needs and wants above her own, and presumably above those of their children. They would always come a very poor second best to his loyalty to his mother. Was that really what she wanted for herself…for her children?

Lisa knew it wasn't.

It was as though the scales had suddenly fallen from her eyes, as though she were looking at a picture of exactly how and what her life with Henry would be—and she didn't like it. She didn't like it one little bit.

In the handful of seconds it took her to recognise the fact, she knew irrevocably that she couldn't marry him, but she still owed him an explanation of what had happened, and from her own point of view. For the sake of her pride and self-respect she wanted to make sure that he and his precious mother knew exactly how she had come to meet Oliver and exactly how he had manipulated them into believing his deliberately skewed view of the situation.

Still seething with anger against Oliver, she refused Henry's father's offer of another drink and some supper. She would choke rather than eat any of Mary Hanford's food, she decided angrily.

Just the thought of the kind of life she would have had as Henry's wife made her shudder and acknowledge that she had had a lucky escape, but knowing that did not lessen her overwhelming fury at the man who had accidently brought it about.

How would she have been feeling right now had she been deeply in love with Henry and he with her? Instead of stalking angrily around the Hanfords' drawing room like an angry tigress, she would probably have been upstairs in her bedroom sobbing her heart out.

Some Christmas this was going to be.

She had been so looking forward to being here, to being part of the family, to sharing the simple, traditional pleasures of Christmas with the man she intended to marry, and now it was all spoiled, ruined… And why? Why? Because Oliver Davenport was too arrogant, too proud…too…too devious and hateful to allow someone whom he obviously saw as way, way beneath him to get the better of him.

Well, she didn't care. She didn't care what he did or what he said. He could tell the whole room, the whole house, the whole world that she had bought her clothes second-hand and that they had belonged to his cousin's girlfriend for all she cared now. In fact, she almost wished he would. That way at least she would be vindicated. That way she could walk away from here…from Henry and his precious mother…with her head held high.

'An outfit bought by a man for his lover…' How dared he…? Oh, how dared he…? She was, she suddenly realised, almost audibly grinding her teeth. Hastily she stopped. Dental fees were notoriously, hideously expensive.

She couldn't leave matters as they were, she decided fiercely. She would have to say something to Oliver Davenport—even if it was to challenge him over the implications he had made.

She got her chance ten minutes later, when she saw Oliver leaving the drawing room alone.

Quickly, before she could change her mind, she followed him. As he heard her footsteps crossing the hallway, he stopped and turned round.

'Ah, the blushing bride-to-be and her borrowed raiment,' he commented sardonically.

'I bought in good faith my second-hand raiment,' Lisa corrected him bitingly, adding, 'You do realise what impression you gave Henry and his mother back there, don't you?' she challenged him, adding scornfully before he could answer, 'Of course you knew. You knew perfectly well what you were doing, what you were implying…'

'Did I?' he responded calmly.

'Yes, you did,' Lisa responded, her anger intensifying. 'You knew they would assume that you meant that you and I had been lovers…that *you* had bought my clothes—'

'Surely Henry knows you far better than that?' Oliver interrupted her smoothly. 'After all, according to the local grapevine, the pair of you are intending to marry—'

'Of course Henry knows me…' Lisa began, and then

stopped, her face flushing in angry mortification. But it was too late.

Swift as a hawk to the lure, her tormentor responded softly, 'Ah, I see. It's because he knows you so well that he made the unfortunate and mistaken assumption that—'

'No… He doesn't… I don't…' Lisa tried to fight back gamely, but it was still too late, and infuriatingly she knew it and, even worse, so did Oliver.

He wasn't smirking precisely—he was far too arrogant for that, Lisa decided bitterly—but there was certainly mockery in his eyes, and if she hadn't known better she could almost have sworn that his mouth was about to curl into a smile. But how could it? She was sure that he was incapable of doing anything so human. He was the kind of man who just didn't know what human emotions were, she decided savagely—who had no idea what it meant to suffer insecurity or…or any of the things that made people like herself feel so vulnerable.

'Have you any idea what you've done?' she challenged him, changing tack, her voice shaking under the weight of her suppressed emotion. 'I came here—'

'I know why you came here,' he interrupted her with unexpected sternness. 'You came to be looked over as a potential wife for Mary Hanford's precious son.

'Where's your pride?' he demanded scornfully. 'However, a potential bride is all you will ever be. Mary Hanford knows quite well who she wants Henry to marry, and I'm afraid it isn't going to be you…'

'Not now,' Lisa agreed shortly. 'Not—'

'Not ever,' Oliver told her. 'Mary won't allow Henry to marry any woman who she thinks might have the slightest chance of threatening her own superior position in Henry's life. His wife will not only have to take second place to her but to covertly acknowledge and accept that fact before she's allowed to marry him. And besides, the two of you are so obviously unsuited to one another that the whole thing's almost a farce. You're far too emotionally turbulent and uncontrolled for Henry… He wouldn't have a clue how to handle you…'

Lisa couldn't believe her ears.

'You, of course, would,' she challenged him with acid sweetness, too carried away by her anger and the heat of the moment to realise what she was doing, the challenge she was issuing him, the risks she was taking.

Then it was too late and he was cutting the ground from beneath her feet and making a shock as icy-cold as the snow melting on the tops of the Yorkshire hills that were his home run down her spine as he told her silkily, 'Certainly,' and then added before she could draw breath to speak, 'And, for openers, there are two things I most certainly would do that Henry obviously has not.'

'Oh, yes, and what exactly would they be?' Lisa demanded furiously.

'Well, I certainly wouldn't have the kind of relationship with you—or with any woman who I had the slightest degree of mild affection for, never mind being on the point of contemplating marrying—which would necessitate you feeling that you had to conceal anything about yourself from me, or that you needed to impress my family and friends with borrowed plumes, with the contents of another woman's wardrobe. And the second…' he continued, ignoring Lisa's quick, indrawn breath of mingled chagrin and rage.

He paused and looked at her whilst Lisa, driven well beyond the point of no return by the whole farce of her ruined Christmas in general and his part in it in particular, prompted wildly, 'Yes, the second is…?'

'This,' he told her softly, taking the breath from her lungs, the strength from her muscles and, along with them, the willpower from her brain as he stepped forward and took her in his arms and then bent his head and kissed her as Henry had never kissed her in all the eight months of their relationship—as no man had ever kissed her in the whole history of her admittedly modest sexual experience, she recognised dizzily as his mouth moved with unbelievable, unbeatable, unbearable sensual expertise on hers.

Ordinary mortal men did not kiss like this. Ordinary mortal men did not behave like this. Ordinary mortal men did not have the power, did not cup one's face with such tender mastery. They did not look deep into your eyes whilst they caressed your mouth with their own. They did not compel you, by some mastery you could not understand, to look back at them. They did not, by some unspoken command, cause you to open your mouth beneath theirs on a whispered ecstatic sigh of pure female pleasure. They did not lift their mouths from yours and look from your eyes to your half-parted lips and then back to your eyes again, their own warming in a smile of complicit understanding before starting to kiss you all over again.

Film stars in impossibly extravagant and highly acclaimed, Oscar-winning romantic movies might mimic such behaviour. Heroes in stomach-churning, body-aching, romantically sensual novels might sweep their heroines off their feet with similar embraces. God-like creatures from Greek mythology might come down to earth and wantonly seduce frolicking nymphs with such devastating experience and sensuality, but mere mortal men…? Never!

Lisa gave a small, blissful sigh and closed her eyes, only to open them again as she heard Henry exclaiming wrathfully, 'Lisa…what on earth do you think you're doing?'

Guiltily she watched him approaching as Oliver released her.

'Henry, I can explain,' she told him urgently, but he obviously didn't intend to let her speak.

Ignoring Oliver's quiet voice mocking, 'To Henry, maybe,

but to Mary, never,' she flushed defensively as his taunting comment was borne out by Henry's furious declaration.

'Mother was right about you all along. She warned me that you weren't—'

'Henry, you don't understand.' She managed to interrupt him, turning to appeal to Oliver, who was standing watching them in contemptuous amusement.

'Tell him what really happened… Tell him…'

'Do you really expect me to give you my help?' he goaded her softly. 'I don't recall you being similarly sympathetic when I asked you for yours.'

Whilst Lisa stood and stared at him in disbelief he started to walk towards the door, pausing only to tell Henry, 'Your mother is quite right, Henry. She wouldn't be the right wife for you at all… If I were you I should heed her advice—now, before it's too late.'

'Henry,' Lisa began to protest, but she could see from the way that he was refusing to meet her eyes that she had lost what little chance she might have had of persuading him to listen to her.

'It's too late now for us to change our plans for Christmas,' he told her stiffly, still avoiding looking directly at her. 'It is, after all, Christmas Eve, and we can hardly ask you to… However, once we return to London I feel that it would be as well if we didn't see one another any more…'

Lisa could scarcely believe her ears. Was this really the man she had thought she loved, or had at least liked and admired enough to be her husband…the man she had wanted as the father of her children? This pompous, stuffy creature who preferred to take his mother's advice on whom he should and should not marry than to listen to her, the woman he had proclaimed he loved?

Only he had not—not really, had he? Lisa made herself admit honestly. Neither of them had really truly been in love.

Oh, they had liked one another well enough. But liking wasn't love, and if she was honest with herself there was a strong chord of relief mixed up in the turbulent anger and resentment churning her insides.

Stay here now, over Christmas, after what had happened…? No way.

Without trusting herself to speak to Henry, she turned on her heel and headed for the stairs and her bedroom, where she threw open the wardrobe doors and started to remove her clothes—her borrowed clothes, not her clothes, she acknowledged grimly as she opened her suitcase; they hadn't been hers when she had bought them and they certainly weren't hers now.

Eyeing them with loathing, her attention was momentarily distracted by the damp chilliness of her bedroom. Thank goodness they had driven north in her car. At least she wasn't going to have the added humiliation of depending on Henry to get her back to London.

The temperature seemed to have dropped since she had left the bedroom earlier, even taking into account Mary Hanford's parsimony.

There had been another warning of snow on high ground locally earlier in the evening, and Lisa had been enchanted by it, wondering out loud if they might actually have a white Christmas—a long-held childhood wish of hers which she had so far never had fulfilled. Mary Hanford had been scornful of her excitement.

As she gathered up her belongings Lisa suddenly paused; the clothes she had bought with such pleasure and which she had held onto with such determination lay on the bed in an untidy heap.

Beautiful though they were, she suddenly felt that she knew now that she could never wear them. They were tainted. Some things were just not meant to be, she decided regretfully as she stroked the silk fabric of one of the shirts with tender fingers.

She might have paid for them, bought them in all good faith, but somehow she had never actually felt as though they were hers.

But it was her borrowed clothes, like the borrowed persona she had perhaps unwittingly tried to assume to impress Henry's family, which had proved her downfall, and she was, she decided firmly, better off without both of them.

Ten minutes later, wearing her own jeans, she lifted the carefully folded clothes into her suitcase. Once the Christmas holiday was over she would telephone the dress agency and explain that she no longer had any use for the clothes. Hopefully they would be prepared to take them back and refund most, if not all of her money.

It was too late to regret now that she had not accepted Alison's suggestion that she join her and some other friends on a Christmas holiday and skiing trip to Colorado. Christmas was going to be very lonely for her alone in her flat with all her friends and her parents away. A sadly wistful smile curved the generous softness of her mouth as she contemplated how very different from her rosy daydreams the reality of her Christmas was going to be.

'You're going to the north of England—Yorkshire. I know it has a reputation for being much colder up there than it is here in London, but that doesn't mean you'll get snow,' Alison had warned her, adding more gently, 'Don't invest too much in this visit to Henry's family, Lisa. I know how important it is to you but things don't always work out the way you plan. The Yorkshire Dales are a beautiful part of the world, but people are still people and—well, let's face it, from what Henry has said about his family, especially his mother, it's obvious that she's inclined to be a little on the possessive side.'

'I know you don't really like Henry…' Lisa had begun defensively.

But Alison had shaken her head and told her firmly, 'It isn't that I don't care for Henry, rather that I *do* care about you. He isn't right for you, Lisa. Oh, I know what you're going to say: he's solid and dependable, and with him you can put down the roots that are so important to you. But, to be honest—well, if you want the truth, I see Henry more as a rather spoiled little boy than the kind of man a woman can rely on.'

It looked as if Alison was a much better judge of character than she, Lisa acknowledged as she zipped her case shut and picked it up.

CHAPTER THREE

LISA WAS HALFWAY down the stairs when Henry walked into the hallway and saw her.

'Lisa, why are you dressed like that? Where are you going?' he demanded as he looked anxiously back over his shoulder, obviously not wanting anyone else to witness what was going on.

'I'm leaving,' she told him calmly. It was odd that she should be able to remain so calm with Henry who, after all, until this evening's debacle had been the man she had intended to marry, the man she had planned to spend the rest of her life with, and yet with Oliver, a complete stranger, a man she had seen only twice before and whom she expected…hoped…she would never see again, her emotions became inflamed into a rage of gargantuan proportions.

'Leaving? But you can't… What will people think?' Henry protested. 'Mother's got the whole family coming for Christmas dinner tomorrow and they'll all expect you to be there. We were, after all, planning to announce our engagement,' he reminded her seriously.

As she listened to him in disbelief Lisa was shocked to realise that she badly wanted to laugh—or cry.

'Henry, I can't stay here now,' she told him. 'Not after what's happened. You must see that. After all you were the one—'

'You're leaving to go to him, aren't you?' Henry accused her angrily. 'Well, don't expect Oliver to offer to marry you,

Lisa. He might want to take you to bed but, as Mother says, Oliver isn't the kind of man to marry a woman who—'

That was it. Suddenly Lisa had had enough. Her face flushing with the full force of her emotions, she descended the last few stairs and confronted Henry.

'I don't care what your mother says, Henry,' she told him through gritted teeth. 'And if you were half the man I thought you were *you* wouldn't care either. Neither would you let her make up your mind or your decisions for you… And as for Oliver—'

'Yes, as for me…what?'

To her consternation Lisa realised that at some point Oliver had walked into the hall and was now standing watching them both, an infuriatingly superior, mocking contempt curling his mouth as he broke into her angry tirade.

'I've had enough of this… I've had enough of both of you,' Lisa announced. 'This is all your fault. All of it,' she added passionately to Oliver, ignoring Henry's attempts to silence her.

'And don't think I haven't guessed why you've done it,' she added furiously, her fingers tugging at the strap of her suitcase. She wrenched the case open and cried out angrily to him, 'You want your precious clothes back? Well, you can have them…all of them…'

Fiercely she wrenched the carefully packed clothes from her case and hurled them across the small space that lay between them, where they landed in an untidy heap at Oliver's feet.

She ignored Henry's anguished, shocked, 'Lisa…what on earth are you doing…? Lisa, please…stop; someone might see… Mother…'

'Oh, and we mustn't forget this, must we?' Lisa continued, ignoring Henry, an almost orgasmic feeling of release drowning out all her normal level-headedness and common sense.

For the first time in her life she could understand why it was some people actually seemed to enjoy losing their temper, giving up their self-control…causing a scene…all things that were normally completely foreign to her.

Triumphantly she threw the beautiful Armani suit which she had bought with such pleasure at Oliver's feet whilst he watched her impassively.

'There! I hope you're satisfied,' she told him as the last garment headed his way.

'Lisa,' Henry was still bleating protestingly, but she ignored him. Now that the sudden, unfamiliar surge of anger was retreating she felt oddly weak and shaky, almost vulnerably light-headed and dangerously close to tears.

In the distance she was aware that Henry was still protesting, but for some reason it was Oliver whom her attention was concentrated on, who filled her vision and her prickly, wary senses as she deliberately skirted around him, clutching her still half-open but now much lighter suitcase, and headed for the front door.

There had been a look in his eyes as she had flung that trouser suit at him which she had not totally understood—a gleam of an emotion which in another man she could almost have felt was humour mixed with a certain rueful respect, but of course she must have been imagining it.

As she tugged open the front door and stepped outside a shock of ice-cold air hit her. She hadn't realised how much the temperature had dropped, how overcast the sky had become.

Frost crunched beneath her feet as she hurried towards her car. Faithful and reliable as ever, it started at the second turn of the key.

As Lisa negotiated the other cars parked in the drive she told herself grimly that she had no need to try to work out whom that gleaming, shiny Aston Martin sports car belonged to. It just had to be Oliver Davenport's.

As she turned onto the main road she switched on her car radio, her heart giving a small forlorn thud of regret as she heard the announcer forecasting that the north of England was due to have snow.

Snow for Christmas and she was going to miss it.

It was half past eleven; another half an hour and it would be Christmas Day, and she would be spending it alone.

Stop snivelling, she told herself as she felt her throat start to ache with emotional tears. You've had a lucky escape.

She knew she had a fairly long drive ahead of her before she reached the motorway. As she and Henry had driven north she had remarked on how beautiful the countryside was as they drove through it. Now, however, as she drove along the empty, dark country road she was conscious of how remote the area was and how alone she felt.

She frowned as the car engine started to splutter and lose power, anxiety tensing her body as she wondered what on earth was wrong. Her small car had always been so reliable, and she was very careful about having it properly serviced and keeping the tank full of petrol.

Petrol. Lisa knew what had happened from the sharp sinking sensation in her stomach even before she looked fearfully at the petrol gauge.

Henry had not bothered to replace the petrol they had used on the journey north and now, it seemed, the tank was empty.

Lisa closed her eyes in mute despair. What on earth was she going to do? She was stranded on an empty country road miles from anywhere in the dark on Christmas Eve, with no idea where the nearest garage was, no means of contacting anyone to ask, dressed in jeans and a thin sweater on a freezing cold night.

And she knew exactly who she had to blame for her sorry plight, she decided wrathfully ten minutes later as the air inside her car turned colder and colder with ominous speed. Oliver Davenport. If it hadn't been for him and his cynical and deliberate manipulation of the truth to cast her in a bad light in front of Henry and his parents, none of this would have happened.

Even now she still couldn't quite believe what she had done in the full force of that final, unexpected burst of temper, when she had thrown her clothes at him.

Lisa hugged her arms tightly around her body as she started to shiver. It was too late to regret her hasty departure from Henry's parents' home now, or the fact that she had brought nothing with her that she could use to keep her warm.

Just how far was it to the nearest house? Her teeth were chattering now and the windscreen had started to freeze over.

Perhaps she ought to start walking back in the direction she had come. At least then the physical activity might help to keep her warm, but her heart sank at the thought. So far as she could remember, she had been driving for a good fifteen minutes after she had passed through the last small hamlet, and she hadn't seen any houses since then.

Reluctantly she opened the car door, and then closed it again with a gasp of shock as the ice-cold wind knifed into her unprotected body.

What on earth was she going to do? Her earlier frustration and irritation had started to give way to a far more ominous and much deeper sense of panicky fear.

One read about people being found dying from exposure and hypothermia, but it always seemed such an unreal fate somehow in a country like Britain. Now, though, it suddenly seemed horribly plausible.

Her panic intensified as she realised that unless she either managed to walk to the nearest inhabited building, wherever that might be, or was spotted by a passing motorist, it would be days before anyone realised that she was missing. There was, after all, no one waiting at home in London for her. Her parents had agreed not to telephone on Christmas Day because they knew she would be staying with Henry's family. Henry would assume—if indeed he gave her any thought at all—that she was back in London.

As she fought down the emotions threatening to overwhelm her Lisa happened to glance at her watch.

It was almost half past twelve…Christmas Day.

Now she couldn't stop the tears.

Christmas Day and she was stuck in a car miles from anywhere and probably about to freeze to death.

She gave a small, protesting moan as she sneezed and then sneezed again, blinking her eyes against the dazzling glare of headlights she could see in her driving mirror.

The dazzling glare of headlights… Another car…

Frantically Lisa pushed on her frozen car door, terrified that her unwitting rescuer might drive past her without realising her plight.

The approaching car was only yards behind her when she finally managed to shove open the door. As she half fell into the icy road in her haste to advertise her predicament any thoughts of the danger of flagging down a stranger were completely forgotten in the more overriding urgency of her plight.

The dazzle of the oncoming headlights was so powerful that she couldn't distinguish the shape of the car or see its driver, but she knew he or she had seen her because the car suddenly started to lose speed, swerving to a halt in front of her.

Now that the car was stationary Lisa recognised that there was something vaguely familiar about it, but her relief overrode that awareness as she ran towards it on legs which suddenly seemed as stiff and wobbly as those of a newborn colt.

However, before she could reach it, the driver's door was flung open and a pair of long male legs appeared, followed by an equally imposing and stomach-churningly recognisable male torso and face.

As she stared disbelievingly into the frowning, impatient face of Oliver Davenport, Lisa protested fatalistically, 'Oh, no, not you…'

'Who were you hoping it was—Henry?' he retorted sardonically. 'If this is your idea of staging a reconciliation scene, I have to tell you that you're wasting your time. When I left him you were the last thing on Henry's mind.'

'Of course I'm not staging a reconciliation scene,' Lisa snapped back at him. 'I'm not staging a scene of any kind… I—it isn't something I do…'

The effect of her cool speech was unfairly spoiled by the sudden fit of shivering that overtook her, but it was plain that Oliver Davenport wouldn't have been very impressed with it anyway because he drawled, 'Oh, no? Then what was all that highly theatrical piece of overacting in the Hanfords' hall all about?'

'That wasn't overacting,' Lisa gritted at him. 'That was…'

She shivered again, this time so violently that her teeth chattered audibly.

'For God's sake, put a coat on. Have you any idea what the temperature is tonight? I know you're from the south and a city, but surely common sense—?'

'I don't have a coat,' Lisa told him, adding bitterly, 'Because of you.'

The look he gave her was incredulously contemptuous.

'Are you crazy? You come north in the middle of December and you don't even bother to bring a coat—'

'Oh, I brought a coat all right,' Lisa corrected him between shivers. 'Only I don't have it now…'

She gritted her teeth and tried not to think about the warmth of the lovely, heavenly cream cashmere coat which had been amongst the things she had thrown at his feet so recklessly.

'You don't… Ah… I see… What are you doing, anyway? Why have you stopped?'

'Why do you think I've stopped? Not to admire the view,' Lisa told him bitterly. 'The car's run out of petrol.'

'The car's run out of petrol?'

Lisa felt herself flushing as she heard the disbelieving male scorn in his voice.

'It wasn't my fault,' she defended herself. 'We were supposed to be coming north in Henry's car, only it was involved in an accident and couldn't be driven so we had to use mine, and Henry was so anxious to get…not to be late that he didn't want to stop and refill the tank…'

Lisa hated the way he was just standing silently looking at her. He was determined to make things as hard for her as he could. She could see that… He was positively enjoying making her look small…humiliating her.

In any other circumstances but these she would have been tempted simply to turn her back on him, get back in her car and wait for the next driver to come by, but common sense warned her that she couldn't afford to take that kind of risk.

Her unprotected fingers had already turned white and were almost numb. She couldn't feel her toes, and the rest of her body felt so cold that the sensation was almost a physical pain.

Taking a deep breath and fixing her gaze on a point just beyond his left shoulder, she said shakily, 'I'd be very grateful if you could give me a lift to the nearest garage…'

Tensely she waited for his response, knowing that he was bound to make the most of the opportunity which she had given him to exercise his obvious dislike of her. But when it came the blow was one of such magnitude and such force that she physically winced beneath the cruelty of it, the breath escaping from her lungs in a soft, shocked gasp as he told her ruthlessly, 'No way.'

It must be the cold that was making her feel so dizzy and light-headed, Lisa thought despairingly—that and her panicky fear that he was going to walk away and simply leave her here to meet her fate.

Whatever the cause, it propelled her into instinctive action, making her dart forward and catch hold of the fabric of his jacket as she told him jerkily, 'It wasn't *my* fault that your cousin sold his girlfriend's clothes without her permission. All *I* did was buy them in good faith… He's the one you should be punishing, not me. If you leave me here—'

'*Leave* you here…?'

Somehow or other he had detached her hand from his jacket and was now holding it in his own. Dizzily Lisa marvelled at how warm and comforting, how strong and safe it felt to have that large male hand enclosing hers. She could almost feel the warmth from his touch—his body—flooding up through her arm like an infusion of life-giving blood into a vein.

'Leave you *here* in this temperature?' he said, adding roughly, 'Are you crazy…?'

She couldn't see him properly any more, Lisa realised, and she thought it must be because the tears that had threatened her eyes had frozen in the intense cold. She had no idea that she had actually spoken her sentiments out loud until she heard him respond, 'Tears don't freeze; they're saline… salty.'

He had let go of her hand and as Lisa watched him he stripped off his jacket and then, to her shock, took hold of her and bundled her up in it like an adult wrapping up a small child.

'I can't walk,' she protested, her voice muffled by the thickness of the over-large wrapping.

'You're not going to,' she was told peremptorily, and then, before she knew what was happening, he was picking her up and carrying her the short distance to his car, opening the passenger door and depositing her on the seat.

The car smelled of leather and warmth and something much more intangible—something elusive and yet oddly familiar… Muzzily Lisa sniffed, trying to work out what it was and why it should inexplicably make her want to cry and yet at the same time feel oddly elated.

Oliver had gone over to her car, and as he returned Lisa saw that he was carrying her case and her handbag.

'I've locked it…your car,' he told her as he slid into the driver's seat alongside her. 'Not that anyone would be likely to take it.'

'Not unless they had some petrol with them,' Lisa agreed drowsily, opening her mouth to give a yawn which suddenly turned into a volley of bone-aching sneezes.

'Here.' Oliver handed her a wad of clean tissues from a pack in the glove compartment, telling her, 'It's just as well I happened to be passing when I did. If you're lucky the worst you'll suffer is a bad cold; another hour in these temperatures and it could have been a very different story. This road is never very heavily trafficked, and on Christmas Eve, with snow forecast, the locals who do use it have more sense than to…'

He went on talking but Lisa had heard enough. Did he think she had wanted to run out of petrol on a remote Yorkshire road? Had he forgotten whose fault it was that she had been there in the first place instead of warmly tucked up in bed at Henry's parents' home?

Tears of unfamiliar and unexpected self-pity suddenly filled her eyes. 'It isn't Christmas Eve,' she told him aggressively, fighting to hold them back. 'It's Christmas Day.'

It was the wrong thing to say, bringing back her earlier awareness of how very fragile were the brightly coloured, delicate daydreams that she had cherished of how this Christmas would be—as fragile and vulnerable as the glass baubles with which she had so foolishly imagined herself decorating that huge, freshly cut, pine-smelling Christmas tree with Henry.

It was too much. One tear fell and then another. She tried to stop them, dabbing surreptitiously at her eyes, and she averted her face from Oliver's as he started the engine and set the car in motion. But it was no use. He had obviously witnessed her distress.

'Now what's wrong?' he demanded grimly.

'It's Christmas Day,' Lisa wept.

'Christmas Day.' He repeated the words as though he had never heard them before. 'Where would you have been spending it if your car hadn't run out of petrol?' he asked her. 'Where were you going?'

'Home to London, to my flat,' Lisa told him wearily. Despite the fact that at some point, without her being aware of it, he had obviously noticed that she was shivering and had turned the heater on full, she still felt frighteningly cold.

'My parents are both working away in Japan so I can't go to them, and my friends have made other plans. I could have gone with them, but…'

'But you chose to subject yourself to Henry's mother's inspection instead,' he taunted her unkindly.

'Henry and I were planning to get engaged,' Lisa fought back angrily. 'Of course he wanted me to meet his parents, his family. There was no question of there being any "inspection".'

'No? Then why the urgent necessity for a new wardrobe?'

Lisa flushed defensively.

'I just wanted to make a good impression on them, that's all,' she muttered.

'Well, you certainly did that all right,' he mocked her wryly. 'Especially—'

'I would have done if it hadn't been for your interference,' she interrupted him hotly. 'You had no right to imply that you and I had been…that those clothes…' She paused, her voice trailing away into silence as she saw the way he lifted one eyebrow and glanced unkindly at her.

'I spoke nothing but the truth. Those clothes were bought by my cousin for his girlfriend—his lover…'

'It might have been the truth, but you twisted it so that it seemed…so that it sounded…so that…'

Lisa floundered, her face flushing betrayingly as he invited helpfully, 'So that what?'

'So that people would think that you and I…that you had bought those clothes for me and that you and I were lovers,' she told him fiercely.

'But surely anyone who really knows you…a prospective fiancé, an established lover, for instance…would automatically know that it was impossible for us to be lovers?' he pointed out to her.

'Henry and I are not lovers.'

Lisa bit her lip in vexation. Now what on earth had prompted her to tell him that? It was hardly the sort of thing she would normally discuss with someone who was virtually a stranger.

Again the dark eyebrows rose—both of them this time—his response to her admission almost brutally comprehensive as he asked her crisply, 'You're not? Then what on earth were you doing thinking of getting engaged to him?'

Lisa opened her mouth but the words she wanted to say simply wouldn't come. How could she say them now? How could she tell him, I loved him, when she knew irrevocably and blindingly that it simply wasn't true, that it had possibly and shamingly never been true and that, just as shamingly, she had somehow managed to delude herself that it might be and to convince herself that she and Henry had a future together?

In the end she had to settle for a stiff and totally unconvincing, 'It seemed a good idea at the time. We had a lot in common. We were both ready to settle down, to commit ourselves. To—' She stopped speaking as the sound of his laughter suddenly filled the car, drowning out the sound of her own voice.

He had a very full, deep, rich-bodied and very male laugh, she acknowledged—a very…a very…a very sensual, sexy sort of laugh…if you cared for that sort of thing…and of course she didn't, she reminded herself firmly.

'Why are you laughing?' she demanded angrily, her cheeks flying hot banners of scorching colour as she turned in her seat to glare furiously at him. 'It isn't…there isn't anything to laugh at…'

'No, there isn't,' he agreed soberly. 'You're right… By rights I— How old are you? What century are you living in? "We had a lot in common. We were both ready to settle down…"' he mimicked her. 'Even if that was true, which it quite patently is not—in fact, I doubt I've ever seen a couple more obviously totally unsuited to one another—I have never heard of a less convincing reason for wanting to get married.

'Why haven't you been to bed with him?' he demanded, the unexpectedness of the question shocking her, taking her breath away.

'I don't think that's any of your business,' she told him primly.

'Which one of you was it who didn't want to—you or him?'

Lisa gasped, outraged. 'Not everyone has…has a high sex drive…or wants a…a relationship that's based on…on physical lust,' she told him angrily. 'And just because…'

Whilst they had been talking Oliver had been driving, and now unexpectedly he turned off the main road and in between two stone pillars into what was obviously the drive to a private house—a very long drive, Lisa noted, before turning towards him and demanding, 'What are you doing? Where are you taking me? This isn't a garage.'

'No, it isn't,' he agreed calmly. 'It's my home.'

'Your home? But—'

'Calm down,' Oliver advised her drily. 'Look, it's gone one in the morning, Christmas morning,' he emphasised. 'This isn't London; the nearest large petrol station is on the motorway, nearly thirty miles away, *if* it's open—and personally what I think you need right now more than anything else is a hot bath and a good night's sleep.'

'I want to go home,' Lisa insisted stubbornly.

'Why?' he challenged her brutally, and reminded her, 'You've already said yourself that there's no one there. Look,' he told her, 'since it is Christmas, why don't we declare a cease-fire in our…er…hostilities? Although by choice neither of us might have wanted to spend Christmas together, since we are both on our own and since it's patently obvious that you're in no physical state to go anywhere, never mind drive a car—'

'You're spending Christmas on your own?' Lisa interrupted him, too astonished to hold the question back.

'Yes,' he agreed, explaining, 'I was to have spent it entertaining my cousin and his girlfriend, but since they've made up their quarrel their plans have changed and they flew to the

Caribbean yesterday morning. Like you, I'd left it too late to make alternative plans and so—'

'I can't stay with you,' Lisa protested. She was, she recognised, already starting to shiver as the now stationary car started to cool down, and she was also unpleasantly and weakly aware of how very unappealing the thought of driving all the way back to London actually was—and not just unappealing either, she admitted. She was uncomfortably conscious that Oliver had spoken the truth when he had claimed that she was not physically capable of making the journey at present.

'We're strangers…'

'You've already accepted a lift in my car,' he reminded her drily, adding pithily, 'And besides, where else can you go?'

All at once Lisa gave in. She really didn't have the energy to argue with him, she admitted—she was too cold, too tired, too muzzily aware of how dangerously light-headed and weak she was beginning to feel.

'Very well, then,' she said, adding warningly, 'But only until tomorrow…until I can get some petrol.'

'Only until tomorrow,' he agreed.

CHAPTER FOUR

'YOU LIVE HERE ALL ALONE?' Lisa questioned Oliver, breaking into his conversation as she curled up in one corner of the vast, deep sofa where he had taken her and told her sternly she was to remain until he returned with a hot drink for her.

'Yes,' he said. 'I prefer it that way. A gardener comes twice a week and his wife does the cleaning for me, but other than that—'

'But it's such a big house. Don't you…?'

'Don't I what?' Oliver challenged her. 'Don't I feel lonely?' He shook his head. 'Not really. I was an only child. My mother died when I was in my teens and my father was away a lot on business. I'm used to being on my own. In fact I prefer it in many ways. Other people's company, their presence in one's life isn't always a pleasure—especially not when one has to become responsible for their emotional and financial welfare.'

Lisa guessed that he was referring obliquely to his cousin, and she sensed that he was, by nature, the kind of man who would always naturally assume responsibility for others, even if that responsibility was slightly irritably cynical rather than humanely compassionate. It also probably explained why he wasn't married. He was by nature a loner—a man, she suspected, who enjoyed women's company but who did not want to burden himself with a wife or children.

And yet a house like this cried out for children. It had that kind of ambience about it, that kind of warmth; it was a real family home for all its obviously priceless antiques. It had a lived-in, welcoming feel to it, Lisa acknowledged—a sense of having been well used and well loved, a slightly worn air which, to her, gave it a richness that far surpassed the sterile, elegant perfection of a house like Henry's parents'.

It didn't surprise Lisa to learn that the house had been in Oliver's family for several generations but what did surprise her was how at ease, how at home she actually felt here, how unexpectedly easy it was to talk to Oliver after he had returned from the kitchen with a huge mug of piping-hot chocolate which he insisted she drink, virtually standing over her until she had done so.

She had suspected from the taste of it that something very much more alcoholic than mere milk had been added to it, but by that stage she had been so grateful for the warmth of her comfortable niche in the deep sofa, so drowsily content and relaxed that there hadn't seemed to be any point in mentioning it, never mind protesting about it.

Now, as she yawned sleepily, blinking owlishly, her forehead pleating in a muzzy frown as she tried to focus on the fireplace and discovered that she couldn't, she was vaguely aware of Oliver getting up from his own chair and coming over to her, leaning down towards her as he firmly relieved her of the now empty mug.

'Bath for you, and then bed, I think,' he told her firmly, sounding so much as her father had when she had been a little girl that Lisa turned her head to look at him.

She hadn't realised that he was quite so close to her, nor that his grey eyes had a darker outer rim to them and were not flat, dead grey at all but rather a mystical mingling of so many silvers and pewters that she caught her breath a little at the male beauty of them.

'You've got beautiful eyes,' she heard herself telling him

in a soft, slightly slurred…almost sexy voice that she barely recognised as her own.

She was unaware that her own eyes were registering the shock of what she had said as Oliver responded gravely, 'Thank you.'

She was, she recognised, still holding onto her mug, even though his own fingers were now wrapped securely around it—so securely in fact that they were actually touching her own.

Some of that molten silver heat from his eyes must have somehow entered his skin, his blood, she decided dizzily. There could be no other reason for those tiny, darting, fiery sensations of heat that she could feel where her own flesh rested against his.

'So are yours…'

'So are yours'? Uncomprehendingly, Lisa looked at him and watched as he smiled a slow, curling, sensual smile that made her heart soar and turn over and do a bellyflop that left her as shocked and winded as though her whole body had actually fielded a blow.

'Your eyes,' Oliver told her softly. 'Your eyes are beautiful too. Do you always keep them open when you kiss?'

'Why?' Lisa heard herself croak shakily. 'Do you?'

As she spoke her glance was already drifting down to his mouth, as though drawn there by some potent force that she couldn't control.

'That depends,' Oliver was drawling, 'on who I'm kissing…'

He was looking at her mouth now, and a panicky, unfamiliar feeling of mingled excitement and shock kicked into life inside her, bringing with it some much needed sobering sanity, bringing her back to reality.

Lisa gulped and turned her head away, quickly withdrawing her hand from the mug.

'I...I...'

As she fought to find the words to explain away her totally uncharacteristic behaviour and conversation, she was overcome by a sudden fit of sneezing.

Quickly reaching for the box of tissues that Oliver had brought her, she hoped that he would put her flushed complexion down to the fever or the cold that she had obviously caught rather than to her self-conscious embarrassment at what she had said.

What on earth had come over her? She had practically been flirting with him...asking him...inviting him...

Thankfully, Lisa buried her face in another tissue as she sneezed again.

When she had finished, determined to dispel any erroneous ideas that he might have gained from her unguarded and totally foolish comments, she said quickly, 'It must have been wonderful here at Christmas when you were young—your family...this house...'

'Yes, it was,' he agreed, before asking, far too perceptively for Lisa's peace of mind, 'Weren't your childhood Christmases good?'

'Yes, of course they were,' Lisa responded hastily.

'But?' he challenged her.

'My parents travelled a lot with their work. They still do. Whilst I dreamed of traditional Christmases in a house with log fires and a huge tree surrounded by aunts and uncles and cousins, going to church on Christmas morning and doing all the traditional British Christmas things, the reality was normally not roast turkey with all the trimmings but ice cream on an Australian beach or sunshine in Japan.

'My parents did their best, of course. There were always mounds of presents, and they always made sure that we spent Christmas and Boxing Days together, but somehow it just wasn't the same as it would have been if we'd been here...

It's silly of me, really, but I suppose a part of me still is that little girl who—'

She stopped, embarrassed by how much of herself she had inadvertently revealed. It must be whatever it was he had obviously added to her hot chocolate that was making her so loquacious and communicative, she thought. She certainly wasn't normally so open or confiding with people she barely knew, although in some odd way it felt as though she had actually known Oliver for a very long time.

She was still frowning over this absurdity when he handed her a glass of amber liquid that he had just poured.

'Drink it,' he told her when she looked at it doubtfully. 'It's pure malt whisky and the best antidote for a heavy cold that I know.'

Reluctantly, Lisa took the glass he handed her. Her head was already swimming slightly, and she felt that the last thing she needed was any more alcohol, but her father was also a great believer in a hot toddy as a cure for colds and so hesitantly she began to sip the tawny golden liquid, closing her eyes as it slid smoothly down her throat, spreading the most delicious sense of beatific warmth throughout her body.

There was something so comforting, so safe, so…so pleasurable about being curled up cosily here in this house…with this man… With this man? What did that mean? Where had that thought come from?

Anxiously Lisa opened her eyes and started to sit up.

'Was that why you wanted to marry Henry, because you thought he could provide you with the traditional lifestyle you felt you'd missed out on?' she heard Oliver asking her.

'Yes…yes, I suppose it was,' she agreed huskily, caught too off guard to think of prevaricating or avoiding the question, and then flushing slightly as she saw the way Oliver was looking at her.

'It would have been a good marriage,' she defended herself.

'We both wanted the same things…' As she saw the way his eyebrows rose, she amended herself shakily, 'Well, I thought that we did.'

'I've heard of some odd reasons for getting married,' she heard Oliver telling her drily, 'but marrying someone because you think he'll provide you with a traditional Christmas has to be the oddest…'

'I wasn't marrying him for that—' Lisa began indignantly, stopping when another volley of sneezing mercifully prevented her from having to make any further response or explanation.

'Come on,' Oliver told her. 'I think it's time you were in bed.'

The whisky that she had drunk was even more potent than she had realised, Lisa acknowledged as Oliver led the way back into the warm, panelled entrance hall and up the stairs.

Just where the stairs started to return towards the galleried landing, Lisa paused to study two large oil paintings hung side by side.

'My grandparents,' Oliver explained, adding informatively, 'My grandfather commissioned the artist to paint them as a first wedding-anniversary present for my grandmother.'

'You look very like him,' Lisa told him. And it was the truth, only the man in the portrait somehow looked less acerbic and much happier than Oliver—much happier and obviously very much in love with his young wife. In the portrait his face was turned slightly towards her matching portrait, so that for a moment it seemed as though the two of them were actually looking at one another.

'It's this way,' Oliver told Lisa, touching her briefly on her arm as he directed her across the landing and towards one of the bedrooms.

'Since my cousin Piers and his girlfriend were supposed to

be spending Christmas here a room had already been made up for them and you may as well sleep there.' As he spoke he pushed open one of the seven wooden doors leading off the landing. Lisa blinked dizzily as she stepped inside the room.

It seemed huge—almost as large, she was sure, as the entire floor space of her own small flat. It was so large, in fact, that in addition to the high, king-sized bed there was also a desk and chair and a small two-seater sofa drawn up close to the open fireplace.

'The bathroom's through that door,' Oliver told her, indicating one of a pair of doors set into the wall. 'The other door opens into a walk-in wardrobe.'

A walk-in wardrobe. Lisa blinked owlishly before reminding him, 'Well, that's something I shan't be needing.' When he frowned she explained, 'I don't have any other clothes with me. The others are the ones I—'

'Hurled at me in a fit of temper,' Oliver finished for her.

She had started to shiver again, Lisa noticed, hugging her arms around herself despite the warmth of the bedroom, with its soft fitted carpet and heavy damask curtains.

That whisky really had gone to her head, she acknowledged as a wave of dizziness swept over her, making her sway and reach out instinctively for the nearest solid object to cling onto—the nearest solid object being Oliver himself.

As he detached her hand from his arm she looked up at him muzzily, only to gasp in startled surprise as she was suddenly swung very firmly up into his arms.

'What…what are you doing?' she managed to stammer as he strode towards the bed, carrying her.

'Saving us both a lot of time,' he told her drily as he deposited her with unexpected gentleness on the mattress before asking her, 'Can you manage to get undressed or…?'

'Yes, of course I can,' Lisa responded in a flurry of mingled indignation and flushed self-consciousness, adding defensively, 'I…I just felt a little bit dizzy, that's all…I'm all right now…'

He didn't look totally convinced, and Lisa discovered that she was holding her breath as she watched him walk towards the bedroom door, unable to expel it until she was sure that he had walked through it and closed it behind him.

He really was the most extraordinary man, she decided ten minutes later as she lay in a huge bath of heavenly, deep hot water.

At Henry's parents' house both baths and hot water had been rationed and now it was sheer bliss to ease her aching limbs into the soothing heat, even if something about the steamy atmosphere of the bathroom did somehow seem to increase the dizzying effect that the whisky had had on her system. She felt, she recognised when she eventually reluctantly climbed out of the bath and wrapped herself in one of the huge, warm, fluffy towels on the heated rail, not just physically affected by the alcohol but mentally and emotionally affected by it as well, as though she was on some sort of slightly euphoric high, free of the burden of her normal, cautious, self-imposed restraints.

Shaking her head, she towelled herself dry, remembering only when she had finished that she had no night-clothes.

Shrugging fatalistically, she wrapped herself in another towel instead and padded towards the bed, discarding it as she climbed into the bed's welcoming warmth.

The bedlinen was cotton and deliciously soft against her skin. It smelled faintly of lavender. She breathed in the scent blissfully as she closed her eyes. After the austere regime of Henry's parents' home this was luxury indeed.

She was just on the point of falling asleep when she heard the bedroom door open. In the half-light from the landing she could see Oliver walking towards the bed carrying something.

As he reached the bed she struggled to sit up.

'I've brought you a hot-water bottle,' he told her. 'Just in case you get cold during the night.'

His thoughtfulness surprised her. He was the last person she would have expected to show such consideration, such concern.

Tears filled her eyes as she took it from him, and on some impulse, which when she later tried to rationalise it she could only put down to the effects of the whisky on her system, she reached out and lifted her face towards his, kissing him.

He must have moved, done something…turned his head, because she had never intended to kiss him so intimately, only to brush her lips against his cheek in a small gesture of gratitude for his care of her. She had certainly never planned to do anything so bold as kiss him on the lips, but oddly, even though her brain had registered her error, her body seemed to be having trouble responding to its frantic message to remove her mouth from the male one which confusingly, instead of withdrawing from her touch, seemed to be not merely accepting it but actually actively…

Lisa swallowed, panicked, swallowed again and jerked her head back, only to find that somehow or other Oliver's hand was resting on her nape, preventing her from doing anything other than lift her lips a mere breath away from his.

'If that's the way you kissed Henry, I'm not surprised the two of you never went to bed together,' she heard him telling her sardonically. 'If you want to kiss a man you should do it properly,' he added reprovingly, and then before she could explain or even object he had closed the small distance between them and his mouth was back on hers, only this time it wasn't merely resting there against her unintended caress but slowly moving on hers, slowly caressing hers, slowly and then not so slowly arousing her, so that…

It must be the drink, Lisa decided giddily. There could be no other reason why she was virtually clinging to Oliver with both her hands, straining towards him almost as though there was nothing she wanted more than the feel of his mouth against her own.

It *had* to be the drink. There could be no other explanation for the way her lips were parting, positively inviting the masterful male thrust of his tongue. And it had to be the drink as well that was causing her to make those small, keening, soft sounds of pleasure as their tongues meshed.

And then abruptly and shockingly erotically Oliver's mouth hardened on her own, so that it was no longer possible for her to deceive herself that what they were sharing was simply a kiss of polite gratitude. No longer possible at all, especially when the rest of her body was suddenly, urgently waking up to the fact that it actively liked what Oliver was doing and that in fact it would very much like to prolong the sensual, drugging pleasure of the way his mouth was moving on hers and, if at all possible, to feel it moving not just on her mouth but on her…

Shocked by her own reactions, Lisa sobered up enough to push Oliver away, her eyes over-bright and her mouth trembling—not, she admitted inwardly, because he had kissed her, but because he had stopped doing it.

'I never meant that to happen,' she told him huskily, anxious to make sure that he understood that even though she might have responded to him she had not deliberately set out to encourage such intimacy between them.

'I just wanted to say thank you for—'

'For making Henry think you're having an affair with me,' he mocked her as he sat back from her. 'Go to sleep,' he advised her, adding softly, 'unless you want me to take up the invitation these have been offering me…' As he spoke he reached out and very lightly touched one of her exposed breasts.

The bedclothes must have slipped down whilst he'd been kissing her, revealing her body to him, even though she herself hadn't realised it, Lisa recognised. And they hadn't just revealed her body, either, she admitted as her face flushed to a pink as deep as that of her tight, hard nipples.

Quickly she pulled the bedclothes up over herself, clutching them defensively in front of her, her face still flushed, and flushing even deeper as she saw the fleeting but very comprehensive and male glance that Oliver gave her now fully covered body.

'Forget about Henry,' he advised her as he turned to leave. 'You're better off without him.'

He had gone before Lisa could think of anything to say—which in the circumstances was probably just as well, she decided as she settled back into the warmth of the bed. After all, what was there she possibly could have said? Her body grew hot as she remembered the way he had kissed her, her toes curling protestingly as she fought down the memory of her own far from reluctant reaction.

No wonder there had been that male gleam of sensual triumph in his eyes as he'd looked at her body—a look which had told her quite plainly that he enjoyed the knowledge that he had been responsible for that unmistakable sexual arousal of her body—his touch…his kiss…*him*.

It had been an accident, that was all, Lisa reassured herself. A fluke, an unfortunate sequence of events which, of course, would never be repeated. Her toes had relaxed but there was a worrying sensual ache deep within her body—a sense of…of deprivation and yearning which she tried very firmly to ignore as she closed her eyes and told herself sternly to go to sleep.

CHAPTER FIVE

LISA OPENED HER EYES, confused by her unfamiliar surroundings, until the events of the previous evening came rushing back.

Some of those events were quite definitely ones that she did not want to dwell on and which had to be pushed very firmly back where they belonged—in a sealed box marked 'very dangerous'. And some of those events, and in particular the ones involving that unexpectedly passionate kiss she had shared with Oliver, were, quite simply, far too potentially explosive to be touched at all.

Instead she focused on her surroundings, her eyes widening in disbelief as she looked towards the fireplace. She rubbed them and then studied it again. No, they were not deceiving her; there was quite definitely a long woollen stocking hanging from the fireplace—a long woollen stocking bulging with all sorts of odd shapes, with a notice pinned to it reading, 'Open me.'

Her curiosity overcoming her natural caution, Lisa hopped out of bed and hurried towards the fireplace, removed the stocking and then returned to the sanctuary of her bed with it.

As she turned it upside down on the coverlet to dislodge its contents, a huge smile curled her mouth, her eyes dancing with a mixture of almost childlike disbelief and a rather more adult amusement.

Wrapped in coloured tissue-paper, a dozen or more small

objects lay on the bed around her. Some of them she could recognise without unwrapping them: the two tangerines, the nuts, the apple…

There could, of course, only be one person who had done this; the identity of her unexpected Father Christmas could not be in doubt, but his motivation was.

Her fingers trembled slightly as she removed the wrapping from what turned out to be a tube of thick white paper. As she unrolled it she began to frown, her frown turning to a soft gasp as she read what had been written on it in impressive copperplate handwriting.

In this year of our Sovereign Queen Elizabeth it is hereby agreed that there shall be a formal truce and a cessation of hostilities between Mistress Lisa and Oliver Esquire in order that the two aforenamed may celebrate the Festival of Christmas in true Christian spirit.

Beneath the space that he had left for her to sign her own name Oliver had signed his.

Lisa couldn't help it. She started to laugh softly, her laugh turning into a husky cough and a fit of sneezes that told her that she had not, as she had first hoped, escaped the heavy cold Oliver had warned likely the previous evening.

At least, though, her head was clear this morning, she told herself severely as she scrabbled around amongst the other packages on the bed, guessing that somewhere amongst them there must be a pen for her to sign their truce.

It touched her to think of Oliver going to so much trouble on her behalf. If only Henry had been half as thoughtful… But Henry would never have done anything like this. Henry would never have kissed her the way Oliver had done last night. Henry would never…

Her fingers started to tremble as she finally found the parcel containing the pen.

It hurt to think that the future that she had believed she and Henry could have together had been nothing more than a chimera…as childish in its way as her daydreams of a perfect Christmas which she had revealed to Oliver last night, under the effects and influence of his malt whisky.

Her eyes misted slightly with fresh tears, but they were not, this time, caused by the knowledge that she had made a mistake in believing that she and Henry had a good relationship.

After she had signed the truce she noticed that her signature was slightly wobbly and off balance—a reflection of the way she herself had felt ever since Oliver had thrust his way into her life, demanding the return of his cousin's girlfriend's clothes.

Thinking of clothes reminded Lisa that she had nothing to wear other than the things she had discarded the previous evening. Hardly the kind of outfit she had planned to spend Christmas Day in, she acknowledged as she mourned the loss of the simply cut cream wool dress that she had flung at Oliver's feet before her departure from Henry's parents' house.

Still, clothes did not make Christmas, she told herself, and neither did Christmas stockings—but they certainly went a long way to help, she admitted, a rueful smile curling her mouth as she pictured Oliver painstakingly wrapping the small traditional gifts which for generations children had delighted to find waiting for them on Christmas morning.

It was a pity that after such an unexpected and pleasurable start the rest of her Christmas looked so unappealingly bleak. She wasn't looking forward to her return to her empty flat. She glanced at her watch. She had slept much later than usual and it was already nine o'clock—time for her to get up and dressed if she was going to be able to retrieve her car, fill it with petrol and make her return journey to London before dark.

She had just put one foot on the floor when she heard Oliver knocking on the bedroom door. Hastily she put her foot back under the bedclothes and made sure that the latter were secured firmly around her naked body as she called out to Oliver to come in. She didn't want there to be any repeat of last night's still blush-inducing *faux pas* of not realising that her breasts were clearly on view.

The sight of him carrying a tea-tray complete with a china teapot, two cups and a plate of wholemeal toast made her eyes widen slightly.

'So you found it, then. How are you feeling?' he asked her as he placed the tray on the empty half of her bed, half smiling as he saw the clutter of small objects still surrounding her and the evidence of her excitement as she had unwrapped them in the small, shredded pieces of paper torn by her impatient fingers.

'Much better,' Lisa assured him. 'Just as soon as I can get my car sorted out I should be off your hands and on my way back to London. I still haven't thanked you properly for what you did,' she added, half-shyly. Last night the intimacy between them had seemed so natural that she hadn't even questioned it. This morning she was acutely conscious of the fact that he was, after all, a man she barely knew.

His soft, 'Oh, I wouldn't say that,' as he looked directly at her mouth made her flush, but there was more amusement in his eyes than any kind of sexual threat, she acknowledged.

'I haven't thanked you for the stocking either,' she hurried on. 'That was… I… You must think me very childish to want… I'm not used to drinking, and your whisky… I've signed this, by the way.' She tried to excuse herself, diving amongst her spoils to produce the now rerolled truce.

As she did so she suddenly started to sneeze, and had to reach out for the box of tissues beside the bed.

'I thought you said you were feeling all right,' Oliver reminded her sardonically.

'I am,' Lisa defended herself, but now that she was fully awake she had to acknowledge that her throat felt uncomfortably raw and her head ached slightly, whilst yet another volley of sneezes threatened to disprove her claim to good health.

'You're full of a cold,' Oliver corrected her, 'and in no fit state to drive back to London—even if we could arrange for someone to collect your car.'

'But I have to… I must…' Lisa protested.

'Why…in case Henry calls?'

'No,' Lisa denied vehemently, her face flushing again as she suddenly realised how little thought she had actually given to Henry and the end of their romance.

But it was obvious that Oliver had mistaken the cause of her hot face because he gave her an ironic look and told her, 'It will never work. He'll always be tied to his mother's apron strings and you'll always have to take second place to her…

'It's half past nine now,' he told her, changing the subject. 'The village is only ten minutes away by car and we've got time to make it for morning service. I've put the turkey in the oven but it won't be ready until around three…'

Lisa gaped at him.

'But I can't stay here,' she protested.

'Why not?' he asked her calmly. 'What reason have you to go? You've already said that you'll be alone in your flat, and since I'll be alone up here—if you discount a fifteen-pound turkey and enough food to feed the pair of us several times over—it makes sense for you to stay…'

'You want me to stay?' Lisa asked him, astonished. 'But…'

'It will be a hell of a lot easier having you to stay than

trying to find a reputable mechanic to sort out and make arrangements for a garage to collect your car, check it over and refuel it. And having one guest instead of two is hardly going to cause me any hardship…' He gave a small shrug.

It was a tempting prospect, Lisa knew. If she was honest with herself she hadn't been looking forward to returning to her empty flat, and even though she and Oliver were virtually strangers there was something about him that… Severely she gave herself a small mental shake.

All right, so maybe last night her body *had* reacted to him in a way that it had certainly never reacted to Henry… Maybe when he had kissed her she *had* felt a certain…need…a response…but that had only been the effect of the whisky… nothing more.

She opened her mouth to decline his invitation, to do the sensible thing and tell him firmly that she had to return home, and instead, to her chagrin, heard herself saying in a small voice, 'Could we really go to church…?' As she realised what she was saying she shook her head, telling him hastily, 'Oh, no, I can't… I haven't anything to wear. My clothes…your cousin's girlfriend's clothes…'

'Are hanging in the closet,' Oliver informed her wryly.

Lisa looked at him. 'What? But they can't be… I left them at Henry's parents'.'

'I didn't,' Oliver informed her succinctly.

'But…but you wanted to give them back to Emma.'

'Originally, yes, but only because Piers was so convinced that the moment she knew what he had done she'd walk out again. However, it transpires that she's off Armani and onto Versace so Piers was allowed to make his peace with her by taking her out and buying her a new wardrobe.'

'So you went to all that trouble for nothing,' Lisa sympathised, knowing how she would have felt in his shoes.

The look he gave her in response made her heart start to

beat rather too fast, and for some reason she found it impossible to hold his gaze and had to look quickly away from him.

His slightly hoarse, 'You'd have been wasted on a man like Henry,' made her want to curl her toes in much the same way as his kiss had done last night, and the small shiver that touched her skin had nothing to do with any drop in temperature.

'I'll meet you downstairs in half an hour,' Oliver was saying to her as he moved away from the bed.

Silently, Lisa nodded her agreement. What had she done, committing herself to spend Christmas with him? She gave a small, fatalistic shrug. It was too late to worry about the wisdom of her impulsive decision now.

Thirty-five minutes later, having nervously studied her reflection in the bedroom mirror for a good two minutes, Lisa walked hesitantly onto the landing.

The cream wool dress looked every bit as good on as she had remembered; the cashmere coat would keep her warm in church.

Her hair, freshly washed and dried, shone silkily, and as yet the only physical sign of her cold was a slight pinky tinge to her nose, easily disguised with foundation.

At the head of the stairs she paused, and then determinedly started to descend, coming to an abrupt halt as she reached the turn in the stairs that looked down on the hallway below.

In the middle of the large room, dominating it, stood the largest and most wondrous Christmas tree that Lisa had ever seen.

She gazed at it in rapt awe, unaware that the shine of pleasure in her eyes rivalled that of the myriad decorations fastened to the tree.

As excited as any child, she positively ran down the remaining stairs and into the hall.

'How on earth…?' she began as she stood and marvelled at the tree, shaking her head as she was unable to find the words to convey her feelings.

'I take it you approve,' she heard Oliver saying wryly beside her.

'Yes. Yes. It's wonderful,' she breathed, without taking her eyes off it to turn and look at him. 'But when… How…?'

'Well, I'm afraid I can't claim to have gone out last night and cut it down. It had actually been delivered yesterday. Piers and I were supposed to be putting it up… It's a bit of a family tradition. He and I both used to spend Christmas here as children with our grandparents, and it was our job to "do the tree". It's a tradition we've kept up ever since, although this year…

'I brought it in last night after you'd gone to bed. Mrs Green had already brought the decorations down from the attic, so it was just a matter of hanging them up.'

'Just a matter…' Lisa's eyebrows rose slightly as she studied the rows and rows of tiny lights, the beautiful and, she was nearly sure, very valuable antique baubles combined with much newer but equally attractive modern ones.

'It must have taken you hours,' she objected.

Oliver shrugged.

'Not really.'

'It's beautiful,' she told him, her throat suddenly closing with emotion. He hadn't done it for her, of course. He had already told her that it was a family tradition, something he and his cousin did together. But, even so, to come down and find it there after confiding in him last night how much she longed for a traditional family Christmas…suddenly seemed a good omen for her decision to stay on with him.

'It hasn't got a fairy,' she told him, hoping he wouldn't notice the idiotic emotional thickening in her voice.

As he glanced towards the top of the tree Oliver shook his

head and told her, 'Our fairy is a star, and it's normally the responsibility of the woman of the house to put it on the tree, so I left it—'

'You want me to do it?' Fresh emotion swept her. 'But I'm not… I don't belong here,' she reminded him.

'But you are a woman,' he told her softly, and there was something in the way he said the words, something in the way he looked at her that warned Lisa that the kiss they had shared last night wasn't something he had forgotten.

'We'll have to leave it for now, though,' he told her. 'Otherwise we'll be late for church.'

It had been a cold night, and a heavy frost still lay over the countryside, lending it a magical quality of silvered stillness that made Lisa catch her breath in pleasure.

The village, as Oliver had said, was ten minutes' drive away—a collection of small stone houses huddled together on one side of the river and reached by a narrow stone bridge.

The church was at the furthest end of the village and set slightly apart from it, small and weathered and so old that it looked almost as though it had grown out of the craggy landscape around it.

The bells were ringing as Oliver parked the car and then led her towards the narrow lych-gate and along the stone-flagged path through a graveyard so peaceful that there was no sense of pain or sorrow about it.

Just inside the church, the vicar was waiting.

The church was already almost full, but when Lisa would have slipped into one of the rear pews Oliver touched her arm and directed her to one at the front. A family pew, Lisa recognised, half in awe and half in envy.

The service was short and simple, the carols traditional, the crib quite obviously decorated by very young hands, and yet to Lisa the whole experience was more movingly intense than if they had been in one of the world's grandest cathedrals.

Afterwards the vicar was waiting to shake hands and exchange a few words with all his congregation, including them, and as they ambled back to where Oliver had parked the car the final magical seal of wonderment was put on the day when the first flakes of the forecast snow started to fall.

'I don't believe it,' Lisa whispered breathlessly as Oliver unlocked the car doors. 'I just don't believe it.'

As she whirled round, her whole face alight, Oliver laughed. The sound, so spontaneous and warmly masculine, had the oddest effect on Lisa's body. Her heart seemed to flip helplessly, her breathing quickening, her gaze drawn unerringly to Oliver's mouth.

She shouldn't be feeling like this. It wasn't fair and it certainly wasn't sensible. They barely knew one another. Yesterday they had been enemies, and but for an odd quirk of fate they still would be today.

Shakily she walked towards the car, the still falling snowflakes forgotten as she tried to come to terms with what was happening to her.

What exactly *was* happening to her? Something she didn't want to give a name to... Not yet... Perhaps not ever. She shivered as she pulled on her seat belt.

'Cold?' Oliver questioned her, frowning slightly.

Lisa shook her head, refusing to give in to the temptation to look at him, to check and see whether, if she did, she would feel that heart-jolting surge of feminine awareness and arousal that she had just experienced in the car park for a second time.

'Stop thinking about him,' she heard Oliver say harshly to her as she turned away from him and stared out of the window. It took her several seconds to realise that he thought that Henry was the reason for her sudden silence. Perhaps it was just as well he did think that, she decided—for both their sakes.

Through the now drifting heavy snowflakes Lisa could see how quickly they had obscured the previously greeny-brown landscape, transforming it into a winter wonderland of breathtaking Christmas-card white.

Coming on top of the poignant simplicity of a church service which to Lisa, as an outsider, had somehow symbolised all she had always felt was missing from her own Christmases—a sense of community, of sharing…of involvement and belonging, of permanence going from one generation to the next—the sight of the falling snow brought an ache to her throat and the quick silvery shimmer of unexpected tears to her eyes.

Ashamed of her own emotionalism, she ducked her head, searching in her bag for a tissue, hoping to disguise her tears as a symptom of her cold. But Oliver was obviously too astute to be deceived by such a strategy and demanded brusquely, 'What is it? What's wrong?' adding curtly, 'You're wasting your tears on Henry; he isn't—'

'I'm not crying because of Henry,' Lisa denied. Did he really think that she was so lacking in self-esteem and self-preservation that she couldn't see for herself what a lucky escape she had had, if not from Henry then very definitely from Henry's mother?

'No? Then what are these?' Oliver demanded tauntingly, reaching out before she could stop him to rub the hard pad of his thumb beneath one eye and show her the dampness clinging to his skin. 'Scotch mist?'

'I didn't say I wasn't crying,' Lisa defended herself. 'Just that it wasn't because of… It's not because of Henry…'

'Then why?' Oliver challenged, obviously not believing her.

'Because of this,' Lisa told him simply, gesturing towards the scene outside the car window. 'And the church…'

She could see from the look he was giving her that he didn't really believe her, and because for some reason it had suddenly become very important that he did she took a deep breath and told him quickly, 'It's just so beautiful… The whole thing… the weather, the church service…'

As she felt him looking at her she turned her head to meet his eyes. She shook her head, not wanting to go on, feeling that she had perhaps said too much already, been too openly emotional. Men, in her experience, found it rather discomforting when women expressed their emotions. Henry certainly had.

If Oliver was discomforted by what she had said, though, he certainly wasn't showing it; in fact he wasn't showing any kind of reaction that she could identify at all. He had dropped his eyelids slightly over his eyes and turned his face away from her, ostensibly to concentrate on his driving, making it impossible for her to read his expression at all, his only comment, as he brought the car to a halt outside the house, a cautionary, 'Be careful you don't slip when you get out.'

'Be careful you don't slip…!' Just how old did he think she was? Lisa wondered wryly as she got out of the car, tilting up her face towards the still falling snowflakes and breathing in the clean, sharp air, a blissful expression on her face as she studied her surroundings, happiness bubbling up inside her.

'I still can't believe this…that it's actually snowing…on Christmas Day… Do you realise that this is my very first white Christmas?' As she whispered the words in awed delight she closed her eyes, took a deep breath of snow-scented air and promptly did what Oliver had warned her not to do and lost her footing.

Her startled cry was arrested almost before it had begun as Oliver reached out and caught hold of her, his strong hands gripping her waist, holding her tightly, safely…

Holding her closely, she recognised as her heart started

to pound with unfamiliar excitement and her breath caught in her throat. Not out of shock, Lisa acknowledged, her face flushing as she realised just what it was that was causing her heart and pulse-rate to go into overdrive, and she prayed that Oliver wouldn't be equally quick to recognise that her shallow breathing and sudden tension had nothing to do with the shock of her near fall and everything to do with his proximity.

Why was this happening to her? she wondered dizzily. She didn't even like the man and he certainly didn't like her—even if he *had* offered her a roof over her head for Christmas.

He was standing close enough for her to smell the clean man scent of his skin—or was it just that for some extraordinary reason she was acutely sensitive to the scent and heat of him?

Her legs started to tremble—in fact, her whole body was trembling.

'It's all right,' she heard Oliver saying calmly to her. 'I've got you…'

'Yes,' Lisa heard herself responding, her own voice unfamiliarly soft and husky, making the simple affirmation sound something much more sensual and inviting. Without having had the remotest intention of doing any such thing—it simply wasn't the kind of thing she did, ever—Lisa found that she was looking at Oliver's mouth, and that her gaze, having focused on it for far, far too long, was somehow drawn even more betrayingly to his eyes.

Her breath caught in her throat as she saw the way he was looking back at her, his head already lowering towards hers—as well it might do after the sensually open invitation that she had just given him.

But instead of avoiding what she knew was going to happen, instead of moving away from him, which she could quite easily have done, she simply stood there waiting, with her lips softly parted, her gaze fixed on the downward descent of his head and his mouth, her heart thudding frantically against her chest wall—not in case he kissed her, she acknowledged in semi-shock, but rather in case he didn't.

But of course he did. Slowly and deliberately at first, exploring the shape and feel of her mouth, shifting his weight slightly so that instead of that small but oh, so safe distance between them and the firm grip of his hands on her waist supporting her, it was the equally firm but oh, so much more sensual strength of his body that held her up as his arms closed round her, holding her in an embrace not as intimate as that of a lover but still intimate enough to make her powerfully aware of the fact that he was a man.

Lisa had forgotten that a man's kiss could be like this—slow, thorough and so sensually inventive and promising as he hinted at all the pleasures that there could be to come. And yet it wasn't a kiss of passion or demand—not yet—and Lisa was hazily aware that the slow stroke of his tongue against her lips was more sensually threatening to her self-control than to his, and that she was the one who was having to struggle to pull herself back from the verge of a far more dangerous kind of arousal when he finally lifted his mouth from hers.

'What was that for?' she asked stupidly as she tried to drag her gaze away from his eyes.

'No reason,' he told her in response. But as she started to turn her head away, expecting him to release her, he lifted one hand to her face, cupping the side of her jaw with warm, strong fingers, holding her captive as he told her softly, 'But this is.'

And he was kissing her again, but this time the passion that she had sensed was missing in his first kiss was clearly betrayed in the way his mouth hardened over hers, the way his body hardened against hers, his tongue probing the softness of her mouth as she totally abandoned her normal, cautious behaviour and responded to him with every single one of her aroused senses—every single one.

Her arms, without her knowing quite how it had happened, were wrapped tightly around him, holding him close, her fingertips absorbing the feel of his body, its warmth, its hardness, its sheer maleness; her eyes opened in dazed arousal as she looked up into his, her ears intensely attuned to the sound of his breathing and his heartbeat and their tell-tale quickened rate, the scent of him reaching her with every breath she took, and the taste of him. She closed her eyes and then opened them again as she heard him whispering against her mouth, 'Happy Christmas.'

'Happy Christmas'! Lisa came back to earth with a jolt. Of course. Hot colour flooded her face as she realised just how close she had been to making a complete fool of herself.

He hadn't kissed her because he had wanted her, because he had been overwhelmed by desire for her. He had kissed her because it was Christmas, and if that second kiss had been a good deal more intense than their extremely short-lived acquaintanceship really merited then that was probably her fault for… For what? For responding too intensely to him the first time?

'Happy Christmas!' she managed to respond as she hurriedly stepped back from him and turned towards the house.

As Oliver opened the door for her Lisa could smell the rich scent of the roasting turkey mingling with the fresh crispness of the tree.

'The turkey smells good,' she told him, shakily struggling to appear calm and unaffected by his kiss, sniffing the richly scented air. The kiss that they had so recently exchanged might never have been, judging from the way he was behaving towards her now, and she told herself firmly that it was probably best if she pretended that it hadn't too.

Oliver could never play a permanent role in her life, and this unfamiliar and dangerous intensity of physical desire that she had experienced was something she would be far better off without.

'Yes, I'd better go and check on it,' Oliver agreed.

'I'll come and give you a hand,' Lisa offered, adding as she glanced down at her clothes, 'I'd better go and get changed first, though.'

It didn't take her long to remove her coat and the dress she was wearing underneath it, but instead of re-dressing immediately she found that she was standing staring at her underwear-clad body in the mirror, trying to see it as a man might do… A man? Or Oliver?

Angry with herself, she reached into the wardrobe and pulled out the first thing that came to hand, only realising when she had started to put it on that it was the cream trouser suit which had caused so many problems already.

She paused, wondering whether or not to wear something else, and then heard Oliver rapping on the bedroom door and calling out, 'Lisa, are you all right…?'

'Yes, yes. I'm fine… I'm coming now,' she told him quickly, pulling on the jacket and fastening it. Hardly sensible apparel in which to help cook Christmas lunch, but with the sleeves of the jacket pushed back, she thought… And she could always remove the jacket if necessary. So what if the pretty little waistcoat that went underneath it was rather brief? Oliver was hardly likely to notice, was he?

He was waiting for her outside the bedroom door, and caught her off guard by catching hold of her arm and placing his hand on her forehead.

'Mmm…no temperature. Well, that's something, I suppose. Your pulse is very fast, though,' he observed as his hand circled her wrist and he measured her pulse-rate.

Quickly Lisa snatched her wrist away. 'I've just got a cold, that's all,' she told him huskily.

'Just a cold,' he reiterated. 'No broken heart…'

Lisa flashed him a doubtful look, half suspecting him of deliberately mocking her, but unable to make any response, knowing that she would be lying to him if she tried to pretend that she felt anything other than half-ashamed relief at breaking up with Henry.

'You might not want to accept it now, but you didn't really love him,' Oliver told her coolly. 'If you had—'

'You have no right to say that,' Lisa objected suddenly, angry with him—and, more tellingly, with herself, without wanting to analyse or really know why.

'What do you know about love?'

'I know enough about it to recognise it when I see it—and when I don't,' Oliver countered as she fell silent, but Lisa wasn't really listening; she was too caught up in the shock of realising that the pain spearing her, pinning her in helpless, emotional agony where she stood, was caused by the realisation that for all she knew there could have been, could still be a woman in Oliver's life whom he loved.

'Stop thinking about it,' she heard Oliver telling her grimly, her face flushing at the thought that he had so easily read her mind and guessed what she was feeling, until he added, 'You must have seen for yourself that it would never have worked. Henry's mother would never have allowed him to marry you.'

Relief made her expel her breath in a leaky sigh. It had been Henry whom he had warned her to stop thinking about and not him. He had not guessed what she had been thinking or feeling after all.

'I thought we'd agreed a truce,' she reminded him, adding softly, 'I still haven't thanked you properly for everything you've done. Helping—'

'Everything?'

For some reason the way he was looking at her made her feel closer to the shy teenager she had once been than the adult woman she now was.

'I meant…' she began, and then shook her head, knowing that she wouldn't be able to list all the reasons she had to thank him without at some point having to look at him, and knowing that once she did her gaze would be drawn irresistibly to his mouth, and once it was…

'I… That turkey smells wonderful.' She gave in cravenly. 'How long did you say it would be before we could eat?'

She could tell from the wry look he gave her as she glanced his way that he wasn't deceived, but to her relief he didn't push matters, leaving her to follow him instead as he turned back towards the stairs.

CHAPTER SIX

'I NEVER IMAGINED you'd be so domesticated.'

They were both in the large, well-equipped, comfortable kitchen, Lisa mixing the ingredients for the bread sauce whilst Oliver deftly prepared the vegetables, and she knew almost as soon as she had voiced her surprise that it had been the wrong thing to say. But it was too late to recall her impulsive comment because Oliver had stopped what he was doing to look frowningly across at her.

'I'm sorry,' she apologised ruefully. 'I didn't mean to—'

'To sound patronising,' Oliver supplied for her.

Lisa glanced warily at him and then defended herself robustly, telling him, 'Well, when we first met you just didn't seem the type to—'

'The "type".' Oliver pulled her up a second time. 'And what "type" would that be, exactly?'

Oh, dear. He had every right to sound annoyed, Lisa acknowledged.

'I didn't mean it the way it sounded,' she confessed. 'It's just that Henry—'

'Doesn't so much as know how to boil an egg,' Oliver supplied contemptuously for her. 'And that's something to be admired in a man, is it?'

Lisa's face gave her away even before she had protested truthfully, 'No, of course it isn't.'

'The reason Henry chooses to see even the most basically necessary domestic chores such as cooking for himself as beneath his male dignity is because that's the way his mother has brought him up and that's the way she intends him to stay. And woe betide any woman who doesn't spoonfeed her little boy the way she's taught him to expect.'

There was no mistaking the disgust in Oliver's voice as he underlined the weakness of Henry's character, and Lisa knew that there was no real argument that she could put forward in Henry's defence, even if she had wanted to do so.

'It might come as something of a surprise to you,' Oliver continued sardonically, obviously determined to drive home his point, 'but, quite frankly, the majority of the male sex—at least the more emotionally mature section of it—would not take too kindly at having Henry held up to them as a yardstick of what it means to be a man. And neither, for future reference, do most of us relish being classified as a "type".'

'I didn't mean it like that,' Lisa protested. 'It's just that when we first met you seemed so… I could never have imagined you…us…' She was floundering, and badly, she recognised, adding lamely, 'I wasn't comparing you to Henry at all.'

'No?' Oliver challenged her.

'No,' Lisa insisted, not entirely truthfully. She *had* been comparing them, of course, but not, as Oliver fortunately had incorrectly assumed, to his disadvantage. Far from it… She certainly didn't want to have to explain to him that there was something about *him* that was so very male that it made laughable the idea that he should in any way fail to measure up to Henry.

Measure up to him! When it came to exhibiting that certain quality that spelled quite essential maleness there was simply no contest between them. Oliver possessed it, and in abundance, or so it seemed to Lisa, and Henry did not have it at all. She was faintly shocked that she should so clearly recognise this—and not just recognise it, she admitted uneasily. She was quite definitely somehow or other very sensitively aware of it as a woman—too aware of it for her peace of mind.

'I happen to have an orderly mind,' Oliver was telling her, thankfully unaware of what she was thinking, 'and I loathe any unnecessary waste of time. To live in the midst of chaos and disorder seems to be totally counter-productive, and besides...' he gave a small shrug and drained the peeled and washed potatoes, turning away from her as he started to cut them, so that she could not see his expression '...after my mother died and my father and I were on our own, we both had to learn how to look after ourselves.'

Lisa discovered that there was a very large lump in her throat as she pictured the solemn, lonely little boy and his equally lonely father struggling together to master their chores as well as their loss.

'The behavioural habits one learns as a child have a tendency to become deeply ingrained, hence my advice to you that you are well rid of Henry. He will never cease being his mother's spoilt and emotionally immature little boy...' His tasks finished, he turned round and looked directly at her as he added drily, 'And I suspect that you will never cease thinking of Christmas as a specially magical time of year...'

'No, I don't expect I shall,' Lisa admitted, adding honestly, 'But then I don't really want to. I don't suppose I'll ever stop wanting, either, to put down roots, to marry and have children and to give them the stability and permanence I missed as a child,' she confessed, wanting to be as open and honest with him as he had been with her.

'I know a lot of my friends think that I'm rather odd for putting more emphasis on stability and the kind of relationship that focuses more on that than on the romantic and sexual aspects of love—'

'Does there have to be a choice?' Oliver asked her.

Lisa frowned. 'What do you mean?'

'Isn't it possible for there to be romance and good sex between a couple, as well as stability and permanence? I thought the modern woman was determined to have it all. Emotional love, orgasmic sex, a passionately loyal mate, children, career…'

'In theory, yes,' Lisa agreed ruefully. 'But I suppose if I'm honest…I'm perhaps not very highly sexed. So—'

'Who told you that? Henry?'

'No,' she said, stung by the mocking amusement that she could see in his eyes, aware that she had allowed herself to be drawn onto potentially very treacherous ground and that sex was the very last topic she should be discussing with this particular man—especially when her body was suddenly and very dangerously reinforcing the lack of wisdom in her laying claim to a low libido when it was strongly refuting that. Too strongly for her peace of mind. Much, much too strongly.

'I…I've always known it,' she told him hastily, more to convince herself, she suspected, than him.

'Always…?' The way the dark eyebrows rose reminded her of the way he had looked when he had come round to see her and demand the return of Emma's clothes, and that same frisson of danger that she had felt then returned, but this time for a very, very different reason.

'Well, from when I was old enough… When I knew… After…' she began, compelled by the look he was giving her to make some kind of response.

'You mean you convinced yourself that you had a low sex drive because, presumably, that was what your first lover told you,' Oliver challenged her, cutting through her unsuccessful attempts to appear breezily nonchalant about the whole thing.

'It wasn't just because of that,' Lisa defended herself quickly and, she realised uneasily, very betrayingly.

'No?' Oliver's eyebrows rose again. 'I'll take a bet that

there haven't been very many… Two, maybe three at the most, and that, of course, excludes Henry, who—'

'Three…?' Lisa was aghast. 'Certainly not,' she denied vehemently. 'I would never…' Too late she realised what she was doing…what she was saying.

It was one thing for her to feel that, despite the amusement of her peers, she had the sort of nature that would not allow her to feel comfortable about sharing the intimacy of her body with a variety of lovers and that her low sex drive made it feel right that there had only been that one not really too successful experience in her late teens, and it was one thing to feel that she could quite happily remain celibate and wait to re-explore her sexuality until she found a man she felt comfortable enough with to do so, but it was quite another to admit it to someone like Oliver, who, she was pretty sure, would think her views archaic and ridiculous.

'So, there has only been one.' He pounced, immediately and humiliatingly correct. 'Well, for your information, a man who tells a virgin that she's got a low sex drive tends to be doing so to protect his own inadequacy, not hers.'

Her inadequacy! Lisa drew in a sharp breath of panic at the fact that he should dare so accurately and acutely to put her deepest and most intimate secret fears into words, and promptly fought back.

'I'm twenty-four now, not eighteen, and I think I know myself well enough to be able to judge for myself what kind of sex drive I have…'

'You're certainly old enough and, I would suspect, strong-willed enough to tell yourself what kind of sex drive you think it safe to allow yourself to have,' Oliver agreed, staggering her with not just his forthrightness but his incisive astuteness as well.

Pride warred with caution as Lisa was torn between demanding to know exactly what he meant and, more cravenly, avoiding what she suspected could be a highly dangerous confrontation—highly dangerous to her, that was. Oliver, she thought, would thoroughly enjoy dissecting her emotional vulnerabilities and laying them out one by one in front of her.

In the end caution won and, keeping her back to him, she told him wildly, 'I think this bread sauce is just about ready… What else would you like me to do?'

She thought she heard him mutter under his breath, 'Don't tempt me,' before he said far more clearly, 'Since it's Christmas Day I suppose we should really eat in the dining room, although normally I prefer to eat in here. I'll show you where everything is, and if you could sort it all out—silver, crystal, china…'

'Yes…of course,' Lisa agreed hurriedly, finding a cloth to wipe her hands on as she followed him back into the hall.

The dining room was a well-proportioned, warm, panelled room at the rear of the house, comfortably large enough to take a table which, Oliver explained to her, could be extended to seat twelve people.

'It was a wedding present to my grandparents. In those days, of course, twelve was not a particularly large number. My grandmother was one of seven and my grandfather one of five.'

'Oh, it must be wonderful to be part of a large family,' Lisa could not help commenting enviously. 'My parents were both onlys and they only had me.'

'Being an only child does have its advantages,' Oliver told her firmly. 'I'm an only myself, and—'

'But you had the family—aunts, uncles, cousins…'

'Yes,' Oliver agreed.

But he had also lost his mother at a very vulnerable age, Lisa recognised, and to lose someone so close must inevitably have a far more traumatic effect on one's life than the mere absence of a non-existent extended family.

'I can guess what you're thinking,' she told him wryly. 'I just sound pathetically self-absorbed and self-pitying. I know how much both my parents need their work, their art, how important it is to them. It's just that...'

'There have been times when you needed to know that you came first,' Oliver guessed shrewdly. 'There are times when we all feel like that,' he told her. 'When we all need to know that we come first, that we are the most important person in someone else's life... What's wrong?' he asked when he saw the rueful acknowledgement of his perception in Lisa's eyes.

'Nothing,' she said. 'It's just that I can't...that you don't...' She shook her head. 'You seem so self-contained,' was the only thing she could say.

'Do I?' He gave her a wry look. 'Maybe I am now. It wasn't always that way, though. The reason for the breakup of my first teenage romance was that my girlfriend found me too emotionally demanding. She was right as well.'

'You must have loved her an awful lot,' was all she could find to say as she tried to absorb and conceal the unwanted and betraying searing surge of envy that hit her as she listened to him.

'I certainly thought I did,' Oliver agreed drily, 'but the reality was little more than a very intense teenage crush. Still, at least I learned something from the experience.'

What had she been like, the girl Oliver had loved as a teenager? Lisa wondered ten minutes later when he had returned to the kitchen and she was removing silverware and crystal from the cupboards he had shown her.

She found it hard to imagine anyone—*any* woman—rejecting a man like him.

Her hand trembled slightly as she placed one of the heavy crystal wineglasses on the table.

What was the matter with her? she scolded herself. Just because he had kissed her, that didn't mean… It didn't mean anything, and why should she want it to? If she was going to think about any member of the male sex right now she ought to be thinking about Henry. After all, less than twenty-four hours ago she had believed that she was going to marry him.

It unnerved her a little bit to realise how far she had travelled emotionally in such a short space of time. It was hard to imagine now how she could ever have thought that she and Henry were suited—in any way.

'I really don't think I should be drinking any more of this,' Lisa told Oliver solemnly as she raised the glass of rich red wine that he had just refilled to her lips.

They had finished eating fifteen minutes earlier, and at Oliver's insistence Lisa was now curled up cosily in one corner of the deep, comfortable sofa that he had drawn up close to the fire and where she had been ordered to remain whilst he stacked the dishwasher.

The meal had been as good as any Christmas dinner she could ever remember eating and better than most. It had amazed her how easily the conversation had flowed between them, and what had surprised her even more was to discover that he was a very witty raconteur who could make her laugh.

Henry had never made her laugh.

Hastily she took a quick gulp of her wine. It was warm and full-bodied and the perfect accompaniment for the meal they had just enjoyed.

When they had left the table to come and sit down in front of the fire to finish their wine, Oliver had closed the curtains, and now, possessed by a sudden urge to see if it was still snowing, Lisa abandoned her comfortable seat and walked rather unsteadily towards the curtained window.

The wine had been even stronger than she had believed, she admitted. She wasn't drunk—far from it—but she certainly felt rather light-headed and a little giddy.

As she tugged back the curtain she gave a small, soft sigh of delight as she stared through the window.

It was still snowing—thick, whirling-dervish-like, thick white flakes, like those in a child's glass snowstorm. As she looked up into the darkening sky she could see the early evening stars and the thin sickle shape of the moon.

It was her childhood dream of a white Christmas come true. And to think that if she had returned to London as she had originally planned to do she would have missed it! Emotion caught her by the throat.

She dropped the curtain, turning back into the room, stopping as she saw Oliver watching her. She hadn't heard him come back in and unaccountably she could feel herself starting to tremble slightly.

'What is it? What's wrong?' he asked her.

'Nothing,' she denied. 'It's just…' She gave a small shrug, closed her eyes and then opened them again as the darkness increased the heady effects of the wine. 'It's just that all of this…is so…so perfect,' she told him huskily, gesturing to the room and then towards the window and the view that lay beyond it. 'So…so magical… This house…the weather…the tree…church this morning…my stocking and…'

'And…?' Oliver prompted softly.

He was looking at her very intently—so intently, in fact, that she felt as though she could drown in the dark intensity of his eyes, as though she was being compelled to…

'And you,' she breathed, and as she said it she felt her heart slam fiercely against her chest wall, depriving her of breath, whilst the silence between them seemed to pulse and quicken and to take on a life of its own.

'I really shouldn't drink any more of this,' she heard herself whispering dizzily as she picked up her glass and took a nervous gulp, and then watched as Oliver walked softly towards her.

'No, you really shouldn't,' he agreed as he reached her and took the glass from her unresisting fingers, and then he took her equally unresisting body in his arms and her quiescent mouth into the warm captivity of his.

'We shouldn't be doing this,' she reproached him, mumbling the words against his mouth, her arms wrapped around him, her fingers burrowing into the thick darkness of his hair, her eyes luminous with the desire that was turning her whole body into molten liquid as she gazed up into his eyes.

'Oh, yes, we should,' was his sensuously whispered response. 'Oh, yes, we most definitely, assuredly should.' And then he was kissing her again. Not forcefully, but oh, so compellingly that it was impossible for her to resist him—impossible for her to want to resist him.

'You've already kissed me once for Christmas,' Lisa reminded him unsteadily as he slowly lifted his mouth from hers and looked down at her.

'This isn't for Christmas,' he whispered back as his hand slid under her hair, tilting her head back up towards him, sliding his other hand down her back, urging her closer to his own body.

Lisa could feel her heart hammering against her ribs as sensations that she had never experienced before—not with Henry and certainly not with the man who had been her first and only lover—flooded her body.

'Then what is it for?' she forced herself to ask him huskily.

'What do you think?' Oliver responded rawly. 'I wanted you the first time I saw you—did you know that?'

'How could you have done?' Lisa argued. 'You were so furious with me, and—'

'And even more furious with myself...with my body for the way it was reacting to you,' Oliver told her, adding rawly, 'The same way it's reacting to you right now.'

Uncertainly Lisa searched his face. Everything was happening so quickly that she couldn't fully take it all in. If she had felt dizzy before, with the combination of the rich wine and the warm fire, that was nothing to the headiness affecting her now, clouding her ability to reason logically, making her heart thump dangerously, heavily as her body reacted to what was happening to her—to them.

'I'll stop if you want me to,' she heard Oliver telling her hoarsely as he bent his head and gently nuzzled the soft, warm flesh of her throat. As she stifled the small, betraying sound she made when her body shuddered in shocked pleasure Lisa shook her head.

'No. No. I don't want you to stop,' she admitted huskily.

'Good,' Oliver told her thickly. 'Because I don't want to either. What I want is you, Lisa... God, how I want you.'

'I'm not used to this,' Lisa said shakily. 'I don't—'

'Do you think that I am...that I do?' he interrupted her almost roughly. 'For God's sake, Lisa, have you any idea how long it is since I was this intimate with a woman...since I wanted to be this intimate with a woman? I'm not a teenager,' he half growled at her when she shook her head. 'I don't normally... It's been a hell of a long time since anyone has affected me the way you do... One hell of a long time.'

Lisa was trembling as he took her back in his arms, but not because she was afraid. Oh, no, not because of anything like that.

At any other time the eagerness with which she met Oliver's

kiss would have shocked her, caused her to deny what she was experiencing, but now, for some reason, things were different—*he* was different. This was Christmas, after all—a special, magical time when special, magical things could happen.

As she felt the probing thrust of Oliver's tongue she reached out towards him, wrapping her arms around him, opening her mouth to him.

Somewhere outside this magical, firelit, pine-scented world where it seemed the most natural thing of all for her and Oliver to come together like this there existed another, different world. Lisa knew that, but right now…right now…

As she heard the rough deep sound of pleasure that Oliver made in his throat when he tasted the honeyed interior of her mouth Lisa gave up trying to think and behave logically. There was no point and, even more important, there was no need.

Instead, as she slid her fingers through the thick softness of Oliver's hair, she let her tongue meet his—slowly, hesitantly at first, such intimacy unfamiliar to her. The memories of her much younger, uncertain teenage explorations recalled sensations which bore no resemblance whatsoever to the sensations she was experiencing now as Oliver's tongue caressed hers, the weight of his body erotically masculine against the more slender femininity of her own as his hands caressed her back, her waist, before sliding down over her hips to cup the soft swell of her buttocks as he lifted her against him.

Lisa knew already that he was aroused, but until she felt the taut fullness of his erection against her own body she hadn't realised how physically and emotionally vulnerable and responsive she was to him. A sensation, a need that was totally outside her previous experience overtook her as she felt the liquid heat filling her own body, her hips lifting automatically, blindly seeking the sensual intimacy that her flesh craved.

'So much for your low sex drive,' she heard Oliver muttering thickly against her ear, before he added throatily, 'You're one hell of a sexy lady, Lisa. Do you know that? Do you know what you're doing to me…? How you're making me feel…? How you've made me feel since you stood there in your flat in that damned suit, with your breasts…?'

Lisa heard him groan as his hand reached upwards towards her breast, sliding beneath the fabric that covered it to cup its soft, eager weight, his thumb-tip caressing the hard peak of her nipple.

'Let me take this off,' he urged her, his hands removing her jacket, and then starting on the buttons of the waistcoat underneath it, his eyes dark with arousal as he looked deeply into hers. And then, without waiting for her to respond, his mouth curled in a small, sensual half-smile and he bent his head and kissed her briefly but very hard on her half-parted mouth. 'I want to see you, Lisa—all of you. I want to touch you, hold you, taste you, and I want you to want to do the same as me.'

Lisa knew that he must have felt the racking, sensual shudder that convulsed her body even if he hadn't heard her immediate response to the mental image that his words had aroused, in the low groan she was not quite able to suppress.

'You want that,' he pressed huskily. 'You want me to undress for you. You want to see me…to touch me…' He was kissing her again now—slow, lingering kisses all over her face and throat—whilst his hands moved deftly, freeing her from her clothes. But it wasn't the thought of her own nakedness beneath his hands that was causing her breath to quicken and her heart to lurch frantically against her ribs, but rather the thought of his nakedness beneath hers.

What was happening to her? she wondered dazedly. Her, to whom the thought of a man's naked body was something which she normally found rather discomforting and not in the least erotic. What was happening that she should now be so filled with desire that her whole body ached and pulsed with it at the mere thought of seeing Oliver's? The mere thought… Heaven knew what she would be like when that thought became a reality, when she was free to reach out and touch and taste him too.

Helplessly she closed her eyes, and then opened them again to find Oliver watching her.

'*Is* that what you want, Lisa?' he asked her softly whilst his thumb-tip drew a sensual line of pleasure around her sensitised mouth. 'Is that what you want—to see me…touch me…feel me…?'

Dry-mouthed, Lisa nodded. Her top was unfastened now, and she was vaguely aware of the half-exposed curves of her breasts gilded by the firelight, but her own semi-nudity seemed unimportant and irrelevant; her whole concentration was focused on Oliver, on the deft, steady movements of his hands as he unfastened the buttons on his shirt, his gaze never wavering from her as he started to remove it.

His chest was broad and sleekly muscled, tanned, with a dark arrowing of silky black hair down the centre, the sight of which made her muscles clench and her breath leak from her lungs in a rusty ache of sensory overload. His nipples, flat and dark, looked so different from her own.

As his hands reached for the fastening on his trousers, Lisa leaned forward, acting on impulse. The scent of him filled her nostrils, clouding her thought processes, drugging her…

As her lips closed around the small dark nub of flesh, she made a soft sound of feminine pleasure deep in her throat. Her tongue-tip circled his flesh, stroked it, explored the shape and texture of it before she finally returned to sucking gently on it.

'Lisa.'

The shock of being wrenched away from him was like having her whole body plunged in icy-cold water after it had been lapped in tropical warmth, the pain so great that it made her physically ache and cry out, her shocked gaze focusing in bewilderment on Oliver's, quick emotional tears filming her eyes as she wondered what it was she had done, why it was that he was being so cruelly brutal with her.

'It's too much, too soon,' she heard him telling her harshly. 'I can't… It's…'

Still half in shock she watched him as he shook his head.

'You're turning me on too much,' he told her more gently, 'and I can't…'

Lisa could feel the shock of it all the way through her body—the shock and an intensely feminine thrill that she could have such a powerful effect on him. As though he had guessed what she was feeling, she heard Oliver groan softly, and then he was reaching for her, holding her in his arms before she could evade them, kissing her now tightly closed eyelids, and then her mouth, and then he was telling her, 'Another few seconds of that and right now I'd be inside you and without—' He broke off and then added, 'That isn't how I want it to be for our first time together.'

Lisa moved instinctively against him, and then tensed as she felt the rough brush of his body hair against her naked breasts.

As she bent her head to look down at where her top had slid away from her Oliver's gaze followed hers, and then he bent his head, slowly easing her top completely away from her as he gradually kissed his way down her body, stopping only when he had reached the dark pink tautness of her nipple.

As he closed his mouth on it, repeating on her the caress she had given him, Lisa tensed in shock beneath the surge of pleasure that arced through her, arching her spine, locking her hands against his head, making her shudder as her body, beneath the weight of the flooding waves of pleasure that pulsed through her, was activated by the now urgent suckle of his mouth on her breast.

Was this how *he* had felt when she had caressed him in the same way? No, it couldn't have been, she denied. She could feel what he was doing to her, right deep down within her body, her womb. She could feel… With a small, shocked gasp she started to push him away.

'What is it?' she heard Oliver asking thickly as he released her nipple. He was breathing heavily and she could feel the warmth against her skin resensitising it, making her…

'I…' Nothing, she had been about to respond, but instead she heard herself saying helplessly in an unfamiliar and huskily sensual voice, 'I want you, Oliver… I want you.'

'Not one half as much as I want you,' he responded tautly as she quickly removed the remainder of her clothes and his own, and then, like a mystical, almost myth-like personification of all that was male inspired by some Greek legend, and filling her receptive senses with that maleness, he knelt over her, his dark head bowed as he gently eased her back against the soft fabric of the sofa and made love to her with a sensuality that took her breath away.

It didn't matter that no man had ever touched her, caressed her, kissed her so intimately before or that she had never imagined wanting one to do so. Somehow, when it was Oliver's hands, Oliver's mouth that caressed her…

So this was desire, need, physically wanting someone with an intensity that could scarcely be borne.

Lisa gasped, caught her breath, held out her arms, her body opening to him, wanting him, enfolding him as she felt the first powerful thrust of him within her and then felt it again and again until her whole world, her whole being was concentrated on the powerful, rhythmic surge of his body within her own and the sensation that lay beyond it—the ache, the urgency…the release…

Lisa heard herself cry out, felt the quickening thrust of Oliver's body, the hard, harsh sound of his breathing and his thudding heartbeat as she clung to him, moved with him, against him, aching, urging and finally losing herself completely, drowning in the liquid pulse of pleasure that flooded through her.

Later, still drowsy, sated, relaxed as she lay within the protective curve of Oliver's body, she told him sleepily, 'I think this is the best Christmas I have ever had.'

She could feel as well as hear him laughing.

'You do wonders for my ego, do you know that?' he told her as he tilted her face up to his own and kissed her lingeringly on the mouth.

'It's the truth,' Lisa insisted, her eyes clouding slightly as she added more self-consciously, 'I…I never realised before that it could be so… That I could feel…'

'It?' Oliver teased her.

'Sex,' Lisa told him with dignity.

'Sex?' She heard the question in his voice. She looked uncertainly up at him. He looked slightly withdrawn, his expression stern, forbidding…more like the Oliver she had first met than the man who had just held her in his arms and made such wonderful, cataclysmic, orgasmic love to her.

'What's wrong?' she asked him hesitantly, her heart starting to thump nervously. Wasn't this what all the books warned you about—the man's withdrawal and coldness after the act of sex had been completed, his desire to separate himself from his partner whilst she wanted to maintain their intimacy and to share with him her emotional awe at the physical pleasure their bodies had given one another?

'What we just shared may have been sex to you,' he told her quietly, 'but for me it was more than that. For me it was making love in the true sense of those words. Experimenting teenagers, shallow adults without maturity or sensitivity have sex, Lisa…'

'I don't understand,' she told him huskily, groping through the confusion of her thoughts and feelings to find the right words. 'I… You… We don't really know one another and…'

'And what?' Oliver challenged her. 'Because of that we can't have any feelings for one another?' He shook his head. 'I disagree.'

'But until today…until now…we didn't even like one another… We…'

'We what?' Oliver prompted her as she came to an uncertain stop. 'We were very physically aware of one another.'

Lisa opened her mouth to deny what he was saying and then closed it again.

'Not so very long ago you told me that you wanted me,' Oliver reminded her softly, 'and I certainly wanted you. I agree that the circumstances under which we met initially clouded our ability to judge one another clearly, but fate has given us an opportunity to start again…a second chance.'

'Twenty-four hours ago I was still planning to marry Henry,' Lisa protested helplessly.

'Twenty-four hours ago I still wanted to wring your pretty little neck,' Oliver offered with a smile.

'What's happening to us, Oliver?' she asked him uneasily. 'I don't understand.' She sat up and pushed the heavy weight of her hair off her face, her forehead creased in an anxious frown. 'I just don't do things like this. I've never… I thought it must be the wine at first… That…'

'That what? That the effect of three glasses of red wine was enough to make you want me?' He gave her a wry look. 'Well, I haven't even got that excuse. Not then, and certainly not now,' he added huskily as he reached towards her and took hold of her hand, guiding it towards his body whilst he bent his head and kissed her slowly.

To be aroused by him the first time might just possibly have been some kind of fluke, Lisa acknowledged, but there was no way she could blame her desire for him now on the wine. Not a second time, not now. And she did desire him, she acknowledged shakily as her fingers explored the hard strength of him. Oh, yes, she did want him.

It was gone midnight before they finally went upstairs, Lisa pausing to draw back the curtains and look out on the silent, snow-covered garden.

'It's still snowing,' she whispered to Oliver.

'Mmm…' he agreed, nuzzling the back of her neck. 'So it is… Lovely…'

But it wasn't the view through the window he was studying as he murmured his rich approval, and Lisa laughed softly as she saw the way he was studying her still naked breasts.

'No,' Oliver said to her, shaking his head as she paused outside the guest-bedroom door. 'Tonight I want you to sleep with me…in my bed…in my arms,' he told her, and as she listened to him Lisa felt her heart flood with emotion.

It was too soon yet to know just how she really felt about him, or so she told herself. And too dangerous, surely, when her body was still flooded with the pleasure he had given it? She was by nature cautious and careful; she always had been. It wasn't possible for her to fall in love over the space of a few hours with a man she barely knew.

But then less than twenty-four hours ago she would also have vehemently denied that it was possible for her to want that same man so much and with such a degree of intensity that, as he drew her towards his bed and held out his arms to her, her body was already starting to go liquid with pleasure and yearning for him.

CHAPTER SEVEN

'OUCH. THAT'S NOT FAIR. I was retying the snowman's scarf.'

Lisa laughed as Oliver removed from his collar the wet snow of the snowball she had just thrown at him, quickly darting out of the way as he bent down mock-threateningly to make a retaliatory snowball of his own.

She had been awoken two hours earlier by the soft thud of a snowball against the bedroom window, Oliver's half of the bed that they had shared all night being empty. Intrigued and amused, she had slid out of bed, wrapping the quilt around her naked body as she'd hurried across to the window. As she'd peered out she'd been able to see beneath the window Oliver standing in the garden next to a huge snowman, a pile of snowballs stacked at his feet.

'At last, sleepyhead, I thought you were never going to wake up,' he'd teased her as she had opened the window, laughing at her as she'd gasped a little at the cold shock of the frosty air.

'I'm not sleepy,' Lisa had corrected him indignantly. 'It's just that I'm…' she had begun, and then had stopped, flushing slightly as she'd acknowledged the real reason why her body was aching so deliciously, why her energy was so depleted.

As Oliver had looked silently back at her she had known that he too was remembering just why it was that she had fallen into such a deep sleep in the early hours of the morning.

She was remembering the night, the *hours* they had spent

together again now as she went to help him brush the snow from his collar, the scent of him, overlaid by the crisp, fresh smell of the snow, completely familiar to her now and yet at the same time still headily erotic.

When previously she had read of women being aroused by the body smell of their lover she had wrinkled her own nose just a little fastidiously, never imagining that there would ever come a time when she not only knew just how those women had felt but also actively wanted—no, *needed,* she corrected herself as her stomach muscles clenched on a weakening surge of emotion—to bury her face against her lover's body and breathe his scent, to trace the outline of his bones, his muscles, absorb the texture of his flesh and the whole living, breathing essence of him.

'It's too soon for this…for us…' she had whispered shakily last night in the aftermath of their second loving. 'We can't be…'

'Falling in love,' Oliver had supplied for her, and had challenged her softly between kisses. 'Why not? People do.

'What is it you're really afraid of, Lisa?' he had asked her later still, after his mouth had caressed every inch of her body, driven her to unimaginable heights of ecstasy and he had whispered to her that she was everything he had ever dreamed of finding in a woman…everything he'd begun to think he would never find, and she had tensed in his arms, suddenly afraid to let herself respond to him as her senses were urging her to do, to throw caution to the wind to tell him what she was feeling.

'I'm afraid of this,' she had whispered huskily back, 'of you…'

'Of me?' He held her slightly away from him, frowning at her in the darkness. 'Look, I know the circumstances surrounding our initial meeting weren't exactly auspicious, and yes, I agree, I did rather come the heavy, but to be confronted with Piers within thirty minutes of my plane landing from New York after a delay of over five hours and to discover what he'd done—'

'No, it's not that,' Lisa assured him quickly. She was fully aware now that the arrogance that she had believed she had seen in him was simply part of a protective mask behind which he hid his real personality. 'It's us…us together,' she told him, searching for the right words to express her feelings. 'I'm afraid that…everything's happening so fast. And it's not…I'm not…

'This isn't how I ever thought it would be for me,' she told him simply in the end. 'I never imagined I could feel so…that I could…' She paused, fumbling for the words and blushed a little as she tried to tell him how bemused, how shocked, almost, she still was by the intensity not just of his desire for her but of her own for him. It was so out of character for her, she told him, so unexpected…

'So unwanted,' he guessed shrewdly.

'It isn't how I thought my life was going to be,' she persisted. 'None of it seems quite real, and I'm afraid. I don't know if I can sustain this level of emotional intensity, Oliver… I feel like a child who has been handed a Christmas gift so far outside its expectations that it daren't believe it's actually got it. I'm afraid of letting myself believe because I'm afraid of the pain I'll suffer if…if it proves not to be real after all.'

'Don't you think I feel exactly the same way?' Oliver challenged her.

'You've been in love before,' she told him quietly. 'You've experienced this kind of sexual intimacy…sexual ecstasy before, but I—'

'No.' He shook his head decisively. 'Yes, I'm more sexually experienced than you are, but *this*… Take my word for it, Lisa—this is something different…something special.

'Look,' he added when she said nothing. 'With all this

snow, there's no way either of us can leave here now until it thaws; let's use the time to be together, to get to know one another, to give our feelings for one another a chance. Let's suspend reality, if you like, for a few days and just allow ourselves to feel instead of questioning, doubting…'

He had made it all sound so easy, and it was easy, Lisa acknowledged now as his arms closed around her. Too easy… That was the trouble.

Already after only a few short, fateful hours she was finding it hard to imagine how she had ever lived without him and even harder to imagine how she could ever live without him in the future. It would be so easy simply to close her eyes, close her mind to her thoughts and concentrate instead on her feelings. She could feel her heart starting to thump heavily with the intensity of her emotions.

'Stop worrying,' Oliver whispered against her mouth, correctly guessing what she was thinking. 'Everything's going to be fine. We're going to be fine.'

'This really is the best Christmas I have ever had,' she told him huskily ten minutes later as he lifted his mouth from hers.

'*You* are the best Christmas I have ever had,' Oliver responded. 'The best Christmas I ever will have.'

In the end they had four full days together, held for three of them in a captivity from which neither of them truly wanted to escape by the icy frost that kept the roads snowbound. And during those four days Lisa quickly discovered how wrong she had been in her original assessment of Oliver as being arrogantly uncaring.

He did care, and very deeply, about those who were closest to him but, as he freely admitted, the loss of his mother whilst he had still been so young had made him cautious about allowing others to get too close to him too quickly.

'But of course there are exceptions to every rule,' he had told her huskily, 'and *you* are my exception.'

She had given up protesting then that it was too soon for them to be in love. What was the point in denying what she knew she felt about him?

'I still can't believe that this…that we…that it's all really happening,' she whispered to Oliver on the fourth morning, when the thaw finally set in, her voice low and hushed, as though she was half-afraid of even putting her doubts into words.

'It *is* happening,' Oliver reassured her firmly, 'and it's going to go on happening for the rest of our lives.'

They were outside, Lisa watching as Oliver chopped logs to replace those they had used. Dressed in jeans and a black T-shirt, he had already discarded the checked woollen shirt that he had originally been wearing, the muscles and tendons on his upper arms revealed by the upward swing of the axe as he chopped the thick fir trunks into neatly quartered logs.

There was something about watching a man engaged in this kind of hard physical activity that created a feminine frisson of awareness of his masculinity, Lisa acknowledged as Oliver paused to wipe the sweat from his skin. She didn't want this special time that they were sharing to come to an end, she admitted. She was afraid of what might happen when it did. Everything had happened so fast—too fast?

'Nearly finished,' Oliver told her, mistaking the reason for her silence. 'I should be back from New York by the end of the week,' he added as Lisa bent down to retrieve the logs that he had already cut and carry them over to where the others were neatly stacked.

Lisa already knew that he was booked on a flight to New York to complete some protracted and difficult business talks he had begun before Christmas—the reason he had been so irritable and uncompromising the first time they had met, he had explained to her.

'I wish I didn't have to go,' he added, 'but at least we'll be able to spend New Year's Eve together and then… When are your parents due back from Japan?'

'Not until the end of February,' Lisa told him.

'That long.' He put down the axe and demanded hastily, 'Come here.'

Automatically Lisa walked towards him. The hand he extended to cup the side of her face and caress her skin smelled of freshly cut wood and felt slightly and very, very sensually abrasive, and the small shiver that ran through her body as he touched her had nothing to do with being cold.

'I could take some leave at the end of January and we could fly out to Japan together to see them then…'

Lisa knew what he was suggesting and her heart gave a fierce bound. So far they had not talked seriously about the future. Oliver had attempted to do so but on each occasion she had forestalled him, not wanting to do or say anything that might destroy the magic of what they were sharing, fearing that by allowing reality and practicality into their fragile, self-created world they might damage it. Their relationship, their love was so different from anything she had ever imagined experiencing or wanting to experience that part of her was still half-afraid to trust it…half of her?

And besides, she had already written to her parents to tell them that she and Henry would be getting engaged at Christmas and, whilst she suspected that they would never have been particularly keen on the idea of having Henry for a son-in-law, she felt acutely self-conscious about suddenly informing them that she had fallen head over heels in love with someone else.

It was so out of character for her, and the mere thought of having to confess her feelings for Oliver to anyone else made her feel defensive and vulnerable. She had always taken such a pride in being sensible and level-headed, in making carefully thought-out and structured decisions about her life. She wasn't sure how she herself really felt about this new aspect to her personality yet, never mind being ready to expose it to anyone else.

'What's wrong?' Oliver asked her as he felt her tensing against his touch. 'You don't seem very happy with the idea of me meeting your parents.'

'It's not that,' Lisa denied. There was, she had discovered, an unexpected corner of vulnerability in him which she suspected sprang from the loss of his mother—something that, if not exactly a fear of losing those close to him, certainly made him slightly more masculinely possessive than she would have expected in such an otherwise controlled and strongly emotionally grounded man. And it was, at least in part, because of this vulnerability that she had felt unable to tell him of her own fears and uncertainties.

'No? Then what exactly is it? Or is that yet another subject you don't want to discuss?' Oliver asked her sarcastically as he released her and picked up the axe, hefting it, raising it and then bringing it down on the log that he had just positioned with a force that betrayed his pent-up feelings.

Dismayed, Lisa watched him. What could she say? How could she explain without angering him still further? How could she explain to him what she felt when she truthfully didn't fully understand those feelings herself?

'It isn't that I don't want you to meet them,' she insisted. 'It's just...well, they don't even know yet that Henry and I aren't...' She knew immediately that she had said the wrong thing and winced as she witnessed the fury with which Oliver sliced into the unresisting wood, splitting it with one unbelievably powerful blow, the muscles in his arms cording and bunching as he tightened his grip on the axe.

'You're saying that they'd prefer you to be marrying Henry, is that it?' he suggested dangerously.

'No, of course they wouldn't,' Lisa denied impatiently. 'And besides, I'm old enough to be able to make up my own mind about who I want to commit myself to.'

'Now we're coming to it, aren't we?' Oliver told her, throwing down the axe and confronting her angrily, his hands on his hips, the faded fabric of his jeans stretching tautly against his thighs.

Just the sight of him made her body ache, Lisa acknowledged, but physical desire, sexual desire, could surely never be enough to build an enduring relationship on? And certainly it was not what she had envisaged building a lifetime's commitment on.

'It's not your parents who might reject me, is it, Lisa? It's you… Despite everything that has happened, all that we've shared.'

'No, that isn't true,' Lisa denied.

'Isn't it?' Oliver bit out grimly as he turned away from her to pick up another large chunk of wood.

Numbly Lisa watched him manhandling it onto the trestles that he was using to support the fir trunks whilst he chopped them into more easily manageable pieces. Above them the sky had started to cloud over, obliterating the bright promise of the morning's sunshine, making her feel shivery and inadequately protected from the nasty, raw little wind which had sprung up, even in the fine wool jacket she was wearing.

The weather, she recognised miserably, was very much only echoing what was happening to them—the bright promise of what they had shared was being threatened by the ominous thunderclouds furrowing Oliver's forehead and her own fear that what he had claimed he felt for her might prove too ephemeral to last.

After all, wasn't the classic advice always to treat falling in love too quickly and too passionately with caution and suspicion? Wasn't it an accepted rationale that good love—real love—needed time to grow and didn't just happen overnight?

As she watched Oliver silently releasing his anger on the wood, his jaw hardening a little bit more with each fierce blow of the axe, Lisa knew that she couldn't blame him for what he was feeling, but surely he could understand that it wasn't easy for her either? She was not programmed mentally for the kind of thing that had happened to her with him; she had not been prepared for it either, not…

'There's no need for you to stay.'

Lisa stared at Oliver as she heard the harsh words, the cutting edge to his voice reminding her more of the man she had first met than the lover she had become familiar with over the last few precious days.

'The wind's getting cold and you're shivering,' he added when she continued to stare mutely at him. 'You might as well go back inside; I've nearly finished anyway.'

He meant that there was no need for her to stay outside and wait for him, Lisa realised, and not that she might as well leave him and start her return journey home, as she had first imagined.

The relief that filled her was only temporary, though. Didn't the fact that she had so easily made such a mistake merely confirm what her sense of caution was already trying to make her understand—that she didn't really *know* Oliver, that no matter how compatible they might be in bed out of it there were still some very large and very important gaps in their knowledge of each other?

Quietly she turned away from him and started to walk back towards the house. Behind her she heard the sound of the axe hitting a fresh piece of wood. She had almost reached the house when she heard Oliver calling her name.

Stopping, she turned to watch him warily as he came running towards her.

As he reached her he took hold of her, wrapping her in his arms, telling her fiercely, 'God, Lisa, I'm such a… I'm sorry… the last thing I want us to do is fight, especially when we've got so little time left… Lisa?'

As she looked up at him he cupped her face in his hands, his thumbs caressing her skin, his hair tousled from the wind, his eyes dark with emotion.

Standing close to him like this, feeling the fierce beat of his heart and the heat of his body, breathing in the scent of him, unable to resist the temptation to lift her hand and rub away the streak of dried earth on his cheek, to feel already the beginning of the growth of his beard on his jaw which he had shaved only that morning, Lisa acknowledged that she might just as well have downed a double helping of some fatally irresistible aphrodisiac.

'Lisa…'

His voice was lower now, huskier, more questioning, and she knew that the shudder she could feel going through him had nothing to do with the after-effects of the punishing force he had used to cut up the logs.

She was the one who was responsible for that weakness, for that look in his eyes, that hardness in his body, and she knew that she was responding to it, as unable to deny him as he was her, her body nestling closer to his, her head lifting, her lips parting as he started to kiss her, tenderly at first and then with increasing passion.

'I can't bear the thought of losing you,' he whispered to her minutes later, his voice husky and raw with emotion. 'But you don't seem so concerned. What is it, Lisa…? Why won't—?'

'It's too soon, Oliver, too early,' Lisa protested, interrupting him, knowing that if she didn't stand her ground now, if she allowed her brain to be swayed not just by his emotions but by her own as well, it would be oh, so fatally easy, standing with him like this now, held in his arms, to believe that nothing but this mattered—it would be too late, and there would be no one but herself to blame if at some future date she discovered…

'I could make you commit yourself to me,' Oliver warned her, his mood changing as his earlier impatience returned. 'I could take you to bed now and show you…'

'Yes, you could,' Lisa agreed painfully. 'But can't you see, Oliver…? Please try to understand,' she begged him. 'It isn't that I don't love you or want you; it's just that…this…this…us…isn't how I envisaged it would be for me. You're just not the kind of man I—'

'You mean that I'm not Henry,' Oliver supplied harshly for her, his arms dropping back to his sides as he stepped back from her.

Lisa closed her eyes. Here we go again, she thought tiredly. She had meant one thing and Oliver had taken the words to mean something completely different—just as she had misunderstood him earlier when she had thought he was telling her to leave. And if they could misunderstand one another so easily what real chance did they have of developing the harmonious, placid relationship that she had always believed she needed? Some people enjoyed quarrels, fights, emotional highs and lows, but she just was not one of them.

'I don't want to fight with you, Oliver,' she told him quietly now. 'You must know that you have no possible reason to feel…to think that I want you to be Henry…'

'Haven't I?' he demanded bitterly. 'Why not? After all, you were prepared to marry him. Wanted to marry him… Wanted to so much in fact that you were prepared to let his mother browbeat and bully you and—'

'That's not true,' Lisa interrupted him swiftly. 'Look, Oliver, please,' she protested, spreading her hands in a gesture of emotive pleading for his temperance and understanding. 'Please… I can't talk. I don't want us to argue…not now, when everything has been so…perfect, so special and—'

'So perfect and special in fact that you don't want to continue it,' Oliver cut across her bitterly.

'You've given me the most wonderful Christmas I've ever had,' she whispered huskily, 'in so many different ways, in all the best of ways. Please don't spoil that for me…for us…now. I need time, though, Oliver; we *both* need time. It's just…'

'Just what?' he demanded, his eyes still ominously watchful and hard. 'Just that you're still not quite sure…that a part of you still thinks that perhaps Henry—?'

'No. Never,' Lisa insisted fiercely, adding more emotionally, 'That's a horrible thing to say. Do you really think that if I had any doubts about…about wanting you, that I would have—?'

'I didn't say that you don't prefer me in bed,' Oliver told her curtly, correctly guessing what she had been about to say, 'but the implication was there none the less—in the very words you used to describe what you wanted from marriage the first time we discussed it, the fact that you've been so reluctant to accept what's happening between us…the fact that you don't seem to want me to meet your parents.'

'You've got it all wrong,' she protested. 'My feelings…my doubts,' she amended when he snorted derisively over her use of the word 'feelings', 'they…they don't have anything to do with you. It isn't because I don't…because I don't care; in fact—'

'Oh, no,' Oliver told her cynically, not allowing her to finish what she was saying.

'It's me…not you,' Lisa told him. 'I've always been so cautious, so…so sensible… This…this falling in love with you—well, it's just so out of character for me and I'm afraid.'

'You're afraid of what?' he demanded.

The wind had picked up and was flattening his T-shirt against his body, but, unlike her, he seemed impervious to the cold and Lisa had to resist the temptation to creep closer to him and beg him to wrap his arms protectively around her to hold her and warm her.

'I don't know,' she answered, lifting her eyes to meet his as she added, 'I'm just afraid.'

How could she tell him without adding to his anger that a good part of what she feared was that he might fall out of love with her as quickly as he had fallen in love with her? He was quite obviously in no mood to understand her vulnerability and fear and she knew that he would take her comment as an indication that she did not fully trust him, an excuse or a refusal to commit herself to him completely.

'Please don't let's quarrel,' she repeated, reaching out her hand to touch his arm. His skin felt warm, the muscles taut beneath her touch, and the sensation of his flesh beneath her own even in this lightest of touches overwhelmed her with such an intense wave of desire that she had to bite down hard on her bottom lip to prevent herself crying out her need to him.

They were still standing outside, and through the windows she could see the tree that he had decorated for her, the magic he had created for her.

'Oh, Oliver,' she whispered shakily.

'Let's go inside,' he responded gruffly. 'You're getting cold and I'm… You're right,' he added rawly. 'We shouldn't be spoiling what little time we've got left.'

'It is still Christmas, isn't it?' Lisa asked him semi-pleadingly as he turned to open the door for her.

'Yes, it's still Christmas,' he agreed, but there was a look in his eyes that made her heart ache and warned her that Christmas could not be made to last for ever—like their love?

Was *that* why she doubted it—him? Because it seemed too perfect, too wonderful…too precious to be real?

They said their private goodbyes very early in the morning in the bedroom they had shared for the last four nights, and for Lisa the desolation which swept over her at the thought that for the next two nights to come she would not be sleeping within the protection of his arms, next to the warmth and intimacy of his body, only confirmed what in her heart of hearts she already knew.

It was already too late for her to protest that it was too soon for them to fall in love, too late to cling to the sensible guidelines that she had laid down for herself to live her life by: the sensible, cautious, pain-free guidelines which in reality had been submerged and obliterated days ago—from the first time that Oliver had kissed her, if she was honest—and there were tears in her eyes as she clung to him and kissed him.

What was she doing? she asked herself helplessly. What did guidelines, common sense, caution or even potential future heartache matter when they had this, when they had one another; when by simply opening her mouth and speaking honestly and from her heart she could tell Oliver what she was feeling and that she had changed her mind, that the last thing she wanted was to be apart from him?

'Oliver…' she began huskily.

But he shook his head and placed his fingertips over her mouth and told her softly, 'It's all right—I know. And I do understand. You're quite right—we do need time apart to think things through clearly. I've been guilty of trying to bully you, to coerce you into committing yourself to me too soon. Love—real love—doesn't disappear or vanish when two people aren't physically together; if anything, it strengthens and grows.

'I didn't mean to put pressure on you, Lisa, to rush you. We both have lives, commitments, career responsibilities to deal with. The weather has given us a special opportunity to be together, to discover one another, but the snow, like Christmas, can't last for ever.

'If I'd managed to get you to come to New York with me as I wanted, I probably wouldn't have got a stroke of work done,' he told her wryly. 'And a successful conclusion to these negotiations is vitally important for the future of the business—not just for me personally but for everyone else who is involved in it as well. Oh, and by the way, don't worry about not taking your car now; I'll make arrangements to have it picked up and returned to you later. I don't want you driving with the roads like this.'

Oliver had already told her about a large American corporation's desire to buy out part of his business, leaving him free to concentrate on the aspects of it he preferred and giving him the option to work from home.

'If Piers goes ahead and marries Emma, as he's planning, he's going to need the security of knowing he has a good financial future ahead of him. Naturally the Americans want to get the business as cheaply as they can.' He had started to frown slightly, and Lisa guessed that his thoughts were not so much on her and their relationship but on the heavy responsibility that lay ahead of him.

Her throat ached with pain; she desperately wanted to reach out to him and be taken in his arms, to tell him that she had made a mistake, that she didn't want to let him go even for a few short days. But how could she now after what he had said?

Suddenly, illuminatingly, she realised that what she had feared was not loving him but losing him. The space that she had told herself she needed—they both needed—had simply been a trick her brain had played on her, a coping mechanism to help her deal with the pain of being without his love.

Quietly she bowed her head. 'Thank you,' Lisa whispered to him as tears blurred her eyes.

'Are you sure there's nothing else you want…a book or…?'

Lisa shook her head. 'You've already bought me all these magazines,' she reminded Oliver huskily, indicating the pile of glossies that he had insisted on buying for her when they'd reached the station and which he was still carrying for her, together with her case, as he walked her along the platform to where the train was waiting.

She had tried to protest when he had insisted on buying her a first-class ticket but he had refused to listen, shaking his head and telling her, 'That damned independence of yours. Can't you at least let me do something for you, even if it's only to ensure that you travel home in some degree of comfort?'

She had, of course, given in then. How could she not have done so? How could she have refused not just his generosity but, she sensed, from the expression in his eyes at least, his desire to protect and cherish her as well?

'Make sure you have something to eat,' he urged her as they reached the train. 'It will be a long journey and…'

And she wouldn't be spending it eating, Lisa thought as he went on talking. Nor would she be doing anything more than flipping through the expensive magazines he had bought her. No, what she would be doing would be trying to hold back the tears and wishing that she were with him, thinking about him, reliving every single moment they had spent together…

A family—mother, father, three small children—paused to turn round and hug the grandparents; the smallest of them, a fair-haired little boy, clung to his grandmother, telling her, 'I don't want to go, Nana… Why can't you come home with us…?'

'I have to stay here and look after Grandpa,' his grandmother told him, but Lisa could hear the emotion in her voice and see the tears she was trying not to let him see.

Why did loving someone always seem to have to cause so much pain?

'Oh, to be his age and young enough to show what you're feeling,' Oliver murmured under his breath.

'It wouldn't make any difference if I did beg you to come home with me,' Lisa pointed out, trying to sound light-hearted but horribly aware that he must be able to hear the emotion in her voice. 'You'd still have to go to New York. We'd still have to be apart…'

'Yes, but I… At least I'd know that you want me.'

It was too much. What was the point in being sensible and listening to the voice of caution when all she really wanted to do was to be with him, to be held in his arms, to tell him that she loved and wanted him and that all she wanted—all she would ever want or need—was to be loved by him?

He was looking at her…watching…waiting almost.

'Oliver…' She wanted so desperately to tell him how she felt, to hear him tell her that he understood her vulnerability and that he understood all the things she hadn't been able to bring herself to say, but the guard was already starting to close the carriage doors, advancing towards them, asking her frowningly, 'Are you travelling, miss, because if so…?'

'Yes… Yes…'

'You'd better get on,' Oliver advised her.

She didn't want to go. She didn't want to leave him. Lisa could feel herself starting to panic, wanting to cling to him, wanting him to hold her…reassure her, but he was already starting to move away from her, lifting her case onto the train for her, bending his head to kiss her fiercely but far, far too briefly.

She had no alternative. She had to go.

Numbly Lisa stepped up into the train. The guard slammed

the door. She let down the window but the train was already starting to move.

'Oliver. Oliver, I love you...'

Had he heard her, or had the train already moved too far away? She could still see him...watching her...just.

Oliver waited until the train had completely disappeared before turning to leave, even though Lisa had long since gone from view. If only he didn't have these damned negotiations to conclude in New York. He wanted to be with Lisa, wanted to find a way to convince her.

Of what...? That she loved him?

Lisa pushed open the door of her flat and removed the pile of mail which had accumulated behind it. Despite the central heating, the flat felt cold and empty, but then that was perhaps because *she* felt cold and empty, Lisa recognised wryly—cold without Oliver's warmth beside her and empty without him... his love.

In her sitting room the invitation she had received from her friend Alison before Christmas to her annual New Year's Eve party was still propped up on the mantelpiece, reminding her that she would have to ring Alison and cancel her acceptance. The telephone started to ring, breaking into the silence. Her heart thumping, she picked up the receiver.

'You got home safely, then.'

'Oliver.'

Suddenly she was smiling. Suddenly the world was a warmer, brighter, happier place.

'Lisa, I've been thinking about what you said about us not rushing into things...about taking our time...'

Something about the sombreness in his voice checked the happiness bubbling up inside her, turning the warmth at hearing his voice to icy foreboding.

'Oliver...'

Lisa wanted to tell him how much she was missing him, how much she loved him, but suddenly she wasn't sure if that was what he wanted to hear.

'Look, Lisa, I've got to go. They've just made the last call for my flight...' The phone line went dead.

Silently she replaced the receiver. Had it really only been this morning that he had held her in his arms and told her how much he loved her? Suddenly, frighteningly, it was hard to believe that that was true. It seemed like another world, another lifetime, already in the past...over...as ephemeral as the fleeting magic of Christmas itself.

'No...it's not true,' she whispered painfully under her breath. 'He loves me; he said so.' But somehow her reassurance lacked conviction.

Even though she had been the one to insist that it was too soon for them to make a public commitment to one another, that they both needed time, she wished passionately now that Oliver had overruled her, that he had confirmed the power and strength of his love for her. How? By refusing to let her leave him?

What was the matter with her? Lisa asked herself impatiently. Could she really be so illogical, saying one thing, wanting another, torn between her emotions and her intelligence, unable to harmonise the two, keeping them in separate compartments in much the same way as Oliver had accused her of doing with sex and marriage?

Had she after all any real right to feel chagrined at the sense of urgency, almost of impatience in his voice as he had ended his brief call? She had, she admitted, during the last few days grown accustomed to being the sole focus of his attention, and now, when it was plain that he had something else on his mind...

She frowned, aware that instead of feeling relief when he

had told her that he agreed that they did need time to think things over she had actually felt—*still* felt—hurt and afraid, abandoned, vulnerably aware that he might be having second thoughts about his feelings for her.

How ironic if he had—especially since she had spent almost the entire journey home dwelling on the intensity of her own feelings and allowing herself to believe…

It would only be a few days before they were together again, she reminded herself firmly. Oliver had promised that he would be back for the New Year and that they would spend it together. There would be plenty of time for them to talk, for her to tell him how much she loved and missed him.

Even so… Sternly she made herself pick up her case and carry it through to her bedroom to unpack. A small, tender smile curled her mouth as she picked up the stocking that she had so carefully packed—the stocking that Oliver had left for her to find on Christmas morning.

There were other sentimental mementoes as well—a small box full of pine needles off the tree, still carrying its rich scent, the baubles that Oliver had removed from it and hung teasingly on her ears one night after dinner, a cracker that they had pulled together… She touched each and every one of them gently.

Through what he had done for her to make her Christmas so special Oliver had revealed a tender, compassionate, emotional side to his nature that made it impossible for her not to love him, not to respond to the love he had shown her. *Had* shown her?

Stop it, she warned herself. Stop creating problems that don't exist. Determinedly, she started to unpack the rest of her things.

CHAPTER EIGHT

IT WAS NEW YEAR'S EVE and almost three o'clock in the afternoon, and still Oliver hadn't rung. Lisa glared at the silent telephone, mentally willing it to ring. She had been awake since six o'clock in the morning and gradually, as the hours had ticked by, her elation and excitement had changed to edgy apprehension.

Where *was* Oliver? *Why* hadn't he been in touch? Was he just going to arrive at her door without any warning so that he could surprise her, instead of telephoning beforehand as she had anticipated?

Nervously she smoothed down the skirt of her dress and just managed to restrain herself from checking her reflection in the mirror for the umpteenth time.

She had spent most of her free time the previous day cleaning the flat and shopping for tonight. The lilies she had bought with such excitement and pleasure were now beginning to overpower her slightly with their scent. The champagne waiting in the fridge was surely chilled to perfection; the special meal she had cooked last night now only required reheating. Oliver might be planning to take her out somewhere for dinner, but the last thing she wanted was to have to share him with anyone else.

And even if she had dressed elegantly enough to dine at the most exclusive restaurant in town and her hair was immaculately shiny, her make-up subtly enhancing her features, it was not to win the approval of the public at large that she had taken such pains with her appearance, or donned the sheer, silky stockings, or bought that outrageously expensive and far too frothily impractical new silk underwear. Oh, no!

Where *was* Oliver? Why hadn't he been in touch? The small dining table which was all her flat could accommodate was lovingly polished and set with her small collection of good silver and crystal—unlike Oliver's grandparents she did not possess a matching set of a dozen of anything, and her parents, peripatetic gypsy souls that they were, would have laughed at the very idea of burdening themselves with such possessions.

However, through her work Lisa had developed a very good eye for a bargain, and the small pieces that she had lovingly collected over the years betrayed, she knew, the side of her nature that secretly would have enjoyed nothing better than using her dormant housewifely talents to garner a good old-fashioned bridal bottom drawer.

To help pass the time she tried to imagine Oliver's eventual arrival, her heartbeat starting to pick up and then race as she visualised herself opening the door to him and seeing him standing there, reaching out for her, holding her, telling her how much he had missed her and loved her.

Oliver, where are you? Where are you…?

Almost on cue the telephone started to ring—so much on cue in fact that for several seconds Lisa could only stand and listen to the shrill sound of it, before realising that she wasn't merely imagining it and that it had actually rung, was actually ringing.

A little to her own disgust she realised as she picked up the receiver that her hand was actually trembling slightly.

'Lisa…'

Her heart sank.

'Oliver…where are you? When will you—?'

'Bad news, I'm afraid.' Oliver cut her off abruptly.

'I'm not going to be able to make it after all; I'm stuck in New York and—'

'What?'

There was no way Lisa could conceal her feelings—shock, disappointment, almost disbelief, and even anger was sharpening her voice as she tried to take in what he was telling her. A horrid feeling of sick misery and despair was beginning to fill her but Lisa's pride wouldn't let her give in to it, although her hand was clenched so tightly on the receiver that her skin was sharp white over her knuckles.

'I'm still in New York,' she heard Oliver telling her, his voice curt and almost—so her sensitive ears told her—hostile as he added brusquely, 'I know it's not what I'd planned but there's simply nothing I can do…'

Nothing he could do or nothing he *wanted* to do?

All the doubts, the fears, the insecurities and the regrets that Lisa had been holding at bay ever since they had had to part suddenly began to multiply overwhelming and virtually obliterating all her self-confidence, her belief in Oliver's love. She had been right to be mistrustful of his assurances, his promises; she had been right to be wary of a love that had sprung into being so easily and now, it seemed, could just as easily disappear.

'Lisa?' Oliver said sharply.

'Yes, I'm still here.'

It was an effort to keep her voice level, not to give in to the temptation to beg and plead for some words of reassurance and love, but somehow she managed to stop herself from doing so, even though the effort made her jaw ache and her muscles lock in painful tension.

'You do understand, don't you?' he was asking her.

Oh, yes, she understood. How she understood.

'Yes,' she agreed indistinctly, her voice chilly and distant as she tried to focus on salvaging her pride instead of giving in to her pain. 'I understand perfectly.'

She wasn't going to weaken and let herself ask when he would be coming home, or why he had changed his mind… so obviously changed his mind.

Before he could say any more and before, more importantly, she could break down and reveal how hurt and let down she was feeling, Lisa fibbed tersely, 'I must go; there's someone at the door.' And without waiting to hear any more she replaced the receiver. She must not cry, she *would* not cry, she warned herself fiercely.

In the mirror she caught sight of her reflection; her face was paper-white, her eyes huge, revealing all too clearly what she was feeling, the contrast between her carefully made-up face and the misery in her eyes somehow almost pathetically grotesque.

Her flat, her clothes, her whole person, she decided angrily, made her feel like some modern-day Miss Havisham, decked out all ready for the embrace of a man who had deserted her. The thought was unbearable. She couldn't stay here, not now… not when everything around her reminded her of just how stupid she had been. Why, even now she was still emotionally trying to find excuses for Oliver, to convince herself that she had overreacted and that he felt as bad as she did and that he wasn't having second thoughts.

Alison's invitation was still on her mantelpiece. She reached for the telephone.

'Of course you can still come, you didn't need to ask,' Alison reproved her when she'd explained briefly that there had been a change in her plans and that she was now free for the evening. 'What happened? Has Henry—?'

'It's all off with Henry,' Lisa interrupted her.

There hadn't been time to explain to Alison just what had happened when she had telephoned her to ask her how her skiing holiday had gone and cancel her acceptance to her party and now Lisa was grateful for this omission, even though it did give her a small twinge of guilt when Alison immediately and staunchly, like the good friend she was, declared, 'He's let you down, has he? Well, you know my feelings about him, Lisa. I never thought he was the right man for you. Look, why don't you come over now? Quite a few people are coming early to help but we can always use another pair of hands.'

'Oh, Alison…'

Ridiculously, after the way she had managed to control herself when she'd been speaking to Oliver, she could feel her eyes starting to fill with tears at her friend's sturdy kindness.

'Forget him,' Alison advised her. 'He's not worth it…he never was. You may not believe me now, but, I promise you, you are better off without him, Lisa. Now go and put your glad rags on and get yourself over here… Are we going to party!'

As she replaced the telephone receiver Lisa told herself that Alison's words applied just as much to Oliver as they did to Henry, although for very different reasons.

Forget him. Yes, that was what she must do.

Tonight, with the old year ending and the new one beginning, she must find a way of beginning it without Oliver at her side. Without him in her life.

On impulse she went into the kitchen and removed the champagne from the fridge, pouring herself a glass and quickly drinking it. It was just as well that Alison's flat was within reasonably easy walking distance, she decided as the fizzy alcohol hit her empty, emotionally tensed stomach.

There was no need for her to get changed; the little black dress she was wearing—had put on for Oliver—was very suitable for a New Year's Eve celebration. All she had to do was redo her make-up to remove those tell-tale signs of her tears.

She poured herself a second glass of champagne, realising too late that instead of filling the original glass, which still had some liquid in the bottom, she had actually filled the empty one—Oliver's glass. Grimacing slightly, she picked them both up and carried them through to her bedroom with her, drinking from one before placing them both on the table beside her bed and then quickly repairing her make-up.

In New York Piers frowned as he walked into his cousin's hotel suite and saw Oliver seated in a chair, staring at the telephone.

'Is something wrong?' he asked him. His curiosity had been alerted earlier by the fact that Oliver had been extremely impatient to bring their discussions with the Americans to a conclusion, stating that he had to return to England without explaining why. Piers had happened to be looking at him when they had heard the news that the talks would have to continue. Oliver had been none too pleased.

'No,' Oliver responded shortly. Why had Lisa been so distant with him—so uninterested, so curt to the point of dismissal? She had every right to be angry and even upset about the fact that he had had to change their plans, but she had actually sounded as though she hadn't wanted to see him.

'Well, Jack Hywell is anxious to get on with the negotiations,' Piers told him. 'Apparently he's due to take his kids away the day after tomorrow, which is why he wants to take the discussion through the New Year period.

'Oh, by the way, Emma rang me this morning. She's been up to Yorkshire, and whilst she was up there she heard that Henry is getting married. Apparently, he's marrying someone he's known for a while. I must admit I'm surprised his mother finally sanctioned a marriage. Still, good luck to him, I say, and to her.

'What is it?' he asked Oliver. 'Hey, Oliver, watch it…'

he warned his cousin as he watched the latter's hand clench tightly on the glass he was holding. 'Look, I know how much pressure these negotiations are putting you under,' he commiserated, 'but with any luck they'll be over soon now, and… Oliver, where are you going?'

'Home,' Oliver told him brusquely.

'Home? But you *can't*,' Piers protested. 'The negotiations.'

Oliver snarled at him, telling him in no uncertain terms what should be done with the negotiations and leaving the room.

Piers stared open-mouthed at his departing back. Oliver hardly ever swore, and he certainly never used the kind of language that Piers had just heard him use. He was normally so laid back… Something was obviously wrong, but what?

'Ugh?'

Reluctantly Lisa opened her eyes. What *was* that noise? Was someone really banging a hammer inside her head or was someone at the door?

Someone was at the door. Flinging back the duvet, she reached for her robe, wincing at both the pain in her aching head and the state of her bedroom—clothes scattered everywhere in mute evidence of the decidedly unsober state in which she had returned to her flat in the early hours of the morning. She had never had a strong head for alcohol, she admitted to herself, and Alison's punch had been lethal. She would have to ring her later and thank her for the party, and for everything else as well.

'Don't even think about it,' Alison had advised Lisa drolly the previous evening after she had determinedly rescued her from the very earnest young man who had buttonholed her.

'He's even worse than Henry,' she had warned Lisa, rolling her eyes. 'He still lives with his parents and his hobby is collecting beetles or something equally repulsive. I only invited him because it was the only way I could escape from his mother. I know how much you like a lame dog, but really, Lisa, there are limits. Has he invited you round to look at his beetle collection yet?' she asked wickedly, making Lisa laugh in spite of herself.

'That's better,' she had approved, adding more seriously, 'I hadn't realised that Henry meant quite so much to you, but—'

'It isn't Henry,' Lisa had started to say, but someone had come up and dragged Alison away before she could explain properly and after that, rather than cause her friend any more concern, she had forced herself to be more enthusiastic and convivial, the result of which was her aching head this morning. No, this afternoon, she acknowledged as she saw in horror what time it was.

The doorbell was still ringing. Whoever it was was very determined. What if Oliver had changed his mind and come back after all? What if…?

Her fingers were trembling so much that she could hardly tie the belt of her robe. Quickly she hurried into the hallway, leaving her bedroom door open, and went to open the door, her heart beating so fast that she could hardly breathe.

Only it wasn't Oliver, it was Henry.

Henry!

Dumbly Lisa stood to one side as he walked self-importantly into her flat without bothering to close the door. Henry—what on earth was he doing here? What did he want? He was the last person Lisa wanted to see.

She pressed her fingers to her throbbing head. How could she have been stupid enough to think it might be Oliver? So much for all her promises to herself last night, as they'd all waited for midnight to come and the new year to start, that she would put him completely out of her mind and her heart.

'Henry, what is it? What are you doing here? What do you want?' she demanded shortly.

As she watched him breathe in then puff out his cheeks disapprovingly when he looked at her, she wondered how on earth she could ever have contemplated marrying him, how she had ever been so blind to the true reality of his character, his small-mindedness and fussiness, his lack of humour and generosity. Disapproval was written all over him as he looked at her.

'Surely you weren't still in bed?' he criticised her.

'No, I always dress like this. Of course I was still in bed,' Lisa snapped, losing her patience with him. She could hear him clearing his throat, the sound grating on her over-stretched nerves. If she had known it was only Henry at the door she would have stayed where she was.

'Mother thought I should come and see you,' he told her.

Lisa stared at him in angry disbelief.

'Your mother wanted you to come and see *me*… What on earth for? I would have thought I was the last person she would want you anywhere near. In fact, if I remember correctly, she said—'

'Er—yes, well…' Henry was flushing slightly as he cut her off. Why had she never noticed that slightly fishy bulge to his eyes when he was under pressure? Lisa wondered distastefully. Why had she never noticed, either, how very like his mother's his features were? She shuddered.

'The thing is, Lisa, that Mother thought I should make the situation absolutely clear to you, and—'

'What situation?' she demanded.

'Well…' Henry tugged at his collar. 'The thing is that I'm getting married to…to someone I've known for some time. She and I… Well, anyway, the wedding will be in June and we're having our official engagement party in February and…'

'And what?' Lisa pressed, irritated, wondering what on

earth Henry's engagement and intended marriage had to do with her and why his mother should think she might want to hear about them.

He coughed and told her. 'Well, Mother didn't want there to be any misunderstandings…or embarrassment… She felt that it was best that you knew what was happening just in case you tried…'

Lisa couldn't believe what she was hearing.

'Just in case I tried what?' she demanded with ominous calm. 'Just in case I tried to resuscitate our relationship—is *that* what you're trying to say?' she asked him sharply. 'Is that what your mother is afraid of?'

Did either of them really think…after what had been said, after the accusations which had been made, that she wanted anything…*anything* to do with Henry? Heavens, she wouldn't so much as cross the street to say hello to him now, never mind try to resuscitate a relationship which Oliver had been quite right to tell her she was better off without, and she opened her mouth to tell Henry as much and then closed it again.

There was no point in losing her temper with Henry; rather, she ought to be pitying him.

'Who is the lucky bride-to-be?' she asked him with acid sweetness instead. 'Or can I guess…? Your aunt's goddaughter…?'

She saw from his expression that her guess had been right. Poor girl—Lisa hoped she knew what she was taking on.

'It's all right, Henry,' she reassured him calmly. 'I *do* understand and you are quite safe. In fact I wish you and your wife-to-be every happiness.'

And as she spoke she pulled open her front door and firmly pushed Henry backwards towards it whilst at the same time raising herself on her tiptoes to place her hands on his shoulders and deposit a dismissive and cold contemptuous kiss on his cheek—just as Oliver crossed the foyer outside her flat and to all intents and purposes saw her with her arms around Henry and kissing him.

There was a second's tense silence as Lisa saw Oliver over Henry's shoulder, his face set in a mask of furious anger, and then Henry was backing away from her and almost scurrying past Oliver as he headed for the stairs, whilst Oliver strode towards her, ignoring him.

'Oliver!' Lisa exclaimed weakly. 'What are *you* doing here? I wasn't expecting you. I thought you were in New York.'

'Very evidently,' Oliver agreed tautly as he slammed the front door behind him, enclosing them both in the suddenly far too small space of her hallway.

'It's just as well your fiancé has decided to leave. I want to have a few words with you… Not very brave of him, though. Some husband he's going to make… When I heard that your engagement was back on I couldn't believe it. I thought there must have been some mistake.'

'There has,' Lisa agreed. If only her head would stop aching, she thought.

'I tried to ring you from the airport,' she heard Oliver tell her.

'I was out at a party,' she responded.

'A party—to celebrate your engagement, no doubt,' he accused her grittily, adding savagely as he suddenly stiffened and looked past her and through her open bedroom door to where the clothes she had discarded the previous evening lay scattered all over the floor, 'Or did you save *that* until you were back here alone with him? My God, and to think I believed you when you told me that sexually he had never meant anything to you, that there had never been anything between you. What else did you lie to me about, Lisa? Not that it matters now…'

'I haven't lied to you,' Lisa protested, reminding him, 'And if anyone should be making any accusations surely it should be me? After all, I'm not the one who promised to be back for New Year's Eve and then broke that promise.'

Furious with herself, she closed her eyes. What on earth had prompted her to say that, to betray to him how much his broken promise had hurt her…how much *he* had hurt her?

'I had no choice,' she heard Oliver telling her angrily, 'but you did, Lisa, and you chose—'

'I chose nothing,' she interrupted him, as angry with him now as he patently was with her.

What right, after all, did he have to come back and make such ridiculous accusations—accusations he must surely know couldn't possibly be true? And how come he could manage to get back *now* when he hadn't been able to do so before?

'No?' Oliver strode past her and walked into her bedroom, demanding dangerously, 'No? Then would you mind explaining to me what the hell has been going on here?' He picked up the half-empty champagne glass that she had abandoned the previous evening and gestured to its now flat contents contemptuously as he snarled, 'Couldn't he even wait to let you finish this? *His* glass is empty I note…'

His glass?

Indignantly Lisa opened her mouth to put him right, but before she could say anything Oliver demanded savagely, 'It must have been quite some celebration the two of you had. What the hell did he do—tear the clothes off your back? You should have told me that that was what you liked,' he advised her, his voice suddenly dropping dangerously, his eyes glittering as his glance raked her from head to toe. 'I'd no idea your sexual tastes ran to such things. If I had—'

'Oliver, no…' she protested as he reached for her, catching hold of her arm and dragging her towards him as he ignored her angry denial.

'You don't understand,' she said, but he was beyond listening to reason or to any of her explanations, she realised, her heart lurching against her chest wall as she saw the way his gaze raked her, his look a mingling of loathing and desire.

'I think it's you who doesn't understand,' Oliver was correcting her softly, but there was nothing remotely soft about the way he was holding onto her or the way he was watching her. Her body trembled, her toes curling protestingly into the carpet. 'I thought we had something special, you and I… I thought I could believe in you, trust you… Like a fool I thought, when you told me you needed me, that you…

'What is it, what's wrong?' he asked her as he felt her body shiver and his apparent concern almost caught her off guard, until she saw the steely, almost cruel look in his eyes.

'Nothing's wrong,' Lisa denied. 'I just want you to let me go.'

'You're trembling,' Oliver pointed out, still in that same nerve-wrenchingly soft voice. 'And as for letting you go… I will let you go, Lisa, but not until I've reminded you of exactly why you shouldn't be marrying Henry…'

I'm not marrying Henry, Lisa wanted to say, but she only got as far as, 'I'm not—' before Oliver silenced her mouth, coming down hard on hers in a kiss of angry possession.

She tried to resist him and even physically to repel him, her own anger rising to meet his as she alternately tried to push him away and twist herself out of his grasp, but the more she fought to escape, the more her body came into contact with his, and as though something about her furious struggles only added extra fuel to the flames of his anger Oliver responded by propelling her back against the bedroom wall and holding her there with the hard strength of his body whilst he lifted her arms above her head and kept them pinioned there as he continued to brutalise her mouth with the savagery of his punishing kiss.

Lisa could feel his heart thudding heavily against her body, her own racing in frantic counterpoint, her breathing fast and uneven as her anger rose even higher. How dared he treat her like this? All thoughts of trying to explain and pacify him fled as she concentrated all her energy on trying to break free of him.

She could feel the heat coming off his body, the rough abrasion of the fabric of his clothes on her bare skin where her robe had come unfastened. Her mouth felt swollen and bruised from the savagery of his kisses, but there was no fear or panic in her; she recognised only an unfamiliar and fierce desire to match Oliver's fury with her own.

'You want me… Me…' she heard Oliver telling her thickly between plundering kisses.

'No,' she denied, but the sound was smothered by the soft moan that rose up in her throat as her body responded to its physical contact with his. Somehow, against all logic, against everything she herself had always thought she believed in, she was becoming aroused by him and by the furious force of their mutual anger, Lisa recognised. And so was he.

On a wave of shocked despair she closed her eyes, but that only made things worse; the feel of him, the scent of him, the weight of him against her—these were all so familiar to her aching, yearning body that they immediately fed her roaring, feral need, turning her furious attempt to wrench herself free from him into something that even to her came closer to a deliberately sensual indication of her body's need to be possessed by his than a genuine attempt to break free.

Her anger now wasn't just directed at him, it was directed at herself as well, but with it now she could feel a surge of sensual, languid weakness, a heat which seemed to spread irresistibly throughout her body, so that under the hard pressure of Oliver's searing kiss, instead of resisting him, her body turning cold and lifeless in rejection of him, she was actually moving, melting, yielding, moaning softly beneath her breath.

'Lisa, Lisa...' She could hear the responsive urgency in Oliver's voice, feel it in his hands as he released her pinioned arms to push aside her robe and caress her body.

Her anger was still there, Lisa saw as she watched him studying her semi-naked body, and so was his, but somehow it had been transmuted into a form of such intense physical desire that she could barely recognise either herself or him in the two human beings who had suddenly become possessed of such a rage of physical passion.

She had never dreamed that she could feel like this, want like this, react like this, she acknowledged dazedly several minutes later as she cried out beneath Oliver's savage suckling of her breast, clawing at his back in a response born not of anger or pain or fear but rather of a corresponding degree of intensity and compulsion.

And she made the shocking acknowledgement that there was something—some hitherto secret and sensually dark part of her—that actually found pleasure...that actually wanted savagery, a sensation that was only seconds away from actual pain, that a part of her needed this release of her pent-up emotions and desires, that this dark self-created floodtide of their mutual fury and arousal possessed a dangerously addictive alchemy that made her go back for more, made her cling dizzily to him as he wrenched off his clothes and lifted her, still semi-imprisoning her, against the wall.

He entered her with an urgency that could have been demeaning and unwanted and even painful but which was, in fact, so intensely craved and needed by her body that even she was caught off guard by the intensity of her almost instantaneous orgasm and by her inner knowledge that this was how she had wanted him, that part of her had needed that kind of appeasement, as Oliver allowed her to slide slowly down towards the floor.

Shocked, not just at what had happened but by Oliver's

behaviour and even more so by her own, Lisa discovered that she was trembling so much that she had to lean against the wall for support. Ignoring the hand that Oliver put out to steady her, she turned away from him. She couldn't bear to look at him, to see the triumph and the contempt she knew would be in his eyes.

'Lisa…'

Whatever it was he was going to say she couldn't bear to listen to it.

'Just go,' she told him woodenly. 'Now… I never want to see you again… Never…'

She could hear her voice starting to rise, feel herself starting to tremble as shock set in. Her face burned scarlet with mortification as she reached for her abandoned robe and pulled it around her body to shield her nakedness as Oliver got dressed in grim-faced silence. Now that it was over she felt sick with disbelief and shock, unable to comprehend how she could have behaved in the way that she had, how she could have been so…so…depraved, how she could have wanted…

'Lisa…'

Oliver was dressed now and standing by the door. A part of her could sense that he too had behaved in a way that was out of character but she didn't want to listen to him. What was the point? He had shown her with damning clarity just what he thought of her.

'No…don't touch me…'

For the first time panic hit her as she saw him turn and start to walk towards her. She couldn't bear him to touch her now, not after…

She could sense him, feel him willing her to look at him but she refused to do so, keeping her face averted from him.

'So that's it, then,' she heard him saying hoarsely. 'It's over…'

'Yes,' she agreed. 'It's over.'

It wasn't until well over an hour after he had gone, after she had cleaned the bedroom from top to bottom, changed the bed, polished every piece of furniture, thrown every item of discarded clothing into the washing machine and worked herself into a furore that she realised that she had never actually told Oliver that she and Henry were not getting married. She gave a small, fatalistic shrug. What did it matter? What did *anything* matter any more after the way the pair of them had destroyed and abused their love?

Their *love*… There had never been any love—at least not on Oliver's side. Only lust; that was all.

Lisa shuddered. How had it happened? How could anger—not just his but, even worse, her own—become so quickly and so fatally transmuted into such an intensity of arousal and desire? Even now she could hardly believe it had happened, that *she* had behaved like that, that she had felt like that.

Later she would mourn the loss of her love; right now all she wanted to do was to forget that the last few hours had ever happened.

CHAPTER NINE

LISA WOKE UP WITH A START, brought out of her deep, exhausted sleep, which she had fallen into just after the winter dawn had started to lighten the sky, by the shrill bleep of her alarm.

Tiredly she reached out to switch it off. She had spent most of the night lying in bed trying not to think about what had happened—and failing appallingly. Round and round her thoughts had gone until she'd been dizzy with the effort of trying to control them.

Shock, anger—against herself, against Oliver—grief, pain, despair and then anger again had followed in a relentless, going-nowhere circle, her final thought before she had eventually fallen asleep being that she must somehow stop dwelling on what was now past and get on with her life.

Her head ached and her throat felt sore—a sure sign, she suspected, that she was about to go down with a heavy cold. The faint ache in her muscles and her lethargy were due to another cause entirely, of course.

Quickly she averted her gaze from the space on the bedroom wall—the place where Oliver had held her as he…as they… The heat enveloping her body had nothing to do with her head cold, Lisa acknowledged grimly, and nor had the hot colour flooding her face.

It was bad enough that she had actually behaved in such an…an abandoned, yes, almost sexually aggressive way in the first place, but did her memory *have* to keep reminding her of what she had done, torturing her with it? she wondered wretchedly. She doubted that Oliver was tormented by any such feelings of shame and guilt, but then, of course, it was different for a man. A man was allowed to be sexually driven, to express anger and hurt.

But it hadn't been Oliver's behaviour—hurtful though it had been—that had kept her awake most of the night, she acknowledged; it had been her own, and she knew that she would never be able to feel comfortable about what she had done, about the intensity of her passion, her lack of control, her sexuality, unchecked as it had been by the softening gentleness of love and modesty.

Women like her did not behave like that—they did *not* scratch and bite and moan like wild animals, they did *not* urge and demand and incite…they did *not* take pleasure in meeting…in matching a man's sexual anger, they did *not*… Lisa gave a low moan and scrambled out of bed.

There was no point in going over and over what had happened. It wouldn't change anything; *she* couldn't change anything. How on earth *could* Oliver have possibly thought that she could want *any* other man, never mind a sorry specimen like Henry…? How could he have misinterpreted…accused her…?

Angrily she stepped into the shower and switched it on.

That was the difference between men and women, she decided bitterly. Whereas she as a woman had given herself totally, emotionally, physically, mentally to Oliver, committing herself to him and to her love in the act of love—an act which she naïvely had believed had been a special and a wonderful form of bonding between them—to Oliver, as a man, they had simply had sex.

Sex. She started to shudder, remembering. Stop thinking about it, she warned herself grimly.

As she dried her hair and stared into the mirror at her

heavy-eyed, pale-faced reflection she marvelled that such a short space of time could have brought so many changes to her life, set in motion events which had brought consequences that she would never be able to forget or escape.

Such a few short days, and yet they had changed her life for ever—changed *her* for ever. And the most ironic thing of all was that even if Henry or another man like him were to offer her marriage now she could not accept it. Thanks to Oliver she now knew that she could never be content with the kind of marriage and future which had seemed so perfect to her before.

Fergus her boss gave her an uneasy look as he heard her sneezing. He had a thing about germs and was a notorious hypochondriac.

'You don't sound very well,' he told Lisa accusingly as she started to open the mail which had accumulated over the Christmas break. 'You've probably caught this virus that's going round. There was something on last night's TV news about it. They're advising anyone who thinks they've got it to stay at home and keep warm…'

'Fergus, I've got a cold, that's all,' Lisa told him patiently. 'And besides, aren't we due to go down to Southampton on Thursday to start cataloguing the contents of Welton House?'

Welton House had been the property of one of Fergus's clients, and following her death her family had asked Fergus to catalogue its contents with a view to organising a sale. Normally it was the kind of job that Lisa loved, and she thought that it would do her good to get away from London.

'That's next week,' Fergus told her, his voice quickening with alarm as Lisa burst into another volley of sneezes. 'Look, my dear, you aren't well. I really think you should go home,' he said. 'In fact, I insist on it. I'll ring for a taxi for you…'

There was no point in continuing to protest, Lisa recognised wearily; Fergus had quite obviously got it into his head that she was dangerously infectious, and, if she was honest, she didn't feel very well. Nothing to do with her slight head cold, though. The pain that was exhausting her, draining every bit of her energy as she fought to keep it at bay had its source not in her head but in her emotions.

Her telephone was ringing as she unlocked her door; she stared at it for a few seconds, body stiffening. What if it was Oliver, ringing to apologise, to tell her that he had made a mistake, that he…?

Tensely she picked up the receiver, unsure of whether to be relieved or not when she heard her mother's voice on the other end of the line.

'Darling, I'm glad I caught you. I'm just ringing to wish you a Happy New Year. We tried to get through yesterday but we couldn't. How are you? Tell me all about your Christmas with Henry…'

Lisa couldn't help herself; to her own consternation and disbelief she burst into tears, managing to tell her mother between gulped sobs that she had not, after all, spent Christmas with Henry.

'What on earth has happened?' she heard her mother enquiring solicitously. 'I thought you and Henry—'

'It's not Henry,' Lisa gulped. 'He's getting married to someone else anyway. It's Oliver…'

'Oliver. Who's Oliver?' her mother asked anxiously, but the mere effort of saying Oliver's name had caused her so much pain that Lisa couldn't answer her questions.

'I've got to go, Mum,' Lisa fibbed, unable to bear any more. 'Thanks for ringing.'

'Lisa,' she could hear her mother protesting, but she was already replacing the receiver.

There was nothing she wanted to do more than fling herself on her bed and cry until there were no more tears left, until she had cried all her pain away, but what was the point of such emotional self-indulgence?

What she needed, she acknowledged firmly, was something to keep her thoughts away from Oliver not focused on him. It was a pity that the panacea that work would have provided had been taken away from her, she fretted as she stared round her sitting room, the small space no longer a warm, safe haven but a trap imprisoning her with her thoughts, her memories of Oliver.

Impulsively she pulled on her coat. She needed to get away, go somewhere, anywhere, just so long as it was somewhere that wasn't tainted with any memories of Oliver.

Oliver was in a foul mood. He had flown straight back to New York after his confrontation with Lisa, ostensibly to conclude the negotiations he had left hanging fire in his furious determination to find out what was going on. Well, he had found out all right. He doubted if he would ever forget that stomach-sickening, heart-destroying, split second of time when he had seen Lisa—*his* Lisa—in Henry's arms.

And as for what had happened... His mouth hardened firmly as he fought to suppress the memory of how easily—how very and humiliatingly easily—with Lisa in his arms he had been on the point of begging her to change her mind, of pleading with her at least to give him a chance to show her how good it could be for them.

He had known, of course, how reluctant, how wary she had been about committing herself fully to him, how afraid she had been of her own suppressed, deeply passionate nature. Then it had seemed a vulnerability in her which had only added to his love for her. Then he had not realised... How could he have been so blind—he of all people? How could *she* have been so blind? Couldn't she see what they had had… what they *could* have had?

The American negotiations were concluded now and he and Piers were on their way back north. They had flown back into London four hours ago to cold grey skies and thin rain.

'Oliver, is something wrong?'

He frowned, concentrating on the steely-grey ribbon of the motorway as he pulled out to overtake a large lorry.

'No, why should there be?' he denied, without looking at his cousin.

'No reason. Only you never explained why you had to fly back home like that and since you flew back to the States… well, it's obvious that something is bothering you. You're not having second thoughts about selling off part of the business, are you?' Piers asked him.

Oliver relaxed slightly, and without taking his eyes off the road responded, 'No, it was the right decision, but the timing could, perhaps, have been better. When is Emma due back?' he asked, changing the subject.

His cousin's girlfriend had been away visiting her family, and to his relief Piers, not realising that he was being deliberately sidetracked, started to talk enthusiastically about the reunion with her.

'It's official, by the way,' he informed Oliver. 'We're definitely going to get married this summer. In Harrowby if that's OK with you. We thought…well, I thought with Emma's family being so scattered… We…we're not sure how many of them will want to come up for the wedding yet, but the house is big enough to house twenty or so and…' He paused and gave Oliver a sidelong glance.

'I…I'd like you to be my best man, Oliver. Funny things, women,' he added ruminatively. 'Up until we actually started talking properly about it Emma had always insisted she didn't want a traditional wedding, that they were out of date and unnecessary, and yet now…she wants the whole works—bridesmaids, page-boys… She says it's to please her mother but I know different.

'That will mean two big weddings for Harrowby this summer. I still can't get over old Henry getting married—or rather his mother allowing him to… Hell, Oliver… watch out!' he protested sharply as his cousin suddenly had to brake quickly to avoid getting too close to the car in front.

'You're sure you're OK?' he asked in concern. 'Perhaps we should have stayed in London overnight instead of driving north straight from the flight. If you're tired, I can take over for a while…'

Oliver made no reply but his mouth had compressed into a hard line and there was a bleak, cold look in his eyes that reminded Piers very much of a younger Oliver just after he'd lost his mother. Something was bothering his cousin, but Piers knew him well enough to know that Oliver wasn't likely to tell him or anyone else exactly what it was.

'What the hell is that still doing here?'

Piers frowned as Oliver glared at the Christmas tree in the hallway. There was nothing about it so far as he could see to merit that tone of icy, almost bitter hatred in his cousin's voice. In fact, he decided judiciously, it was a rather nice tree—wilting now slightly, but still…

'It's not Twelfth Night until tomorrow,' he pointed out to Oliver. 'I'll give you a hand dismantling it then, if you like, and—'

'No,' Oliver told him curtly. 'I'll give Mrs Green a ring and ask her to arrange for Tom to come in and do it. We're going to be too busy catching up with everything that's been going on whilst we've been in New York.'

Thoughtfully Piers followed Oliver into the kitchen. It wasn't like his cousin to be so snappy and edgy, and, in point of fact, he had planned to drive across to York to see his parents whilst they were in the north, but now it seemed as though Oliver had other plans for him.

'Well, if we're going to work I'd better go and unpack and have a shower, freshen up a bit,' he told Oliver.

Upstairs he pushed open the door of the room which traditionally was his whenever he visited. The bed was neatly made up with crisp, clean bedlinen, the room spotless apart from…

Piers' eyes widened slightly as he saw the small, intimate item of women's clothing which Mrs Green had obviously laundered and left neatly folded on the bed, no doubt thinking that the small pair of white briefs belonged to Emma.

Only Piers was pretty sure that they didn't. So who did they belong to and where was their owner now?

Piers knew enough about his cousin to be quite sure that Oliver would not indulge in any kind of brief, meaningless sexual fling. Piers had endured enough lectures from his elder cousin on that subject himself to know that much.

So what exactly was going on? Oliver had made no mention to him of having any visitors recently, either male or female. He could always, of course, show him the briefs and ask him who they belonged to, but, judging from his current mood, such an enquiry was not likely to be very well received.

Another thought occurred to Piers. Was there any connection between the owner of the briefs and his cousin's present uncharacteristic bad mood?

When Piers returned downstairs Oliver was in his study opening the mail that had accumulated in his absence.

'Mmm…isn't it amazing how much junk gets sent through the post?' Piers commented as he started to help him. 'Oh, this one looks interesting, Oliver—an invite to Henry's betrothal party. Well, they certainly are doing things the traditional way, aren't they?'

'Give that to me,' Oliver instructed, his tone of voice so curt that Piers started to frown. He knew that Oliver had never particularly liked either Henry or his parents, especially his mother, but, so far as he knew, the anger he was exhibiting now was completely different from his normal attitude of relaxed indifference towards them.

Silently Piers handed him the invitation and saw the way Oliver's hands trembled slightly as he started to tear the invitation in two, and then he abruptly stopped, his concentration fixed on the black script which he had previously merely been glancing at furiously, his whole body so still and tense that Piers automatically moved round the desk to stand beside him, wondering what on earth it was that was written on the invitation that was causing such a reaction.

It had seemed unremarkable enough to him.

'"The betrothal is announced of Miss Louise Saunders, daughter of Colonel and Lady Anne Saunders, to—" Henry is marrying Louise Saunders,' Oliver intoned in a flat and totally unfamiliar voice.

'That's what it says,' Piers agreed, watching him in concern. 'It makes sense. They've known one another for ever and, of course, there's money in the family. Louise stands to inherit quite a considerable sum from her grandparents.

'Oliver, what is it, what's wrong?' he demanded as he saw the colour draining out of his cousin's face, leaving it grey and haggard, the skin stretched tightly over his facial bones as he lifted his head and stared unseeingly across the room.

'Nothing,' he told Piers tonelessly. 'Nothing.' And then he added in a sharper more incisive voice, 'Piers, there's something I have to do. I need to get back to London. I'll leave you here...'

'London...? You can't drive back there now,' Piers protested. 'It's too late. You haven't had any sleep in the last twenty-four hours that I know of, and not much in the three days before that. Oliver, what's going on? I—'

'Nothing's going on,' Oliver denied harshly.

'Look, if you must go back to London, at least wait until the morning when you've had some sleep,' said Piers. 'Surely whatever it is can wait that long?'

'Maybe it can,' Oliver agreed savagely, 'but *I* can't.'

In London Lisa's cold had turned into the full-blown virus, just as Fergus had predicted. Common sense told her that she ought to see a doctor but she felt too full of self-pity, too weak, too weighed down with misery to care how ill she was. And so instead she remained in her flat curled up in her bed, alternately sweating and shivering and being sick, wishing that she could just close her eyes and never have to open them again.

At first when she heard the sound of someone knocking urgently on her door after ten o'clock at night she thought she was imagining things, and then when the knocking continued and she realised that it was, in fact, real her heart started to bang so fiercely against her chest wall that it made her feel even more physically weak.

It was Oliver! It had to be. But it didn't matter what he had to say because she wasn't going to listen. She had always known that sooner or later he would discover his mistake. But nothing—no amount of apologising on his part—could take away the pain he had caused her.

If he had really loved her he would never have doubted her in the first place. *If* he had really loved her he would never…

The knocking had stopped, and Lisa discovered that she was almost running in her sudden urgency to open the door.

When she did so, flinging it wide, Oliver's name already on her lips, it wasn't Oliver who was standing there at all…

It was…

She blinked and then blinked again, and then to her own consternation she burst into tears and flung herself into the arms that had opened to hold her, weepingly demanding, 'Mother, what are you doing here?'

'You sounded so unhappy when I rang that I was worried about you,' her mother told her.

'You came all the way home from Japan because you were worried about me?'

Lisa stared at her mother in disbelief, remembering all the times when, as a child, she had refused to give in to her need to plead for her parents to return from whatever far-flung part of the world they were working in, telling herself stoically that she didn't mind that they weren't there, that she didn't mind that they didn't love her enough to be with her all the time.

'Don't sound so surprised,' her mother chided her gently. 'You may be an adult, Lisa, but to us, your father and me, you are still our child… Your father wanted to come with me, but unfortunately…' She spread her hands.

'Now,' she instructed as she smoothed Lisa's damp hair back from her forehead and studied her face with maternal intuition, 'tell me what's really wrong… All of it… Starting with this Oliver…'

'Oliver…'

Lisa shook her head, her mouth compressing against her emotions.

'I can't,' she whispered, and then added, 'Oh, Mum, I've been such a fool. I thought he loved me… I thought…'

'Oh, my poor darling girl. Come on, let me put the kettle on and make us both a drink and something to eat. You need it, by the looks of you. You're so thin… Oh, Lisa, what have you been doing to yourself?'

Half an hour later, having been bullied into having a hot bath by her mother, Lisa was ensconced on her small sofa, wrapped in her quilt, dutifully eating the deliciously creamy scrambled eggs that her mother had cooked for her whilst the latter sat on a chair opposite, waiting for her to finish eating before exclaiming as she removed the empty plate, 'Right, now! First things first—*who* is this Oliver?'

'He's… He's…' Lisa shook her head. 'I hate him,' she told her mother emotionally, 'and it hurts so much. He said he loved me but he couldn't have done—not and said what he did…'

Slowly, under her mother's patient and gentle questioning, the whole story came out. Although Lisa would not have said that she was particularly close to her parents, she had always felt able to talk to them. But, even so, she was slightly shocked to discover how easy it was to confide in her mother and how much she wanted to talk to her. Of course, there were bits she missed out—things so personal that she could not have discussed them with anyone. But she sensed from her mother's expression that she guessed when Lisa was withholding things from her and why.

Only when it came to outlining what had happened the night that Oliver had discovered her kissing Henry did her voice falter slightly.

'It must have been a shock for him to find Henry here,' her mother suggested when Lisa had fallen silent.

'He seemed to think that I was going to marry Henry. I…'

'And you told him, of course, that you weren't?' her mother offered.

Lisa shook her head. 'I tried to but…' She bit her lip, turning away, her face flushing slightly. 'He was so…

'I had been honest with him right from the start, told him why I was marrying Henry, told him that I hadn't…that I didn't think that sex…' She bit her lip again and stopped.

'After what had happened between us I don't understand

how he could possibly have thought that I'd go back to Henry and to use what we had…all that we'd shared, to abuse it and destroy… To make me feel… How could he do that?' she whispered, more to herself than her mother.

'Perhaps because he's a man and because he felt jealous and insecure, because a part of him feared that what he had to offer you wasn't enough…that *he* wasn't enough.'

'But how could he possibly think that?' Lisa demanded, looking at her mother, her eyes dark and shadowed with pain. 'He knew how I felt about him, how I… He knew…'

'When you were in bed together, yes,' her mother agreed, softening the directness of her words with a small smile. 'But it isn't only our sex who fear that the emotions aroused when two people are sexually intimate may not be there once that intimacy is over.

'Your Oliver obviously knew he could arouse you, make you want him physically, but you had already told him that he was not what you wanted, what you had planned for. He already knew that a part of you feared the intensity of the emotions he had for you and aroused in you. You said yourself that he was anxious for you to make a commitment to him.'

'Initially, yes. But later…when I tried to tell him how I felt just before he left for New York, he didn't seem to want to listen.'

'Perhaps because he was afraid of what you might say,' her mother suggested gently, adding, 'He had no way of knowing you were going to tell him that you had changed your mind, that you were ready to make the commitment you had previously told him he must wait for. For all he knew, you might have wanted to say something very different—to tell him in fact that you had changed your mind and didn't want him at all.'

'But he couldn't possibly have thought that,' Lisa gasped,

'could he? It isn't important now anyway,' she said tiredly. 'I can never forgive him for—'

'Is it really *Oliver* you can't forgive, or yourself?' her mother interposed quietly, watching as Lisa stared at her and then frowned.

'You said that he was angry…that he made love to you,' she reminded Lisa. 'That he used your feelings to punish and humiliate you. But you never said that you didn't want him, or that he hurt or abused you. Anger against the person we love when he is our lover can result in some very passionate sex.

'For a woman, the first time she discovers that fact, it can be very traumatic and painful because it goes against everything that society has told us we should want from sexual intimacy. It can seem very frightening, very alien, very wrong to admit that we found pleasure in expressing our sexuality and desire in anger and, of course, that it was the only way we could express it…'

'He was so angry with me,' Lisa told her mother, not making any response to what she had said but mentally digesting it, acknowledging that her mother had a point, allowing herself for the first time since it had happened to see her own uninhibited and passionate response to Oliver as a natural expression of her own emotions.

'Oliver was probably as shocked and caught off guard by what happened as you were,' her mother told her wryly.

'You're not the only one something like this has happened to, you know,' she added comfortingly. 'I can still remember the first time your father and I had a major row… I was working on a piece for a gallery showing and I'd forgotten that your father was picking me up to take me out to dinner… He came storming into my work room demanding to know what was more important to me—my work or him… I had just finished working on the final piece for the exhibition. He picked it up and threw it against the wall.'

Lisa stared at her mother in shock.

'Dad did that? But he always seems so laid back…so…'

'Well, most of the time he is, but this particular incident was the culmination of a series of small misunderstandings. He didn't take second place to my work at all, of course, but…'

'Go on—what happened, after he had broken the piece?' Lisa demanded, intrigued.

'Well, I'm ashamed to say that I was so angry that I actually tried to hit him. He caught hold of me, we struggled for a while and then…'

As her mother flushed and laughed, Lisa guessed what the outcome of their fight had been.

'Afterwards your father stormed off and left me there on my own… I vowed I wasn't going to have anything more to do with him, but then—well, I started to miss him and to realise that what had happened hadn't been entirely his fault.'

'So what did you do?' Lisa asked.

Her mother laughed. 'Well, I made a small ceramic heart which I then deliberately broke in two and I sent him one half of it.'

'What did he do?' Lisa demanded breathlessly.

'Well, not what I had expected,' her mother admitted. 'When I sent him the heart I had been trying to tell him that my heart was broken. I kept the other half hoping he would come for it and that we could mend the break, but when several days went by and he didn't I began to think that he had changed his mind and that he didn't want me any more.

'I was in despair,' she told Lisa quietly. 'Exactly the same kind of despair you are facing now, but then, just when I had given up hope, your father turned up one night.'

'With the broken heart,' Lisa guessed.

'With the mended heart,' her mother told her, smiling. 'The reason he had delayed so long before coming to see me had been because he had been having a matching piece to the broken one I had sent him made, and where the two pieces were bonded together he had used a special bond to, as he put it, "make the mended heart stronger than it had been before and unbreakable".'

'I never dreamed Dad could be so romantic!' Lisa exclaimed.

'Oh, he can,' her mother told her. 'You should have seen him the night you were born. He had desperately wanted you to be a little girl. He was overjoyed when you were born—we both were—and he swore that no matter where our work might take us, as long as it was physically possible, we would take you with us…'

Lisa could feel fresh tears starting to sting her eyes. All these years and she had misunderstood the motivation behind her parents' constant uprooting of her, had never known how much she was actually loved.

As they looked at one another her mother reached out and took Lisa's hand, telling her firmly, 'When Oliver comes to see you—and he will—listen to what he has to say, Lisa—'

'When,' Lisa interrupted her. 'Don't you mean if…?'

'No, I mean when.'

'But how could he believe I could go behind his back and return to Henry?'

'He's a man and he's vulnerable, as I've already told you, and sometimes, when we feel vulnerable and afraid, we do things which are out of character. You said yourself that losing his mother when he did made him feel wary of loving someone in case he lost them too. Such emotions, even when they're only felt subconsciously, can have a very dramatic effect on our actions.'

'He won't come back,' Lisa protested dully. 'I told him I never wanted to see him again. We both agreed it was over.'

'Well, in that case, why don't you come back to Japan with me?' her mother suggested prosaically.

'I can't… My job… Fergus—'

'Fergus would give you some extended leave if you asked him,' her mother told her. 'He adores you, you know that…'

'Not when he thinks I'm full of germs,' Lisa told her ruefully. 'I'd like to come back with you,' she added hesitantly, 'but…'

'But not yet,' her mother finished for her, getting up to kiss her gently on the forehead and tell her, 'Well, I'm going to be here for a few days so you've got time to change your mind. But right now you're going to bed and I'm going to ring your father. I promised him I would. He'll be worrying himself to death wondering if you're all right. Now, bed…'

'Yes, Mum.' Lisa yawned obediently.

It felt so good to have her mother here with her, to know that she was cared for and loved, but no amount of parental love, no matter how valued, could erase the pain of losing Oliver.

He'll be back, her mother had promised her. But would he? Had they perhaps between them destroyed the tender, vulnerable plant of their love?

CHAPTER TEN

PIERS HAD BEEN RIGHT to caution him against driving back to London tonight, Oliver admitted as his concentration wavered and he found himself having to blink away the grittiness of his aching eyes as he tried to focus on the road. With all that adrenalin and anxiety pumping through his veins it should have been impossible to start drifting off to sleep, but the compulsion to yawn and close his eyes kept on returning.

Up ahead of him he could see the lights of a motorway service station. Perhaps it would be wiser for him to stop, even if it was only for a hot, reviving cup of coffee. He knew there was no point in his trying to sleep; how could he when all he could think of was Lisa and the injustice he had done her?

The motorway services were closer than he had thought; he had started to pull into the lane taking him off the motorway, when the metal barrier at the edge of the road loomed up in front of him. The shrill squeal of brakes was followed by the harsh sound of metal against metal and his head jolted forward, pain exploding all around him.

'If it's that bad why don't you go out for a walk? It will be cheaper than wearing the carpet out.'

Lisa frowned as she looked at her mother.

'You've been pacing up and down the sitting room for the last half-hour,' her mother pointed out. 'And besides, it will do you good to get some fresh air.'

'Yes, perhaps you're right,' Lisa agreed. 'A walk might do me good.'

'Put your jacket on and some gloves,' her mother instructed her as Lisa headed for the hallway. 'I know the sun is out but we had frost last night.'

'Yes, Mother,' Lisa agreed dutifully, amusement briefly lightening her eyes and touching her mouth.

It had been three days since her mother's unexpected arrival now; in another two she would be returning to Japan. She was still pressing Lisa to return with her, and Lisa knew that she had spoken the truth when she had said that Fergus would give her the extra leave. There had been plenty of occasions in the past when she had put in extra hours at work, given up weekends and been cheerfully flexible about how long she worked. No, it wasn't the thought of Fergus that was stopping her.

'Why don't you come with me?' she suggested to her mother as she pulled on her jacket and found her gloves. The virus she had picked up had been thankfully short-lived, but Fergus had insisted that she did not return to work for at least a full week, and although she was enjoying her mother's company there were times when she was filled with restless energy that nothing seem to dissipate—a sense of urgency and anxiety.

Both of them knew what was causing it, of course, but since the night she had confided in her mother neither of them had ever referred to Oliver—Lisa because she couldn't bear to, couldn't trust herself to so much as think, never mind say his name, without losing control and being swamped by her emotions, and her mother, she suspected, because despite her initial conviction that Oliver would discover the truth and want to make amends she too was now beginning to share Lisa's belief that it was over between them.

'I won't be too long,' she told her mother as she opened the front door.

'No...there's an exhibition on at the Tate that I thought we might go to this afternoon, and then I thought we might have dinner at that Italian place in Covent Garden that your father likes so much.'

Her mother was doing her best to keep her occupied and busy, Lisa knew, and she was doing all she could to respond, but both of them also knew that she was losing weight and that she didn't sleep very well at night, and that sometimes when she did she woke up crying Oliver's name.

Her head down against the sharp January wind, she set off in the direction of the park.

Once she had gone Lisa's mother picked up the receiver and dialled her husband's number in Japan.

'I still haven't managed to persuade Lisa to come back with me,' she told him after they had exchanged hellos. 'I'm worried about her, David. She looks so pale and thin... I wish there was some way we could get in touch with this Oliver. No, I know we mustn't interfere,' she agreed, 'but if you could see her. She looks so... I must go,' she told him. 'There's someone at the door.' Quickly she replaced the receiver and went to open the front door.

The tall, dark-haired man wearing one arm in a sling with a huge, purpling bruise on his cheekbone and a black eye and a nasty-looking cut on his forehead was completely unfamiliar to her and yet she knew who he was immediately.

'You must be Oliver,' she told him simply, extending her hand to shake his. 'I'm so glad you're here. I'd just about begun to give up on you. Silly of me really, especially when... You look rather the worse for wear; have you been in an accident...? I'm Lisa's mother, by the way; she's out at the moment but she'll be back soon. Do come in...'

'I had a bump in my car a few days ago,' Oliver told her as

he followed her into the flat. 'Fortunately nothing too serious. I say fortunately because it was my own fault; I virtually fell asleep at the wheel…' He caught the frowning look that Lisa's mother gave him and explained tersely, 'I was on my way back to London to see Lisa. Where did you say she was…?'

'She's gone out for a walk; she shouldn't be too long. She's been ill and I thought some fresh—'

'How ill?' Oliver pounced sharply.

Hiding her small, satisfied smile, Lisa's mother responded airily, 'Well, as a matter of fact, the doctor seemed quite concerned, but I'm a great believer in the efficacy of plenty of fresh air myself. She did say she felt a bit weak but—'

'A bit weak… Should she be out on her own?'

Poor man, he really had got it badly, Lisa's mother decided. As she witnessed his obvious concern Lisa's mother relented a little; this was no uncaring sexual predator, this was quite definitely a man very, very deeply in love.

'She's a lot better than she was,' she told him more gently.

Her half-hour in the park might have brought a pink flush to her skin and made her fingertips and toes tingle, Lisa acknowledged, but it had done nothing to alleviate the pain of loving Oliver. Only one person could do that, and with every day that passed her common sense told her that there was less and less chance of Oliver doing what her mother had claimed he was bound to do and coming in search of her, to tell her that he had discovered his mistake and to beg her to forgive him.

Grimly, Lisa retraced her steps towards her flat. Part of her wished desperately that she had never met Oliver, that she had never been exposed to the agony of loving him and then losing him, and yet another part of her clung passionately to the memory of their brief time together.

As her mother opened the door to her knock she told

Lisa, 'I'm just going out. Oh, and by the way, you've got a visitor.'

'Oliver?'

Hope, disbelief, the desire to push open the door and run to him and the equally strong desire to turn on her heels and run from him were all there in Lisa's eyes.

'Treat him gently,' her mother advised her as she took hold of her and gave her a supportive hug.

'Treat him gently', after what he had done to her? In a daze Lisa walked past her mother and into the flat, closing the door behind her. Oliver was actually here…here. The angry relief that flooded her was that same emotion so familiar to parents when a child had emerged unscathed from a forbidden risk—relief at its safety and anger that it should have taken such a risk with itself, with something so precious and irreplaceable.

In fact she was so angry that she was actually shaking as she pushed open the sitting-room door, Lisa discovered, her mouth compressing, and without even waiting to look directly at Oliver, without daring to take the risk of allowing her hungry heart, her starved senses to feast on the reality of him, she demanded tersely, 'What are you doing here?'

He was standing with his back to her, facing the window, apparently absorbed in the view outside. He must have seen her walking back to the flat, Lisa recognised, her heart giving a small, shaky bound. He turned round and every single thought, every single word she had been about to voice vanished as Lisa saw his cut and bruised face, his arm in a sling.

'Oliver…' Her voice cracked suddenly, becoming thready and weak, her eyes mirroring her shock and anxiety as she whispered, 'What's happened? Why…?'

'It's nothing…just a minor bump in my car,' Oliver assured her quickly. 'In fact I got off far more easily than I deserved.'

'You've been in an accident. But how?' she demanded, ignoring his attempts to make light of his injuries and instinctively hurrying towards him, realising only when it was too late and she was standing within easy distance of the free arm he stretched forward to her just how physically close to him she actually was.

Immediately she raised her hand in an automatic gesture of rejection, but Oliver had already stepped forward and the hand she had lifted in the body-language sign that meant 'No, keep away from me' was somehow resting against his shirt-covered chest with a very different meaning indeed.

'Oliver,' she protested weakly, but it wasn't any use; it wasn't just her legs and her body that were trembling now, her mouth was trembling as well, tears spilling over from her eyes as she said his name, causing Oliver to groan and reach for her, cradling her against his body with his good arm as he said, 'Lisa, darling, please don't…please don't cry. I can't bear to see you unhappy. I'll never forgive myself for what I've done—*never*. My only excuse is that I was half-crazed with jealousy over Henry.'

'Jealous?' Lisa questioned. 'You actually believed…? You were jealous of Henry?' She couldn't quite keep the disbelief out of her voice.

'Yes,' Oliver admitted ruefully. 'It all seemed to slot so neatly into place—your reluctance to commit yourself to me, the news that Henry was marrying an old flame, the sight of the two of you together. I know I overreacted. I was jealous, vulnerable,' he told her simply. 'You'd already made it plain that I wasn't the kind of man you wanted for a husband. I knew how reluctant you'd been to commit yourself to me, to our love.

'I knew, as well, how much I was rushing you, pressurising you, using the intensity of what we both felt for one another to win you over. I suppose a part of me will always be the child who felt that in dying my mother deliberately abandoned me. Logically I know that isn't what happened, but there's always that small worm of fear there—fear of losing the one you love—and the more you love someone, the greater the fear is. And I love you more than I can possibly tell you. I'm not trying to look for excuses for myself, Lisa; there aren't really any. What I did was…' He paused and shook his head as she touched his hand gently with understanding for what he was trying to say. 'At the time it seemed logical that you should have changed your mind, decided you preferred the safe life you had already mapped out for yourself.'

'Oh, Oliver.' Lisa shook her head.

'I was wrong, I know, and what I did was…unforgivable…'

The bleakness in his eyes and voice made Lisa want to reach out and hold him, but she restrained herself. She was already in his arms, and once she touched him…

'I…I didn't know that loving someone could be like that,' she told him in a husky voice. 'That anger could… That physically… I felt so ashamed after you had gone,' she admitted shakily.

'To have wanted you the way I did, to have responded to you, said the things I did, when I knew that you weren't touching me out of love. I felt so…' She shook her head, unable to find the words to express her own sense of horror at what, at the time, had seemed to her to be her own totally unacceptable and almost abnormal behaviour.

'Being angry with someone doesn't stop you loving them,' Oliver told her quietly. 'I was angry, bitter—furiously, destructively so; I can't deny that. I wanted to hurt you in the same way that I felt you had hurt me, but those feelings, strong as they were, destructive as they were, did not stop me loving you. In fact…'

He paused and looked down into her upturned face,

searching her eyes before telling her roughly, 'I tried to tell myself that I was punishing you…that I *wanted* to punish you…but almost from the moment I held you in my arms…' He stopped and shook his head. 'No matter what I might have *said*, my *body* was loving you, Lisa—loving you and wanting you and hating me for what I was trying to do.'

'What made you think I was marrying Henry in the first place?' Lisa questioned him.

'My cousin,' he informed her briefly. 'Emma had phoned from Yorkshire and she'd heard that Henry was getting married to someone he had already known for some time.'

'And you assumed it was me…'

'I assumed it was you,' Oliver agreed.

A little uncertainly Lisa looked up at him. The sadness she could see in his eyes made her heart jolt against her ribs.

'Have I completely ruined everything between us?' he asked her huskily. 'Tell me I haven't, Lisa. I can't… Being without you these last few days has been hell, but if you…'

He paused and Lisa told him shakily, 'I've missed you as well…'

Missed him!

'I should have rung you from New York and talked to you instead of flying back like that, but it looked like those damned negotiations were going to go on for ever and I'd already missed being with you on New Year's Eve. And then when I reached your flat and saw you there with Henry…'

'He came to tell me that he was getting married. His mother had sent him,' Lisa explained drily. 'She was concerned that I might get in touch with him and try to patch up our differences… I had just finished telling Henry that there was absolutely no chance whatsoever of that happening when you appeared. I thought when you didn't make New Year's Eve that you were having second thoughts…about us,' she confessed.

'*Me* having second thoughts… There's no way I could ever have second thoughts about the way I feel about you…about what I want with you…'

Lisa took a deep breath. There was something she had to tell him now, whilst they were both being so open and honest with one another.

'I did,' she confessed. '*I* had second thoughts…the day we parted…' She looked anxiously up at him; his face was unreadable, grave, craven almost, as he watched her in silence.

'I tried to tell you then,' she hurried on. 'I tried to say that I had changed my mind, but you didn't seem to want to listen and I thought that perhaps you had changed yours and that—'

'Changed your mind about what?' Oliver demanded hoarsely, cutting across her.

'About…about wanting to make a commitment,' Lisa admitted, stammering slightly as she searched his face anxiously, looking for some indication as to how he felt about what she was saying, but she could see none. Her heart started to hammer nervously against her ribs. Had she said too much? Had she…? Determinedly she pushed her uncertainty away.

'I knew then that it was just fear that had stopped me from telling you what I already knew… That I *did* love you and that I did want to be with you… I was even going to suggest that I went to New York with you.' She paused, laughing shakily. 'When it came to it I just couldn't bear the thought of not being with you, but you seemed so preoccupied and distant that I thought—'

'You were going to tell me that…?' Oliver interrupted her. 'Oh, my God, Lisa… Lisa…'

Any response she might have made was muffled by the hard pressure of his mouth against hers as, ignoring her protests that he might hurt his injured arm, he gathered her up, held her against his body and kissed her with all the hungry passion she had dreamed of in the time they had been apart.

'Lisa, Lisa, *why* didn't you say something to me?' Oliver groaned when he had finally finished kissing her. 'Why…?'

'Because I didn't think you wanted to hear,' Lisa told him simply. 'You were so distant and—'

'I was trying to stop myself from pleading with you to change your mind and come with me,' Oliver told her grimly. '*That* was why I was quiet.'

'Oh, Oliver…'

'Oh, Lisa,' he mimicked. 'How long do you suppose your mother will be gone?' he asked her as he bent his head to kiss her a second time.

'I don't know, but she did say something about going to see an exhibition at the Tate,' Lisa mumbled through his kiss.

'Mmm…' He was looking, Lisa noticed, towards the half-open bedroom door, and her own body started to react to the message she could read in his eyes as she followed his gaze.

'We can't,' she protested without conviction. 'What about your arm? And you still haven't told me about the accident,' she reminded him.

'I will,' he promised her, and added wickedly, 'They said at the hospital that I should get plenty of rest and that I shouldn't stand up for too long. They said that the best cure for me would be…' And he bent his head and whispered in Lisa's ear exactly what he had in mind for the two of them for the rest of the afternoon.

'Tell me about the accident first,' Lisa insisted, blushing a little as she saw the look he gave her when he caught that betraying 'first'.

'Very well,' he agreed, adding ruefully, 'Although, it doesn't make very good hearing.

'I didn't find out until we were back in Yorkshire that you weren't marrying Henry, but once I did and I realised what I'd done I broke all the rules and drove straight back here despite the fact that I hadn't had any sleep for going on three days and that I was jet-lagged into the bargain. Hardly a sensible or safety-conscious decision but…' He gave a small, self-deprecatory grimace. 'I was hardly feeling either sensible or safety-conscious; after all, what else had I got left to lose? I'd already destroyed the most precious thing I had in my life.

'Anyway…I must have started to doze off at the wheel; fortunately I'd already decided to stop at a motorway service station and I'd slowed down and pulled onto the approach road, and even more fortunately there was no other vehicle, no other person around to be involved in my self-imposed accident. The authorities told me that I was lucky my car was fitted with so many safety features…otherwise…'

'No, don't,' Lisa begged him, shuddering as her imagination painted an all too vivid picture of just how differently things could have turned out.

'Lisa, I know there is nothing I can say or do that can take away the memory of what I did; all I can do is promise you that it will never happen again and ask if you can forgive me.'

'It did hurt that you could think such a thing of me,' Lisa admitted quietly, 'and that you could…could treat me in such a way, but I *do* understand. In a way both of us were responsible for what happened; both of us should have trusted the other and our love more. If we had had more mutual trust, more mutual faith in our love then… Oh, Oliver,' she finished, torn between laughter and tears as she clung onto him. 'How could you possibly think I could even contemplate the idea of marrying anyone else, never mind Henry, after you…after the way you and I…?'

'Even when mentally I was trying to hate you I was still loving you physically and emotionally,' Oliver told her huskily. 'The moment I touched you… I never intended things to go so far; I'd just meant to kiss you one last time, that was all, but once I had…'

'Once you had what?' Lisa encouraged him, raising herself up on tiptoe to feather her lips teasingly against his.

'Once I had…this,' Oliver responded, smothering a groan deep in his throat as he pulled her against him with his good arm and held her there, letting her feel the immediate and passionate response of his body to her as he kissed her.

'We really ought to get up,' Lisa murmured sleepily, her words belying her actions as she snuggled closer to Oliver's side. 'The day's almost gone and…'

'Soon it will be bedtime. I know,' Oliver finished mock-wickedly for her. 'It was very thoughtful of your mother to telephone and say that she'd decided to go and visit some friends this evening and to stay overnight with them…'

'Mmm…very,' Lisa agreed, sighing leisurely as Oliver's hand cupped her breast.

'Mmm…that feels nice,' she told him.

'It certainly does,' Oliver agreed, and asked her softly, 'And does this?' as he bent his head and started to kiss the soft curve of her throat.

'I'm not sure… Perhaps if you did it for a bit longer,' Lisa suggested helpfully. 'A lot longer,' she amended more huskily as his mouth started to drift with delicious intent towards her breast… 'A lot, *lot* longer.'

EPILOGUE

'HOW DOES THAT LOOK?'

Lisa put her head to one side judiciously as she studied the huge Christmas tree that Oliver had just finished erecting in the hallway.

'I think it needs moving a little to the left; it's leaning slightly,' she told him, and then laughed as she saw his pained expression.

'No, darling, it's perfect,' she added with a happy sigh. They had been married for eight months, their wedding having preceded both Henry's and Piers'. Lisa's parents had both flown home for the wedding and Lisa and Oliver had flown out to Japan to spend three weeks with them in October.

Fergus had been disappointed when Lisa had handed in her notice, but she and Oliver were talking about the possibility of her setting up her own business in the north in partnership with Fergus. It seemed almost impossible to Lisa that it was almost twelve months since that fateful night when Oliver had found her stranded on the road and brought her home with him. Her smile deepened as she glanced down at the Armani suit she was wearing—a surprise gift from Oliver to mark the anniversary of the day they had initially met.

'Happy?' Oliver asked her, bending his head to kiss her.

'Mmm…how could I not be?' Lisa answered, snuggling closer to him. 'Oh, Oliver, last Christmas was wonderful, special, something I'll never forget, but this Christmas is going to be special too; I'm so glad that everyone's been able to come—your family and my parents.'

'We're certainly going to have a houseful,' Oliver agreed, laughing.

He had raised his eyebrows slightly at first when Lisa had suggested to him that they invite all his own relatives and her parents to spend their Christmas with them, but Lisa's enthusiasm for the idea had soon won him over.

'You really do love all this, don't you?' he commented now, indicating the large hallway festooned now for Christmas with the garlands and decorations that Lisa had spent hours making.

'Yes, I do,' Lisa agreed, 'but not anything like as much as I love you. Oh, Oliver,' she told him, her voice suddenly husky with emotion, 'you've made me so happy. It's hard to imagine that twelve months ago we barely knew one another and that—I love you so much.'

'Not half as much as I love you,' Oliver whispered back, his mouth feathering against hers and then hardening as he felt her happy response.

'We still haven't put the star on the tree,' Lisa reminded Oliver through their kiss.

'*You* are my star,' he told her tenderly, 'and without you I'd be lost in the darkness of unhappiness. You light up my life, Lisa, and I never, ever want to be without you.'

'You never, ever will,' Lisa promised him.

'Hey, come on, you two, break it up,' Piers demanded, coming into the hallway carrying a basket of logs for the fire. 'You're married now—remember?'

'Yes, we're married,' Oliver agreed, giving Lisa a look that made her laugh and blush slightly at the same time, as he picked up the star waiting to be placed at the top of the tree—the final touch to a Christmas that would be all the things that Christmas should be, that Christmas and every day *would* be for her from now on.

Oliver *was* her Christmas, all her special times, her life, her love.

* * * * *

Figgy Pudding

PENNY JORDAN

Dear Reader,

To me, there is no more magical and traditional time of the year than Christmas—perhaps because, as a Sagittarian, a small part of me has always retained my childhood wonder in the specialness of Christmas: its bright shining warmth in the darkest time of the year, a time to celebrate the triumph of hope over adversity and of love over pain.

These are all emotions that are strongly expressed in this story, with its heroine who is my favourite type of woman—strong, gutsy, determined to stand true to what she believes in and yet at the same time endearingly vulnerable. My hero in this story also embodies, I believe, the very best of traditional male values, 'magicked' by a special sprinkling of that extra ingredient that makes a man *the* man!

Since my own home is old and traditional, a cosy cottage nestling in the countryside, it is the traditional things in life in which I tend to take most pleasure. The Figgy Pudding recipe on which this story is based is as traditional as Christmas itself—although my heroine, Heaven, has added her own special *extra* ingredients! In bygone centuries every member of the household would have taken a turn in stirring the rich fruity pudding mixture, uniting them all in its preparation. I hope that in reading this story you will share this special sense of Christmas as it unites us all in spirit and in love, no matter how much we may be divided in other ways.

Penny Jordan

(Letter from the original version of this story)

PENNY JORDAN'S FIGGY PUDDING

(Makes two large puddings)
This is a traditional English recipe.

110g/1 cup chopped almonds
110g/ ¾cup chopped figs
450g/3 cups raisins
225g/ ½ lb currants
225g/1½ cups sultanas
110g/ ¾ cup mixed peel
110g/ ¾ cup chopped glacé cherries
110g/ ¾ cup plain flour
2 tsp ground mixed spice
2 tsp ground cinnamon
1 tsp ground nutmeg
225g/1¼ cups firmly packed brown sugar
225g/ ½ lb shredded suet or vegetarian suet
225g/4 cups fresh white breadcrumbs
225g/ ½ lb grated apple (about 2 medium apples)
1 large grated carrot
Juice and grated zest of 2 large lemons
2 tbsp molasses
4 large eggs, beaten
225 ml/1 cup Guinness or milk
4 tbsp rum or brandy

Combine the chopped almonds, figs, raisins, currants, sultanas, mixed peel and cherries. Add the sifted flour, spices, sugar, suet and breadcrumbs and mix thoroughly. Add the grated apple, carrot, lemon juice and zest and molasses and mix again. Stir in the beaten eggs, followed by the Guinness (or milk) and rum (or brandy). Spoon into two buttered casseroles (2½ pint capacity each) and cover with a double layer of waxed paper. Leave overnight to mature. Cover the casseroles with a double layer of foil, pleated down the centre and tied securely with string. Steam for 8 hours, checking regularly to see that the pan hasn't boiled dry. Remove and set aside to cool. Cover with fresh waxed paper and foil, then store somewhere cool and dark, ideally for 4 to 6 weeks. When ready to be eaten, steam the puddings for an additional 3 hours before turning out into serving dishes. Warm a ladleful of brandy, set alight and pour over the puddings.

PROLOGUE

'MMM...well, I suppose he's all right,' Christabel announced as she looked critically at her less than one-week-old cousin as he lay contentedly in his mother's arms.

In four weeks' time it would be Christmas and Heaven and Jon would be going up to the Scottish Borders to spend the Christmas season in their home there, but right now they were still in London where Jon was enjoying showing off his newborn son to his sister, her two daughters and their doting stepfather.

'What I don't understand, though,' young Christabel continued seriously, 'is why you've called him Figgy.'

Over the dark downy head of Charles Christopher Hugo, nicknamed 'Figgy', Heaven grinned at her husband.

'Well, it's a long story,' she began 'and let's just say that figgy pudding is a very special Christmas treat and "Figgy" here—'

'I think you'd better stop there,' Jon warned her ruefully, but his niece, picking up on the very interesting adult messages passing between her uncle and her new aunt, decided she wanted to hear more.

She had just reached the age where adult secrets, adult conversations were beginning to make her curious.

'Tell me,' she demanded imperiously. 'I like stories…'

Heaven laughed into Jon's eyes. In his mother's arms Figgy continued to sleep despite his father's attempts to make him wake up.

'Well,' Heaven began importantly, 'just as figgy pudding is a pudding with a difference, so too is this a story with a difference, and it all began like this…'

CHAPTER ONE

'YOU'RE really going to go ahead and do it, then—take the job, despite…everything?'

Looking up from the pudding mixture she was stirring, Heaven Matthews grimaced at her best friend and nodded emphatically, confirming, 'Yep, Janet, I'm really going to go ahead and do it.'

'Well, I can understand why,' Janet Viners acknowledged. 'Anyone would, and after the way Harold Lewis treated you—after what he did to you—he certainly deserves to receive a taste of his own medicine!'

'Oh, he will,' Heaven said fervently, the stern look on her small, heart-shaped, vivacious face not really masking the pain Janet knew she was still suffering from the traumatic events which had so catastrophically affected her life. 'He quite definitely will,' Heaven averred, adding quietly, 'Revenge, so they say, is a dish best eaten cold. We shall see. In this instance the proof of the pudding will quite definitely be in the eating—his eating, not mine. He always was a greedy pig, and not just for food.'

The smile which had brought into prominence the pretty dimples on either side of her generously curved mouth had faded again and as she watched her Janet reflected sadly on how much the last months had sapped her friend's normal joie de vivre and how rarely she had heard the infectious happy laughter that had always been such a wonderful part of Heaven's personality. The fact that she was the kind of person—woman—who was loved and valued by all those who knew her only made what had happened to her seem all the more unbelievable, all the more unpalatable—if Janet was to follow Heaven's humorous habit of using food metaphors and clichés in a tongue-in-cheek fashion to illustrate her conversation and to underline and emphasise her passionate love of good food.

Not that you would ever know it from her enviably slender figure, Janet acknowledged wistfully as she contrasted her own much plumper frame with Heaven's delicate sylph-like figure.

Even when they had been at school together Heaven had been determined that one day when she was grown up she was going to be famous for her cooking.

Some months ago when Janet had reminded her of that childhood dream Heaven had given her a bitter smile and said painfully, 'Well, I was nearly right, wasn't I? Only instead of becoming famous what I've become is infamous…infamous, notorious and unemployable…' And her strikingly beautiful dark blue eyes had filled with painful tears which, true to character, she had dashed impatiently away. The last thing that Heaven was was the kind of person who wallowed in self-pity, despite the fact that right now she had every reason to feel sorry for herself, Janet acknowledged, reflecting on the events of the last eighteen months.

A promising career totally ruined, her life turned upside down by the media interest the whole affair had created, and as if that wasn't bad enough poor Heaven had also had to live with the fact that no matter how often she protested her innocence there would always be those who were going to disbelieve her.

'Who's going to want to employ me as a private cook now?' she had demanded bitterly some months earlier, when Janet had called round to find her friend busily trying to compose an ad for the classified pages of certain magazines.

'Even if my name wasn't recognised then sooner or later my face would be. I doubt there's a hostess in London who hasn't heard about the cook who tried to steal her employer's husband.'

'Are you really sure you're doing the right thing?' Janet tried now to counsel her friend gently. Perhaps because Heaven was so petite, too naively inclined to believe the best of everyone and she herself was so much taller, so much more wary, despite the fact that they were both the same age—twenty-three—Janet had always been inclined to be protective of Heaven.

They were standing in the kitchen of a pretty Georgian town house in Chelsea. Heaven's father had inherited it from his great-aunt who had in turn inherited it from her parents, so there was a good deal of family history attached to it. Too much for the house to be sold, and since there was no way that Heaven's parents were going to uproot themselves from the comfortable Shropshire village to which they had retired her father had suggested that Heaven should live there rent-free until she could restore some sort of order to her shattered life.

'After all,' Janet continued, 'you're starting to build up quite a nice little business for yourself and—'

'Selling puddings through the classified ads and at country fairs,' Heaven interrupted her in self-contempt. 'Janet, I'm a trained cordon bleu cook. Making home puddings…'

'It's a living,' Janet reminded her gently.

'It's an existence,' Heaven corrected her. 'If Dad wasn't allowing me to live here rent-free…'

'Have you thought of looking for work abroad, somewhere…?'

'Where no one knows me?' Heaven supplied for her, shaking her head. 'Perhaps I should, but I haven't. This is where I want to work, Janet. Here… London…my home…the place where I should be able to work, where I would be able to work if it wasn't for that rat Harold.' Angry tears filled her eyes. Determinedly she blinked them away. 'I was just beginning to make a proper name for myself. I would have made a name for myself if that creep hadn't gone and destroyed everything I'd worked for and…'

Heaven put the mixing bowl to one side and gave Janet a woeful look as she pushed her fingers into her already tousled dark curly hair.

'I'm sorry to be such a wet lettuce, Jan, but you know…'

'Yes, I know,' Janet agreed sympathetically.

'I just wish that Lloyd was earning enough for us to be able to employ you,' she added with a grin. 'He keeps complaining that he's getting sick of microwave cooking. I think, of course, he's using that as an excuse for getting me to go to his parents' for Christmas. Not that I mind. I get on really well with his family. Have you made any plans yet? After all, it's only next week…'

Heaven shook her head.

'Mum and Dad have offered to pay for me to fly out to Adelaide with them. They're off to spend Christmas and all of January with Hugh.'

Hugh, as Janet knew, was Heaven's married brother who lived in Australia with his wife and children.

'Why don't you go with them?' Janet urged her. 'Who knows? You might even find you like it so much that you decide to stay there.'

'Shipped off to Australia, like the family black sheep?' Heaven countered painfully. 'No…that isn't what I want, Jan, even if the days are long gone when someone in disgrace was sent away from home. I feel that if I run away now people will think I'm running because I'm guilty, because I was to blame for the break-up of Harold's marriage, because all those things he said…' She stopped and gulped in a steadying breath.

'I was not having an affair with him,' she told her friend fiercely. 'And even if he hadn't been the completely loathsome and reptilian thing that he is I still wouldn't have been tempted…not with another woman's man. That just isn't me, Jan… Mind you, some of it was my own fault,' Heaven admitted with what Janet privately considered was far too much generosity; she had her own opinion of Harold Lewis and it wasn't good—creep was far too kind a description of him, so far as she was concerned.

'I should have guessed what lay ahead when he pretended he didn't have enough cash to reimburse my travelling expenses when I went for the initial interview, but I was still green then and the job seemed such a good one. Residential, with summers with the family in Provence and the opportunity not just to cook for him and his wife and the two girls and do all their private entertaining, but also to cook for his business lunches and dinners as well…'

'I do understand how you must feel,' Janet consoled her. Heaven gave her a small smile.

'I'm sorry, I don't mean to rant and rave at you. It's just the unfairness of it all that gets to me still. He deliberately used me, set me up, lied about me by pretending that we were having an affair to Louisa, his wife, so that she would walk out on him, so that he could then divorce her and get away with keeping the house and hardly give her any proper settlement. She's the one I should be feeling sorry for…'

'Have you seen anything of her since?'

'Since I so publicly got the sack and my name and my supposed role in their divorce, not to mention his bed, got so much media attention?' Her pretty mouth twisted. 'No, not really. Oh, she did try to make amends; she apologised for the fact that I'd been dragged into things and she told me that she recognised with hindsight just how cleverly she'd been tricked into believing I was having an affair with her husband.

'Apparently he'd been dropping hints about "us" virtually even before I'd gone to work for them and had, in fact, insisted on employing me above her head; and he'd then gone on to deliberately arouse her suspicions and undermine her by letting her think that he was attracted to me.

'You'd never think he was virtually a millionaire, would you—not after the way he's been so mean with Louisa?'

'Sometimes the richer a man is the meaner he is,' Janet pointed out.

Heaven grimaced in distaste. 'If you ask me Louisa

is well rid of him, and I suspect from what she hinted at that she has started to feel the same way since their divorce. She did say that she had tried to tell her friends that Harold had lied about me and about my role in the break-up of their marriage, but let's face it, no one is really going to believe her.'

As she saw the way Heaven's expressive eyes filled with sad tears, Janet felt her own eyes fill up in sympathy.

It wasn't just her job she had lost, Heaven reflected inwardly as she determinedly pulled the pudding mixture towards her and started to finish a fresh batch of puddings. The money she was earning from the small classified ad she had taken, offering 'Mrs Tiggywinkle's traditional figgy puddings by post', had brought her a much needed small income even if she was beginning to get sick of the sight and smell of her very saleable and mouthwatering puddings.

No, it wasn't just the job she had lost. Not even Janet knew about those delicate, fragile private hopes that had begun to grow after Louisa's brother had casually asked if she would like to take up a spare ticket he had for one of London's newest plays.

Jon Huntingdon, Louisa's brother, was an eminent financial consultant. Tall, dark-haired and suavely handsome. He had set Heaven's all too vulnerable heart beating just that little bit too fast the very first time she had been introduced to him by Louisa, several days after she had first taken up her new job. Unmarried and in his thirties, Jon Huntingdon was almost too swooningly male, too darkly handsome, with a heart-melting sense of humour betrayed by the twitch of his mouth as he gently teased Louisa's daughters, his nieces.

Heaven had prepared for their date in a fever of excitement; she had even cajoled an early birthday cheque out of her father in order to splash out on a new outfit. A Nicole Farhi dress and jacket, the dress a silver shimmer of thick matt jersey cut in a halter-neck style and supported simply by a thin silver collar.

She hadn't really needed to see the appreciative male gleam of sensual pleasure in Jon's eyes the evening he had picked her up to know that the dress looked good on her, but she had enjoyed seeing it there none the less.

After the play had ended he had taken her out for supper at a small French restaurant she had never even heard of, but when she had ordered and tested the French onion soup she had known that his taste in good food was as impeccable as his taste in well-made clothes.

After dinner he had driven her home, parking his silver-grey Jaguar discreetly in the drive of the Lewises' house and then switching off the lights.

Heaven, who had been awaiting this moment ever since he had made his casual invitation to take up his spare ticket, hadn't been sure if it was exhilarated excitement that was churning her stomach so nervously, or pure fear.

She had been out with good-looking men before, but she had never previously met anyone who'd affected her as quickly and overwhelmingly as Jon had done, and she had known even then, with that heart-deep instinct that all women possessed, that he was a man who could be something very special in her life…perhaps even be the man.

And then he had kissed her.

Briefly, decorously, unthreateningly…the first time!

After the world had stopped turning around her, after

she had stopped feeling like one of those small figures in a child's toy snow storm, he had kissed her again.

And she had responded, totally unable to stop herself from letting her emotions show.

'I'm not used to this,' she told him shakily and plaintively when he eventually released her.

'Do you think I am?' he countered rawly before drawing her back into his arms. 'You smell of cinnamon and honey, and everything good that was ever created,' he told her huskily as he breathed in the scent of her with heart-rocking sensuality, 'and I could eat you—every tiny last bit of you.'

He didn't do that, but he certainly kissed her again, deeply, lingeringly, like someone relishing every mouthful of a delicious meal, parting her lips and tasting her mouth as though he were enjoying some sweet, juicy-fleshed fruit.

There wasn't anything else. He didn't make any attempt to touch her more intimately, and, despite the way he had aroused her, irrationally she was glad… glad of the fact that already he liked her enough, cared enough not to want to rush things, to gobble down the pleasure she knew instinctively the two of them could share.

'I have to go away tomorrow,' he whispered to her as he held her face and kissed her gently on the mouth a final time. 'Business in Europe. But once I get back I'll be in touch…'

But of course he hadn't been, she mused now. She hadn't been there for him to get in touch with. The storm had broken two days later, and she had gone to ground, with Louisa accusing her of having an affair with her husband and him having admitted it. Refusing to listen to Heaven's denials, Louisa had left her husband, taking their two children with her.

Although he had strenuously denied it Heaven had had a pretty shrewd suspicion that it had been Harold himself who had leaked the story to the press. The initial story had quickly turned into a nationally covered media debate on Heaven's supposed treachery in having an affair with Harold—a debate which had left her reputation in tatters and her self-esteem so low that she had been more than grateful to accept her parents' suggestion that she leave London and stay with them until the fuss had died down.

She had no idea just when Jon had returned from abroad but she had not been surprised when he had not got in touch with her, and, even though on a chance meeting in the street Louisa had apologised for not listening to her when she had originally tried to explain that Harold had been lying about the supposed relationship between them, no mention had been made of her brother and Heaven had not felt able to ask about him.

Over the last few months she had had the scales so well and truly ripped from her eyes where the male sex was concerned that she had few illusions left, and besides, right now she had far more important and immediate concerns to deal with.

Things like making sure that Harold Lewis paid for what he had done to her. Oh, not in money. No, something far more satisfactory… Something that would damage his reputation, his self-esteem, his standing in the eyes of the world, just as he had damaged hers.

'The proof of the pudding,' she reminded herself, muttering the words under her breath so that Janet shook her head slightly.

'I'm sorry.' She apologised again to her friend. 'It just makes me so mad, that's all. He gets away scot-free with what he's done and I'm left not just without a job but also without a reputation. What sane woman is going to employ me now when the whole world knows the risk she'd be taking? When everyone thinks I'm a cook from hell, the kind of employee who is more interested in making the man of the house than in making the dinner? Well, it's my turn now and fate has given me an opportunity to well and truly butter his bread for him. It's almost too good to be true…'

'Mmm…' Janet agreed doubtfully. 'Tell me in more detail what you plan to do.'

'Just let me get these puddings on,' Heaven said. 'I've got an order for fifty to fill and get sent off by tomorrow.'

'Fifty…' Janet groaned, watching as Heaven moved deftly around the kitchen.

'Right,' Heaven announced when she had finished. 'As you know I've been advertising in the classified ads as Mrs Tiggywinkle, selling figgy puddings, but saying that I can cater for private functions as well. Well, I got a phone call three days ago from someone who introduced herself to me as Tiffany Simons. She said that she was desperate to find someone to cook a special celebration pre-Christmas dinner for her fiancé who was returning from the States with a couple of important business clients who he wanted her to entertain along with some close friends and business associates. None of the agencies could supply her with a cook so close to Christmas and at such short notice—so she was literally ringing round every number she could find in the hope of getting a cook from somewhere.

'To add to her problems, as well as dropping this dinner on her it transpired that her fiancé had also left her with full responsibility for getting the work completed on a house he was having renovated for them both.

'We arranged to meet to have lunch and discuss everything. And that was when I knew…'

'When you knew what?' Janet questioned her.

'When I knew that she—Tiffany—must be engaged to Harold… She was wearing Louisa's old engagement ring,' Heaven told her simply. 'I recognised it straight away. Louisa threw it back at him the day she walked out. Later she told me that she'd never liked it and had always considered it too vulgar. It was a huge brilliant-cut solitaire. Very flashy.'

'Louisa's engagement ring and now this Tiffany's wearing it?' Janet gasped.

'Yes, but I doubt that she knows it was Louisa's. She's very young—I feel quite sorry for her. She's obviously terrified of doing anything to annoy or upset Harold and it's typical of him that he should have sprung this dinner thing on her—and typical as well that the fee he's willing to pay the cook he's told her to hire is nowhere near enough—not for the type of meal he's ordered her to organise.

'She's panicking like mad that the guest bedrooms aren't going to be finished on time. She confided to me that Harold's refusing to pay the interim payments he promised the designers and suppliers unless they get everything ready ahead of schedule. I don't know who these people are he's so keen to impress but they must be pretty important to him…'

'More important than his new fiancée,' Janet suggested shrewdly.

'Oh, much more important,' Heaven agreed. 'I could tell from the way she was talking about him that she hardly knows him at all. There's some kind of distant business connection between Harold and her father, apparently, and that's how they met.

'Anyway, once she told me what was happening, I realised that if I took on the job of cooking this dinner for her it would give me the ideal opportunity to get my own back on Harold. He always did have a sweet tooth,' she added inconsequentially, a wide, cat-like smile curling her mouth as her eyes danced.

'Heaven…' Janet said uncertainly. 'You're not thinking of doing anything too over the top, are you?'

She was suddenly remembering the scrapes her friend's irrepressible sense of humour had got them into as schoolgirls and remembering too just how much reason Heaven had to want to punish Harold for the damage he had done to her.

'That depends,' Heaven answered soberly, but Janet could see that her eyes were still gleaming with amusement.

'On what?' she asked warily.

'On what one considers to be too over the top,' Heaven replied promptly, but unsatisfactorily—at least so far as Janet was concerned.

Janet tried again.

'What I meant was, you're not planning on doing something illegal…?'

'Illegal?' Heaven's eyebrows rose. 'Certainly not,' she denied emphatically. 'What I have in mind is designed quite simply to hurt Harold's pride, to damage it just as he damaged mine. Poisoning him and ending up in prison for it—if that's what that anxious mother-hen look in your eyes means you're worrying about—is the last thing I'd want to do, although…' A thoughtful far-away look in her eyes made Janet's anxiety increase. 'There are certain hallucinogenic mushrooms which I could—'

'No, no, you mustn't do anything like that,' Janet intervened quickly.

'No, I mustn't,' Heaven agreed, adding with mock primness, 'It would be quite unethical.

'No, what I've got in mind will teach Harold a much more salutary lesson than anything like that…'

'If he doesn't recognise you and throw you out,' Janet warned her.

'He won't recognise me,' Heaven assured her positively. 'For a start Tiffany only knows me by my new professional name of Mrs Tiggywinkle and she obviously hadn't a clue who I was when we met. She was at great pains and rather embarrassed to ask me if I would mind keeping a very low profile—apparently Harold wants his guests to think that she cooked their meal.

'He would, of course, since he's obviously being too mean to take them out to an expensive restaurant or pay the fees charged by the kind of frantically up-market caterers he'd enjoy boasting about hiring. He's decided it will give him more kudos to have his victims—sorry, his guests—believe that poor Tiffany has cooked their dinner, so I'm to lie low in the kitchen whilst she serves the meal.

'Knowing Harold as I do, I very much doubt he'll come anywhere near the kitchen—for a start he'd think he was demeaning himself and no doubt he'll try his best to get away with delaying paying me for as long as he can—I've asked to be paid cash on the night. No, Harold won't see me to recognise me.

'It won't matter, not so long as they eat their dinner—and they will.

'Revenge is sweet, so they say, and, as I've already told you, Harold has an extremely sweet tooth, so he shall have an extremely generous portion of revenge,' Heaven told her, giving Janet a kind smile when she saw that she was still looking anxious.

'I wish you weren't doing this,' Janet told her.

'I don't,' Heaven responded cheerfully. 'You can't imagine how much better I've felt these last few days knowing that at last Harold is going to get his comeuppance, or rather his just deserts! Do you know, I think I'm going to enjoy Christmas this year after all?' she added conversationally as the timer on her oven pinged and she went to attend to the puddings she had made earlier.

'All alone here?' Janet asked her doubtfully. 'I wish you would change your mind and come with us to Lloyd's parents'. I know they'd make you welcome.'

'No…I want to be alone… Next year is going to be my year and I want to be ready for it.'

'Those puddings smell marvellous,' Janet told her.

'Mmm…they do, don't they?' Heaven agreed with a small smile that made Janet's maternal heart beat even more anxiously.

CHAPTER TWO

'I HOPE you don't intend to allow him to get away with this.'

Louisa gave her brother an unhappy look as he put down the letter he had just been reading. She had received it from her ex-husband's solicitor only that morning and had telephoned Jon straight away to tell him what had happened.

'I don't want to. If he does insist on refusing to pay the girls' school fees they'll have to change school and Belle is already having a few problems following the divorce...but I don't know what I can do to stop him.'

'My God, when I think...' Jon began, and then stopped when he saw the unhappiness on his sister's face.

'I know what you're thinking, Jon,' she told him. 'I admit I have only myself to blame for the fact that Harold has made such a fool of me financially. If I hadn't walked out on him and insisted on an immediate divorce and if I hadn't been so desperate to let my pride rule my head I could have obtained a much better financial settlement from him.'

'The fact that he's depriving not just you but also his own children of the financial comfort you've all every reason to expect has nothing to do with your pride and everything to do with his greed,' Jon told her gently. 'I just wish I hadn't been working abroad and away so much when the divorce was going through. I'd give a lot to know just how he managed to convince the divorce judge that he didn't have the assets to give you what you were fully entitled to.'

'He manipulated me,' Louisa admitted grimly, 'by pretending that he was having an affair with Heaven. He tricked me into walking out on him. I should have stayed where I was. After all, it wasn't as though she was his first affair—not that they were having an affair, of course,' Louisa corrected herself hastily. 'She was just as much a victim of his machinations as I was myself—even more of one, really, when I think what that poor girl suffered…'

'Have you seen her at all since?' Jon asked her casually, turning slightly to one side as he did so so that Louisa couldn't see his face.

'Only once,' she told him. 'Not unnaturally I don't think she really wanted anything to do with me but we literally bumped into one another in the street. At least I was able to apologise to her. Even now, you know, I've still got friends who quite plainly don't believe that she wasn't involved with Harold even though I've told them that it was all a mistake. Harold treated her almost as vindictively as he did me and I've wondered since if he did actually make a play for her and got turned down. That would explain the obvious pleasure he took in deliberately blackening her character…

'Jon, what am I going to do about this?' she asked her brother, returning to the original subject of her urgent phone call to him. 'If I accept this reduced level of maintenance and Harold's refusal to pay the girls' school fees, I just don't know what we're going to do.'

'I'm more than happy to cover the cost of the girls' education. After all, they are my nieces,' Jon told her firmly.

'Your nieces, yes, but one day you could well have children of your own, a wife of your own who might not look too kindly on you having to virtually support my children as well as your own.'

'Any woman who felt like that would never be my wife,' Jon told her truthfully, and Louisa hugged him.

'It says in this letter that the reason Harold is seeking to reduce his payments to you is the fact that he is planning to remarry and he and his new wife intend to have their own family…'

'Has he said anything to you about wanting to cut my maintenance payments?'

'No,' Jon told her, shaking his head. 'I have managed to convince him that I'm more interested in maintaining the friendship I've struck up with him than I am in whatever problems you might be facing, but as yet he still hasn't opened up to me as much as I'd hoped about how and where he's managed to conceal so much of his wealth. But I am still trying.

'He's invited me to a pre-Christmas dinner he's giving at the end of the week. He faxed me from New York to tell me about it. He's over there on business at the moment.'

'A pre-Christmas dinner?' Louisa questioned.

'Mmm…his new fiancée is arranging everything, apparently, and it's being held at the house he's been having renovated in Knightsbridge.'

'The house he bought with the profit he made on selling our house,' Louisa said fiercely.

'Yes,' Jon agreed grimly.

'That poor girl. I hope that, unlike me, she finds out what he's really like before they get married,' Louisa told her brother bitterly. 'Oh, Jon, what am I going to do?' she asked him plaintively. 'The parents have offered to help but they've already done more than enough, and so has Rory…'

Jon noticed the way his sister's skin changed colour slightly as she mentioned the old family friend who had done so much to support her both emotionally and practically since the break-up of her marriage. It was no secret to Jon that Rory Stevens loved his sister and Jon suspected that she was now beginning to return his feelings.

'Do you think Harold believes that you want his friendship and that you approve of what he's done?'

'He seems to,' Jon told her, 'but I must admit I had hoped by now to at least have some proof for you that he deliberately concealed the major part of his assets in order to pay you far less money than he should.'

'We already know that he did,' Louisa pointed out fiercely.

'We know it, yes, but we can't prove it,' Jon reminded her patiently.

Later, as he set off back to his own apartment—a set of traditional and old-fashioned rooms in Fulham which he owned along with a home in the Scottish Borders where he spent as much time as he could, and another large apartment in a renovated Belgian château which he used whenever he had business in Brussels—he was still thinking over his sister's financial problems.

It infuriated him that a man like Harold could use the law as he had done and he had to admit it was getting harder and harder to keep his real feelings about the man to himself whenever they were together.

He had no idea why Harold should be so keen to pursue their 'friendship', unless he felt that in doing so he was somehow or other getting one up on Louisa.

Well, Jon was damned if he was going to let Harold get away with cheating Louisa and more importantly their children out of their financial due a second time, especially when Harold could well afford to be far more generous with them than he had been. At the very least Louisa should have had the family home—would have had it if she hadn't been manipulated into walking out on him.

When he opened the door of his car Jon froze momentarily as a girl walked into his line of vision, thick dark curls bouncing softly on her shoulders as she hurried down the street wrapped up against the raw December wind in a coat which looked three or four sizes too big for her slender frame.

And then she turned her head and he saw her face. When was he going to stop doing this? When was he going to stop reacting blindly and ridiculously every single time he saw a woman who bore the slightest resemblance to Heaven?

Heaven. What a name...what a woman. He had been attracted to her the moment he saw her, attracted to her, enchanted by her, instinctively aware of the importance of not rushing her...not panicking her by coming on too strong too soon. He could still remember the way her lips had quivered so softly and tellingly under his, still see the way her eyes had opened and widened as she'd looked back at him, unable to conceal what she was feeling.

God knew where she was now, but wherever it was it was obvious that she wanted nothing to do with him. The man whose sister had been responsible for the destruction of her reputation, the man whose brother-in-law had dragged her name through the tabloids, publicly labelling her as his mistress—publicly and completely untruthfully. Jon had known that immediately and instinctively but by then it was too late. She had gone and no one had seemed able to tell him where.

Her parents, when he had approached them, had been polite but pointedly determined. Their daughter had told them quite categorically that she wished to have no contact whatsoever with anyone connected with Harold—no matter who—and they'd been afraid that they could not tell him where she was or how to get in touch with her.

At one point he had actually thought of employing a private detective to find her for him but just in time he had come to his senses and recognised what an appalling intrusion of her privacy that would be—but that hadn't stopped him searching every even half-familiar face glimpsed in the street just in case…

Did she still have that irrepressible sense of humour, that impish smile? He hoped so. Had she got over the trauma of what had been inflicted on her? Did she ever think of him? Somehow he doubted it.

Grimly he climbed into his car and started the engine. It was pointless now cursing the fate that had led to him being out of the country when the whole nasty affair of Harold's manipulation of Louisa's vulnerable emotions had blown up, but of course that didn't stop him from doing so.

They had only shared one date…a few chaste kisses…and two far more memorable ones that had been anything but chaste…but that had been enough to have him comparing every woman he had been tempted to date since with Heaven and finding them wanting—and finding himself even more wanting for being so emotionally hung up on a woman he had known so briefly and so tenuously.

Thank goodness for that, Heaven puffed, heaving a sigh of relief that the last of the large batch of puddings she had received orders for had been passed over to the post-office clerk for onward despatch.

It was a fine if cold winter's day, the sky a pale smudgy blue over the steel-grey waters of the Thames as she walked back towards the house. As always the river fascinated her, causing her to stop and look at it.

Had her ancestors, her great-grandparents, who had lived in the house before her, been equally fascinated by the ebb and flow of its tides, the magnificence of it?

The weather forecasters had predicted a heavy frost for the next few days and idly Heaven wondered what it must have been like to be alive when the Thames had actually frozen over. She remembered reading that it had once frozen so deeply and so hard that a fair had actually been held on it complete with burning braziers to warm the skaters and provide the excited crowds who had flocked to enjoy the novel experience of actually walking on the solid surface of the river with tasty snacks. What exactly would they have served? she wondered dreamily.

Eel pie, whelks, whitebait, hot bread and buns, confectionery of all descriptions. She had a much treasured recipe book from the eighteenth century which had been a twenty-first-birthday present from her parents and just reading the lists of some of the ingredients brought forcibly to her a mental image of the merchant vessels which had once thronged the Thames, bringing home their cargoes of exotic and expensive spices and sugar.

This afternoon she was due to meet with Tiffany Simons to go through the menu she had produced for her. With the dinner scheduled for the end of the week that wouldn't leave her very much time to do her shopping and she still had the kitchen to inspect and to check on.

Her thoughts firmly back in the present, she turned her back on the river and hurried home.

'Figgy pudding… What exactly is that?' Tiffany enquired, her forehead crinkling in a small frown.

She and Heaven were seated opposite one another at the table of the kitchen of the house she had explained to Heaven she was going to share with Harold once they were married.

'My parents are rather old-fashioned,' she had told Heaven with a small sigh. 'They wouldn't be happy about me moving in with anyone before we were married. Mummy didn't have me until she was forty. They had given up all hope of having a family when she became pregnant with me and so…' She had paused, but Heaven could guess just how precious she was to her parents and just how protective of her they were—but not apparently protective enough—not if they thought that Harold would make her a good husband.

'Figgy pudding,' she started to explain now in response to Tiffany's question, 'it is an old-fashioned, traditional and very rich pudding mixture. Men love it,' she added when she saw the doubt shadowing Tiffany's pretty soft brown eyes.

Instantly the other girl's expression cleared.

'Oh, do they? Well, in that case that's all right, then,' she declared ingenuously, adding, 'I'm afraid I'm not much of a cook. That's why Harold said I had to find someone to prepare this dinner.

'Apparently the people he's bringing back from New York are some very important new business contacts he's made. Harold owns his own software company,' she told Heaven importantly. 'These Americans want him to sell the business to them. Harold's brilliantly clever, though,' she went on, giving Heaven a proud smile, 'because if he does sell the company to them he's still going to keep a new software program he's been working on, although he won't be able to sell it in America, not at first; but Harold says there's a huge market for it in the Middle East and Taiwan.'

Heaven had to shade her eyes with her lashes to conceal her true thoughts as she listened to Tiffany's artless prattle. Knowing Harold as she did, Heaven suspected that the kind of deal he was hoping to pull off with the Americans would not only benefit him financially but would also involve him practising the same sort of deliberate manipulation he had used with his wife, to gain yet another financial victory just as underhandedly as he had Louisa's divorce settlement.

As she listened to Tiffany enthusing about Harold's

supposed cleverness Heaven couldn't help but feel sorry for her. The girl really had no idea what Harold was about at all. Heaven, though, could well understand why Harold wanted to marry her. Her naivety would appeal to him almost as much as her undoubted prettiness.

'So you're quite happy with the menu we've decided on,' Heaven checked with Tiffany as she started to gather up the notes she had made, giving the kitchen a thorough professional visual inspection whilst she did so. She hadn't missed the nervous half-whispered telephone conversation Tiffany had had with the kitchen designer halfway through their own conversation, from which it had been obvious that the designers still had to be paid, not just for their own work but for the units and equipment as well. Well, that didn't really surprise Heaven, not knowing Harold as she did.

'Oh, yes, it's perfect,' Tiffany was assuring her now happily. 'especially the pudding. Harold adores sweet things.'

The menu Heaven had suggested was simple enough: a thick home-made winter soup followed by a fish course, a sorbet to clear the palate and then the main course, for which she had suggested a rich casserole of red meat with accompanying vegetables, filling but not so filling that Harold's guests wouldn't have room for her piÈce de résistance—the figgy pudding on which as Mrs Tiggywinkle she had based her small new mail-order business.

'And you'll have everything ready here in the kitchen for me to carry through to the dining room?' Tiffany checked anxiously.

'Yes, everything will be ready,' Heaven told her, adding reassuringly, 'Don't worry, no one will ever know that you haven't cooked everything yourself.'

Quickly she stifled her own uncomfortable qualm at the thought of Harold blaming Tiffany for her wrongdoing—but of course Harold would know that Tiffany hadn't actually done the cooking. He simply didn't want to admit as much to his guests—he would, of course, try to discover who had cooked the meal but she would be safely hidden behind the anonymity of Mrs Tiggywinkle.

Tiffany blushed.

'I wouldn't normally be so…so deceitful, but Harold says it's vitally important that we make a good impression on these Americans and apparently there's nothing they like more than home-cooked food.'

'You said there'd be eight of you to cater for,' Heaven reminded her.

'Yes, that's right. Harold and me, the three businessmen who are coming back with him, his accountant and his wife and a friend of Harold's who's a business consultant.'

A business consultant and his accountant. Heaven might not know the former but she certainly knew Harold's accountant and his wife, an avaricious, acid-tongued woman whom Heaven had overheard on more than one occasion running Louisa and the children down to Harold. She had even tried to tell Heaven herself how to do her job and had, Heaven knew, been instrumental in spreading the completely untrue rumours about her supposed affair with Harold. She was a thoroughly unpleasant woman whom Heaven had no qualms about allowing to share Harold's fate. Harold obviously wasn't taking any chance on letting the big fish he had landed slip away from him, Heaven decided sardonically as she gave Tiffany a small smile and stood up. She found herself liking Tiffany. Somehow she would have to find some way of ensuring that Tiffany herself didn't eat any of the figgy pudding.

Not that there was anything wrong with her figgy pudding—far from it—at least not when she made it without the addition of the certain extra ingredients she planned to put in the one for this dinner party!

CHAPTER THREE

NERVOUSLY Heaven smoothed her hands down over the crisp white apron she was wearing over the simple short-sleeved black dress she had picked up at a bargain price because of its small size.

It wasn't any worries about her cooking that were making her feel so jittery, her stomach muscles clenching every time she heard a noise on the other side of the very firmly closed kitchen door. Despite her stalwart assurances to Janet that she knew exactly what she was doing and that her plan was completely fireproof, it was still a fact, as Janet had pithily pointed out to her, that all it would take for her to be run out of the house in very short order would be for Harold to walk into the kitchen and see her.

'Harold won't walk into the kitchen,' Heaven had asserted. 'Harold is the kind of man who boasts about barely knowing how to find the fridge door—he wouldn't dream of visiting any kitchen but most especially not his own.'

But despite the fact that Tiffany had already inadvertently confirmed that view by explaining apologetically to Heaven that although Harold would actually be paying her fee for the evening Tiffany doubted that Heaven would actually see him she still felt nervous.

'This business deal is so very, very important to him, that I doubt he's even going to have time for me. He rang me three times yesterday just to check on how things were going. He says it's vitally important that he gets the Americans to sign the purchase contract for his business before the end of the year. Something to do with some patent he's taking out on this new software he's designed,' she had told Heaven vaguely.

Tiffany had in fact told Heaven rather a lot over the past couple of days, and Heaven couldn't help feeling sorry for her, quickly coming to realise how lonely and bereft of any real friends the other girl was and how, in many ways, she was much more naive and unworldly than one would have expected a young woman of twenty-one to be. Heaven herself at only two years older felt so much more mature.

The sound of the kitchen door being opened had her tensing and automatically turning her back towards it, but it was only Tiffany who came in.

'Harold has just rung from the airport,' she announced breathlessly. 'They will be here within the hour; he wants dinner to be served promptly at eight-thirty…'

'That will be fine,' Heaven assured her.

'It's eight o'clock now,' Tiffany jittered. 'I'd better go just in case anyone arrives early. Thank goodness all the bedrooms are finished at least…'

Heaven gave her an understanding smile. It would be interesting to say the least to discover Harold's reaction when he found out that the elegant en suite bathrooms which complemented every bedroom might look fully fitted and finished, with their impressive reproduction Victorian sanitary ware, but that look at them was all one could do because the owner of the firm who had supplied and installed them had been so incensed by Harold's refusal to pay him a single penny until after he had inspected everything that none of it had actually been connected up to the mains.

'You do know he's got guests staying, don't you?' Heaven had pointed out to the contractor who had poured out his grievances to her over a cup of coffee and a generous bowl of her delicious soup in the kitchen.

'Yup…they'll have to make do with the downstairs cloakroom; that's all in order,' he had told Heaven with a wink.

Perhaps she ought to have warned Tiffany about what the contractor had told her, Heaven acknowledged, but why add to the poor girl's problems?

A sharp thrill of fear-cum-excitement drilled through her as she heard the front doorbell ring.

Well it was too late for second thoughts now. Everything was ready. Everything…everything, just as she had planned.

She swallowed hard as she looked across at the hob where the pudding was still steaming gently.

Figgy pudding…

She glanced down at the handwritten recipe she had used, all of the ingredients delicious and sinfully rich, especially the almonds, cherries and mixed peel.

That was the basic recipe but because these puddings were going to be extra-special she had added three extra ingredients, ingredients which never in a lifetime would she actually commit to paper, and those ingredients were a generous pouring of liquid paraffin, an equally generous measure of cascara and, just to make sure no one could detect the suspicious taste of such strong laxatives, a large glass of very rich, full-bodied sherry.

A naughty smile curled her mouth as she contemplated the results of her inventive additions to the pudding.

Harold and his guests were going to find it a serious inconvenience that the contractor had omitted to connect all the plumbing. Oh, she hadn't added enough cascara or liquid paraffin to cause any real health risk, but there was certainly enough to cause anyone who had a generous portion of the pudding to be seriously embarrassed by its effect on their digestive system… very seriously embarrassed.

Harold would of course be furious and guess that her cooking was to blame but by then she would be long gone and anyway he would only know her as Mrs Tiggywinkle, whom he would never connect with her, Heaven! It would be well worth the fact that she had used some of her carefully hoarded income from the recent sales of her puddings in order to buy the ingredients for tonight's meal to know that Harold was finally having a taste of his own medicine.

She had to admit, though, that she had been extremely relieved when Tiffany had informed her that she would probably pass on the pudding.

'Harold doesn't want me to put on weight,' she had confided to Heaven. 'And this pudding sounds sinfully rich to me.'

Smiling reassuringly at Tiffany, Jon introduced himself. She reminded him of a timid fawn, all gauche movements and nervous eyes. There was no way she was any match for Harold and Jon couldn't help feeling sorry for her. In many ways she was almost more child than woman and so far as he was concerned, despite her obvious prettiness, not really his type at all.

'Am I the first to arrive?' he asked her as she dutifully took his coat.

'Yes. Harold should be here soon. The Concorde flight from New York was delayed by the weather,' she told him nervously.

'Mm…they've had heavy snowfalls in New York, and according to the forecasters, we're due for some soon. If they're right, we could have the first white Christmas for a long time.

'Harold's bringing some business colleagues back with him, I understand…'

'Yes…he is… They're the people he's hoping will buy the company. Oh…' Tiffany blushed. 'I'm not supposed to talk to anyone about business things, but since you're his friend I'm sure it will be all right…'

'Of course it will,' Jon soothed her.

So Harold was intending to sell the business—a business which, according to the accounts he had produced at the time of the divorce, was heavily in debt and not making any money. It would be interesting to see just who would want to buy that kind of company—and why, he decided as Tiffany bustled away with his coat and then returned to ask him what he would like to drink as she invited him into the drawing room.

As he walked past the half-open dining-room door, Jon paused and then stiffened as he recognised the dining-room set which his parents had given Louisa.

Harold had refused to return the furniture to Louisa, claiming that it had been a joint gift to both of them and that she had forfeited her right to it when she had walked out of the house.

In desperation Louisa had actually gone to the expense of hiring a furniture van and going round to the house to reclaim her furniture when she knew that Harold would be away, but Harold had of course had all the locks changed and even though Louisa had eventually managed to gain admittance by persistently hammering on the door until the housekeeper had let her in, as she had told Jon afterwards, the furniture was no longer there and in its place had been a cheap ugly fifties table and chairs.

Through the kitchen door, which Tiffany had left open, Heaven could hear people arriving. She went to close the door and then stiffened as she just caught the sound of a warm deep male voice that sent a sharp volley of shocked emotion surging through her veins.

She must be hearing things, imagining things, her memory distorted by time and thrown into confusion by the fact that she was in some ways resurrecting the past.

It was inconceivable that the male voice she had so tantalisingly heard could possibly belong to Jon. He was, after all, Louisa's brother. Even so, she found that she was lingering by the still half-open door, her ears stretched, her stomach churning even more than it had already been doing.

It was just her own memory playing tricks on her, she told herself as she made herself walk away from the door, but beneath the buoyant determination which had made her so keen to see Harold get his just deserts, in both senses of the word, she was warily aware of a sudden sharp sense of nostalgia and loss, a foolish yearning for what might have been.

Stop daydreaming, she warned herself sternly. Remember why you're here.

Whilst Tiffany hovered uncertainly, obviously wondering why Jon was staring so intently into the dining room, the front doorbell pealed again.

The new arrivals were Harold's accountant and his wife, neither of whom Jon particularly liked although he always made a point of concealing the fact from them.

'Harold not here yet?' Jeremy Parton asked, rubbing his hands together as he went to stand in front of the fake log fir in the equally fake Regency fireplace.

'No, but he should arrive soon. I hope he does… He told me he wanted dinner served at eight-thirty and—' Tiffany fluttered.

'Who have you got in to do the catering?' Freda Parton interrupted Tiffany sharply. 'Some of the caterers are dreadfully over-priced and as for the food they serve…'

'Er—'

'Whoever it is, it won't be a certain deliciously sexy and mouthwateringly tasty little brown-haired nymphet of a cook,' Jeremy interrupted with what Jon privately considered to be totally inappropriate licentiousness.

What was it about the man's face that made him want to punch it—extremely hard? Jon wondered angrily. He certainly wasn't normally so easily provoked and physical expressions of anger just weren't his style at all.

'Jeremy,' Freda Parton warned her husband curtly.

'Oh, come on; it's no secret that old Harold had the hots for the girl, and who could blame him? I wouldn't have minded a little taste of what she had on offer myself.'

'Jeremy!' Freda Parton warned a second time even

more curtly, turning to explain to Tiffany, who looked both embarrassed and confused.

'Jeremy is just joking, my dear. He's referring to the young woman who was the cause of the break-up of Harold's first marriage. A most tenacious type of girl. She deliberately set out to trap Harold into having an affair with her…'

'He—he's never mentioned anything about that to me,' Tiffany stammered.

Freda Parton gave her husband another dire look and soothed, 'No, well, of course not. Although Harold had nothing to blame himself with, men being what they are, I'm sure quite naturally the whole subject is something he wants to put behind him, but then, of course, if Louisa had had her wits about her she would have realised what was going on sooner and— How is Louisa, Jon?' she asked Jon pointedly.

'She's fine,' Jon responded calmly. 'She and the children are spending Christmas with our parents.'

Still smiling, he turned to Tiffany and explained, 'Louisa, Harold's first wife, is my sister…'

Tiffany blushed hotly. 'Oh, I—I didn't know…' she started to stammer, but Jeremy ignored her discomfiture to challenge Jon.

'Some people might find it rather odd that you should have chosen to remain so close to Harold; after all, the divorce was pretty aggressive.'

'I'm a businessman,' Jon returned with a casual shrug. 'I don't allow my emotions to get in the way of my judgement. Harold has put some very good business my way…'

'And you're hoping for some more? Well, you could be in luck; I expect the reason he's asked you here tonight is to make sure this sale he's planning for the business is all sound and watertight.'

For some reason the smile Jeremy was giving him made the tiny hairs at the back of Jon's neck lift atavistically but he had too much self-control to allow his feelings to show as he responded calmly, 'Well, I would certainly be pleased to advise Harold on whatever aspect of the proposed sale he chose to consult me on. I take it he's planning to sell off the company in its entirety…?'

'Lock, stock and barrel,' Jeremy agreed cheerfully, breaking off as they saw the lights of the taxi that was drawing up outside the house through the window.

'Oh here's Harold now,' Tiffany announced in relief. 'I'd better go and let them in.'

Twenty past eight. Heaven had heard Harold arriving, recognising the familiar loud aggressiveness of his voice; another ten minutes and Tiffany should arrive to collect the soup plates and the soup.

Whilst Tiffany was serving it to their guests, Heaven intended to finish off the second course—a fish dish of which she was particularly proud.

'They loved the soup.'

'Good, then they'll love the fish even more,' Heaven promised as she and Tiffany exchanged conspiratorial smiles some time later.

'Freda Parton keeps on asking who the caterers are… I fibbed a little bit and said I'd just had some help from a friend… Well, it isn't entirely untrue… I do feel that we have become friends these last few days.'

It amazed Heaven just how protective she was beginning to feel towards the other girl. How could she have become involved with Harold? Louisa, too, must have loved him once, but Heaven had sensed that Jon had never really liked his brother-in-law. Jon—what on earth was she doing thinking about Jon when she ought to be concentrating on what she was doing, not daydreaming over a man who was past history?

Only the sorbet and the main course to go before they had their pudding. Heaven could feel the nervous tension beginning to build up inside her stomach.

To keep herself occupied and out of habit she started to clear away the used crockery and cutlery Tiffany had returned to the kitchen.

She had just placed the last plate in the dishwasher when Tiffany came back for the next course.

Jon frowned as he listened to the conversation taking place between Harold and the Americans. On the face of it, there was no reason why he should feel so instinctively suspicious that Harold was concealing something, but then he knew Harold.

Tiffany, looking increasingly hot and bothered, was bringing in the pudding course.

Jon shook his head when she offered him some. He had never had much of a sweet tooth, unlike Harold who was greedily indicating that Tiffany give him an extra-generous helping of the pudding.

'Wow, that was some meal,' one of the Americans commented enthusiastically to Tiffany, gallantly insisting on helping her to remove the dirty dessert plates and carrying them out to the kitchen for her whilst Harold reminded Tiffany that he wanted the men's biscuits and cheese to be served in his study.

In the kitchen Heaven heaved a small sigh of relief. Only the cheese and biscuits and the coffee and petits fours left now and then she could leave, before the disastrous explosive effects of her special additions to her pudding recipe began to make themselves felt!

She stiffened as Tiffany came into the kitchen accompanied by a man. Fortunately it wasn't Harold.

'Hey now, who is this?' the American demanded.

'I've been helping Tiffany with the meal,' Heaven told him quickly before Tiffany herself could say anything.

'Say, isn't that the pudding we've just had?' the American demanded, his attention distracted away from Heaven towards the segment of pudding still left.

'You ought to try it,' he told Heaven. 'It's something else…' And then, to Heaven's horror, he reached for the bowl and, picking up a spoon, dug it into the pudding and then held out a spoonful towards her.

As she stepped back from him Heaven mentally prayed for help. There was no way, no way in this world she could eat that pudding but the American was very large, very determined and, she suspected, slightly drunk.

'Oh, dear,' she suddenly heard Tiffany cry anxiously. 'Mr Rosenbaum…Eddie… Please, we must get back.'

'Where the hell is Tiffany with that cheese?' Harold demanded angrily. 'Jon, be a good chap and see what's doing, will you?'

As he threw the command across the table at him, Jon had to grit his teeth to prevent himself from throwing it right back at him, but for Louisa's sake he couldn't afford to betray any of the antagonism he felt towards his ex-brother-in-law and so instead of telling him in no uncertain terms to go himself he stood up and pushed his chair back, heading for the kitchen, but not before he caught sight of the smirking smile that Jeremy Parton was giving him.

Grimly Jon pushed open the kitchen door and then came to an abrupt halt at the scene in front of him and the woman dominating it.

As Heaven looked up and saw him all the colour drained from her face. For a minute she thought she was actually going to faint. What on earth was Jon doing here?

'Oh, Jon, is everything all right?' she heard Tiffany twittering. 'Is Harold—?'

'Harold sent me to check up on what had happened to the cheese and biscuits,' Jon informed her, causing Tiffany to start scurrying frantically round the kitchen.

The American, sensing an ally, looked at him and announced, 'Say, she won't eat the pudding…'

'I can't. I'm allergic to nuts and it's got almonds in it,' Heaven garbled. Oh, God, what on earth was she going to do now? There was no doubt whatsoever that Jon had recognised her, and no doubt either, she suspected from the thoughtful way he looked first at the pudding and then at her, that her refusal to touch it was arousing his suspicions.

As he reached past the American, for a moment Heaven thought he was actually going to force-feed the pudding to her. The thought made her feel quite giddily sick but to her relief he simply relieved the American of the bowl and spoon and told him firmly, 'Harold wants to talk with you…'

Her relief was short-lived, though, because instead of following the American as he scuttled quickly towards the door Jon simply stood watching her.

'Heaven?' Tiffany started to panic, looking uncertainly from Heaven to the trolley.

'Harold is waiting, Tiffany,' Jon reminded her, and whilst Heaven watched in helpless dismay Tiffany gave her an apologetic look and then followed the American through the kitchen door, letting it swing closed after her, leaving Heaven completely alone with Jon, enclosing her in the now far too small space of the kitchen with a man whose presence had once filled her with excitement but which now filled her with apprehensive dread.

In a voice that warned her he wasn't prepared to play any games, Jon demanded. 'What have you done to the pudding, Heaven?'

'The pudding?' Heaven hedged instinctively. 'Nothing…why should you think I might have done anything?'

Oh, God, if only she had had time to get away before he had come into the kitchen. Desperately she tried to glance at the clock to check the time without him seeing what she was doing. How long before the extras she had added to the pudding started to make their existence felt?

That depended very much on the individual person's digestive system, but at a guess…Heaven's heart started to beat nervously fast. She had to get away before the consequences of her retaliatory actions came to light. As she had good cause to remember, Harold had a nasty temper; she had never actually seen him physically abuse another person but she had sensed that he had the temperament to do so if pushed too hard—he was that kind of man; you could see it in his face… in his eyes…especially now that he was approaching forty and the slightly florid good looks she had seen in photographs of him as a younger man could no longer mask his real personality.

'You were refusing to eat it,' Jon reminded her dryly.

'I told you…I'm allergic to nuts,' Heaven fibbed, hoping he would put the betraying tide of colour warming her throat and face down to nervousness and not guilt.

'You weren't allergic to them the night I took you out,' he told her softly. 'I distinctly remember that the pudding you ordered and ate on that occasion contained them.'

Heaven's eyes widened. He could remember that? She could certainly remember what they had ordered to eat, but then she could remember every single small detail of that evening, and the hopes it had brought her.

'Er, how much pudding did you have?' Heaven asked him warily.

'None,' Jon returned promptly. 'I wasn't very hungry and I don't particularly enjoy sticky puddings.'

'None.' Heaven couldn't manage to keep the relief out of her voice. 'You really mean that?' she checked. 'You didn't have any at all?'

'I didn't have any at all,' Jon confirmed, grimly adding. 'So, I'll ask you once again. What have you done to the pudding, Heaven?'

Heaven hung her head. She knew he wouldn't let her escape until he had got the truth out of her.

'I put cascara in it…cascara and liquid paraffin,' she told him, dry-mouthed.

For a moment Jon simply looked at her in silence and then, when he managed to find his voice, he demanded, 'You did what?'

'I put cascara and liquid paraffin in it,' Heaven repeated. Then, taking a deep breath, she added challengingly, 'And you may as well know that although it had nothing to do with me Harold hasn't paid the contractors so they haven't connected the plumbing upstairs and—'

'Oh my God…'

Heaven could hear someone walking towards the kitchen and immediately she started to panic.

'Jon…' She froze as she recognised the voice of Harold's accountant, knowing that he would recognise her.

Jon obviously realised it too from the look he was giving her, but, to her amazement, as the other man pushed open the door Jon reached for her, wrapping his arms tightly around her and pushing her face against his shoulder so that it was virtually concealed by his body and her own hair.

'What—?' she began indignantly, but Jon quickly silenced her, bending his head to cover her open mouth with his own and then proceeding to kiss her slowly and thoroughly—very slowly and very thoroughly, Heaven acknowledged as her head began to reel with shock and her body literally melted against him with the devastating immediacy of hot chocolate sauce poured over ice cream.

'What the hell is going on in here?' Heaven tensed as she heard Harold's voice and realised that he must have come looking for the other two men. 'And who in hell's name is this?' he demanded, no doubt referring to her, Heaven recognised as she trembled in Jon's arms, instinctively cuddling closer to him as she allowed him to tuck her face back into the protective and concealing curve of his shoulder.

'My girlfriend, Harold. I rang her and asked her to come and pick me up; I don't want to risk losing my licence…' she heard Jon responding smoothly.

'Your girlfriend, great,' she heard Harold snarling. 'Well right now you've got more important things to do than practising for the sexual olympics on my kitchen table, and—'

Harold stopped speaking abruptly, his hands going to his stomach.

'Oh my God…God…' Heaven heard him cry as he clutched his body in desperation and started to run towards the doorway.

In the hallway total pandemonium seemed to have broken out, with everyone—but more especially the men—groaning and clutching their stomachs as they complained of the griping pains gripping them.

'Come on,' Heaven heard Jon saying as he started to release her, but instead of freeing her completely as she had expected he kept hold of her arm, hustling her towards the back door. When she balked at this treatment and tried to break free he shook her arm and warned her, 'If I were you I'd leave whilst I still could. Once Harold—'

'That was exactly what I was trying to do before you interfered,' Heaven informed him indignantly, 'and if you'd just let go of my arm…'

'Tiffany, where the hell's the cook?' Heaven heard

Harold screaming above the cacophony of noise in the hall.

Grimly Jon smiled at her.

'I want to talk to you,' he told her, 'so make up your mind, Heaven. Either you stay here and face Harold or you leave now with me.'

He wanted to talk to her. What about? Heaven wondered nervously as, without waiting for her decision he pulled open the back door and half pushed and half dragged her through it.

'Tiffany...' Harold was still bellowing.

Heaven winced.

'It won't be just Harold you'll have to answer to,' he warned her as he marshalled her towards his car and, still holding her captive with one hand, unlocked the driver's side with the other. 'Those Americans aren't going to feel too happy with you. You do carry professional insurance against being sued, I take it...?'

Heaven's expression, mercilessly revealed by the interior light of the car, gave away her shocked consternation.

'Ah, I see—you don't carry that kind of insurance.' Jon answered his own question. 'Rather foolish of you, I would have thought.

'Get in, Heaven,' he commanded, holding open the passenger door for her.

Reluctantly Heaven did as he instructed. After all, what alternative did she have? She had planned to be well away from the scene of her retribution before the effects of her innovative recipe additions took hold and she shuddered inwardly as she contemplated what might happen to her if Jon chose to turn her over to Harold now.

She still couldn't believe that he was actually working for Harold, but what other reason did he have for being one of Harold's dinner guests?

Which meant that Jon could not possibly be the man she had once thought him to be. And that discovery should surely have meant that her heart could have no possible reason to bounce crazily against her ribs just because she was seated next to him and just because she could still smell the warm, sexy male scent of him, still feel the sensual erotic pressure of his mouth against her own.

'Why did you kiss me?'

As soon as she had blurted out the words, Heaven regretted them. She had quite obviously been spending too much time with Tiffany, she derided herself, because that was the kind of naive, gauche remark more acceptable from someone like Tiffany than from a streetwise life-wary woman like herself.

'Why do you think?' Jon challenged her back as he set the car in motion and activated the central locking system. 'If I hadn't, Jeremy Parton could well have recognised you and Harold most certainly would…'

'Why should you want to protect me from them?' Heaven demanded aggressively. 'After all, you're Harold's business advisor and you're just as—'

Abruptly she stopped, biting down hard on her bottom lip.

'Go on, I'm just as what? Just as dishonest—is that what you were about to say?'

Heaven lifted her head.

'Well, it's the truth, isn't it?' she challenged him. 'Harold is dishonest, morally if not legally, and I'm surprised that you, knowing what he did to Louisa, how he cheated your own sister, should have anything to do with him. Tiffany told me all about the American deal,' she added assertively. 'I know that although Harold is planning to sell the business to them, he's also planning to withhold from them the patent for the new software he's originated.'

'What?'

They had just joined the mainstream of traffic on the road outside the house but, instead of accelerating, much to her shock, Jon actually braked.

'Run that by me again, will you?' he demanded as he took his foot off the brake and the powerful Jaguar started to glide forward again.

'You heard me the first time,' Heaven told him bravely. 'I know that Harold is planning to sell the business to the Americans letting them believe that they've got sole rights to all the software but in reality he's come up with a new program that supersedes the ones they're buying and he's planning to fix it so that the patent takes effect from immediately after the sale. Tiffany told me.'

'He might be planning to do that but the Americans aren't stupid. They're putting certain clauses into the contract which prevent Harold from rewriting any of the programs they're buying or selling any new program within a prescribed area…'

'But that area doesn't include the Far and Middle East, at least not according to Tiffany and that's where Harold Lewis intends to sell it,' Heaven pronounced triumphantly.

As he quickly assimilated the information Heaven had just given him, Jon recognised that she had unwittingly given him the very tool he needed to pressure Harold into giving his sister a much fairer financial settlement; he also recognised that Harold had perhaps guessed all along just why he, Jon had publicly appeared to take his side.

No mention of Harold's plans to withhold the new patent, or even a whisper of their existence, had been included in the information Jon had been given about the deal, which would have meant that had he even the smallest part in helping to draw up any kind of sale contract his reputation would have been destroyed in much the same way and just as effectively as Heaven's had been once the Americans discovered how Harold had cheated them.

But also, and right now far more importantly, once Harold realised who his cook for the evening had been, and if he discovered just how much Tiffany had told her about his business affairs, Heaven herself could be in grave danger.

Quickly he came to a decision. As luck had it he had called at the petrol station on his way out and filled the car up, so he had enough fuel to get most of the way to the Borders before having to stop…

Now that she was over the initial shock of having him walk into Harold's kitchen, and her fear that Harold might discover her presence there, Heaven was growing tense, increasingly aware of the danger of her remaining in Jon's presence for a single second longer than necessary. That kiss he had given her in the kitchen had proved more than well enough to her, thank you very much, just how femininely vulnerable she still was to him.

'You can drop me here,' she announced determinedly, reaching for the door handle as Jon stopped for the lights and then frowning as she discovered that the door was locked.

'Jon,' she started to protest as the lights changed and the car moved away, her initial irritation giving way to disbelief as Jon swiftly changed lanes and she saw the road sign up ahead of them indicating the distance to the M25.

'Jon,' she protested this time more forcefully. 'I want to get out...'

'You can't,' he told her promptly, adding dryly, 'Not in the middle of the traffic.'

'Then pull over to the side,' Heaven insisted irritably. 'I—'

But instead of obeying her Jon changed gear and the car picked up speed as the traffic opened up ahead of them and they started to leave the congested heart of the city behind them.

'I want to go home,' Heaven told him angrily, 'and I—'

'Really...? It won't take long for Harold to track you down, you know,' he warned her grimly.

'Harold doesn't know it was me,' Heaven shot back. 'Tiffany found me in the classified ads: "Mrs

Tiggywinkle's figgy puddings"...'

'Maybe she did, Mrs Tiggywinkle, but I noticed she referred to you as Heaven and it isn't the most common of Christian names, is it?'

Heaven bit her lip. She had forgotten about that, deeming it unimportant in the heat of her determination to pay Harold back for the damage he had inflicted on her.

'No doubt you gave Tiffany your telephone number, where she could reach you even if you didn't give her your actual address,' Jon continued remorsefully. 'As I said, it won't take a man like Harold long to track you down, Heaven, and when he does...'

'He won't be in any state to think about tracking me down for at least twenty-four hours.' Heaven retaliated spiritedly, but in truth Jon's warning had made her stomach muscles clench in nervous fear.

'I'll bet you haven't even given a thought to the outcome of your little piece of culinary engineering, have you?' Jon demanded scornfully. 'Harold isn't the kind of man to grin and bear it, Heaven; you should know that already,' Jon reminded her.

'In view of the fact that you have such a low opinion of him I'm surprised that you're working for him,' Heaven shot back, determined not to let him get the better of her, too engrossed in her argument with him to realise that they were now on the M25 and heading north, the large Jaguar picking up speed under Jon's expert touch.

Jon was aware of it, though. Hopefully he could keep her occupied...talking...arguing...until they were far enough away from the city for her to accept what he was planning to do...

The car's speedometer crept upwards and he thanked the fates that the road was relatively quiet and empty of other traffic.

'The reason I'm working for him, as you put it, has nothing to do with any fellow feeling for him,' he told her grimly. 'Far from it.'

'No? You're just earning your living, is that it?' Heaven demanded scathingly. 'What about your sister? What about Louisa?'

'It's because of Louisa that I'm doing this,' Jon returned curtly. 'Heaven…'

'I don't want to hear any more. In fact, what I want right now is for you to stop this car and let me out… At once… Immediately!'

'Heaven, listen to me…'

'No. I don't want to hear another word,' Heaven told him fiercely, lifting her hands to cover her ears.

'Heaven, this is important dammit,' Jon told her grittily. 'I've spent months trying to get Harold's confidence so that I can find out how he managed to conceal his financial assets and persuade the divorce judge that he couldn't afford to give Louisa and the girls a decent settlement. Months…' he stressed as Heaven slowly uncovered her ears and looked uncertainly at him.

'Why should I believe you?' she asked him flatly. 'You might just be trying… You're Harold's business advisor; Tiffany told me so.'

'I was, you mean,' Jon told her grimly. 'Once Harold realises that you were the one who fed them that appalling concoction—and he will find out—and he realises that I concealed the fact—and you—from him, I doubt he's going to have a lot of faith left in my loyalty, don't you?'

'So why did you do it?' Heaven asked him slowly. 'Why did you protect me from him?'

'I'm going to have to claim the fifth amendment on that one,' Jon told her forthrightly. 'At least for the time being.

'Heaven, you said something earlier about some new software Harold is planning—'

He broke off as Heaven's eyes suddenly widened as she caught sight of the motorway sign ahead of them.

She turned furiously towards him, demanding, 'That said "North". North where? Where are you taking me, Jon?'

'To the Borders,' he told her quietly.

'The Borders? What Borders?'

'The Scottish Borders. I've got a property up there and I—'

'You can't be serious,' Heaven interrupted him again. 'I just don't believe this. Pull over and stop this car immediately, otherwise I'll…'

'You'll what?' he asked her dryly. 'You can't get out. I've activated the central locking system.'

'I don't believe this… This is…this is kidnap,' Heaven told him wildly. 'This is…'

'The safest precautionary measure I could come up with,' Jon intervened grimly.

Precautionary measure… Heaven's throat had suddenly gone very tight. Her lips felt dry. She touched them nervously with the tip of her tongue and then wished she hadn't as she saw a sudden certain male gleam flicker in Jon's eyes.

'Yes…precautionary measure,' Jon repeated, 'for both of us. Once Harold discovers that you and Tiffany talked about far more than recipes—and, again, he will—you are going to be in very grave danger. Anyone who has the kind of information you have is going to be in danger, at least until after he's got those contracts safely signed.

'I've no doubt that Harold thought he was being extremely clever, planning to get the contracts signed before Christmas and then having the new patent come into effect with the new year, but what he hadn't bargained for was you and the fact that your figgy pudding will mean that the Americans aren't going to be in any fit state to sign anything for several days. It's probably too late now for him to stop that patent going through and until he gets those contracts signed he's going to be in a very, very vulnerable position. The first thing he's going to want to do is to make sure you can't use the information that Tiffany has given you.'

Despite the heat inside the car Heaven had started to shiver.

'I know that you are deliberately trying to frighten me,' she warned him. 'You're just exaggerating…Harold wouldn't—

Abruptly she stopped.

'Harold would,' he told her softly, and as she looked across at him Heaven knew that the knowledge that what he had just said was true showed in her eyes, and with it her growing apprehension.

'Perhaps what I've done is rather dramatic,' Jon acknowledged, 'but it seemed the best solution for both of us, given the short time I had in which to make a decision.

'Harold's possibly forgotten that I own property in the north and being there will provide you with a safe haven and give me the chance to use the information you've given me to force Harold into giving Louisa the money she's entitled to…'

'Aren't you afraid he might try to retaliate? To…?' She stopped and shivered again.

'To what?' Jon asked her softly. 'To ruin my reputation the way he did yours? Well, I suspect he was intending to do that anyway, but thanks to you that won't now be possible. I know that taking you off like this must seem a trifle dramatic, but believe me, Heaven,

I am not in any way overdramatising when I say that you will be much safer somewhere where Harold can't find you.

'Is there any problem about you being away from home?' he asked her carefully. 'A friend…a lover who might—?'

Quickly Heaven shook her head.

'No. There's nothing…no one like that. My parents are in Australia with my brother and—'

'You were going to be on your own over Christmas?'

Heaven's vulnerable heart gave a small treacherous leap at that past tense 'were'.

'I…I was invited to join a friend and her family but…' She took a deep breath. 'What about you? Was Louisa…? Were you…?'

'Louisa is taking the children to stay with our parents,' Jon told her, shaking his head as he added, 'I did have the option of joining a party of friends who are going skiing but a telephone call is all it will take to notify them that I shan't be going.'

'But surely all this will be over by Christmas?' Heaven pointed out, suddenly panicking at the thought of having to spend several days with him.

'Perhaps, but not necessarily, and you have to remember that it's going to be quite some time before Harold forgets the part you've played in ruining his plans to cheat the Americans. Although, with a bit of luck, he should have rather more on his mind than pursuing you.'

'Quite some time… How…how long?' Heaven asked him dry-mouthed.

'It's hard to say,' Jon told her seriously, but inwardly he was feeling far more light-hearted than he looked and than the situation warranted because, if anything, he had played down rather than over-emphasised the danger they were both potentially in.

'What about Tiffany?' Heaven queried, suddenly remembering the other girl. 'Won't Harold…?'

'Harold won't be able to do anything to harm or hurt Tiffany. I happen to know that her mummy and daddy are very protective of their precious little chick and none too happy about losing her to Harold.'

'But I can't stay with you…I…I don't have any clothes…'

For the first time since their journey had started Heaven saw Jon smile.

'No! What a pity,' he drawled teasingly. 'That means…'

The look he gave her made Heaven turn crimson from the tips of her ears all the way down to her toes. Toes which curled up in her shoes with something that was very, very different from the self-conscious embarrassment burning her skin.

'Well, I'm sure we can remedy that. We're not far from the nearest town.'

'But I can't go out and buy a new wardrobe just like that,' Heaven protested. 'For a start I haven't—'

She stopped, closing her lips over the admission she had been about to make. But Jon had obviously guessed what she had been about to say as he finished her sentence for her by saying, 'You can't afford it. Did Harold pay you for the dinner?'

'No.' Heaven shook her head.

'Well, then as his business advisor I strongly suggest that you write to him in strong terms demanding payment, and in the meantime I will be more than happy to make you a small loan against that payment.'

Heaven was not so easily gulled.

'He won't pay me,' she told Jon positively.

Jon was equally positive back.

'Oh, yes, he will,' he told her softly. 'I shall make sure of that! I've spent months searching for a way to force him to make a decent settlement on Louisa and the girls but he's kept on claiming that the business is losing money even though it's been perfectly obvious that he's lying, that that sleazy accountant he employs has no doubt siphoned off all the assets to some dubious off-shore tax haven. He's even threatening to stop paying the girls' school fees.'

'What makes a person like that? So mean and…and horrid,' Heaven wondered out loud, adding, 'He's even kept the dining-room furniture that Louisa was given by your parents.'

'Yes, I know,' Jon agreed, his mouth growing grim. 'And thank you for reminding me of that, Heaven. That's something else to put on the list.'

'What will you do?' Heaven asked him uncertainly. 'You're not going to let him cheat the Americans, are you? I mean…'

'Oh—' Jon shook his head '—the most he can expect from that is I keep quiet about the potential fraud he was planning to enact; the price for my keeping quiet will be Louisa's settlement and the sale of the company with all its software.

'We have very strong fraud laws in this country and so do the Americans. If what he was planning to do becomes public it won't just be his reputation he'll lose and somehow I can't see Harold settling happily into prison life.'

'Prison…' Heaven's eyes widened.

'Now you see why I'm so concerned for your safety,' Jon pointed out to her.

'What about yours?' Heaven challenged.

'Oh, I shall be safe enough,' he assured her.

'The Borders,' Heaven murmured sleepily, smothering a yawn as the events of the evening began to catch up on her. 'That sounds so romantic…'

Her eyes were already starting to close so she didn't see the look that Jon gave her, but she did hear the softly sensual note in his voice as he told her, 'Then we shall have to see if we can't make them live up to your image, shan't we?'

CHAPTER FOUR

SLEEPILY Heaven struggled to sit up. Outside the car everything was pitch-black.

'Where are we?' she asked Jon groggily.

'Nearly home,' he told her.

Nearly home. Heaven could feel her heart start to beat just a little bit too fast.

'Look, it's starting to snow,' he told her urgently as small fine white flakes started to drift across the car windscreen.

'Snow!' Heaven peered out of the window as excitedly as a small child, whilst Jon watched her and laughed.

'You look about sixteen,' he teased her, 'with your hair all ruffled and your make-up…'

When his glance drifted to her mouth Heaven discovered that she was colouring up again as she remembered how she'd come to be denuded of her lipstick. Self-consciously she touched her lips with her fingertips and then tensed as Jon told her softly, 'Don't do that…'

'Why not?' Heaven whispered back to him, her eyes soft and huge in her small face as she turned uncertainly to look at him.

The road was empty; it was three o'clock in the morning. Swiftly Jon brought the car to a halt and reached for her, gathering her into his arms as he whispered against her mouth, 'Because it makes me want to kiss you.'

Heaven tried to protest as logic and common sense dictated that she must, but happily the very fact that Jon's mouth was already covering hers, caressing hers, meant that her protest never got further than an 'Oh'—and for some reason instead of recognising this for what it was Jon seemed to think that the soft parting of her lips wasn't so much representative of a womanly objection to his kiss-stealing actions but in fact a very feminine invitation to make the kiss even more intimate and devastating to Heaven's vulnerable self-control.

Mmm… Outside the car it might be cold enough to be snowing but inside the temperature was quite definitely rising. The sexual chemistry and magnetism between them were positively making the air sizzle, Heaven recognised dreamily as she snuggled closer to Jon, her hands automatically sliding beneath his jacket to hold him closer.

The deep sound of satisfaction he made in response to her own softer but very recognisable sensual response made Heaven feel as though she was melting, slowly, deliciously, languorously, and as inevitably as a dish of ice cream in the warm summer sun. Jon made her feel all soft and sensual and deliciously, dangerously wanton, as though…as though…

'What happened to you? We should have done this months ago,' she heard Jon groaning as he drew her even closer.

Months ago he had left on a flight to goodness knew where after one brief date, whilst she…

The shudder of remembered revulsion and shame

which had begun to tense her body turned to a shivery muscle reaction of a very different type as Jon's hand slid upwards over her body towards her breast. She could hear her own heartbeat picking up speed, feel her whole body starting to react to the urgent pressure of his hand against her breast.

'Oh-h-h…' Heaven couldn't stop herself from giving a small betraying gasp of pleasure as Jon's thumb circled her nipple, causing it to harden and beg unashamedly and very provocatively for even more of his touch.

'You're making me feel…react…more like a teenager than a grown man,' she heard him whispering, groaning in her ear as he started to drag a passionate line of kisses along her jaw and over her throat.

'Jon…' Heaven could hear the passion in her own voice as she arched her neck, her instinctive response throwing the profile of her body into clear relief, revealing her tightly erect nipples.

Totally lost in what she was feeling, she was unaware of Jon's momentary tension and hesitation, and of the fact that he was muttering something very male and urgent below his breath, but the sudden sensation of his mouth against her body as his hands cupped her breasts sent a thrill of sharp, dizzying feminine pleasure hurtling through her.

In his urgency to taste the delicious nubs of flesh that were being so innocently and irresistibly offered to him, Jon couldn't wait to unzip Heaven's dress, hungrily pulling the fabric down and quickly laying bare one soft round breast.

Heaven felt the shudder that went through him as he studied the feminine softness of her avidly for a heartbeat of time, gently rubbing her bare nipple with his thumb before guiding it into his mouth.

The sensation of his lips closing round her flesh, of him suckling on her bare flesh—carefully at first and then with far more urgency as his reaction to the taste of her overwhelmed him—made Heaven's whole body contort with delicious pleasure. Willingly she gave herself up to the erotic sensation of Jon's mouth tugging on one breast whilst his hand caressed the other.

Yearningly Heaven reached out to touch him, an erotic image of his naked body dancing behind her closed eyelids, her imagination tantalising and arousing her. Her fingertips found the buttons on his shirt and impetuously tugged at them.

The shudder that racked Jon's body as she touched him had nothing to do with the cold beyond the passionate heat they had generated inside the car—and nor had the low male groan of need he gave as the hand that had been caressing her breast captured her wrist, pressing her palm flat against the soft, silky dark hair that arrowed downwards from his chest.

'Lower,' Heaven heard him growl pleadingly. 'Lower, Heaven—touch me here,' he begged rawly, moving her hand down towards his waistband as his mouth released her breast to whisper the tormented words against her lips.

All at once Heaven started to panic. She was behaving as though she and Jon had known one another for ever, as though it was the most natural thing in the world for them to be together like this, as though the intimacy they were sharing was so natural and preordained that to deny or obstruct it would be like denying one another air to breathe.

But their relationship wasn't like that. She knew him, yes, had been attracted to him, yes, and yes, all right, had felt perhaps even more than mere attraction for him—had, if she was honest, hoped, even felt that he had shared the feelings she had experienced the evening he had taken her out. But this—this explosion of passion and intensity between them, this sense of coming home, of being completely at one with him—these were surely far too dangerous emotions for her to put any trust in.

She had, she reminded herself, already been on an adrenalin- and tension-induced high even before she had realised that Jon was one of Harold's guests, and events since she had realised it had done nothing to help her come down from that high—far from it.

'What's wrong?' she heard Jon ask her softly as he felt her tension.

'Nothing…' Heaven denied, and then added shakily, 'This wasn't meant to happen. I didn't want…'

'To be dragged off into the night and driven half the length of the country? Or to be made love to by me?' he asked her wryly. 'Which?'

'Neither,' Heaven lied primly, taking advantage of the fact that he had released her to hurriedly straighten her dress and turn her head slightly away from him so that he couldn't see her face properly.

'I'm sorry,' she heard him apologising. 'It wasn't my intention to. You're a very special woman, Heaven,' he added in an even softer and very deep voice. 'So special in fact that…'

He was starting the engine as he spoke, and set the car back in motion without finishing his sentence, but, even though she was desperately curious to know what he had been about to say, Heaven didn't trust herself to ask him—nor him to answer her.

Along with the intense passion and sensuality of the lovemaking they had just shared there had also been a heart-tugging skein of sweetness and tenderness. Or was she just imagining it? Would the spell he had woven around her by reigning in the urgency of his passion be broken if she forced him to put what he was thinking and feeling into words and then discovered that he was not sharing her thoughts and feelings after all?

So much had happened so quickly—too much and too quickly, perhaps, Heaven rationalised as they rounded a bend in the road and she could see the lights of what looked like a small village ahead of them.

'Not much further,' Jon told her as they drove through the village, which was picturesquely sheltered by the surrounding hills of the Borders, its stone cottages hugging the winding road, the narrowness of the humpback bridge crossing the river that Jon drove over making Heaven breathe in automatically.

Ahead of them lay what was obviously the village's main street, its bare trees currently adorned with Christmas lights.

It had stopped snowing, the sky clearing to reveal the stars, and Heaven couldn't stop herself from exclaiming out loud, 'Oh, Jon, it's so pretty! So Christmassy.'

'It may look pretty now,' he responded, 'but it has a rather bloody history. The actual border with Scotland isn't very far from here and this village was the home of border reivers from the English side of the border and the target from those from the Scots side. When a truce was finally declared it was decreed that it would be celebrated and remembered annually at Christmas time, which means that Christmas for the villagers is a doubly special time of joy and celebration. It's a tradition that everyone attends a special thanksgiving supper. We could go to it if you'd like?'

'Could we…?' Heaven began, her eyes shining, and then abruptly she stopped, reminding herself of just why she was here with Jon in the first place, the excitement dying out of her face as she asked him anxiously, 'But Christmas is a week away and I can't…'

'You can't stay…' Jon finished quietly for her.

Heaven bit her lip and turned to look out of the car window. They had left the village behind and were starting to climb now, the road winding upwards through the hills. The snow lay more thickly on the road here, but not too thickly for Jon's car, thank goodness.

Heaven could feel her eyes starting to close as waves of tiredness washed down over her. Sleepily she snuggled deeper into her comfortable seat and then, as Jon swung the car off the road and down a gravel drive, she sat up abruptly and asked him, 'What on earth is that?'

'Home,' Jon responded, laughing, obviously enjoying her surprise.

'Home?' Heaven stared in bemusement at the ancient tall square slit-windowed tower looming in front of her. 'You live here?'

'Yes,' Jon confirmed with a smile, bringing the car to a halt on the gravel and causing the building's security lights to come on, further illuminating the building and the soft warm stone from which it was built.

'But what is it?' Heaven asked in fascination as she studied the tower's unfamiliar shape, height and its narrow, almost slit-like windows. That it was very old was obvious.

'A peel tower,' Jon told her promptly, and then explained, 'They were fortified homes built by those who lived on the border, very often, I'm afraid to say, using stone they "acquired" from Hadrian's wall. The tower acted as a protective place of retreat for the family should they come under attack, and it has to be said that it was equally used as a means of holding captive goods and even people they themselves had purloined on their own reiving trips across the border.

'Originally there would have been a collection of wooden shelters at the base of the tower to hold their livestock, with the family accommodation at the top of the tower where it was deemed to be safer. Because of their height the towers also served as good lookout points. On a clear day from here you can see right across the border for miles. Of course this particular tower was renovated and modernised quite some time ago—before I bought it in fact.

'I was staying in the village some years ago and heard that it was up for sale. I've always loved the Borders and buying it was certainly a hell of a lot less expensive than going for a Cotswold cottage.'

'Just imagine the stories it could tell,' Heaven breathed.

'Mmm…' Jon agreed. 'It's said locally that one misty November night a long time ago—ideal weather for stealing your neighbour's sheep—the then owner of this tower decided to break the truce which existed between him and his neighbour and set off to reive his cattle. When he reached the farm he discovered that the only person there was the seventeen-year-old niece of the farmer who was visiting from Edinburgh, so as well as taking his cattle he also took his neighbour's niece.

However, apparently she was so beautiful and so good that our border reiver fell completely in love with her, and, much more unlikely, she with him, and rather than leading to another bloody feud his abduction of her led instead to a wedding.'

'They lived happily ever after,' Heaven laughed.

'Can you doubt it?' Jon laughed back as he opened his car door and went round to open Heaven's door for her.

As she followed him towards the tower, Heaven found herself instinctively moving a little closer to him. It wasn't that she was afraid of anything—no, of course not—but she still jumped and gave a small startled gasp as something rustled in the ivy that clothed the front wall of the tower.

'It's all right; it's just an owl,' Jon comforted her as he pushed open the door and switched on the lights, but he still took her hand in his, holding it comfortingly, and Heaven didn't make any real attempt to pull away from him as they walked into the tower together.

As she stood with him in the hallway Heaven blinked in surprise.

'Oh, but this is lovely,' she enthused as she studied the plain soft cream plaster walls and the rustic iron wall sconces that held the lights. Plain coir matting covered the floor and the three doors which opened off the hallway were all of dark polished wood, like the stairs which led upwards.

'That door leads into the kitchen,' Jon informed her, indicating the door immediately in front of them. 'The other two rooms are my study and a rather small, cold sitting room; the main living room is on the next floor.

Come up and I'll show you it and the bedrooms on the floor above that.'

The living room was huge.

'This must take up the whole of this floor,' Heaven guessed.

'It does,' Jon agreed. 'The main drawback of this place so far as I'm concerned is having the kitchen and this room on separate floors, but it's a drawback which is more than made up for by the panoramic views you get of the countryside from here. On a clear day you can virtually see as far as the coast.'

Heaven nodded sleepily as she tried and failed to stifle a yawn.

Like the hallway the living room was furnished simply with coir matting and three huge sofas covered in natural creamy white linen.

Heaven yawned again and immediately Jon frowned, exclaiming, 'You're tired! Come on; I'll take you up and show you your room.'

As he guided her towards the stairs, Heaven reflected that just once in a while it felt surprisingly good to relax and let someone else take charge.

Two doors opened off the upper landing and Jon pushed open the right-hand one for her, switching on the light inside the room and then ushering her inside.

'Both bedrooms have their own en suite bathroom,' he told her as she blinked sleepily around the room, but it was the large and oh, so comfortable-looking bed with its traditional brass bedstead and its heavenly plain bedlinen that her gaze kept on returning to.

'Look, why don't I leave you to get ready for bed,' Jon suggested gently, 'whilst I go down and make us both a hot drink? You'll find plenty of towels in the cupboard in your bathroom, along with a spare toothbrush and all the usual necessities. Mrs Frazer from the village, who comes in to go over the house for me and keep an eye on things, believes in being equipped for all emergencies.'

As soon as she heard the door close behind him Heaven walked over to the bed. She only intended to touch it, to test it, just to see if it was as deliciously comfortable as it looked, but for some inexplicable reason touching it became sitting on it, and sitting on it became lying on it, so that when Jon returned he found her curled up fast asleep on the edge of the bed still fully dressed.

Very gently he tried to wake her but when he realised how deeply asleep she was he hesitated for a moment, wondering whether to simply cover her with a spare duvet and leave her as she was. But he knew enough about women to recognise that when she woke up in the morning and discovered that she had slept in the only clothes she had to wear she would not be very happy and so, still frowning, he bent down and started to remove her shoes.

The bedroom light was still on, and he wasn't sure if it was for her benefit or his own that he stopped what he was doing and went and switched it off before returning to complete his self-appointed task in the semidarkness, which, if he was honest, did little to conceal the feminine beauty and desirability of her naked body from him. In fact he could see far too much, arousing the urgency and intensity of his own male hunger and desire for her.

The temptation to remove his own clothes, to slide beneath the bedclothes with her, to hold her in his arms was so strong, so intense, so demanding that he felt himself literally grinding his teeth together as he fought to control it, bending instead to scoop up the clothes he'd removed, but as he straightened up his resolve wavered. She looked so adorable, so…kissable…so…so Heaven, lying there with only her face and her soft hair visible above the bedclothes, that he just had to bend down and kiss her very gently on the mouth.

In her sleep, Heaven smiled against his lips and her own clung softly, to him—softly, temptingly… Sternly Jon made himself withdraw from her.

If he couldn't share the intimacy of her bed with her then at least his clothes could share the intimacy of the washing machine and dryer with hers, he told himself ruefully as he closed the door behind himself and went to strip off his own things before taking them down to the kitchen to put them in the washing machine.

At least she could have clean clothes in the morning even if they were the same ones she had worn the previous day. After he'd pushed everything into the machine and selected a suitable washing cycle he paused to scoop up the single small item which had fallen onto the floor, quickly picking up the tiny pair of pretty lacy knickers and pushing them hastily into the machine before closing the door on them and on his own tantalising erotic thoughts.

Eighteen months ago when he had first set eyes on Heaven he had been attracted to her. The evening he had taken her out he had known that that attraction was deepening into something more, something much stronger, and by the end of the evening he had known… sensed… But then had come all the trauma and tragedy of Harold's cruel manipulation of her situation and he had forced himself to acknowledge that he was the last person Heaven would want in her life.

But now fate had thrown them together again and it hadn't taken that intoxicating interlude in his car earlier on to make him realise that far from lessening his feelings towards her the intervening months had only strengthened them.

But what about her feelings for him? She had certainly been responsive to him earlier this evening; he knew she was not the kind of woman to indulge in casual sexual intimacy with anyone and the sexual and emotional chemistry they had generated between them certainly argued well for the future he hoped they would have together.

The future. The smile which had begun to curl his mouth suddenly disappeared. Before he could invite her to think about sharing that future with him there was the present to be dealt with—the present and his unpleasant ex-brother-in-law.

His mouth compressing grimly, Jon mentally reviewed the information Heaven had given him.

As he walked out into the hallway he glanced ruefully towards the stairs leading up to Heaven's bedroom, to Heaven, both literally and metaphorically, he acknowledged. He fought the temptation to ignore his responsibility towards his sister, sternly admonishing himself for the highly erotic and passionately emotional nature of his thoughts as he turned away from the stairs and headed instead for his study.

Once inside he firmly closed the door and then sat down at his desk and switched on his computer.

He had begun to think he would never find a lever with which to manoeuvre his ex-brother-in-law into giving his sister and their children a fairer financial settlement, but now, thanks to Heaven, he suspected that at last he had. And what a lever. A grim smile curled his mouth as he set to work.

CHAPTER FIVE

HEAVEN stretched sleepily and luxuriously and then opened her eyes. Abruptly she sat bolt upright in her bed—no, not her bed at all, she recognised as she snatched up the duvet which had fallen away from her body to cover her naked breasts and warily glanced around her unfamiliar surroundings.

She was not at home in London any more, she was in Scotland, in an ancient border fortress which had once been the home of wild border reivers, and which was now the home of Jon.

Jon. Just thinking about him made her toes start to curl and her tummy flutter in a way that had nothing to do with nervousness or apprehension.

If she sat right up in the high bed she could see through the window to the hills that lay beyond it—white with snow beneath a blue sky from which shone a brilliantly sharp winter sun.

In London it would no doubt be dull and grey and damp; in London she would have been waking up in her admittedly very warm and cosy Chelsea home, her haven—but how long would it have remained her haven once Harold had discovered her identity and tracked her down? And in London there would have been no Jon.

A rosy blush suffused her face. She only had a very vague memory of their arrival the previous evening, but one thing she was very clear about and that was that she had most certainly not undressed herself. Which meant…which meant…

Jon stretched his taut muscles under the sharp, hot sting of the shower. He had finally gone to bed at six o'clock in the morning, very pleased with what he had done. He smiled broadly to himself as he contemplated Harold's reaction to the discovery of just how much Jon knew about his underhand, not to mention virtually fraudulent business dealings.

Of course he had already been aware of Harold's dishonesty—after all, he had spent a large part of the last year investigating his affairs—but knowing it and proving it were two very different things, and now, thanks to Heaven, he was well on the way to having that proof. He knew about the trickery Harold had used to carefully conceal the money he had made via a complex network of interlinking off-shore companies—carefully, but not carefully enough, Jon acknowledged jubilantly.

Soon he would have written evidence of just where Harold's assets were, evidence his sister could put before a judge, but Jon cynically acknowledged that once Harold knew just what they had discovered he would never allow Louisa's maintenance petition to get to court. If he did then the whole of his business empire could be destroyed.

No, Louisa should find that she got a much fairer divorce settlement from her ex-husband now, and with it the return of her family furniture, Jon decided grimly as he reached for a towel and quickly dried off his body before pulling on a towelling robe.

Was Heaven awake yet? There was only one way to find out…

Jon! Where had he slept last night after he had undressed her? This bed, her bed, was certainly big enough for both of them. Heaven wriggled uncertainly beneath the duvet. Had they spent the night together? Had Jon…? She gave a small gasp as the bedroom door was pushed open and the subject of her wantonly sensual thoughts came in carrying a tray with two mugs of tea, and her clothes.

'I put these in the washer for you last night,' he began prosaically as he put her clothes down on a chair several yards away from the bed.

'My clothes…?'

Hard though she tried to suppress it, Heaven could feel her blush starting to deepen, and then, unable to keep the suspicion to herself any longer, burst out, 'Last night did we…did you…?'

The hot-faced look she cast in the direction of the opposite side of the double bed made Jon want to smile as he realised what was going through her mind.

She thought he might have done more than remove her clothing, did she? Well, in some respects he almost wished he had, although if he had…

'Don't you know…can't you remember?' he teased her, watching with enjoyment as her eyes rounded with uncertainty. In her consternation Heaven forgot to hang onto the duvet, which started to slither away from her body immediately she released it, causing Jon, who was just in the act of placing her mug of tea on the table at her side of the bed, to react swiftly and with gentlemanly concern to retrieve the errant duvet for her.

It was mere misfortune, of course, that he should fail in his mission to spare Heaven's blushes and protect her modesty, missing the recalcitrant duvet by millimetres—so few millimetres, in fact, that the tips of his fingers actually brushed against the soft warmth of Heaven's breast.

It was the effect of the cool air against her body that was causing her nipples to pout so provocatively, Heaven tried to reassure herself, and their wanton stiffness had nothing whatsoever—could have nothing whatsoever—to do with Jon's proximity, nor his touch.

'You can't remember, can you?' she heard him accusing her as he sat down on the bed next to her.

Heaven gave a small gulp, not so much because of her near-nakedness, or even because the towelling robe he was wearing was, so it seemed to her, very precariously tied at the waist—so precariously in fact that she suspected that all it would take for it to fall open completely would be for…

Hastily she averted her eyes and her hot face from the interesting darkly shadowed area just below his firmly flat belly. No, it was neither of those two things that was responsible for her agitation. What was causing it was her awareness that she could not remember whether or not she and Jon had spent the night together. What she did know, though, was that she did not find the idea that they might have unbelievable—or unappealing.

'So you think I might have taken advantage of your sleeping state and spent the night here in bed with you, do you?' he was asking her.

Heaven rallied enough to remind him, 'You took my clothes off.'

'Mmm… A purely altruistic action, I can assure you, and done merely so that you could have clean clothes to wear this morning.'

'Oh…'

Jon cocked an eyebrow and smiled encouragingly at her.

'Could that have been an "Oh" of apology…or even one of disappointment?' he asked her teasingly.

Heaven gave him a wrathful look but before she could denounce him with the words clamouring for utterance on her tongue he neatly cut the ground away from her by telling her softly, 'Not that I wasn't tempted…very tempted. You've got a very sexy body… And a delicious little mole just here,' he told her, finding with dismaying accuracy despite the duvet the spot on her hip bone where she did indeed have a small mole.

'A very kissable mole,' he whispered, leaning closer to her.

Heaven couldn't help it. Instinctively, as he moved closer to her she moved closer to him. With his lips only a breath away from hers Jon told her huskily, 'No, I didn't sleep with you, and if I had… If I had, you may be sure that you most certainly would have remembered it…'

'Remembered…' Heaven whispered shakily.

'Mmm…' Jon agreed. 'You would. Because I would have made love to you so thoroughly, so…so sensually…starting like this…'

Heaven had been about to speak but it was too late; Jon was already cupping her face with both hands, pressing slow, mouthwateringly delicious kisses against her mouth. The kind of kisses that made her reach out and wrap her own arms around him to hold him closer.

'Mmm…and then what would you have done?' Heaven asked him dizzily.

'Then I would have done this, and you'd certainly have remembered it,' he told her, sweeping her hair to one side and stringing a line of toe-curling little nibbles all the way down her throat and along her shoulder, bringing her whole body out in a rash of responsive goosebumps as he did so.

Heaven gave a small moan of sheer delight, unwittingly digging her nails into the flesh of his arms, but he didn't mind the pain.

'Oh-h-h…' she gasped as he trailed a row of kisses all the way down the inside of her arm to her wrist, planting one in her palm before he closed her fingers over it and carried that hand to his own body, placing it right where his heart was thumping with heavy irregularity.

'And then…what would you have done?' Heaven pressed him, opening eyes heavy with desire and arousal to focus on him.

Jon felt his heart skip a full half a dozen beats. Just that look in her eyes alone, never mind the softer tempting fullness of her naked breasts, was enough to make him want…

'Then I'd have told you that this isn't a game and I want you so much that I ache like hell for you,' he told her rawly, the emotion in his voice and in his eyes making Heaven catch her breath…

'I want you too,' she admitted bravely as she held out her arms to him.

Very gently he reached out and cupped her breasts

and then equally gently leaned forward and started to kiss her.

Heaven gave a soft moan low in her throat as she felt Jon rubbing the pads of his thumbs over and over her sensitive nipples, her whole body writhing in sensual pleasure as she opened her mouth to the deep, pulsing thrust of his tongue.

When he released her mouth to capture one of her nipples and draw it tenderly into his mouth she could feel the soft sensuality of his body hair and the sleek hardness of the muscles that lay beneath his skin.

She wanted to explore every inch of him, to touch and taste all of him, but she hadn't realised she had said so out loud until Jon buried his face between her breasts and groaned, 'Oh, God, Heaven, have you any idea just what you're doing to me?'

'I know what you're doing to me,' Heaven responded bravely.

His robe had fallen completely open. Fascinated, torn between her natural feminine shyness and her equally instinctive female awe and curiosity, she studied him, unable to resist the temptation to reach out and run her fingertips down the hard length of his erection.

'Heaven,' she heard him protest in a satisfactorily guttural moan of mingled torment and pleasure.

'What's wrong?' she teased him. 'Don't you like me doing that?'

'Don't I like it?' Jon groaned, and closed his eyes. 'You wait,' he warned her. 'I'll get my own back.

'You can't know how often I've thought about you,' he told her more seriously as he shrugged off the robe and took her back into his arms, kissing her mouth gently at first and then with increasing passion as he felt her respond to him.

'When you never got in touch with me after…after everything, I thought that you mustn't have been interested,' Heaven admitted hesitantly.

Jon immediately shook his head.

'I couldn't get in touch because no one knew where to find you. I contacted your parents but they refused to tell me where you were. Then I thought about it and reasoned that anyone connected with…with what had happened would be the last person you'd want to see…'

'I did feel a bit like that,' Heaven admitted, ducking her head so that he couldn't see the anxiety in her eyes as she added, 'And I felt…well, people do say there's no smoke without a fire and—'

'Stop right there,' Jon warned her sternly. 'Other people may have made the mistake of believing Harold's lies, but I never did,' he announced grimly. 'I never did, Heaven,' he repeated, cupping her face and holding it so that she was forced to meet the look in his eyes. 'I never did and I never could…'

Heaven couldn't hide it. His words made her eyes fill with emotional tears which she couldn't disguise from him. Gently he wiped them away and then bent his head and licked the last traces of moisture from her skin. The erotic sensation of his tongue moving against her damp skin sent a tell-tale shudder of reaction jolting through Heaven's body.

'Jon,' she whispered shakily as she clung to him, no longer shy of letting him see the effect he was having on her or her need for him.

'I know,' he whispered back. 'I know.'

And then he was laying her down on the bed and

removing the duvet, caressing every inch of her skin, kissing the small mole on her hip as he had intimated he had wanted to do, but Heaven wasn't sure if it was the sensation of his mouth against her mole or the fact that as he kissed it his hand was resting on her belly, covering her sex, that was making her tremble so wildly.

'What's wrong?' he teased her huskily as his hand slid between her legs and he started to caress her with the same gentle explorative intimacy with which she had touched him earlier. 'Don't you like it?'

But Heaven didn't need to make any response; Jon already knew what her answer was and his own body, his own arousal, his own emotions were reacting chaotically to the feel and warmth of her.

He bent his head and Heaven gave a shocked gasp of pleasure as she felt his mouth caressing the most intimate part of her, his tongue stroking, seeking, questing.

Unable to bear the erotic sensuality of the sensation he was giving her, she called out protestingly to him, her sharp, high cry smothered by the fierce pressure of his mouth on hers, instinctively sensing and satisfying her need for that intimacy, and just as instinctively satisfying her need for the powerful, sensually fulfilling thrust of his body within her own.

It was like poetry, a perfect dawn and even more perfect sunset, every good sensation and feeling you could ever experience or imagine experiencing, to feel the harmony that their bodies were creating together, to share the upward gravity-free surge towards the ecstatic moment of release, to lie dazed and replete in one another's arms.

'That was heaven,' Jon whispered gruffly to her.

Heaven started to giggle and then Jon, realising what he had said, joined in.

'Heaven…' he began, but she suddenly tensed.

'I can hear a car outside,' she told him anxiously. 'You don't think…?'

'Wait here,' he cautioned her, reaching for his robe and pulling it on as he walked towards the door.

Whoever it was who'd arrived was ringing noisily on the doorbell, and Heaven shivered as she listened to the piercing, demanding sound.

'Wait here,' Jon had told her, but if they had been pursued by Harold there was no way she was going to be discovered huddled vulnerably in bed.

Picking up the clean clothes Jon had brought her, she headed for the bathroom, firmly locking the door behind her once she was inside. At least the brisk sound of the shower drowned out whatever might be happening downstairs. The women of the family who had originally built and lived in the peel tower would not have been so fortunate, she acknowledged, unable to stop herself wondering how many times they had huddled together in silent terror at the top of the tower whilst downstairs their menfolk repelled the border reivers who had come to attack them and steal away their cattle.

It had been a very thoughtful gesture on Jon's part to wash and dry her clothes for her, Heaven reflected as she quickly dried herself and then pulled on her clean clothes. By the looks of it, he had even had an attempt at ironing her dress.

She flushed a little as she slipped on her lacy briefs. They were a pair that Janet had given her as part of a surprise 'cheer you up' present and as such rather more skimpy and provocative than the ones she normally wore, hardly large enough to cover the palm of Jon's hand, never mind…

Hastily she reached for her dress. Her mind might be overrun with anxious fears, but her body was still clinging to the faintly languorous feeling of voluptuous satisfaction and completion that Jon's lovemaking had given it.

Jon. A delicious little tremor of pleasure ran delicately across her skin. There could be no doubts from the way he had made love to her and responded to her just how much he had wanted her, desired her, but wanting and loving were not necessarily the same thing, she reminded herself starkly as she unlocked the bathroom door and paused uncertainly, trying to gauge the silence. Had whoever it was gone…or…?

Heaven tensed as the bedroom door opened, but to her relief it was only Jon.

'Has he…? Was it…?' Heaven paused and moistened her dry lips.

Jon started to shake his head, but Heaven had guessed the truth from the severity of his expression.

'It was someone after me, wasn't it?' she insisted.

When Jon nodded, she bit her lip nervously, before asking, 'Was it Harold…?' He shook his head, a small smile starting to curl his mouth as he told her, 'No, Harold wasn't on the doorstep. Apparently he isn't feeling very well. It's all right, Heaven,' he reassured her, walking over to her and taking her in his arms, tucking her head under his chin as he wrapped his arms tightly round her.

'There were two men looking for you, yes—contacts of Harold's who work in Glasgow and whom he'd asked to try and locate you, but fortunately, seem to have convinced them that I came up here alone. Harold had told them that you'd left the house with me and they wanted to know if I knew where you were…'

'Couldn't Harold have asked you that over the telephone?' Heaven asked him uneasily. 'Why send people to your home?'

'I think Harold decided that a personal visit might help to reinforce the urgency of his need to discover your whereabouts,' Jon told her gravely, choosing not to add to her anxiety by revealing to her the warning he had been given about the potential consequences if he had been tempted to either help or conceal her.

'What…what did you tell them about…about me?' Heaven asked him quietly.

'I told them that from what you'd said to me I rather suspected that you might have decided to fly out to Australia to join your family for Christmas,' he told her.

Heaven's eyes widened in admiration as she tilted her head back to look at him.

'Did they believe you?'

'For the time being, but Harold's bound to check,' he warned her, 'which means that there's no way it would be safe for you to return to London, not until—well, not for the next few days.'

'Not until what?' Heaven pressed him.

Jon released her and walked over to the bedroom window. He was very fortunate in that the situation of the peel tower meant that it was impossible for anyone to conceal either a man or a car close enough at hand to be able to spy on the house. He felt sure that his unwanted visitors had accepted his story that he had no real idea where Heaven was, but sooner or later Harold would discover that she hadn't flown out to Australia and that neither had she returned home, and once he did, but hopefully before then, Jon would have gathered together all the information he needed to force his ex-brother-in-law's hand.

He looked out of the window, briefly studying the peaceful snow-covered hills and the clear winter blue of the cloudless sky. So very different from the storm clouds looming on the horizon of his life and the lives of those closest to him. The acrimony of his sister's divorce had affected his parents as well as Louisa herself, and his two nieces had also suffered, although thankfully their father had played a very distant role in their short lives. And as for what Harold had done to Heaven…

He looked back across the room and walked towards her, taking both her hands in his, holding them in a close and protective warm clasp as he told her what he had already found out and what he planned to do.

'You're going to do that… Will it work? Is it safe?' Heaven said nervously.

'I am going to do it, yes, it will work, and no, it probably isn't the safest thing I've ever done,' Jon admitted wryly. 'But I have to do it—for Louisa's sake; I'm just sorry that you had to be dragged into it. But without you I doubt that I would ever have got that vitally important bit of information about Harold's plans to cheat the Americans.'

'Tiffany might have told you,' Heaven demurred, but Jon shook his head decisively.

'No, I doubt it; you have the gift of bringing people close to you. Your natural warmth, your ability to give love encourages them to feel safe with you, to confide in you…'

He paused as Heaven's face clouded.

'What is it?' he asked gently.

'I'm worried about Tiffany. If Harold discovers what she's told me…'

'Tiffany will be fine,' Jon assured her.

Heaven bit her lip. 'You can't know that,' she protested.

'Oh, yes, I can,' he argued, then went on quietly, 'Right about now I suspect that Tiffany's parents will be driving into London to collect their lamb and remove her from Harold's presence—and his life. I sent them a fax warning them that Harold was not the man for their daughter and urging them to dig a little deeper into his background and past history. After all, how could a man who had already deserted two children be relied on to support their daughter and any children she might have?'

'Harold could trace the fax back to you,' Heaven responded fearfully.

'Not a chance,' he assured her. 'When the occasion calls for it, I can be just as devious as him. By the time Harold has unravelled the tangled skein of communication I've knotted around my fax, it will all be too late.'

'You make it all sound so simple and…easy, Jon, but I'm frightened,' Heaven admitted. 'If Harold's prepared to go to the lengths of sending someone here to look for me…'

'It's simply his outraged male pride that's caused him to do that,' Jon soothed her. 'After all, you did make him look very foolish in front of the Americans.

'It could be that the men he's sent here to check me out will keep tabs on me for the next day or so and then I expect they'll get bored and give up and go home.

It will mean, of course, that you've got to stick to the tower and its close environs for the next couple of days,' he warned her, gently touching her arm as he added, 'No clothes shopping, I'm afraid, although… Hang on a minute,' he told her, releasing her and striding across the bedroom to open a door in the bank of wardrobes set against one wall.

'Ah…I thought so,' Heaven heard him announcing triumphantly as he pushed open the adjacent door and indicated the half dozen or so items of women's clothing hanging there.

'I don't know if any of these will fit but you're more than welcome to give them a try,' he assured her, giving her a warm smile. But Heaven was already turning away from him, her body set like stone, her head down so that he wouldn't see the wounded pain in her eyes.

How could she have been so foolish as to start weaving fanciful, happy daydreams around the pair of them when it was plain just what kind of light he viewed their intimacy in if he could so casually and carelessly offer her the use of clothes which quite patently must have belonged to a previous incumbent of this room—and no doubt of his bed?

'What's wrong?' he asked with true male confusion when he saw the way she was responding to what he had imagined would be a very well-received suggestion.

'I couldn't possibly wear another woman's clothes,' Heaven told him freezingly.

'Another woman…' Jon began, puzzled, and then enlightenment dawned. 'I'm sure Louisa won't mind,' he told Heaven gently.

'Louisa…your sister? They're Louisa's clothes?'

Heaven asked him, not just her voice but her whole body reflecting her relief.

'They're Louisa's,' Jon confirmed. 'And although I know she's nothing like as petite as you there may be something you could wear. And, for your information,' he added mock sternly, 'apart from Louisa and the girls, you are the only woman I've… Damn,' he cursed under his breath as the telephone started to ring down below them.

'I'd better answer that. I'm expecting several calls in response to the proceedings I've set in motion…'

He was gone before Heaven could ask him what he had been about to say. Was it that she was the only woman apart from his sister and nieces whom he had invited to his border retreat, or was it that she was the only woman apart from them he'd wanted to invite?

'Stop it,' she warned herself firmly. 'Stop trying to read more into things than there might be. More than Jon himself might want there to be.' But not more than she knew she wanted there to be, she acknowledged.

The attraction she had felt for him when they had originally met might have gone to ground, suppressed by the sheer immediacy and shock of everything else that had overtaken her, but as last night—and this morning—had proved it had never really died and had in fact simply been waiting for the right moment to show its true strength.

All those slow, gentle weeks of gradually getting to know him, of talking with him, of seeing the loving way he reacted to his sister and his nieces, of gradually falling in love with him, had shown their true effect on her in his arms. What she felt for him wasn't just something born of the urgent, adrenalin-fuelled trauma of the moment; her love for him wasn't merely some kind of dangerous viral infection—a winter madness brought on by proximity and physical arousal. It was a forever, once-in-a-lifetime love, the kind of love that went with waking up with him every morning, bearing his children, sharing his whole life. But did he feel the same way about her?

'I'm sorry about this,' Jon apologised to Heaven as he walked into the living room where she was busily engaged looking for the final edge piece of a jigsaw she had discovered tucked away in a cupboard. The subject of the puzzle was a real Victorian family Christmas, complete with a dozen or so assorted aunts, uncles and elderly relatives, a mass of small, excited children, a tree, presents and even a small side table groaning with a mouthwatering selection of fruits and sweets. In effect the kind of Christmas that everyone, in a small corner of their heart, had a sentimental place for, whether or not they chose to acknowledge it.

'Why, are you bored? Never mind, we're nearly there. By this time tomorrow with any luck we'll have Harold exactly where we want him.'

'No, I'm not bored,' Heaven assured him, giving him a warm smile and then crowing with triumph as she pounced on the final edge piece of the jigsaw. She grinned up at Jon as she told him, 'This is definitely a figgy pudding sort of family, don't you think?' She made room on the sofa for him as he dutifully peered at the picture on the lid of the box.

'Oh, definitely,' he agreed, and then, unable to keep his face straight, teased her, 'But minus your special extra ingredients, I trust…'

They were both still laughing when they heard the phone ring.

'Keep your fingers crossed,' Jon told her. 'Hopefully this will be the call—the confirmation—that will prove incontrovertibly just what Harold's been up to.'

CHAPTER SIX

FOUR days after their arrival in the Borders Jon walked into the living room in relief.

'So everything is finally settled? You've got Harold's written and witnessed legal agreement to a proper divorce settlement for Louisa and the girls?'

'Yes, thanks in no small part to you,' he agreed warmly. 'Louisa's solicitor has just confirmed by fax that all the legal papers have been signed and Louisa's bank is in receipt of a very large cheque from Harold. The threat of having his underhand business dealings made public and possibly having to face a full-scale fraud investigation were more than enough to make Harold agree that he could be far more generous than he had been to Louisa and the girls.'

'And Tiffany...?'

'Tiffany is safely at home with her parents,' Jon assured her, adding wryly, 'And before you ask, I suspect that Harold's American buyers may very well be, if not having second thoughts about purchasing the business, then at least putting several more legal restraints on his future activities where they might affect their potential profits.'

'So all's well that ends well,' Heaven said slightly

hollowly, getting up from the sofa where she had been sitting to walk across to the window and look at the still snow-covered landscape. 'And it's safe for me to go home?'

'Yes, it is,' Jon agreed tersely. 'It seems that Harold has decided to spend Christmas in the Caribbean—somewhere where I doubt that figgy pudding or anything like it will be on the menu.'

Heaven tried to smile but for some reason her facial muscles were refusing to co-operate. For some reason! She knew perfectly well what the reason was.

Although she and Jon had been living as closely together as any two people who were not true lovers could, not once in the four days which had elapsed since the morning he had made love to her had he shown any inclination, either physical or verbal, to repeat the intimacy.

Why? Because he regretted ever having made love to her? Because he was afraid that she might have read too much into what had happened…? Too damn right she had. Far too much.

'If I left this afternoon, I could be home for Christmas Eve,' she told Jon numbly.

'I'll make the arrangements for you if that's what you want,' he said abruptly.

What was she supposed to say? That what she wanted was to stay with him; that what she wanted was to be with him, to be loved by him?

She dipped her head.

'Please, if you wouldn't mind,' she confirmed formally.

Jon had switched on the television to catch the morning news and suddenly the room was filled with the sweet sound of a youthful choir singing Christmas carols.

To Heaven's consternation, she felt her eyes start to fill with tears in response to the emotional effect of the sound. She had always been a sucker for the sentimentality of Christmas and couldn't so much as pass a high-street store decorated with a Christmas crib without being flooded with a warm feeling of goodwill towards her fellow men.

But right now, when she was feeling so emotionally vulnerable, so heart-achingly aware of all that she felt for Jon and all that it seemed he did not feel for her, the last thing she needed was any additional pressure on her frail emotional self-control. She tried to force back the tears, but it was too late—Jon had already seen them.

'Heaven, what is it…what's wrong?'

He was at her side, reaching for her, before she could push him away. The sleeves of the overlong sweater that she had 'borrowed' from Louisa unravelled, impeding her efforts to free herself from him as he took hold of her, one hand soothingly stroking her sweater-clad arm, whilst the other…

Heaven gulped as she felt him brush away her tears.

'Why?' he asked her quietly. 'What is it? If you're worrying about Harold…afraid…'

'I'm not afraid of Harold; you've seen to it that he'll not be suing me for my foolhardy revenge on him,' Heaven replied. 'It's…' She tried to lift her hand to her mouth to stem her betraying words, but the sweater sleeve got in the way and to her dismay she could only shake her head.

'I should be the one doing this—not you,' she heard Jon telling her huskily as he touched her tear-damp face.

'You?' Heaven stared up at him. 'Why?'

'Because I don't want you to leave… I don't want to lose you again, Heaven. Because I want to keep you here with me for ever…'

'You want me to stay?' Heaven couldn't quite hide her disbelief. 'How can you say that when for the last four days you've behaved as though…?' She stopped and bit her lip.

'Go on… When for the last four days I've behaved as though what?' Jon pressed her.

'As though you don't want me,' Heaven told him bleakly.

'Not want you…?'

The raw passion in his voice made Heaven's stomach muscles quiver. Urgently Jon cupped her face and forced her to look up at him.

'Of course I want you… I more than merely want you, Heaven, I love you, and there's nothing I've wanted more these last few days than to be in a position to tell you so, but first I had to get this whole sorry mess of Louisa's divorce settlement out of the way, not just because the very nature of the information you gave me about Harold meant I had to act quickly, but, even more importantly, because I wanted you and I to have time together that nothing else, no one else, could intrude on.

'Eighteen months ago when we first met I knew you were someone special, very special—that the way I felt about you was very, very real and permanent; but then…well, you disappeared and I felt that anyone connected with Harold, no matter how distantly, would be the last person you'd want in your life, to remind you of what he'd put you through. But then fate decreed that we should meet again and when we did…'

The look he gave her as he carefully brushed a stray strand of hair off her face made Heaven's heart turn over with awed joy. Never even in her most vivid imaginings had she ever imagined she would have the power to make a man look at her the way Jon was looking at her right now—as though she was his whole world, his whole reason, his whole being.

'Nothing's changed, Heaven,' Jon whispered passionately to her. 'My love for you is very, very real and very, very permanent. I love you and if you want to make my Christmas wish come true you—'

'You really love me?' Heaven interrupted him, unable to keep silent any longer, her eyes starry with emotion.

'I love you,' Jon confirmed. 'I really love you. I love you and my Christmas wish is for you to return my love…for you to be my wife…'

Behind them the TV choir launched into a triumphant burst of praise but Heaven barely heard them, her own heart singing too loudly with joy, and besides, Jon was kissing her so passionately that she was blind, deaf and dumb to everything, everyone but him.

'Promise me one thing,' he begged her when he finally, reluctantly released her mouth.

'What?' Heaven asked him, giddy with joy and love.

'That you'll never, ever make me your special version of figgy pudding,' he told her fervently.

Heaven was still laughing as he swept her up into his arms and headed for the stairs, and the bedroom.

EPILOGUE

'IS THAT it—the end?'

Jon looked lovingly at his wife.

'No, not the end; this story will never end,' he told his niece. 'This is just the beginning, and like our love it will last for ever,' he told Heaven in a voice low enough for only her to hear as he leaned across to kiss her.

'Oh, grown-ups—yuck!' Christabel exclaimed. 'You're just like Mum and Dad—they're always hugging and kissing too. I'm never going to get married...'

'You'll change your mind, you wait and see,' Jon warned her with a smile. 'The proof of the pudding's always in the eating—you ask Heaven.'

'Oh, always,' Heaven agreed, laughing.

Grown-ups, Christabel decided crossly, were a complete mystery to her. First of all that silly kissing and now they were laughing for absolutely no reason at all that she could see!

* * * * *